Prai

Little Girls

"Ronald Malfi continues his habit of chilling readers to the bone. Hell, this one seeps through the bone and swims in the marrow. *Little Girls* is a winner through and through."
—Horror Novel Reviews

"Best horror novel of the year."
—Hunter Shea, author of *The Jersey Devil*

"A complex and richly layered ghost story that slowly but surely creeps under your skin."
—The Horror Bookshelf

"The ending . . . God, the ending. It's magnificent in its simplicity. I had to reread it because the punch was given so swift my mind couldn't wrap around it. A fitting ending for this book, delightful and creepy."
—I Heart Reading

"This is a must for Malfi fans and a great read for those of you who love classically told ghost stories."
—iHorror.com

ALSO BY RONALD MALFI

LITTLE GIRLS

RONALD MALFI

PINNACLE BOOKS
Kensington Publishing Corp.
www.kensingtonbooks.com

PINNACLE BOOKS are published by

Kensington Publishing Corp.
119 West 40th Street
New York, NY 10018

All Kensington titles, imprints, and distributed lines are available at special quantity discounts for bulk purchases for sales promotions, premiums, fund-raising, educational, or institutional use.

Special book excerpts or customized printings can also be created to fit specific needs. For details, write or phone the office of the Kensington sales manager: Kensington Publishing Corp., 119 West 40th Street, New York, NY 10018, attn: Sales Department; phone 1-800-221-2647.

PINNACLE and the P logo are Reg. U.S. Pat. & TM Off.

ISBN-13: 978-0-7860-4138-1
ISBN-10: 0-7860-4138-2

First Kensington trade paperback printing: July 2015
First Pinnacle mass market paperback printing: July 2017

10 9 8 7 6 5 4 3 2 1

Printed in the United States of America

First Pinnacle electronic edition: July 2017

ISBN-13: 978-0-7860-4139-8
ISBN-10: 978-0-7860-4139-0

For Sam, who holds the key . . .

Dear, you should not stay so late,
Twilight is not good for maidens;
Should not loiter in the glen
In the haunts of goblin men.
　　　　　—CHRISTINA ROSSETTI,
　　　　　"Goblin Market"

PART I
HOMECOMING:
Laurie

CHAPTER 1

They had been expecting a woman, Dora Lorton, to greet them upon their arrival, but as Ted finessed the Volvo station wagon up the long driveway toward the house, they could see there was a man on the porch. Tall and gaunt, he had a face like a withered apple core and wore a long black overcoat that looked incongruous in the stirrings of an early summer. The man watched them as Ted pulled the station wagon up beside a dusty gray Cadillac that was parked in front of the porch. For one perplexing instant, Laurie Genarro thought the man on the porch was her father, so newly dead that his orphaned spirit still lingered at the house on Annapolis Road.

"Glad to see Lurch from *The Addams Family* has found work," Ted commented as he shut off the car.

"It looks like a haunted house," Susan spoke up from the backseat, a comment that seemed to underscore Laurie's initial impression of the ghostlike man who stood beneath the partial shade of the porch alcove. Susan was ten and had just begun vocalizing her critical observations to anyone within earshot. "And who's Lurch?"

"Ah," said Ted. "When did popular culture cease being popular?"

"I'm only ten," Susan reminded him, closing the Harry Potter book she had been reading for much of the drive down from Connecticut. She had been brooding and sullen for the majority of the trip, having already pitched a fit back in Hartford about having to spend summer vacation away from her friends and in a strange city, all of it because of a grandfather she had never known.

Who could blame her? Laurie thought now, still staring out the passenger window at the man on the porch. *I'd pitch a fit, too. In fact, I just might do it yet.*

Ted cupped his hands around his mouth. "Thank you for flying Genarro Airlines! Please make sure your tray tables are up before debarking."

Susan giggled, her mood having changed for the better somewhere along Interstate 95. "Barking!" she cried happily, misinterpreting her father's comment, then proceeded to bark like a dog. Ted wasted no time barking right along with her.

Laurie got out of the car and shivered despite the afternoon's mild temperature. In the wake of her father's passing, and for no grounded reason, she had expected her old childhood home to look different—empty, perhaps, like the molted skin of a reptile left behind in the dirt, as if the old house had nothing left to do but wither and die just as its master had done. But no, it was still the same house it had always been: the redbrick frame beneath a slouching mansard roof; Italianate cornices of a design suggestive of great pinwheels cleaved in half; a trio of arched windows on either side of the buckling front porch; all of which was capped by a functional belvedere that stood up against the cloudy June sky like the turret of a tiny castle. *That's where it happened,* Laurie thought with a chill as her eyes clung to the belvedere. It looked like a tiny bell tower sans bell, but was really a little room with windows on all four sides. Her parents had used it mostly for storage back when they had all still lived here together, before her parents' separation. Laurie had been forbidden to go up there as a child.

Trees crowded close to the house and intermittent slashes of sunlight came through the branches and danced along the east wall. The lawn was unruly and thick cords of ivy climbed the brickwork. Many windows on the ground floor stood open, perhaps to air out the old house, and the darkness inside looked cold and bottomless.

Laurie waved timidly at the man on the porch. She thought she saw his head bow to her. Images of old gothic horrors bombarded her head. Then she looked over her shoulder to where Ted and Susan stood at the edge of a small stone well that rose up nearly a foot from a wild patch of grass and early summer flowers on the front lawn. *Yes, I remember the well.* Back when she had been a child, the well had been housed beneath a wooden portico where, in the springtime, sparrows nested. She recalled tossing stones into its murky depths and how it sometimes smelled funny in the dead heat of late summer. Now, the wooden portico was gone and the well was nothing but a crumbling stone pit in the earth, covered by a large plank of wood.

Without waiting for Ted and Susan to catch up, Laurie climbed the creaky steps of the porch, a firm smile already on her face. The ride down to Maryland from Connecticut had exhausted her and the prospect of all that lay ahead in the house and with the lawyer left her empty and unfeeling. She extended one hand to the man in the black overcoat and tried not to let her emotions show. "Hello. I'm Laurie Genarro."

A pale hand with very long fingers withdrew from one of the pockets of the overcoat. The hand was cold and smooth in Laurie's own. "The daughter," the man said. His face was narrow but large, with a great prognathous jaw, a jutting chin, and the rheumy, downturned eyes of a basset hound. With the exception of a wispy sweep of colorless hair across the forehead, his scalp was bald. Laurie thought him to be in his late sixties.

"Yes," Laurie said. "Mr. Brashear was my father."

"I'm sorry for your loss."

"Thank you." She withdrew her hand from his, thankful to be rid of the cold, bloodless grasp. "I was expecting Ms. Lorton. . . ."

"I'm Dora's brother, Felix Lorton. Dora's inside, straightening up the place for you and your family. She was uncomfortable returning here alone after . . . well, after what happened. My sister can be foolishly superstitious. I apologize if I've frightened you."

"Not at all. Don't be silly." But he *had* frightened her, if just a little.

Across the front yard, Susan squealed with pleasure. Ted had lifted the corner of the plank of wood covering the well, and they were both peering down into it. Susan said something inaudible and Ted put back his head and laughed.

"My husband and daughter," Laurie said. She recognized a curious hint of apology in her tone and was quickly embarrassed by it.

"Splendid," Felix Lorton said with little emotion. Then he held out a brass key for her.

"I have my own." David Cushing, her father's lawyer, had mailed her a copy of the key along with the paperwork last week.

"The locks have been changed recently," said Felix Lorton.

"Oh." She extended her hand and opened it, allowing Lorton to drop the key onto her palm. She was silently thankful she didn't have to touch the older man's flesh again. It had been like touching the flesh of a corpse.

"Hi, there!" It was Ted, peering up at them through the slats in the porch railing while sliding his hands into the pockets of his linen trousers. There was the old heartiness in Ted's voice now. It was something he affected when in the company of a stranger whom he'd had scarce little time to assess. Ted was two years past his fortieth birthday but could pass for nearly a full decade younger. His teeth were white and straight, his skin unblemished and healthy-looking, and his eyes were both youthful and soulful at the same time, a combination many would have deemed otherwise incompatible. He kept himself in good shape, running a few miles every morning before retiring to his home office for the bulk of the afternoon where he worked. He could work for hours upon end in that home office back in Hartford without becoming fidgety or agitated, classical music issuing from the Bose speakers his only companion. Laurie envied his discipline.

"That's my husband, Ted," Laurie said, "and our daughter, Susan."

Susan sidled up beside her father, her sneakers crunching over loose gravel. Her big hearty smile was eerily similar to his. She had on a long-sleeved cotton jersey and lacrosse shorts. At ten, her legs were already slim and bronze, and she liked to run and play sports and had many friends back in Hartford. She was certainly her father's daughter.

"Nice to meet you folks. I'm Felix Lorton."

"There are frogs in the well," Susan said excitedly.

Lorton smiled. It was like watching a cadaver come alive on an autopsy table, and the sight of that smile chilled Laurie's bones. "I suppose there are," Lorton said to Susan. He leaned over the railing to address the girl, his profile stark and angular and suggestive of some predatory bird peering down from a tree branch at some blissfully unaware prey. "Snakes, sometimes, too."

Susan's eyes widened. "Snakes?"

"Oh, yes. After a heavy rain, and if it's not covered properly, that well fills up and it's possible to see all sorts of critters moving about down there."

"Neat!" Susan chirped. "Do they bite?"

"Only if you bite first." Lorton chomped his teeth hollowly. Then he turned his cadaverous grin onto Laurie. "I suppose I should take you folks inside now and introduce you to Dora."

"Yes, please," Laurie said, and they followed Felix Lorton into the house.

She had grown up here, though the time spent within these shadowed rooms and narrow hallways seemed so long ago that it was now as foreign to her as some childhood nightmare, or perhaps a threaded segment of some other person's life. Her parents had divorced when she was not much older than Susan, and she and her mother had left this house and Maryland altogether to live with her mother's family in Norfolk, Virginia. Subsequent visits to the house were sporadic at best, dictated by the whim of a father who had been distant and cold even when they had lived beneath the same roof. Her mother had never accompanied her on those visits, and when they stopped altogether, Laurie felt a warm relief wash over her. In her adult life, Laurie had chosen to maintain her distance, and she had never returned to this unwelcoming, tomblike place. Why should she force a relationship on a father who clearly had no interest in one? Even now, despite the horrors that had allegedly befallen her father, Laurie felt little guilt about her prolonged absence from his life.

"This place could be a stunner if it was renovated properly," Ted commented as Lorton led them through a grand entranceway. "I didn't realize the house was so big."

"Is it a mansion?" Susan asked no one in particular.

"No," Ted answered, a wry grin on his face now, "but it's close."

The foyer itself was large and circular, from which various hallways speared off like spokes on a wheel. There was an immense crystal chandelier directly above the entranceway and a set of stairs against one wall leading to the second story. The floors were scuffed and dulled mahogany, with some noticeable gashes dug into the dark wood. Some of the floorboards creaked.

Laurie paused at the foot of the stairs. She felt Lorton hovering close behind her. A cool sweat rose to the surface of her skin and the nape of her neck prickled hotly. "I'm sorry," she said, reaching out and grasping the decorative head of the newel post for support. "I just need a minute."

Ted asked if she was okay.

"It's just a bit overwhelming, that's all."

Frightened, Susan said, "Mommy?"

Laurie offered the girl a tepid smile, which Susan returned wholeheartedly. "Mommy's okay, sweetheart," she said, and was glad when her voice did not waver.

Ted came up behind Laurie and squeezed her shoulder with one firm hand.

"It has been a while since you were last here, Mrs. Genarro?" Felix Lorton asked.

"It has, yes," she confirmed. "I spent my childhood here but haven't been back in many years."

Felix Lorton nodded. "Understandable."

After Laurie regained her composure, Felix Lorton led them into the parlor. The walls were drab, the paint cracked and peeling. A comfortable sofa and loveseat sat corralled on a threadbare oriental carpet before a dark stone hearth. A few books stood on a bookshelf, while an ancient Victrola cabinet squatted in one corner, its lacquered hood raised. Beside the phonograph was a small upright piano, shiny and black. A tarnished candelabrum stood on the piano's hood. At the opposite end of the room, a liquor cabinet with a mesh screen for a door displayed a collection of antediluvian bottles. The windows in this part of the house faced a green yard and, beyond, a wooden fence that separated the side of the house and backyard from the neighboring property which, from what Laurie was able to glimpse, looked overgrown with heavy trees and unkempt shrubbery. The whole room smelled unsparingly of Pine-Sol.

"Strange," commented Ted. He was staring at a large gilded frame on one wall. The frame held no lithograph, no portrait, though bits of it still clung to the inside of the frame. Aside from that, it framed nothing but the blank wall on which it sat. "What happened to the picture?"

Felix Lorton cleared his throat and said, "I wouldn't know, sir."

"Did you work for my father as well, Mr. Lorton?" Laurie asked as she walked slowly around the room. Beneath the cloying smell of Pine-Sol, she could detect the stale odor of cigar smoke, and for a brief moment she was suddenly ushered back to her youth. Her father had often smoked the horrid things. The parlor had been arranged differently back then, her mother having brought to it a domestic femininity it now sorely lacked. Cigar smoking had not been permitted in the house, and Laurie recalled a sudden image of her father standing just beyond the windows of this room, firmly planted in the strip of lawn that ran alongside the fence while he puffed away on one of his cigars. The vision was so distant, Laurie wondered if it was a real memory or some nonsense she had just conjured from thin air.

"No, ma'am, I did not. My sister was assigned to take care of your father from the service. When things got . . . more difficult . . . the service brought on another girl to assist with the caretaking responsibilities. A night nurse. You're aware of this, I presume?"

"Yes."

"I had been coming around on occasion in the past few months, Mrs. Genarro, mostly to do minor repairs. Old houses like these . . ." There was no need for him to complete the thought. "When Dora said the locks needed to be changed, I came and changed them. That sort of thing."

"Why *were* the locks changed?" she asked.

"You'll have to speak with Dora about that."

Laurie frowned. "If it was necessary to have someone maintain the property, I wish the service would have told me. I don't like the idea of you having to take care of my father's things for free."

"It wasn't like that at all, ma'am. My sister had simply requested I come with her so she wouldn't have to be here alone."

"What about the other girl?" Laurie asked. "The night nurse?"

"They were never here at the same time. They worked in shifts. Toward the end, your father required around-the-clock care, as I've been told. I presume you were kept up to date on all of this?"

"Yes. I was aware of my father's condition." Then she frowned. "Why wouldn't Dora want to be here alone?"

"You'll have to ask her, ma'am," said Lorton. It was becoming his automatic response. "If you don't mind my asking, where do you folks currently reside?"

"Hartford, Connecticut," Laurie said. She feigned interest in the crumbling mortar of the fireplace mantel. As a child, there had been framed photographs and various other items on the mantelpiece. Now, it was barren. "It took us longer to get here than we thought," she added, as if the distance excused her absence from this place and her father's life.

What do I have to feel guilty about? she wondered. *He was never there for me; why should I have been there for him? Anyway, what business is it of Felix Lorton's?*

"Understandable. Please have a seat and I'll go fetch my sister," Lorton said, extending a hand toward the sofa and loveseat. "Would any of you like something to drink?"

"Ice water would be great," Ted said. He was examining the spines of the few books on the bookshelf.

"Do you have any grape juice, please?" Susan asked.

The question caused Felix Lorton to suck on his lower lip while his eyes narrowed to slits. A sound like a frog's croak rumbled at the back of the man's throat.

"Water will be fine for her, too," Laurie assured him.

"Very well," Lorton said, then disappeared down the hall that led to the kitchen.

"All these books have pages torn out of them," Ted said, replacing one of the leather-bound editions back on the shelf. "How strange."

Laurie went to one of the windows and looked out onto the side yard. The lawn was spangled with sunlight and the wooden fence was green and furry with mildew. Tree branches drooped over the fence from the neighboring yard, the trees themselves all but blotting out the house next door. She could make out shuttered windows and dark, peeling siding. A green car of indeterminable make and model was parked in the neighbor's driveway and there was another vehicle with some sort of emblem on the door parked on the street. The

Russ family had lived there when she was a girl. Laurie wondered who lived there now.

"This house smells funny," Susan said. She was crouching down to peer into the black, sooty maw of the hearth. "It reminds me of Miss Tannis's house back home." Bertha Tannis was the elderly widow who lived two houses down from the Genarros in Hartford. When she was younger, Susan would sometimes go there after school if both Laurie and Ted weren't home to greet her.

Ted went over and sat on the loveseat. He sighed dramatically as he draped an arm over the high back. "I should have asked the old *galantuomo* for a scotch and soda."

"Is this where bats live?" Susan asked, still peering into the fireplace. She was trying to look up into the chimney, but there was a tri-panel screen in the way blocking her view.

"It's a fireplace, Snoozin," Ted said, using their daughter's much hated nickname. "You know what that is."

"I know what it *is*," she retorted, "but there's *animals* out here. Not like we have at home. Didn't you hear what the man said about the snakes in the well?"

"There are no snakes in the well," Ted assured her. He sounded bored, tired. It had been a long drive down from Connecticut for him, too. "He was just pulling your leg."

"What does 'pulling your leg' mean?"

"It means he was joking."

"I know it means *that,* Daddy, but *why* does it mean that?"

"I don't know. That's a good question."

Felix Lorton returned with two tall glasses of ice water. He set them on the coffee table between the sofa and the loveseat. Laurie caught Lorton eyeing Ted ruefully, as if he did not approve of the man lounging on the loveseat in such a casual fashion.

"Thank you," Ted said, picking up his glass and taking a healthy drink from it.

"Why does someone say 'pulling your leg' when they're telling you a joke?" Susan asked Felix Lorton.

The man straightened his back and lifted his head just enough so that the bands of loose flesh beneath his neck hung like a dewlap. He cleared his throat. "To pull one's leg is to make a fool of them, as in to trip them up and make them fall down." Felix Lorton spoke with an authority Laurie found comical, particularly when addressing a ten-year-old girl. Laurie bit the inside of her cheek to keep from laughing.

"Neat," Susan said.

"Yeah, neat," Ted added. "I didn't know that, either."

"My sister will be with you folks shortly. If you'll excuse me, there are some things I need to attend to before we leave."

Laurie thanked him and Lorton effected a slight bow. His black coat flared out around his ankles as he shuffled quickly down the hallway. *Blood thinners,* it occurred to Laurie. *That's why he's wearing the coat and that's why his hand was so cold. He must be on blood thinners for medical reasons.* A moment later, Laurie heard a door far off in the house squeal open and then close again. With little carpeting to dull the noise, the sound echoed throughout the house.

Susan skipped over to the coffee table and scooped

up her glass of water. She hummed a soft melody under her breath.

"Don't spill it," warned her father.

Susan scowled and, for a moment, she looked to Laurie like a grown woman. Those dark eyes, that lustrous black hair, the copper-colored skin and long, coltish legs . . . at times, the girl looked so much like her father that Laurie felt like an outsider among them, an interloper in some other family's life. Laurie was the fair-skinned freckled one with a plain face and eyes that were maybe a hair too far apart. Summertime, while her husband and daughter tanned with the luxuriance of Roman gods, Laurie burned a fiery red, then shed semitransparent sheets of peeled skin for the next several days.

"How come you didn't tell me it was such a nice house, Laurie?" Ted asked from the loveseat.

"Didn't I?"

"A house like this could go for top dollar, even in this lousy economy. I'll bet it's worth a fortune. It just needs a little TLC, that's all."

"I guess we'll find out when we speak to the lawyer."

"What's 'TLC'?" Susan asked.

"You're dripping water on the rug," Ted told the girl.

Susan set her drink down on the coffee table, then went over to the piano.

"B flat," Ted said.

Susan pecked out the correct key. It rang in the stillness of the otherwise silent room.

"D sharp," Ted said.

Susan said, "Oh," and her index finger moved up and

down the keyboard like a dowsing rod, counting the keys silently, but with her mouth moving. She tapped another key, lower on the fingerboard.

"Yuck," Ted said from the loveseat. "Are you sure? D sharp? Try again."

Under her breath, Susan mumbled, "Sharp is . . . *up*. . . ." Her lithe fingers walked up a series of notes until she rested on one. She hammered the note a few times, smiling to herself.

Ted stuck his tongue out between his lips and produced a sound that approximated flatulence. This set Susan to giggling. She turned around, her face red, her eyes squinting in her laughter. Laurie watched her daughter, smiling a little herself now. She was glad to have Susan back to her old cheerful self again, after the sullenness of the long car ride down from Connecticut. Then Susan's laughter died and the girl's smile quickly faded from her face. Laurie followed her daughter's gaze to the alcove that led out into the main hall. A woman stood in the doorway. Her face was sharp and white, her iron-colored hair cropped short like a boy's. She wore a paisley-patterned frock and was in the process of wiping her hands on a dishtowel when Laurie spotted her and offered the woman a somewhat conciliatory smile.

"You must be Dora," Laurie said, moving swiftly across the room with her hand extended.

"That's right," said the woman. She had a clipped, parochial voice. She stuffed the dishtowel partway into a pocket of her frock and shook Laurie's hand with just the tips of her fingers. She looked to be in her early fifties. There were faint lines bracketing her mouth and crow's feet at the corners of her eyes. The eyes themselves were an icy gray.

"It's so nice to finally meet you. I'm Laurie Genarro. That's my husband, Ted, and my daughter, Susan."

"I'm sorry we must meet under these circumstances," Dora Lorton said as she nodded her head at each of them curtly. "My condolences, Mrs. Genarro."

"Thank you."

"If you've got bags with you, Felix can help bring them in from the car."

"That isn't necessary," Laurie told her. "We haven't decided whether we're staying here or not."

"Why wouldn't you stay? It's your house now."

The thought chilled her.

Ted stood from the sofa, straightening the creases in his linen pants. "There's supposed to be an historic inn downtown. It sounded interesting."

"George Washington stayed there!" Susan chimed in.

Dora's brow furrowed. "Downtown?"

"Annapolis," clarified Ted.

"Well, it's your house now," Dora Lorton repeated, and not without a hint of exasperation. "I suppose you folks can do as you like."

Ted shot Laurie a look, one that she interpreted as, *Cheerful old coot, isn't she?* Once again, Laurie had to fight off spontaneous laughter.

"The house is clean and everything in it is functional," Dora went on in her parochial tone. "Your father was not a man of excesses, Mrs. Genarro, as I'm sure you can see, so you'll find very little items of a frivolous nature in the house. There are no televisions, no radios, nothing like that. What items there are—Mr. Brashear's personal items, as opposed to *house* items, I mean—have been relocated to his study. When was the last time you were here at the house, Mrs. Genarro?"

"Not since I was a teenager, and that was just for a brief visit. I can hardly remember. And, please, call me Laurie."

"Do you recall where the study is?"

Laurie considered and then pointed down one of the corridors that branched off the main hall. It had been a small library when she had been a child, and she could easily imagine it as a study now. "Is it the room just at the end of that hall?"

"Yes. Do you require a rundown of the rest of the house?"

"A rundown?"

"A tour of it, in other words. Seeing how it's been such a long time."

"Oh, I don't think that will be necessary. I remember it well enough. And what I don't remember, I can figure out."

"Nonetheless, there are a few things I feel I should show you." Dora's chilly gray eyes volleyed between Laurie and Ted. "Which one of you does the cooking?"

"Mostly, it's me," Laurie said.

"Laurie's a splendid cook," Ted added. His smile was charming, but Laurie could see that it held no influence over Dora. "I can hardly microwave a salad."

"I figured I would ask nonetheless, just so my assumptions wouldn't offend anyone," Dora said, marching right past Ted's attempt at humor.

"Oh," Laurie said, "not at all."

"Very well," said Dora, those cold eyes settling back on Laurie. "You'll come with me then?"

"Of course."

"Can I go play outside?" Susan chirped to her mother.

"Not just yet, Susan."

"But I'm bored!"

"I'll go with her," Ted said, taking up Susan's hand.

"All right," Laurie said. She shared a look with her husband then . . . and wondered if he could decipher the clutter of emotions behind her eyes. Not that she could decipher them herself. She was weak, tired, troubled, overwhelmed. There was a darkness here in this house, she knew—something cold and widespread, like black water gradually filling up behind the walls—and she thought it might have been the residual ghost of her parents' divorce and Laurie's subsequent extraction from this place. *Extraction,* she thought, summoning the image of a diseased tooth being liberated from purpling gums. *That's good.*

Laurie followed Dora into the kitchen. It was a spacious room with brick walls and stainless-steel appliances. A small circular table stood before a bay window that looked out on the backyard and the moldy green fence that separated the property from the house next door. There were plenty of windows and the room was generously bright.

"You lived here as a child?" Dora said. She led Laurie over to the stovetop.

"I did, yes."

"It's a gas range. The appliances are in fair working order, though I can't be certain how old they are. You've cooked on a gas range before?"

"We have a gas range back home."

"Let me show you, anyway," said Dora. She turned
the knob and let the burner tick until a blue flame ignited. The smell of gas rose up to greet them. Dora
turned the stove off and moved to the refrigerator. She
opened the refrigerator door. It was stocked, but not
obnoxiously so. Laurie could see many of the items
within hadn't yet been opened, and it occurred to her
that either Dora or Felix Lorton had recently gone to
the supermarket in anticipation of their arrival. "You'll
find it is stocked with milk, cheese, bread, juices, and
plenty of condiments. There are frozen meats and poul-
try in the freezer as well, Mrs. Genarro, and the pantry
is sufficiently stocked with cereals, pastas, and canned
goods. I didn't bother getting any fruits or vegetables
or other perishables from the market, as they tend to
go bad quickly in the summer if not eaten right away. I
wasn't sure how long you folks planned to stay."

"I'm not sure we know yet, either."

"It's understandable," Dora intoned, sounding just
then like her brother. Next, Dora led her over to the
dishwasher. "Standard functions, quite easy to use.
There is detergent beneath the sink."

Beyond the curved bay windows, Laurie saw Ted
and Susan galloping across the green lawn. They raced
along the fence and up the lawn's slight incline to where
the trees grew denser and wild blackberry bushes and
honeysuckle exploded like fireworks from the ground.
The tree limbs that overhung the fence waved sleep-
ily in the breeze, throwing moving shadows against the
mossy pickets.

"There's a list of emergency numbers beside the

telephone," Dora went on. "For your convenience I've included the number for Mr. Brashear's lawyer, a Mr. Cushing, I believe, though I presume you already have his contact information."

"Yes, but thank you."

"I've left my home number for you as well, in the event you have any further need of me."

"That's very thoughtful of you. Thank you." It seemed all she was capable of saying to the woman. Also, it occurred to Laurie that Dora Lorton hadn't looked at her a single time since they'd entered the kitchen. "Have you been working here the whole time, since I called the care service?"

"Yes. It had just been me for a while, until Mr. Brashear's condition worsened and we had to bring on more help. I was assisted by a younger woman named Ms. Larosche. Do you know of her?"

"No, I don't. I mean, I was aware the service had added a second caretaker because of the need for twenty-four-hour care, but I'd never spoken to her."

"Nor will you need to. She only worked nights. I handled the household chores. Any questions you might have can be answered by me."

"And Felix, your brother? He had been helping out around here, too?"

At last, Dora's eyes ticked up in Laurie's direction. "That's just been recently."

"Did my father get terribly out of hand? I haven't heard the extent of it. I mean, given the way things ended, I could only imagine what it must have been like."

"You've spoken with Mr. Claiborne?"

"Yes," said Laurie. Mr. Claiborne was the managing director of Mid-Atlantic Homecare Services. Their conversations on the phone had been strained but polite. The last call she had received from him had been to inform her that her father had killed himself. While he had offered his sympathy, Laurie could tell Mr. Claiborne's primary concern was toward any potential lawsuit his company might be facing in the wake of such tragedy. Laurie had assured him she would take no legal action against him or his employees. "He explained the situation as best he could," Laurie continued. "Nonetheless, Ms. Lorton, I feel I owe you some sense of gratitude for looking after my father."

"It was my job."

"I just wanted to thank you. And Ms. Larosche, too."

"What's done is done." As if to brush away crumbs, Dora swept a hand across the Formica countertop, though Laurie hadn't seen anything there. "Come along and I'll show you the rest," said Dora.

CHAPTER 2

They went to the laundry room off the kitchen and Dora showed her where the detergents and fabric softeners were kept. "The lint trap in the dryer builds up very quickly. Mind you, keep an eye on it. It's a fire hazard, you know."

"Ours is the same way at home." Laurie could care less about the dryer. "I'm sorry if this sounds rude," she went on quickly, "but I can't help but wonder if you've got a place to go."

"I don't understand."

"It was a fulltime job being my father's caretaker for the last couple of years. Now that he's dead, I hope you've got other work." She laughed nervously. "I feel like I'm firing you."

"Don't be silly." Dora pulled the lint trap out, showed Laurie that the screen had recently been purged of lint, and then snapped it back into place.

"I could tell the dementia had gotten much worse the last time I called him," Laurie confessed. "That was maybe six months ago. Was the dementia really bad toward the end?"

"Wasn't the dementia that killed him, of course. Not directly, anyway."

"Of course," Laurie said. Mr. Claiborne had told her what had killed him. Her father's lawyer had told her as well. She wondered if she would be able to summon enough courage to go up into the belvedere. Despite her lack of empathy for her dead father, she found thinking about it disturbing nonetheless.

"I've readied the bedrooms for you and your family, Mrs. Genarro, and it's up to you if you want to stay here or someplace else. I suppose I'd understand if you wanted to stay away from the house, given what happened. No hard feelings."

"I appreciate all your work," Laurie said. "Were you here when it happened?"

Once again, Dora Lorton's steely eyes settled on Laurie. The question had just found its way out of Laurie's mouth—she hadn't even realized she'd meant to speak it. The heartbeat of silence that resonated now in its wake was as profound as a gunshot.

"No, I wasn't," Dora said evenly. "It happened in the evening, while poor Ms. Larosche was on shift. She didn't know anything had happened until she began one of her periodic checks on Mr. Brashear, only to find the door leading up to that strange little room standing open. The room at the top of the house."

"My father called it the belvedere," Laurie said.

"The door was usually locked, but it wasn't on this night for some reason," Dora went on as if Laurie hadn't said a word. "When Ms. Larosche went up, she found the room . . . the *belvedere* . . . empty, but then she spotted him on the ground below. His neck was broken and his death had been instantaneous."

"It must have been awful for her. I'm so sorry."

Perhaps Dora Lorton was uncomfortable being the sounding board for Laurie's continual apologies, for she actively ignored the comment with a discomfort that was quite palpable. "There are no television sets and no radios in the house, as I've mentioned," she went on. "There are no computers, either. With the exception of the telephone, contact with the outside world, you will find, is quite limited."

"We've got our cell phones. My husband brought his laptop, too, and we can watch TV shows and movies on that. He's a playwright. He's working on a theatrical adaptation of a John Fish novel at the moment. Have you read any work by him?"

Dora looked unimpressed. "Your husband?"

"No, I meant John Fish, the author. Are you familiar with his books? He writes these sweeping epic dramas. He's quite popular."

"I only read nonfiction," Dora said. "What is it you do, if you don't mind me asking?"

"Well, I'm a stay-at-home mom at the moment," Laurie said, feeling a distant chill, "though I used to teach classes at the college by our house. I'm also a painter."

"A house painter or an artist painter?"

"An artist painter, I suppose."

"Do you make money doing it?"

It seemed a rather intrusive question. Nevertheless, Laurie said, "Sometimes. I used to have paintings for sale in some bookstores and art galleries in Hartford, and once I even had a painting in a gallery in Manhattan. But I haven't painted anything new in a long time."

"Well, maybe you're in need of inspiration," Dora said. "With no televisions or radios, you'll find it hard to be pestered by distraction."

"Well, there's always my daughter." *And husband,* she considered adding, and probably would have had Dora Lorton been a more accessible person, but she decided against it in the end.

"Yes, I'm sure she keeps you quite busy." Dora cleared her throat and said, "You'll also notice that some of the floors have been disturbed."

"What do you mean?"

"Gouges in the flooring in places, some carpeting pulled up in some of the rooms, molding stripped away from the walls. Mr. Brashear never made it as far as to actually pry up the floorboards, though I suspect that was on his agenda."

Laurie recalled the damaged look of the floor in the foyer, the gouges and scrapes in the hardwood. "I don't understand. Why would he do that?"

"Wasn't my business to ask him. It wouldn't have done any good near the end, anyway. Mr. Brashear was quite troubled by the end. I just wanted to set the record straight so you know it was your father who did that to the floors and not me or Ms. Larosche. Things may need to be repaired before you can sell the place, and I wouldn't want you to think we had been irresponsible."

"I wouldn't have assumed you were responsible for any of it." Laurie coughed into one fist, somewhat embarrassed, though she couldn't quite pinpoint why. For some reason, Dora Lorton made her nervous. "How did you know we were going to sell the place?"

"You're uncomfortable just spending the night here, why would I think you'd move in for good?" Dora said, moving past Laurie and out of the laundry room.

Lastly, they went back into the foyer where Dora retrieved a lightweight coat and a handbag from the hall closet. The coat was tan canvas with large brown plastic buttons and a fabric belt, like the kind of coat Peter Sellers wore in all the *Pink Panther* movies. "Did Felix tell you about the rug?"

"What rug?"

"An old Persian rug that had been upstairs in that odd little room. On the night of Mr. Brashear's death, the rug had been . . . damaged . . . I suppose you could say," Dora said, tugging on her detective coat. Behind her, out one of the arched windows, Laurie could see Felix Lorton standing by the dusty Cadillac having a cigarette.

"Damaged how?"

"Stained by fluid."

"Blood?"

Dora's mouth went tight. "Not just blood."

"Oh," Laurie said after she realized what the woman meant. "Was that something that happened often?"

"No. Just that once."

"I'm so embarrassed."

"I cleaned it as best I could and then I had Felix roll it up and tuck it away in a corner downstairs. I considered getting rid of it—it's unsalvageable, to speak openly, Mrs. Genarro—but it is also your property now and I didn't want to take liberties throwing things away. It looked like it might have been a fairly expensive rug."

"I understand. Thank you for thinking of it. And again, I'm so sorry you had to deal with it. I'm sorry you got wrapped up in the middle of it all."

"It's my job," she repeated. The woman shouldered the strap of her handbag. "Or so it once was, anyway."

Laurie walked her to the front door, their footfalls echoing in the empty circular foyer. "Oh!" Laurie said quickly. "There was one more thing."

"Yes?"

"Was there a reason the locks had been changed recently?"

"Reason?" Dora pulled her flimsy coat more tightly about herself. "How often did you say you spoke with your father by telephone, Mrs. Genarro?"

"Not very often, I'm afraid. Six months ago would have been the last time."

"He grew quite paranoid in the final weeks of his life."

"I didn't know."

"He was a frightened man. It seemed his thoughts turned on him, as evidenced by his suicide. He would walk around the house as if he were a young boy lost in the woods."

"So the locks were changed to prevent him from getting out?"

"No, Mrs. Genarro. The locks were changed at your father's insistence to prevent people from getting *in*."

Laurie tasted acid at the back of her throat. Slowly, she shook her head. "I don't understand. What people? Who was trying to get in?"

Dora's lips thinned. "Have you spent any time around people with dementia, Mrs. Genarro?"

"No, I'm afraid I haven't." She was becoming annoyed at the woman's tone.

"Quite often they become paranoid. Their fears are irrational and based outside of reality. I once took care of an elderly woman who was terrified of kitchen utensils—knives, forks, spoons. Pure silliness to you and me, but abject horror to her. You've seen the empty picture frame on the wall?"

Laurie recalled the empty frame on the wall in the parlor, the one Ted had remarked upon. She said, "Yes, I did. I was wondering what that was about. Did he remove the picture from the frame?"

"He broke the glass and tore it right out. I took the frame down afterward, but in his dementia, the poor man insisted I hang it back up with no picture in it."

"Why would he do such a thing?"

"Far be it from me to comprehend the things that went through your father's head, Mrs. Genarro. His dementia had gotten the best of him by that point, I'm sorry to say." The older woman glanced quickly down the hall and then back at Laurie. "I had considered taking the frame down before you got here—it is certainly a disturbing sight—but Mr. Claiborne, he insisted I leave things as they had been prior to your father's death. He claimed it would be disrespectful to start moving items around, but I think it was because he feared a lawsuit and wanted you to see just what it had been like taking care of your father."

"I understand."

"I hope that doesn't sound harsh."

"No, not at all."

"Will there be one? A lawsuit, I mean."

"No," said Laurie. "No one's getting sued." On top of everything else, she couldn't think about filing a lawsuit, too . . . even though Ted had brought it up on more than one occasion since they had received Claiborne's telephone call. *They should have been watching him,* Ted had insisted, and it wasn't as if Laurie necessarily disagreed with him. *That's what twenty-four-hour care is for! That's the goddamn definition! Someone should have been keeping an eye on him twenty-four hours a goddamn day, Laurie!*

"All right, then," said Dora. Then her icy eyes grew distant. She took a step back and gazed down the foyer and the corridors that came off it like spokes. "It's your house now," she said.

Once again, the notion chilled her.

Laurie opened the front door for the woman. "I apologize, but I'm a little unsure how all this works," she said before Dora stepped out. "Did my father . . . owe you anything? What I mean is, are you taken care of? You and Ms. Larosche have both been paid in full through the service, correct?"

"Everything has been taken care of."

"I feel silly," Laurie confessed. "Again, it's like I'm firing you from your job."

"There will be more jobs like it," Dora said. Her short stiff hair vibrated like sagebrush in the cool summer breeze. "I'll find another."

She watched Dora Lorton hobble down the porch and make her way to the passenger side of the Cadillac. He brother stood there waiting for her. He opened the door for her and she climbed slowly inside, moving with the lethargy of someone much older. Felix shut the door and walked around the rear of the car to the driver's side. He paused only briefly beside the Cadillac's rear bumper to acknowledge Laurie with a slight nod of his head, much as he had done earlier upon greeting her, then he folded himself into the driver's seat and pulled the door shut. The Cadillac started with a shuddery growl. It backed up and Felix Lorton executed a point-turn in the driveway, just barely avoiding a collision with the Volvo. Laurie caught Dora Lorton's white ghost-face in the tinted glass of the passenger window. The older woman was looking up at the house with an expression Laurie originally misinterpreted as desultory resignation. But then she realized what the look really was: fear.

A moment later, the dusty old Cadillac was rumbling down the driveway toward the road.

CHAPTER 3

Smiling to himself, Ted surveyed the property. The backyard was large and pastoral, heavily wooded beyond the property. Along the side of the house, a fence set the demarcation between this property and the neighboring one, where a shabby little house stood beyond a veil of thinner trees. A hard blue sky rose up beyond the tree line. He inhaled and thought he could smell the briny aroma of river water.

Why Laurie had never told him about the grandeur of her father's home suddenly weighed on his mind. Particularly with all the money problems they had been having lately, exacerbated by Laurie's reluctance to go back to work, it would have been nice to know there was a potential safety net out there. Even if Myles Brashear had no intention of sharing his fortune with his daughter while he was alive—a scenario Ted guessed had more to do with Laurie's pride than her father's unwillingness—it would have been nice to know that once the old fellow passed on, there would be financial spoils waiting for them in the wings.

Susan did a cartwheel across the lawn, her shadow

exaggerated to hugeness on the grass. When she popped up, there was an ear-to-ear smile on her face.

"Pretty neat place, huh, pumpkin seed?" said Ted.

"It's awesome!"

He pointed straight across the lawn to the trees. "I bet there's water back there."

"Like the beach?"

"Well, no, not the beach. Maybe a river or a lake or something. Want to go have a look?"

Susan pointed to a darkened niche in the tree line. "Can we go there first, Daddy? It looks like a path."

"Indeed it does."

"It can be an adventure!" she said, gathering up his hand and dragging him across the yard to the wooded path.

Awe caused the girl to slow her pace after they walked a few yards into the woods. Colorful wildflowers burst from the ground and the trees sighed softly in the early summer breeze. Tiny white petals fluttered down around them like snowflakes. A smorgasbord of smells met Ted's nose. He inhaled the rich fecundity of the forest that, even as a teenage boy, had always reminded him—though not unpleasantly—of semen.

"Look," Susan said, her voice a sudden whisper.

Ted crouched down so he was at eye level with her. She pointed through dense foliage where, at first, Ted saw nothing. But then the geometric shapes of the forest assembled into a pair of antlers, a tapered brown snout, and glossy tar-colored eyes. It was a seven-point buck, still several yards away but nonetheless massive, even at such a distance. It was staring straight at them, seeming to hold its breath, just as Ted and Susan were doing. He had never seen one out in the wild before, and its presence now was nearly transcendent.

"It sees us," Susan whispered. So close to her face, he could smell candy on her breath.

"It does," he whispered back.

"Can we go up to him? Pet him?"

"I think," said Ted, "that if we take another step, the old boy will turn and run off through the woods."

"But Daddy, we could *try.*"

"Go on," he urged her. "Go ahead and try, sweet pea."

Susan released her grip on her father's hand. A strand of her hair had fallen in front of her face, and Ted watched as her exhalations caused it to swing like a metronome. She took one step toward the deer, her arms straight down at her side, as if to keep herself as unimposing a figure as possible. The deer's eyes were still locked on them. Ted found himself holding his breath. Susan executed another step in the deer's direction. He watched her profile. That loose strand of hair kept blowing back and forth, back and forth. A timorous smile tugged at one corner of Susan's mouth.

Go on, kiddo, he thought.

She took a third step, and this time her sneaker came down on a twig. The twig snapped and, in a flash, the deer vanished into the brush. For several seconds thereafter, Ted could hear its powerful legs pistoning through the woods as it fled.

Susan turned to her father, her eyes brilliant and wide. That timorous smile was still there, frozen to her face.

"Wow," she marveled. "Did you see how fast it ran?"

"I did," he said, taking up her hand again.

They walked some more, until they came upon a clearing.

"What is *that*?" Susan said, pointing.

It was a sizable man-made structure, in the vague suggestion of a small house with a cantilevered roof, covered by a heavy blanket of canvas. The canvas was black with mold, its corners held down by chains attached to what looked like railroad spikes driven into the earth.

"Not sure," Ted said. Together they took a few steps closer to the thing before Ted stopped. He noticed shards of broken glass hidden among the underbrush. "Stay here for a sec so I can have a look."

The thing beneath the canvas was about the size and shape of the detached garage they had back in Hartford. As he drew nearer, the rich scents of the forest intensified; they no longer rose up to greet his nose as much as they accosted him and tried to bully him into a sneeze. There was a deeper smell beneath the floral perfume, too—the unmistakable sick-sweet odor of rotting vegetation.

He crouched down and peered beneath one of the canvas flaps. Then he dropped the flap back into place, stood, and rubbed his hands together.

"What is it?" Susan asked.

He waved her over. "Come here, but watch out for the broken glass."

Susan stared at the ground as she closed the distance between them. There was a daintiness to her posture that Ted found endearing. When she arrived beside him, he peeled away a section of the canvas to reveal a matrix of black glass rectangles.

"What *is* it?" Susan still wanted to know.

"It's a greenhouse," Ted said. "A very old one, but that's what it is."

"What's a greenhouse?"

"What's the matter? They don't teach you kids about global warming in school?"

Susan wrinkled her nose, a gesture she implemented whenever she was confronted with rhetoric.

"It's a little house made of glass where people grow plants and flowers," Ted said.

"Why do you need a house to grow plants and flowers? Seems like they grow pretty good out here on their own."

"Pretty well," Ted corrected her.

"Seems like they grow pretty *well* on their own."

Ted smiled and gently squeezed the back of his daughter's neck.

"Let's go see if I'm right about that water on the other side of the trees," he said.

CHAPTER 4

The house was too quiet and empty after Dora left, so Laurie went outside. She walked around the side of the house to the backyard in search of Ted and Susan. At one point, she thought she heard Susan's high-pitched laughter, but when she reached the backyard neither her daughter nor husband was there. She lingered momentarily on the stamped concrete that comprised the walkway along the side of the house that wound to the patio around back, scrutinizing each concrete panel as if to glean some pertinent information from it. A cool breeze came through the trees and rattled the leaves over her head. She backed up into the tall grass while her gaze scaled up the side of the house to the stunted turret of the belvedere at the center of the roof. From this angle, she could see two of the four sides of the belvedere. One of the windows looked funny, like something was propped up over the glass—a sheet or a board or something. She shielded her eyes against the sun, but still could not make out what it was.

That's it. That's where he jumped. The realization chilled her.

She was about to go inside when she heard the laugh again—the same girlish pitch, though much closer this time. She turned around in time to see someone moving along the fence on the other side, a shadow gliding between the slats.

"Susan?"

The fence was too high for her to peer over, so she leaned against it, trying to glimpse through the slats. She could see no one—the trees on the other side of the fence were too abundant, the gap through which she peered too narrow—yet she was certain someone was standing just on the other side. She repeated her daughter's name, her voice now edged with unease. Waited.

After several seconds holding her breath, she went back inside.

Dora Lorton had been right: the house was devoid of almost all personal affectations and any other items Laurie's father might have construed as frivolous in nature. Almost everything served a functional purpose. Laurie spent the next hour wandering from room to room, familiarizing herself with the layout of the house again, and catching glimpses of fleeting memories every time she turned a corner. The trips she had made to the house in her later years, when she had been a teenager and thrust upon her father for brief periodic visits, were less memorable to her than the years of her preadolescence, when she and her mother had lived here. Yet even those memories were hazy at best, sheened in vagueness and populated by questionable details. Myles Brashear had been a large man with huge, calloused hands and a head that looked slightly wider at the bottom than it did at the top. To look upon him was to assume he eked out his profession slogging away at some grist mill, quarry, or foundry. His year-round tan might have suggested a possible career in construction as well. Yet while Myles Brashear had not been afraid to get his hands dirty, he had been a businessman in shirtsleeves and a necktie. He made the first half of his money as the co-owner of an upstart steel-manufacturing company in Sparrows Point that produced steel for both government and private concerns, including bridges, cargo ships, commercial and industrial buildings, and four separate railroads. He made the second half of his money when he allowed his business partners to buy him out in the early 1980s, after recognizing that the steel industry was declining in favor of scrap recycling and the use of oxygenized furnaces. He had retired at fifty-five and spent the rest of Laurie's childhood tending to various gardens he had planted around the property off Annapolis Road. That was mostly how Laurie remembered him now: a large man with big hands digging in potter's soil in the yard.

She recalled an afternoon drive she had taken with her father so many years ago now. It was just before the divorce, and tensions in the household were running high. Laurie couldn't have been more than ten or eleven—young enough to be confused at the breaking apart of her family but powerless to understand the fundamentals of what had gone wrong between her parents. That afternoon, her father had taken her out for ice cream and then out to the park. She had asked him where he worked—she had always thought the name,

Sparrows Point, sounded mystical and beautiful—and her father had smiled with just the corner of his mouth. He turned the car onto the beltway. Soon, they were crossing the Key Bridge, the glittering expanse of the Patapsco River extending like a great panel of smoked glass. As they crossed the bridge, Laurie could see large cylindrical concrete towers rising up against the horizon, many of them spewing thick white clouds. "This is it," Myles Brashear had told her as they reached the opposite end of the bridge. The landscape was filled with steel-and-glass buildings, industrial parks gridded with pipes, scaffolding like jungle gyms, and spacious paved parking lots twinkling with cars. Directly across the street from the factories, Laurie caught intermittent glimpses of marshland and ruinous little one-story houses with large TV antennas on their roofs. Even the air smelled putrid.

Laurie had stared out the window at the sights in horror. This was Sparrows Point? This was no magical wonderland like she had always pictured in her mind. She was about to say something about it all when her father pulled the car onto the shoulder of the road, slipped it into park, and remained staring out the windshield at the collection of foul-looking smokestacks that rose up like medieval turrets along the horizon. They remained there on the side of the road for a while, neither of them speaking a word. She watched her father's profile and could see his cheeks growing flushed and his eyes becoming glassy.

After several more minutes, he rubbed his eyes with the heels of his hands, turned and offered her a wan smile, and said, "Pretty lousy little place, huh?"

She wanted to ask if he was okay, because she could see there was some visible ache within him, but she couldn't bring herself to formulate the words. Then he lightly pinched her cheek and said, "Let's get home." Laurie and her mother had moved out of the house two days later.

She found herself surprised at the welling of emotion that accompanied such a memory. It was one of the few good ones she had of her father, and even that one wasn't actually *good,* just emotional. Sparrows Point had been a hideous industrial park instead of paradise, and so had her parents' marriage. She had been too young to make the comparison back then, but it wasn't lost on her now.

"Stupid," Laurie told herself as she splashed cool water onto her face in the downstairs bathroom. When she heard footsteps out in the hall, she shut the water off and said, "Susan?" When Susan didn't answer, she called out to Ted. But he didn't answer, either. "Are you guys back?"

Beginning to feel foolish for talking to an empty house, she dried her face and hands on the neatly folded plain white towel at the corner of the sink. She was dragging the towel down her neck when she heard the footsteps again. They sounded like they crossed down the hall, through the parlor, and into either the dining room or the kitchen. Laurie dropped the towel and stepped out into the hallway. "Hey," she called again, more sternly this time. "Is that you, Ted? Susan?" She cleared her throat. "Is someone here?"

The fearful look on Dora Lorton's face as she peered up at the house while the Cadillac pulled away suddenly resurfaced in Laurie's head. Again, she felt foolish for allowing her mind to toy with her already frazzled nerves so liberally. Yet she wondered if perhaps the old woman had forgotten something and come back. "Ms. Lorton? Dora?"

She crossed into the parlor and surveyed the empty room—the sofa still creased from where Ted had been sitting, the phonograph and piano, the musty little liquor cabinet, the geometry of daylight coming from the windows and playing across the gouged hardwood floor. Dust motes spiraled in the shafts of light. There were no open windows and thus no breeze circulating in the house, but she thought she heard the faint chiming of the crystal chandelier out in the foyer.

A door slammed at the opposite end of the house. Laurie jumped. It had been the front door. She turned and looked down the hallway to the foyer. The front door was closed, just as she had left it after coming back in from the porch. *Had* Dora Lorton come back?

She went to the door, opened it, and stepped back out onto the porch. The Cadillac had not returned, and there was no sign of Dora or Felix Lorton—or Ted and Susan, for that matter—anywhere in the vicinity. Disquiet settled over her like a shroud. At that precise moment, it was very easy to convince herself that she was the only person left alive on the planet, and that she had imagined the Lortons and had even imagined her husband and daughter—that anyone she had ever cared about had been just a figment of her imagination all along.

She went back inside, shut the door, paused, and then turned the dead bolt.

*   *   *

There were five rooms on the first floor in addition to two bathrooms—the parlor, the kitchen, a dining room with an adjoining antechamber that had once been a small sitting room but was now completely barren, and her father's study. Just as Dora had mentioned, the carpeting in some of the rooms had been pried up in corners while sections of molding had been removed from the walls. Moreover, holes had been punched into the walls—and not figuratively either, as it seemed these depressions had been made from *punching* with someone's actual *fist*. The crenellation of knuckles could be seen in the circumference of the holes. There was a full bath at the end of one of the diverging hallways as well as a small half bath out in the main hallway. With little emotion, she remembered her father had called the main hallway the *thoroughfare*. At the time, the word had sounded impossibly alien to Laurie. Now, it made the place seem less like a home and more like something constructed for strict functionality. It was a *house,* in other words, and not a *home*.

Laurie wended through these rooms, impressed by the cleanliness yet chilled by the emptiness of each of them. She grew uneasy when she noticed that the windows in each of these rooms had been nailed shut—large carpentry nails driven through the base of the windows and into the sill. She recalled Dora saying something about her father having grown paranoid near the end, and that he'd had the locks on the doors changed. Had he also come through these rooms wielding a hammer, frantically pounding nails into the framework like a mad carpenter?

On the way to her father's study, she passed by the empty picture frame hanging on the parlor wall. Disturbed by it, she took it down and dropped it behind the liquor cabinet. Cracking open the stained teakwood door at the end of the hall, she poked her head in. It was a small room outfitted in empty bookshelves and a lush burgundy carpet. There was a handsome rolltop desk at the center of the room. A leather chair piped with brass tacks was tucked into the foot well of the desk. The chair faced a pair of arched windows shuttered in wooden blinds. Bands of fading sunlight issued through the slats. The furniture and carpeting held no memories for her—she couldn't recall if they'd always been here (for they certainly looked old) or if her father had purchased them later in life, after Laurie and her mother had moved away.

She went to the windows, drew back the blinds, and saw that these windows had also been nailed shut. She took a step back. Daylight now streaming through the windows, she saw that crosses of varying sizes had been gouged into the wood-paneled walls. They were everywhere, hacked into the paneling by some blunt object, too many to count. This surpassed religious zealotry. This was madness.

There were a few cardboard boxes on the floor, stacked in front of the desk. Laurie pulled back the flap on the top box and peered inside. There was a cigar box and a few pipes, a silver letter opener that resembled a dagger, some unused white candles still in the cellophane wrapping, a set of keys on a keychain, and various writing implements. Something glittered and she reached in and took out a gold cuff link with a black onyx face. It was heavy. She dropped it back in the box next to its twin and didn't bother going through the rest of the boxes that day.

Upstairs, the second-floor landing cut to the left at the top of the stairs. To the right was the closed door of the master bedroom and nothing else. She cracked open the door and peered in through the sliver at a gloomy room that smelled like the antibacterial cleaners used at hospitals. The window shades were halfway drawn, leaving the scarce few items in the room to suggest their shapes without giving up any details. She made out the poster bed and a nightstand, an armoire, and a set of folded linens on the cushioned seat below the shaded windows. The memories that trailed out of that room were multitudinous but vague in detail. They were more like slides shuttled quickly through a lighted projector—images glimpsed at random and out of logical sequence—than actual memories. Biting her lower lip, she shut the door and moved on.

There were two remaining bedrooms and a full bathroom up here along the length of the hallway, each of their doors closed. The door to the linen closet was closed, too. There was one final door among the others, this one narrower than the rest. Laurie knew it led up into the belvedere. Not only was this door closed just like all the others, but someone had drilled a metal plate into the frame and locked it with a padlock. She was reminded of a story she had read when she was just a girl in high school—something about a man having to choose between a lady and a tiger, each one hidden behind a similarly closed door. The story ended before you found out which door the man chose, thus leaving the reader to guess at the man's fate. For whatever reason, the memory caused her to shudder. She reached out and gripped the doorknob. It turned freely but the padlock prevented the door from opening. She clutched the padlock, and tugged at it. It was certainly secure. Just above the metal plate, the woodwork of the frame was splintered and gouged, as if someone had tried to pry the lock off with a crowbar or screwdriver. Had that been how her father had gained access to the belvedere the night of his death? She thought that was plausible, but then recalled Dora telling her that the door hadn't been locked that evening, so there would have been no need to pry at the lock. Had Dora been mistaken? Had she gotten incorrect information from someone? Moreover, despite *how* her father had managed to access the belvedere, why had the metal plate been replaced and the door relocked *after* his death?

"Hell," she muttered to herself when she realized she didn't have a key for the padlock. She walked down the hall toward the other closed doors and opened each one systematically, not surprised by her lack of sentiment in peering in and seeing the blank walls and sun-bleached carpets. Just like in the rest of the house, the furniture in these rooms was minimal and functional at best— another desk and chair, an armoire, a small bed in the room at the end of the hall. The windows here were all nailed shut, too. *I had no idea he was this bad. Who did he think was going to break in through a second-story window?* This last room had been hers when she had been a young girl. She assumed it was where the night caretaker, Ms. Larosche, had stayed during the night shift. Again, she was unsurprised by her lack of emotion in seeing it all.

A door slammed downstairs. Again, Laurie jumped. Was someone trying to drive her mad? She went back out onto the landing and was about to shout down over the railing when she heard Ted and Susan giggling together. Given the bare wooden floors and the overall emptiness of the large house, sound traveled with almost supernatural efficiency. A moment later, Susan's high-pitched voice called out for her. Laurie heard the girl's rapid footfalls racing along one of the hallways.

Thoroughfare, she thought coldly.

"I'm upstairs," Laurie called back. She went down the stairs and nearly collided with her daughter in the foyer. "There you are, kiddo."

Susan's face was bright and beaming. She had her hands clasped together and held out in front of her. She thrust them toward Laurie now. "Guess what I caught!"

"Caught?" Laurie said. "As in, something is alive in your hands?"

"A baby frog!"

"Oh, my . . ."

"There was a whole bunch of them in this little pond by the woods!"

"Don't let it loose in the house."

"I won't," Susan said, and spun away back down the hall.

Ted was washing his hands in the kitchen. Laurie folded her arms and leaned against the kitchen doorway, watching him for several seconds before he observed her reflection in the windowpane over the sink. Outside, it was beginning to grow dark.

"It's very pretty out there," he commented, shutting off the water and drying his hands on a dishtowel. Laurie thought it might have been the same dishtowel Dora Lorton had been carrying around with her in the pocket of her frock. "The lawn's a little overgrown and the trees and shrubbery need trimming, but the grounds are very nice. That Felix Lorton knew how to maintain the property."

Laurie smiled weakly at him. She felt suddenly very tired. "Most likely, it was my father. He fancied himself a gardener and an amateur horticulturist."

"There's some water out beyond the trees in the back, too."

"That's the Severn River," Laurie said.

"There were some kids flying kites on the other side. We saw them through a break in the trees. Susan yelled to them and I think they heard her. I think they waved, too."

"Go ahead," she said. "You're going to propose something, aren't you?"

He came and kissed the side of her face. He smelled like his cologne and there was a piece of dead leaf in his hair. She left it there and said nothing about it.

"It makes no sense to throw money away on a hotel," he said. "Unless, of course, you're that uncomfortable with the idea of staying here at all. . . ."

"I don't know, Ted. . . ."

"And the place is great. It's the first time Susan's smiled since she learned she was forfeiting summer vacation with her friends." He shrugged. Laurie noted how young he looked when he was excited about something, as if the boy within him was given permission to peek out on these infrequent occasions. More and more, she found she was astonished by Ted's persistent youthfulness. He was three years older than she was yet he looked younger than her. In another five years, she would look like his mother.

"You have a leaf in your hair."

"Also, we don't know how long it's going to take to get everything squared away with your father's estate." He raked fingers through his hair but did not disturb the leaf. "I could really get some good work done here. There has to be a million rooms to choose from. Trying to work on this adaptation in some cramped hotel room . . ." He made a face that finished the sentence for him.

"A million and one rooms," she said. She was thinking of the windows nailed shut, the crosses gouged into the walls of her father's study. "This is what Susan wants, too?"

"It was her idea!" He stood beside the counter with his hips cocked, his arms folded just as Laurie's had been a moment before. "She thinks the place is great."

"All right," Laurie said.

"But only if you're comfortable with it."

"I said all right. I'm okay."

"And only if we take down that creepy empty picture frame." He grimaced but there was still joviality in his eyes.

"I already have."

"Wonderful. You're a saint." Again, he pecked a kiss

on her cheek. Then he bellowed into the next room, "Hey, Snoozin! Guess what!" His voice boomed down the empty halls of the house.

"It got loose!" Susan shouted from somewhere in the house. Then she squealed. "Daddy! The frog got loose!"

Laurie shivered. "Oh, Jesus . . . Ted . . ."

"I'll get it," he said, still grinning his boyish grin. He rushed past Laurie and galloped down the hall. "Where are you, Snoozin?"

He's going to outlive me. The thought lightninged into her brain out of nowhere. *He'll be like Benjamin Button. I'll get older and he'll just keep getting younger and younger.*

She knew dementia was hereditary, and not for the first time since learning of her father's illness, she wondered if the horrible affliction waited for her somewhere in the future. The last conversation with her father had taken place about six months ago. By then, she was already well aware of the dementia settling cloaklike around him. Eighteen months earlier she had hired a full-time caretaker to look after him from a well-reputed service in Baltimore, which had turned out to be Dora Lorton, and Laurie had since received a few phone calls from Dora's boss, Mr. Claiborne, on a number of occasions concerning his recommendation and ultimate inclusion of a night nurse in order to provide her father with twenty-four-hour care. But Laurie had not known the true severity of Myles Brashear's senility until that final telephone conversation with him. Midway through their phone call, the old man's speech became garbled. Several times she had asked him to repeat what he'd said. When his speech became clear again, the words were there, but they were arranged now in a patternless jigsaw, a litany of nonsense. Twice he called her Tanya. Biting her lower lip, Laurie had remained on the phone and did not interrupt the man until he was once again back in his own head. His apology was pitiable, and she thought that maybe he was crying on the other end of the line. She told him not to worry about apologizing to her . . . though what she really wanted to tell him was that if he'd been more available to her as a father all these years, he could have moved in with her, Ted, and Susan, to live out his remaining years with family instead of in a cold and lonely house with no one but paid caretakers to look after him. It had been on the tip of her tongue. She had watched the seconds tick by on the kitchen wall clock. She hadn't said it.

The phone call about his death came a week ago from Charles Claiborne, managing director of Mid-Atlantic Homecare Services. Laurie had been reading a Janet Evanovich novel in the living room when the call came in. Ted had answered the phone. She listened and could tell it wasn't a typical phone call. Just hearing the tone of Ted's voice, she had thought, *It's about my father. He's dead. And now I'm going to have to deal with all that*.

After he hung up the phone, Ted had come into the living room and sat beside her on the couch. He rubbed her back and told her what Mr. Claiborne had said. She had thought that maybe his heart had given out or that he'd suffered a stroke, but it wasn't to be that simple.

Laurie listened to it all in stunned silence. She tried to imagine what he must have looked like lying there on the stamped concrete pavers, all twisted and broken and useless . . . but then realized she had no idea what the man had looked like in old age, and was only able to summon images of him from her youth, when he had been her father and not some desperate recluse barricaded inside some aging old manse. Later, her father's lawyer, David Cushing, called and spoke with her. The house in Maryland—that aging old manse—was now hers, along with all of her father's belongings, as well as what money was in the man's accounts. There were papers to be signed and things to go over, but David Cushing had promised to make it as simplistic and painless as possible. Cushing had given Laurie his condolences and then hung up the phone.

Now, standing in her dead father's kitchen, Laurie was overcome by a tidal wave of erratic emotion. At least guilt wasn't one of them. Not that she could tell, anyway. It angered her that this had been her *mother's* house for a time, too, but the entire place seemed wholly and solely infused with her father—that singular haunting entity. Her mother had been a kind and intelligent woman who did not deserve to have her memories overshadowed by her father's.

Before the anger turned volatile, Laurie went into the parlor to find her husband and daughter on their hands and knees looking under the sofa.

"Don't tell me," Laurie said.

"Mommy, it's under the couch," Susan said, looking up at her mother. The expression on her face was one of worry, as if the sofa had designs to eat her poor frog alive.

"You better get it."

"It's so *tiny*," Susan whined, and Laurie didn't know if the statement was meant to allay Laurie's fears about having a rogue amphibian loose in the house or to state Susan's own concerns about the poor little frog's helplessness.

"There!" Ted said, and vaulted up onto his feet. "It's getting away!"

Susan shrieked and Ted laughed. They both darted between the sofa and loveseat and chased after the tiny black dot that bounced toward the hallway. Still laughing, Ted told Susan to be careful and not to accidentally step on the little fellow.

A phantom coldness overtook Laurie. Shivering, she turned and saw through the adjoining sitting room that the storm door that led out into the side yard stood open. Laurie went to the door and shut it. There was a locking mechanism on the handle which Laurie thumbed to the locked position. Out in the side yard, the slope of the lawn had darkened as the sun began to set. The sky beyond the trees was a brilliant panorama of orange and pink threaded with scudding white clouds. The green moss on the fence now looked black and the trees that drooped over the fence swayed in what looked to be a strong summer wind. On the other side of the fence, she could see the green car in the neighbor's driveway. The second car was still parked at the curb, and she could see now that the emblem on the door was a dark green BGE logo—Baltimore Gas and Electric. There was a light on in the window of one of the upstairs rooms of

the house, too. A silhouette stood framed in the center
of the lighted window. The longer Laurie stared at the
silhouette, the more she was able to convince herself
that the silhouette was staring back at her. For the first
time in what seemed like an eternity, she thought of a
dead girl named Sadie Russ.

CHAPTER 5

Laurie prepared dinner while Ted and Susan brought their bags in from the car. When Susan learned they would be staying in the big house with the nice yard that sloped toward the woods and the gray river beyond, she cheered for joy and hugged Ted around the hips. Laurie told her that there would be ground rules, which they would address in time, but Susan, now basking in the simple pleasures of childhood vindication, was only partially listening. Ted asked where he should bring the bags and Laurie informed him that Susan's stuff could go in Laurie's old room at the end of the upstairs hall, since there was still a bed in there. Ted could take their stuff and put it in the master bedroom, though she confessed that she hadn't yet been in there to look around and did not know the state of it.

Dora had done a noteworthy job stockpiling the refrigerator and cupboards with suitable groceries, so Laurie whipped up some stir-fry with shrimp, which was Ted's favorite, and promised Susan they could make brownies together after dinner. Again, Susan cheered—it seemed the world was smiling down on this young girl who, as recently as yesterday evening, had planted herself obstinately in her bedroom closet with her headphones on and cried about having to leave Hartford and all her friends for the summer. Susan helped Laurie set the dining room table—there were good Wedgwood dishes in one of the cupboards—and the three of them ate with great relish. It had been a long and exhaustive day, and they hadn't realized just how ravenous they'd been.

"So what's the deal with the locked door upstairs?" Ted asked after he'd finished eating, setting his fork down on his plate. "You got a deformed stepsister locked away up there or something?"

Susan's mouth made an O.

"There's a set of stairs behind it leading up into a little room above the second floor," Laurie said. "My father called it the belvedere."

"That tower-looking room on the roof?"

"The very same."

"How come it's locked?"

"I'm not sure."

"What's a . . . a belve—" Susan asked.

"It's like a loft," Ted explained. "A little room."

"I'll have to call Dora Lorton and see if she has a key for the lock," Laurie said. Yet for some reason she couldn't explain, the idea of speaking to Dora Lorton again made her uncomfortable.

After dinner and dessert were finished, they retired to the parlor. Susan's cheerfulness was short-lived when she realized what not having a television in the house actually meant. Even Ted grumbled about this under his breath but didn't make an actual show of it. Instead, Susan played the piano while Ted addressed the antique liquor cabinet with a hungry sort of curiosity. Laurie sat on the sofa and looked over the paperwork the lawyer David Cushing had FedEx'd to them back in Hartford. The meeting with Cushing was set for tomorrow afternoon. Back in Hartford, during the phone call with Cushing, Laurie had agreed to have her father's body disposed of as expediently as possible. Myles Brashear was cremated, and that had been the end of him. There had been no funeral, since there were no family members alive who might be willing to attend—none that Laurie was aware of, anyway.

Laurie only hoped the meeting with Cushing wouldn't be too strenuous. Cushing had already agreed to assist Laurie in organizing an estate sale . . . for a nominal fee, of course. She had no use for any of her father's belongings, minimal as they were. As for the house itself, they would put it on the market and hopefully be rid of it as soon as possible. Once it was all over, she would never have to think about this place again.

"Will you look at this stuff?" Ted said as he peered into the liquor cabinet. "Harvey's Bristol Cream, an unopened bottle of Hiram Walker triple sec that looks like it was pillaged off an old pirate ship. . . ." He whistled. "This stuff is ancient."

"Was granddad a pirate?" Susan asked while seated at the piano. She was chugging through minor scales with a slow, unpracticed concentration. Now she stopped and turned sideways on the piano bench to look at her father.

"Do you see any parrots flying around?" Ted responded. "Do you see any eye patches or peg legs in the umbrella stand?"

Susan turned red-faced with laughter. The whole thing made Laurie uncomfortable. She didn't like hearing Susan refer to Myles Brashear as "granddad," and the young girl's laughter echoing hollowly through the house struck Laurie as offensive, though she didn't understand exactly why. "Why don't you go upstairs and get ready for bed?"

"It's still early!"

"It's been a long day. No talkbacks, Susan."

Susan whined to Ted, who shrugged his shoulders offhandedly. "Listen to your mother. No talkbacks."

"Can I at least check on Torpedo? Please?"

It was the name she had given to the frog. Earlier, following the little creature's escape, Ted had cornered it in the dining room and managed to trap it underneath a Tupperware container. "Speedy little torpedo," he'd said, and Susan had liked the name, though Laurie did not think the girl understood its meaning. Laurie had retrieved the old cigar box from her father's study, poked some holes in it, and had given it to Susan for her pet. Now, the cigar box sat on the front porch. Susan had filled it with twigs and grass and some small crickets she had chased around the yard so the frog would have something to eat.

"Okay," Laurie relented, "but do it quickly. No dillydallying."

Susan hopped off the piano bench and raced down the hall. Laurie heard the front door swing open.

"Are you feeling okay?" Ted asked. He was replacing the bottles back inside the liquor cabinet.

"I feel fine." She set the legal paperwork down on the coffee table. "This paperwork is just making my head spin."

"I'll have a look for you."

"It's fine. The lawyer will tell us all we need to know tomorrow."

"Is it something else?" He came up behind her and massaged her shoulders. "Is it about your dad?"

"No. Strangely, no." She hadn't been thinking of her father at all, in fact. She had been thinking of Dora Lorton. The way the woman had looked at the house as the Cadillac pulled out of the driveway . . .

Ted kissed the top of her head. "If you change your mind about staying here . . ."

"It's okay. I'm okay." Wearily, she smiled up at him.

Susan appeared in the doorway. Her cheeks were slick with tears and her chin was a wrinkled knot—what Ted often called her "walnut chin" when she was upset, because that's what it most closely resembled.

Laurie sat up stiffly. "What?" she said. "What is it?"

"He's dead. Torpedo's dead."

"Oh, honey," Ted said. Susan ran to him and he scooped her up in his arms. She sobbed against his neck. Ted made shushing sounds and swung her gently from side to side.

Laurie got up and went down the hall to the front door. Susan had left the door open. Laurie stepped out onto the porch and immediately felt the chill in the air. Beyond the porch, the world was comprised of infinite darkness. This sort of darkness did not exist back in Hartford, where the suburban streets were overcrowded with houses and vapor lamps and there were always cars cruising up and down the neighborhood streets. This darkness was nearly primordial in its depth and magnitude. Just beyond the porch, the lawn resounded in a chorus of crickets.

Laurie bent down to examine the cigar box that sat on the porch beside the door. She opened the lid and there it was, the little thing gray and stiff among a spongy mat of dry grass and bits of twigs. The frog's eyes bulged, its mouth frozen open. Laurie could see its individual ribs, thinner than toothpicks. Some of them appeared broken. She jostled the box until the stiff little amphibian rolled obediently onto its back.

She considered tossing the contents of the cigar box off the porch, but then thought better of it. If she knew anything about her daughter, it was that the girl possessed unwavering sentimentality. Susan would want to dispose of the frog herself. And Ted would humor her. He would probably help her dig a hole in the yard, maybe even say a few words: a makeshift funeral for a stiff little amphibian. That this frog might receive the service her dead father had not was a notion that was not lost on Laurie. Yet the thought did not upset her.

Back in the house, Ted was still cradling Susan in his arms. Susan had stopped crying but Laurie could hear her snuffling against Ted's shoulder.

"Okay, Susan," Laurie said. "Calm down, hon. It's just a frog."

Susan's grip around her father intensified as she issued a shrill whine. Ted frowned at Laurie from over Susan's hair.

"Come on," he said, patting Susan on the back. He moved past Laurie and out into the hall. "Let's go upstairs and brush those teeth."

Laurie listened to him climb the stairs to the second floor. The whole house creaked. *We baby her too much. We're turning her into a needy, spoiled child.* Perhaps she had agreed to stay here instead of the hotel too quickly. Susan was as fickle as any ten-year-old; she would have wound up adjusting to the hotel just as easily as this old house. In fact, probably more so, since there would have been a lot to keep her occupied in downtown Annápolis, not to mention a TV in the hotel room. What was there for a ten-year-old to do hanging around an old house all day?

In the kitchen, Laurie loaded the dirty dishes from dinner into the dishwasher. The plate of leftover brownies looked as unappetizing to Laurie as a plate of charred wood. Disgusted, she dumped them into the trash pail beneath the sink. They had turned into hard little cassettes and sounded like stones striking the bottom of the pail.

She went into the hall and paused, listening to Ted and Susan talking in hushed voices upstairs. Quietly, she climbed the stairs and stood at the top. The bedroom door at the far end of the hallway was open and there was a light on in there, but she couldn't see Ted or Susan. Holding her breath, she listened.

At first, it sounded like Ted was consoling her in the loss of her frog, but then Laurie realized they were talking about her—she could hear Ted saying "mommy" over and over again to their daughter in a placating tone. Heedful of loose floorboards, Laurie crept closer to the open bedroom door. She paused halfway down the hall when she heard the squeak of bedsprings.

"It's like when Sissy O'Rourke's dog was hit by that car," she heard Ted say. "Remember? You had to be extra nice to Sissy for a while. Remember how we went over and brought her those chocolate chip cookies?"

"I helped bake those cookies," Susan said.

"Yes. And you did a splendid job," Ted said. "But now you have to be that way for Mommy, if just for a little bit. Does that make sense?"

"Yes," Susan said, her voice hushed now. "I think so."

"That's good. So we'll try to be a little tougher for Mom, okay?"

"Okay."

"Let's see your tough face."

Susan must have pulled a face, because she began giggling and then Ted laughed, too.

"Good," Ted said. "Now plant a kiss right here, sugar-pie."

The bedsprings squealed again.

Something solid seemed to wink into existence in the upper part of Laurie's chest. She didn't approve of Ted talking to Susan about her that way. It made her feel weak and feebleminded. She had spoken to him about it in the past, particularly after an inexplicable episode had happened to Laurie last year—the episode Ted referred to as the "highway incident." At the time, Ted had agreed with her, yet wound up doing what he wanted later on. She considered confronting him about it again, but the thought made her weary. She didn't have it in her. Not tonight. Not here in this house.

She went downstairs, locked up the house, and then crawled back up to the second floor. This time, the bedroom door at the far end of the hall was closed, which meant Susan had gone to sleep. To her right, the door to the master bedroom stood open. She realized that it was the one room in the house—with the exception of the basement—that she had not gone into yet. She approached slowly, hesitant to enter her father's old room. There was a four-poster bed, the sheets fresh and crisp. On the wall above the headboard was a massive wooden crucifix. Jesus was a wraith with a look of idiot madness on his face. Laurie pried it from the wall and slid it under the bed.

Exhaustion settling fully down around her now, Laurie went to the side of the bed and sat down. She kicked off her shoes and tucked them neatly beneath the bed. She pulled her shirt up over her head and draped it over the footboard. The button on her jeans required some finesse and, given her distracted state, it took her nearly a full minute to get it undone and the jeans off. Movement across the room drew her attention to the bedroom door. It eased silently closed on its own accord, until only a vertical sliver of dark hallway remained. The door to their bedroom in Hartford did the same thing: It never wanted to stay open. There was a full-length mirror on the back of this door, and it displayed to her the bedroom in reverse, including her own reflection. In the mirror, she looked like some boardwalk artist's hasty rendition of a human being. Even from across the room, she could make out the terrible dark hollows beneath her eyes. Her skin was the color of old parchment.

Her eyes were then drawn to the reflection of the ornate vase on the nightstand. It was shaped like a cocktail shaker but carved from shiny beige stone marbled with blue veins. There was a lid on it. Vases didn't have lids. Laurie rolled to the other side of the bed and looked closely at the vase that was, in actuality, not a vase at all.

In the adjoining bathroom, the shower turned off. Ted's melodic whistling sounded from behind the bathroom door. When he stepped out amidst a billow of steam, he had a towel wrapped around his waist like a sarong and his hair slicked back. His reddened body was beaded with water.

Laurie was still staring at the urn. She hadn't moved.

"Hey," he said.

"Please," she told him in a small voice. "Please get this out of the bedroom."

"What?"

She continued to stare at the urn.

"What is . . ." he began, moving around the bed to the nightstand. He stopped when he realized what she was looking at.

"It hadn't occurred to me to ask what happened to his ashes," Laurie said. She drew her bare knees up under her chin. "That was stupid of me."

"No," said Ted. "It was stupid for someone to put this in here. It was probably one of those two from earlier today. That Felix Lorton, most likely. Stupid son of a bitch."

"It's not their fault. Just please take it away."

"Where should I—"

"I don't care, Edward." It was his real name, and he

hated it. She knew to use it only when she was deadly serious about something and wanted to show it. "Just put it downstairs for now. It makes me uncomfortable."

He scooped it off the nightstand. Still clutching his towel to his hip with his other hand, he went quickly out of the bedroom and down the stairs. She heard him fumbling around down there. In agitation, he mumbled something to himself, though his words were unintelligible. It was a big house. The echo was terrible.

She was asleep by the time Ted came back upstairs.

CHAPTER 6

She saw what she believed to be a ghost the next morning.

Laurie rose from bed before Ted and Susan were awake. Early morning sunlight streamed through the bedroom windows. She looked around, momentarily disoriented. Then it all came back to her in a solid wave. She sat up and climbed out of bed, careful not to wake up Ted. He was snoring soundly and looked very peaceful. She was almost envious of his apparent tranquility. He never had trouble sleeping. At the foot of the bed, Laurie rooted through her suitcase in silence, opting for a pair of sweatpants and a long-sleeved cotton jersey. She dressed quickly and, without stopping in the bathroom to brush her teeth and wash her face, she went downstairs.

Her father's urn was in the parlor, on the mantel of the fireplace. She paused slightly as she walked through to the kitchen, her gaze lingering on the veined ceramic jar.

With its large bay windows that faced east, the kitchen was bright. Peeking in the cupboards, Laurie found them stocked with various flavors of coffee. She selected a hazelnut blend, then spent the next several moments searching around the countertop for the coffee machine. There was none. It wasn't until she located an old pitted percolator among the pots and pans did the prospect of coffee look feasible again. A wry grin tugged at the corner of her mouth. She filled the percolator at the sink, then dumped in several spoonsful of coffee into the basket. She set the whole contraption on the stove, cranked the dial until the *click-click-click* of the gas gave way to a substantive *whump!* as the gas ignited into blue flame.

When she turned around, she saw a girl of about ten or eleven—Susan's age—run across the yard beyond the bay windows. The girl darted up the incline of the yard and disappeared behind the rippling tendrils of a willow tree. She had long, wavy hair the color of the hazelnut coffee and wore a knee-length dress of a breezy, light blue fabric. Before she disappeared behind the willow tree, the girl had cast a look over at Laurie through the bay windows, as if able to see Laurie standing there through the darkened glass.

Laurie's heart seized. It took her several moments before she was able to regain her composure. There was a door that led from the kitchen out onto a series of cement slabs that formed a porch in the backyard. Laurie went to the door now, unlatched it, and hesitantly pushed it open. The day had warmed considerably from yesterday, even at this early hour, though there was still a strong and chilly breeze in the air. She could smell the trees surrounding the property and, far beyond, the brackish scent of the Severn River.

In bare feet, she stepped out into the yard. She let the

kitchen door slam against the frame behind her as she walked up the slight incline toward the shaggy willow tree. The grass was damp with dew and cold against the bottoms of her feet. She reached the willow tree and saw that the girl was nowhere in evidence. There were many trees on both sides of the property, and it would be easy for someone to hide . . . but why would someone want to hide from her?

"Hello?" She wasn't surprised to find that her voice was horribly unsteady. She lifted some of the willow tree branches and saw that there was a hinged gate in the fence. It was closed but not properly latched. Laurie let the boughs slap back into place and then took a few steps backwards to where the lawn swelled so that she could better see over the fence and into the neighboring yard. The house next door was in poor condition, its siding overgrown with vines, its roof patchy with missing shingles. Some of the window shutters hung at crooked angles. From this vantage she couldn't see if the dusty green car was still in the driveway.

Looking at the house, it was impossible not to think of the Russes, and of Sadie Russ, who had once lived there. The visage of the girl running across the yard just a moment ago only encouraged such memories. *Sadie Russ,* Laurie thought, feeling the bare flesh of her arms prickle despite the warmth of the morning sun. *Sadie Russ, the girl next door, the horrible little wretch.* A nanosecond later, she hated herself for thinking such thoughts about the dead.

Laurie turned and continued up the incline toward the crest of the backyard. At the top of the hill, the property was overcome by sparse trees through which, after a distance, the vastness of the Severn River could be glimpsed. From what she could make out, the water looked to be the color of slate and filigreed with a fine cap of fog that made it nearly impossible to see across to the other side. Much of the shoreline was overrun by thick shoots of bamboo. As a little girl, she had played in these woods and along the riverbank quite often. *With Sadie,* her mind reminded her. *For a while, anyway.*

Shivering, Laurie cut to the left and followed the wooden fence as it trailed off into the woods. The damp cushion of the lawn surrendered to a rutted dirt footpath that wound through encroaching trees. It diverged from the moldy fence and wended deeper into the trees. Being early summer, the foliage was already bright green and thick. She followed the path, knowing from memory where it would ultimately end, though she was uncertain of what she would find when she arrived there. Her bare feet kicked at small stones and prickly balls that looked like cherries covered with sharp teeth. She looked up and saw the sunlight shining in dazzling arrays through a canopy of semitransparent leaves. Carved hastily in the trunk of a large oak was the word FUCK. The base of the tree was wreathed in wildflowers.

And then she came upon the clearing and saw it.

Her heart became infused with equal parts amazement, disbelief, and terror at the revelation that the thing *still existed* after all these years. One could call it a temple, a house of worship which had been constructed as a testament to her father's obsession. When she was just a child, it had been a shimmering glass box that reflected the sunlight and looked like something out of a fairy tale. She could go to any of the windows and look inside at the profusion of plants with their waxy green leaves and colorful explosions of flowers. Often, her father would spend hours here, tending to his flora.

It was the greenhouse.

Now, the little glass house was like a bad secret that had been hidden from the world. The glass panels were brown and grimy with muck so thick they were opaque. The glass itself was thick and unforgiving, unlike the polycarbonate panels used in modern greenhouses. Some of the panels were riddled with cracks, while others had been busted out completely. Triangular shards of glass lay scattered atop the dirt and grass. The roof of the greenhouse, once a cantilevered A-frame, was now a partially sunken pit beneath a weathered sheet of heavy brown canvas. The canvas itself was held in place by a series of long chains that ran down the side of the structure and were bolted to the bottom of the frame.

It was still here. After all that had happened and all the time that had passed, the goddamn thing was still here.

Laurie's mouth went dry. Beside the forgotten greenhouse, the immense oak tree still stood, its massive leafy boughs stretching out over the shattered and covered roof of the greenhouse.

What does it look like on the inside? She couldn't help but wonder. *After all these years, would there still be blood?*

She went around to the front of the structure. Beneath the rumpled and weather-ruined canvas tent, the greenhouse looked smaller than she had remembered it. But of course, the last time she had seen it she had just been a little girl. The front of the greenhouse was covered by two heavy-looking flaps of canvas. A thick rope had been wound through an eyelet at the corner of each flap and tied in a sturdy-looking knot. Frayed and colorless, even the rope looked ancient. Laurie was able to peel back one of the flaps a few inches and peer underneath without untying the rope. A smell like rotting vegetation accosted her. Behind the flap, she could make out the rectangle of the greenhouse door. The door was comprised of several panels of glass, but the glass had blackened with mold over the years, making it impossible to see beyond. With her free hand, she reached out and pressed two fingers against the door. She felt it give, as if the framework was made of sponge. Her eyes traced down to the handle, expecting to find a lock on the door. There was no lock. There was no handle, either—only a sheared metal bolt, burnt orange with rust, protruding from where the handle had once been.

She had suffered many nightmares about this little glass house, all of them immediately after Sadie Russ had died. And while those nightmares faded over time and with age and maturity, the sense of dread and terror that had come from them rushed over her now as if they had never left her. And perhaps they never had, that they had simply lain dormant and in wait for just this moment.

With a series of tugs, she undid the rope. It took some effort, but it eventually fell away and coiled in the dirt at her feet. She parted the canvas flaps like a stage actress parting a curtain for her encore, tucking each flap behind the lengths of chain that secured the canvas covering to the ground. The entire glass front was black. Things grew against the inside of the panes, dark green and furry. The smell coming from the structure was rank enough to transcend olfaction; it was as if all of her five senses were capable of being brutalized by the horrific odor of rotting vegetation. Regardless, she reached out and slipped fingers between the narrow space between the door and the spongy frame, and pulled it open.

The hinges didn't so much whine as growl. Hunks of black, springy mildew pattered to the ground. She managed to get the door open just a few inches when the smell from within breathed out into her face, warm and fetid, and no less potent than a punch to the stomach. With the canvas covering overtop the structure, the inside of the greenhouse was absolute darkness. Only hesitant milky light could be seen through some of the glass panels lower to the ground. Squinting against the darkness, she thought she could see dark, immobile shapes huddled within.

Is there still blood in there somewhere? she wondered yet again. *Has the blood seeped into the soil? Are there parts of Sadie Russ still hidden in there? The black, sightless tomb of a dead girl . . .*

Startled by the sound of someone crunching along a carpet of dead leaves, Laurie spun around and scanned the dense foliage at her back. At first she saw nothing. Then a shape parted from behind a tree and crossed hesitantly behind a scrim of saplings. Laurie glimpsed a cascade of dark hair and a dress that looked bleached from the sun. It was the girl she had seen running across the lawn just moments ago.

"Hello," Laurie called to the girl. Her voice frightened tiny birds, causing them to burst out of the trees and take to the sky. A squirrel that had been loping from branch to branch in a nearby tree froze. Through the trees, the young girl said nothing. She was perhaps twenty or thirty yards away, too far and too well hidden behind the foliage for Laurie to make out her face.

Laurie called to the girl again, this time trying to sound more pleasant. The girl took a step back toward the tree and then looked as though she wanted to crouch down and hide behind the screen of spindly saplings. When Laurie raised her hand and, smiling, waved to the girl, the girl turned around and ran off into the woods. Laurie heard her timid little footfalls trampling dead leaves, which confirmed for Laurie that the girl was not a ghost or some figment of her overworked imagination after all.

Feeling strangely unwelcome, Laurie walked back through the woods toward the house.

Before they left for David Cushing's law office, Ted and Susan went out to the backyard with the little cigar box with the holes punched into the lid. As Laurie predicted, Ted dug a shallow grave beside the moldy fence. With a doleful expression on her face that made her look eerily mature, Susan opened the lid of the cigar box and dumped its contents into the freshly dug grave. Ted rubbed the back of Susan's head and Susan laced a thin arm around her father's waist. Laurie watched from the kitchen windows.

CHAPTER 7

David Cushing's office was on the second floor of a two-story brick colonial on Duke of Gloucester Street in downtown Annapolis. There was ample parking in the rear and a cherubic-faced receptionist seated at a cluttered desk outside Cushing's office. The woman beamed a smile at the Genarro family as they came into the office and she told them Mr. Cushing would be with them shortly. Susan quickly grew agitated and began to pilfer candy from the little crystal bowl on the receptionist's desk. The receptionist smiled dully at Susan, but Laurie could tell she was growing increasingly annoyed. When Susan began talking playfully to the fish in the tank, the receptionist picked up her phone and spoke in a low voice into the receiver, muffling much of what she said with one meaty hand over her mouth. After she hung up, she told them that Mr. Cushing could see them now.

Cushing's office looked more like that of a high school gym teacher's than an attorney's. There were baseball and football trophies on shelves and framed print articles from local magazines and newspapers on the walls. The articles spoke not of David Cushing's lawyerly achievements but of his love of sport fishing, bicycling, and his frequent involvement in charity marathons. The screen saver on his computer was of two monkeys in boxing gloves exchanging punches in a ring with swollen red asterisks in place of eyeballs. Among the files and printouts on his desk, there were several Lego race cars and photos of small children with hair so blond it was nearly white.

David Cushing himself was surprisingly young. He possessed the keen eyes of a hawk, and he sported a short haircut that was perfectly styled. His shirt was crisp and white and his tie looked expensive. A pin-striped suit jacket hung from a coatrack in one corner of the office. David Cushing showed them his perfect teeth and shook their hands while a nice watch glittered on his wrist.

Laurie and Ted sat in comfortable chairs that faced Cushing's desk. Susan lingered behind them, finally resigning herself to sit on an ottoman outfitted in a Navajo design.

"The will is straightforward," Cushing said. He spoke with the charisma of a frat boy, with one corner of his mouth turned up into a sardonic grin. "Being the only living relative, Mrs. Genarro, he left pretty much everything to you. You've got the house and the property, the items inside the house, and the remaining money in his bank account."

Cushing slid a stack of paper across his desk to Laurie. She took it and looked at it. The numbers on the printout made her dizzy.

"There were no outstanding debts in your father's name at the time of his death, although there is still some money owed to the Mid-Atlantic Homecare Services. It isn't much—it's all there in the paperwork—and that will be taken off the top." Cushing reclined in his chair. "As you probably know, the house had been paid off years ago. The only real bills he had, aside from the monthly payments to his homecare service, were for food, utilities, insurance premiums, property tax, and the like. There's ten thousand dollars in his savings account after the payout to the homecare provider and another two thousand or so in checking. Some of that will go toward covering some of the medical bills when they come in, but your father had Medicare, so it shouldn't be too much."

"What medical bills?" Ted asked. "I thought he died instantly in the fall."

"Well, sure . . . but there were paramedics, an ambulance, and all the stuff that goes along with it. The police report details all of that."

Laurie blinked. "There was a police report, too?"

"Of course," said Cushing. "As well as a coroner's report. You never received it?"

In unison, both Laurie and Ted said, "No."

"I apologize. My assistant should have told you," Cushing said, playing with his sparkly gold watch.

"I never spoke with your assistant," Laurie told him. She rolled the papers into a cone and held it in her lap. "I just didn't realize there had been police involved. I guess it should have occurred to me. . . ."

"I don't understand. We were told it was a suicide," Ted cut in. "What's the purpose of a coroner's report? He broke his neck in the fall, didn't he?"

Cushing displayed the palms of his hands in a lazy shrug. "It isn't unusual in cases where there is an untimely death."

Untimely, Laurie thought. Her feet felt cold in her shoes. *My father jumped out a window.*

"Please don't be concerned about any medical costs. They will be minimal, as I've said." Cushing looked at a printout he had on his ink blotter. "Besides," he went on, "the real worth is in the house itself. I had my secretary run some comps on houses in the area. Your father's place has been assessed at seven hundred thousand dollars."

"Wait," Ted said, leaning forward in his chair. "What?"

"Seven hundred thousand dollars," Cushing repeated. His dark, sculpted eyebrows arched. "Back before the housing market crashed you could have put it on the block for closer to eight, but what with the status of the economy at the moment . . ." Cushing seesawed one hand to illustrate the instability of the current housing market.

Ted gaped at the man. Then he turned his ridiculous gaze onto Laurie. She smiled at him without much emotion, then looked back down at the rolled up papers in her lap. She feared she would burst out laughing if she kept staring at the flabbergasted look on Ted's face.

"I've already filed the will with the probate court on your behalf," Cushing said.

"Thank you," Laurie said. She glanced at Ted again and saw him smiling as he looked out one of the office windows.

"You mentioned your desire to liquidate your father's remaining assets," Cushing said. "The items in the house, for example."

Laurie nodded. "Yes."

"I've contacted a liquidator I've worked with a number of times in the past. She's quite good."

"That's good," Laurie said, although she had no idea what was involved in being "quite good" at selling a dead man's things. Was it any different than having a yard sale? When Laurie's mother had died, her aunts had taken care of the details. This was all new to her.

"She'll take thirty percent of the proceeds, which you'll find is standard. Of course, you're more than welcome to find someone else if you want to. Or to sell the stuff yourself, if that's more amenable to you. However, given the circumstances, most family members don't have the wherewithal to oversee such an undertaking, so I usually assist."

Ted nodded. "Okay. We've never done this before."

"I can have the liquidator contact you folks directly. Or, if you prefer, you can contact her." Cushing flipped through a rolodex, then presented Ted with a business card. "Her name is Stephanie Canton."

"All right," Ted said, looking at the card.

"Bored," Susan said from the back of the office.

"Hush down," Laurie told her from over one shoulder.

The corner of David Cushing's mouth tugged up a bit higher. "Cute kid," he said. Then he pointed at the business card in Ted's hand. Laurie could see that Cushing's fingernails had been recently manicured. "Stephanie's a peach. She'll be able to answer any of the questions you good folks might have. I'm sure you've got quite a few."

"Spectacular," said Ted as he tucked the business card into the pocket of his Izod polo shirt.

"Now," Cushing said, leaning back in his chair again, "there was that other issue we spoke about over the phone, I believe." Cushing was looking at Ted. "A claim against the health-care provider."

"Yeah," Ted said. He folded his legs.

Laurie frowned. "What are you talking about?"

"It was just something I had mentioned to Mr. Cushing, Laurie. We went over this back in Hartford."

"You're talking about a lawsuit," she said. She glanced at Cushing and, for the first time, saw that prideful little grin slide off his face.

"I just thought it would be beneficial to hear what our options are before you slam the door, Laurie," Ted said.

"I told you I had no interest in a lawsuit."

"It couldn't hurt to hear the man out."

"Mrs. Genarro," Cushing cut in. "Your husband and I merely discussed the possibility of holding Mid-Atlantic Homecare Services accountable for what happened to your father. Their negligence—"

"With all due respect, Mr. Cushing, my father suffered from horrible dementia and was undoubtedly a handful for the two women who looked after him. The only thing I want to do is hurry up and put this whole mess behind me, not drag it through the courts and relive it every minute of every day."

"Of course," Cushing said.

Laurie looked at Ted. "We've talked about this already. I just don't have it in me to prolong this any more than it needs to be. Okay?"

"Sure," Ted said, placing a hand on her knee. "Okay."

Behind the desk, David Cushing stood up. He tried the smile again but it seemed even phonier than before. "Well, then. There are just a few papers for you to sign, Mrs. Genarro, and then I can get you nice folks on your way. . . ."

Afterward, they walked down Main Street and had lunch at an outdoor bistro that overlooked the inlet. Boats pulled circles around the inlet and Susan cheered when one of them unleashed two resounding bleats from an air horn. Halfway down Main Street, a small white door in an alley between two shops had a sign on it that read PALM READINGS and there was a neon hand glowing in the door's window. Susan rushed up to the window and placed her palm against the neon hand. "Ooh. It's warm," she commented.

Ted was in high spirits. Every time Laurie looked at him she thought she saw dollar signs in his eyes, like some cartoon character. Several times over a lunch of steamed mussels, crusty bread, some crab dip, and quite a few mojitos, Ted commented on how stupefied he was at the assessed value of the house.

"Why the hell had you never told me your father had so much money?"

"I wasn't exactly sure how much he had," Laurie responded. Instead of a mojito, she had a glass of ice water in front of her. She ran one finger around the rim now. "I had no reason to think he'd leave me anything at all, anyway."

"Who else would he leave it to?"

"It just wasn't something I sat around and thought about. Like I said back at the lawyer's office, I just want this stuff over and done with."

Ted glanced at a busty woman who jogged by in a Lycra top and spandex running shorts. "I didn't mean to go behind your back and talk with Cushing about the lawsuit," he said. "I apologize. It was wrong of me. I was just worried you weren't thinking clearly at the time. I was only trying to look out for you."

For one second, she recalled the way Ted had whispered about her to Susan while tucking her into bed last night. He had done a lot of whispering about her after the incident on the highway last year. She knew it was only Ted looking out for her, and she felt a sudden pang of compassion for him.

"An old man in the throes of senility wanders up to the roof of his house and jumps off while Dora Lorton is being paid good money to keep an eye on him," Ted went on, just as she was getting ready to offer him a truce. "Cushing is exactly right. It's negligence. I just wish you'd listen to reason, that's all."

"You know as well as I do that Claiborne called us a number of times to inform us about my father's worsening condition," she countered. "He even suggested we send him to a home. But we both agreed we didn't have the money for that. So we're just as much to blame as anyone else. And besides," she added, knocking around a few ice cubes in her glass with a straw, "it wasn't Dora Lorton at the house that night. It was the other girl."

"What girl?"

"The girl they brought on for the night shift. Don't you remember approving a second caretaker?"

He shrugged. "I guess. Who's this girl?"

"Her last name's Larosche."

"What is that? French?"

"I have no idea."

"Have you spoken to her?"

"No. Dora Lorton mentioned her to me."

"Okay, whatever. So then this Larosche woman is to blame."

Laurie pushed her ice water aside. "Does it really matter? Do we really need the hassle of a lawsuit? We've got the house. Even if it sells for half the assessed value—"

He held up one hand. "Yeah, yeah, yeah. But it's the *principle,* Laurie. You get it?"

"Mr. Ryan, my principal, lost his hair during an assembly," Susan piped up. She had half a cheeseburger on the plate in front of her, though she had been spending most of her time cramming her mouth full of fries sprinkled with Old Bay seasoning. "He sneezed and it, like, flopped off. Did you know hair could do that?"

"It's called a toupee, doll," Ted told her. Then he looked back at Laurie. "I'd really like to hear from this Larosche about exactly what went on that night."

"You're being ridiculous," said Laurie.

"What's a toupee?" Susan asked through a mouthful of potato.

"Am I?" Ted said.

Laurie sighed. "I'm tired, Ted. I feel sick just being back here and at that house, and I hate dealing with all this stuff. I just want it put behind me, okay? Is that so goddamn hard to understand?"

Ted held up both hands, palms out. "Hey. I'm just giving you some food for thought, darling."

"I don't need anything else to think about right now."

Susan tugged at Laurie's arm. "Are you guys fighting?"

"We're not fighting, Snoozin," Ted answered. "We're just discussing."

"It sounds like fighting."

"It's not," Laurie told her.

"Oh." Susan pulled her hand away from her mother's arm. To her father, she said, "Don't call me Snoozin no more."

"Any more," Ted corrected her.

Frowning, Susan said, "What?"

CHAPTER 8

They picked up a pizza on the way home and were back at the house by six o'clock. Laurie was quiet for much of the drive back from downtown and Ted was in no mood to goad her into talking. Susan kept opening the pizza box in the backseat and plucking off slices of pepperoni which she stuffed into her mouth and then giggled to herself. The house loomed up over the incline as the Volvo approached it up the winding driveway. They had left some lights on, and the downstairs windows glowed now in the darkness like eyes. The moonlight glinting off the windows of the strange little room at the top of the house—the belvedere— made it look as though there was a soft light burning from within.

They ate at the dining room table in silence. Ted had never realized how much they relied on the TV back in Hartford for background noise until they had come to this place, where televisions, radios, and computers were things of science fiction. What kind of whack job had Laurie's father been, anyway? Ted ate two slices of pizza, then went to the liquor cabinet in the parlor, selected one of the ancient bottles—this one a dark cognac—and poured himself a couple of fingers into a crystal rocks glass. His laptop was in the bedroom upstairs, still packed away with their luggage. It had wireless Internet, and he supposed he could attempt to harness a signal from one of the neighbors, though he did not hold out much hope for this endeavor; the other houses along Annapolis Road looked even less contemporary than this one, particularly the rundown little cottage next door. Even on the drive back from downtown, he had only spied a few houses with lights on in the windows. Was this part of the city nothing more than a graveyard waiting to happen?

He knew he should sit down at the computer and work on the Fish adaptation, but his head wasn't in the game at the moment. It had taken him months to wend through John Fish's bloated tome and, upon finishing it, he'd been left with a hollow dissatisfaction he knew would be nothing short of a miracle to overcome. Overcoming it was necessary to his role in adapting the work for the stage, and his inability to lose himself in Fish's novel reflected in the ambiguous treatment and the uninspired pages he'd already written himself. Add to that the extra stress he felt in the knowledge that this could prove his biggest break to date, and he found himself reticent to make a single false move. Was he being overly careful with the pages he wrote, the outline he'd drawn up? Of course he was. His future depended on the moves he made. Yet he knew from experience that too much caution rendered him useless. *Writing was easier when I was younger and none of it truly mattered.*

Taking on the adaptation of John Fish's bestselling

novel *The Skin of Her Teeth* was his biggest compromise to date . . . but it had been five years since his play,
Whippoorwill, had seen its final performance at the little Greenwich Village theater, and an equal amount of
years since Ted had received a steady paycheck.

Now, carrying his cognac down the front hall and out
onto the porch, Ted wondered if the death of Laurie's
estranged father hadn't been a godsend. Over a half-
million dollars for the house? Laurie was right—even
if they sold it for half that amount, the money would
afford him enough peace of mind to really focus on the
Fish adaptation and whatever waited for him on the horizon after that. As it was, he laid awake at night worrying about money when he should be worrying about
the play.

Things had been tougher since Laurie had quit teach-
ing. Her quitting was the result of a singular episode that
had occurred during the stasis of time between *Whippoorwill*'s off-Broadway run and the John Fish gig—
what Ted eventually termed the "highway incident."
Despite the insecurity of his burgeoning profession and
worry over the influx of money to the household, Ted
had agreed that it might be a good idea for Laurie to
take some time off and eliminate some stress from her
life. What he hadn't realized at the time was that her
time off would turn into a full year of unemployment.
Moreover, she still showed no desire to return to work.
She used to paint from time to time, but they never saw
any substantial money from the small Hartford galleries that hung her work. He couldn't remember the last
time she had sat down to paint something, let alone the
last time she had sold a piece. So here he was, sell-

ing his creative soul to write an adaptation of someone
else's lousy story. *Funny how life can reach out and
grab you like that.* Yet he couldn't bring himself to say
anything to Laurie because there was a part of him that
believed he might have been the cause of what had happened to her on the highway that afternoon. . . .

Her name was Marney Owen. She was twenty-three,
and possessed a slim figure and a face that reminded
Ted of a wide-eyed Disney heroine. Yet she was anything but unworldly. She was a Marxist or a Maoist
(Ted hardly understood the difference) and she wore
kitschy berets and wool scarves even in the springtime.
She was also a grad student at CUNY and quite talented. She had also had a small role in *Whippoorwill,*
which was how they'd met. He knew very quickly that
he could sleep with this girl if he so desired. And, of
course, he desired.

He had been at Marney's one afternoon, lazing naked beside her in bed, when his cell phone rang. It was
Laurie's number, but there had been a man on the other
end of the phone. The man was a coworker of Laurie's,
and he'd found her car parked up on the shoulder of the
highway, Laurie seated in a catatonic state behind the
wheel.

What had happened? To this day, no one knew for
sure. Not even Laurie herself. She had been heading
to work at the university when she had been suddenly
overwhelmed by what her doctor would later term a
"fugue state." She remained buckled into the driver's
seat, her hands on the steering wheel . . . but for an un-
disclosed amount of time, she was unsure of who she
was or where she had been headed. Later, she would

describe it to Ted like having the power go out in the middle of a television program. "And when the program finally came back on," she had told him, "I was a little lost, having missed the part in-between."

There were some CT scans, an MRI. Yet nothing was found to be wrong with Laurie. It seemed everyone was ready to chalk it up to stress—Laurie included—but Ted began to wonder if she hadn't grown wise to his unfaithfulness and had suffered a moment of collapse, a mental breakdown. If this was the case, she never admitted such a thing to him, nor could he summon the courage to ask her. If she had learned of his infidelity and was willing to put it aside, so was he. And if she didn't know, then he certainly wasn't going to burden her with it. Overwhelmed by this unspoken guilt, he ended his relationship with Marney, who seemed hardly surprised or disappointed, and he had supported Laurie with her decision to quit work in order to give her mind some relaxation.

That had been roughly one year ago. There hadn't been another recurrence of the incident, whatever the incident had actually been, since that first time. At least as far as Ted knew. . . .

He downed the rest of his cognac, then dropped down off the porch and into the damp grass. The sky was alive with stars. Taking a deep breath, he could smell the river over the crest beyond the property. Once again, he was stupefied at just how much the house and the property was worth. Why hadn't Laurie ever mentioned this place to him?

His bladder full, he waded across the driveway and

stopped at the edge of the old well. Briefly, he contemplated kicking the plank of wood off to the side, unzipping his fly, and pissing down into the black chasm. But that seemed like too much work. Instead, he crossed the lawn and sidled up in front of the wooden fence that separated the two properties. Through the heavy foliage that grew over the top of the fence, he could see the house next-door, dark against the night. There was a flickering bluish light in one of the ground-floor windows that Ted recognized as the glow from a television set. Maybe they weren't all hillbilly Luddites around here after all.

Still watching the house, he unleashed a stream of urine against the fence. Above, small bats darted across the starry sky. He listened and thought he could hear the distant growl and mutter of boat engines along the river, even at this hour. Ted knew nothing about boats.

Something struck him squarely in the chest. He looked down but found nothing there. He hadn't seen anything, either, which caused a pang of fear to rise up in him as he considered that the sensation might have actually been internal. They say you feel a heart attack in the left arm first, but was that true one hundred percent of the time?

When something whizzed by his right ear, stinging the rim of cartilage there, he knew it wasn't a heart attack. He quickly shook off and zipped up his fly. Taking a few steps back from the fence, he tried to peer straight into the darkness and through the tangle of overgrown foliage above the pickets. A moment later, he saw something shoot out from the darkness and rush toward his eyes, quick as a bullet fired from a gun. He blinked and jerked his head to one side just as something hard struck his forehead, just above his left eyebrow. It stung.

He scrambled back toward the driveway, his hands up over his face now in a defensive posture. He listened but could hear nothing. The item that had struck him rolled across the lawn and came to rest beside the old well. It was a small stone.

"Hey! Is someone over there?" His voice was both a whisper and a shout. "I see you," he lied. "Come out."

There was a rustling sound on the other side of the fence, like someone treading on a carpet of dead leaves.

But no one came out.

Slowly lowering his hands, he looked up and surveyed the surrounding greenery, pitch-black now in the darkness. The trees rose high over the small fence, their boughs weighty with leaves and birds' nests. He listened and could hear squirrels or birds or bats moving around up there. Had they dropped acorns or stones down on him? He supposed it was possible, though it seemed unlikely. Besides, the force with which that last stone had hit him couldn't have been from a bird or a squirrel. And it hadn't fallen from above, either. It had come from over the fence.

Embarrassed by his own apprehension, he laughed. Then he trotted back across the lawn to the house, where there were lights on in many of the windows and where his girls awaited his return.

CHAPTER 9

The next morning, Laurie awoke to find Ted's side of the bed empty. His running shoes and preposterous-looking spandex shorts were gone, too. She washed and dressed in the adjacent bathroom, then stood for a moment looking at the rumpled bedclothes while trying to remember what it had been like when her parents had still been together and she had lived here. She found it nearly impossible to do so.

As she stepped out onto the second-floor landing, a muted thump caused her to pause. She went down the hall to Susan's bedroom, opened the door, and was surprised to find the bed empty. Susan rarely got up early on her own accord.

Back out in the hall, Laurie lingered for a moment, waiting to see if the sound would repeat itself. Old houses suffered all sorts of ailments, made all sorts of noises. It could have been the clang of a water pipe or the struts settling in the attic. It could have been anything. Yet her eyes arrived at the locked belvedere door. The padlock was still in place.

She went to the door and pressed her ear against it. The sound on the other side of the belvedere door was no different than the imaginary murmurings of the sea in a conch shell—muffled nothingness.

She looked down. A hazy strip of daylight filtered from beneath the door. Laurie got down on her hands and knees and peered beneath the door. On the other side of the door, she could see the bottom of the first step that ascended into the belvedere. Daylight glowed on the wood floor from above. She pressed the right side of her face down against the hall floor to attempt a better view of the stairwell on the other side of the door. As she did so, a shadow passed quickly through the panel of sunlight.

Laurie gasped and sat up. She felt her scalp prickle. Bending back down to the floor, she peered beneath the door again. There were no shapes, no shifting shadows. What she had seen must have been nothing more than the shadow of a tree branch in motion, projected through one of the belvedere windows and onto the floor like a strip of film on a screen.

Downstairs, Laurie found Susan seated alone at the kitchen table eating a large bowl of Cheerios. Laurie smiled at her daughter. "You're up early."

"It's after ten, Mom."

"Is it?" She looked around and realized there were no clocks in the kitchen. "I guess I'm just being a bum then." Laurie went to the sink and rinsed out the percolator, then refilled it with fresh coffee, opting this time for raspberry swirl. *Who the heck comes up with these coffee flavors, anyway?* She imagined a gnomish old man hunched over a series of test tubes and Bunsen burners in the basement of some remote warehouse in the New Mexico desert.

"How did granddad die?"

The question caught Laurie off guard, not because of the inquiry itself but in just hearing Susan refer to Myles Brashear as "granddad" once again. The girl had never met the man, and the familiarity with which she referred to him struck Laurie as absurd.

For a moment, Laurie considered how to respond, including an evasiveness she didn't think Susan would swallow. In the end, she opted for the truth.

"He fell out of a window and broke his neck."

Susan set her spoon down in her bowl. "What window?"

This is why I wanted to stay in a hotel, Laurie thought, sucking on her lower lip. She went to the refrigerator and took out a carton of milk and some eggs. Briefly, she considered lying to her daughter. Then she decided against it. "The window upstairs, in that little room above the second floor. The belvedere, remember?"

"In the *house?*" Susan said. *"Here?"*

"Don't tell me you're a superstitious old biddy, too." Laurie was thinking of what Felix Lorton had said to her about his sister, Dora, on that first day: *She was uncomfortable returning here alone after . . . well, what happened. My sister can be foolishly superstitious.*

"What does that word mean?"

"Superstitious means you believe in spirits and omens and karma. And karma is like, you know—what goes around comes around."

"No. The other word."

"What word?"

"Biddy."

"Oh." Laurie realized she didn't actually know the true definition. "A nosey old lady, I guess."

Susan scrunched up her face. "Why would you call me *that?*"

"It's just an expression. Eat your cereal."

"Did the police come here?"

"Why would the police come here?"

"I don't know. But that's what that lawyer said, remember? That's what they do on TV when someone dies, too."

Laurie took a frying pan out from the cupboard and set it on the stove. She turned the burner on, then went to the fridge and took out the butter. "Yes, Susan, there were police here. When someone has a bad accident like . . . like granddad did . . . you're supposed to call the police. And an ambulance, in case they need medical attention." As an afterthought, Laurie added, "We've talked about you watching those kinds of programs on TV, haven't we?"

"Did that lady find him dead?"

"What lady?"

"The lady who was here in the house when we got here, Mom." She sounded exasperated.

"Dora Lorton? No, honey."

"Who did?"

"There was another woman here when it happened."

"Do you like her?"

"Who's that?"

"The Dora lady," said Susan. "Dora the Explorer."

"I don't even know her."

"Did she seem nice?"

"I suppose," said Laurie.

"Oh."

"What's with all the questions this morning?"

"I'm just bored."

Laurie could see the wheels continuing to turn behind her daughter's eyes, but no more questions followed. It was the closest Susan had ever come to dealing with death. Ted's parents had died before he and Laurie had married, and Susan had been too young when Laurie's mother had passed away.

"You know," Laurie said, knocking a pat of butter into the frying pan, "if you have any questions about it, you can ask me."

"I already did," Susan said matter-of-factly.

"I mean any other questions."

"Like what?"

"Do you know what it means when someone dies?"

Susan wrinkled her face at her mother. "When you're dead, you're dead," said the girl. "Like Sissy's dog."

"That's pretty logical."

"Like Torpedo, too."

"Ah," said Laurie. "Torpedo the frog."

"He died and now he's not coming back. He's in frog heaven with all the other dead frogs. It's different than human heaven. There's just frogs there. And maybe some flies, so they can eat." She clanked her spoon against her bowl. "Do you believe in heaven?"

"For frogs?"

"For people, too," Susan said. "People mostly, I guess."

No, Laurie did not believe in heaven. Neither she nor Ted was religious and they had decided long ago that they wouldn't impinge any organized religion's contradictory and judgmental sentiments on their daughter. Now, however, in the face of Susan's question, she wasn't sure what the right response should be. There was a latent hopefulness in her daughter's voice and Laurie didn't want to be the one to smash that hope.

"What do you think?" Laurie said, turning the question around on her daughter.

Without missing a beat, Susan said, "I think Torpedo is still buried in the yard where me and Daddy put him. I bet if I dig him up, he'll still be there. And if there was a heaven that people go to, then who is buried in all those graveyards? If they're in the ground, they can't be in heaven, too."

"Some people believe only your spirit goes to heaven," Laurie said. "Not your whole body."

"Oh."

"Do you understand the difference?"

"I don't know."

"Does it bother you staying in this house now that you know what happened here?"

"No way. It's a neat house. I like it a lot." The girl didn't appear to fully understand the question. "Daddy said it's ours now."

"Well, yes, but we're going to sell it."

"How come?"

"Because we don't live in Maryland. We live in Connecticut."

"Can't we just move here? I like it here. I like Maryland."

"Wouldn't you miss your friends back home?"

"I could make new friends."

"You don't know anything about living here."

"I do! I know there's a river on the other side of the woods and Daddy said he would take me out to swim there someday. And I know there's a neat little house made out of glass in the woods, too."

Laurie had just broken an egg into the frying pan and now held the two halves of the eggshell in midair, frozen. She looked up sharply at the girl to find her wrinkling her nose again. "You saw it?" Laurie's voice was nearly a whisper.

"It looks like a big dollhouse," said Susan enthusiastically. "But it's all old and dirty and covered under a big tent."

"When did you see it?"

"The day we got here. Daddy and I went walking down a path through the woods and we found it."

"I don't want you to go back there."

"Why?"

"Because I said so. It's dangerous and there's broken glass everywhere. I don't want you playing back there."

"I'm careful."

"No. This is not up for discussion. Promise me you won't go back there."

Even at ten, it seemed Susan was able to harness some sense of trepidation from Laurie's voice, or perhaps from the look on Laurie's face. The young girl's eyes hung on her, slightly wider than they generally were. One palm lay flat down on the tabletop beside her bowl of Cheerios and Laurie could see the little pink fingers working in agitation. "Okay," she said quietly and at last. "I promise."

And now I've just scared the poor kid half to death. . . .

To lighten the tension, Laurie raised her right hand and said, "Girl Scout's honor?"

"I'm not a Girl Scout."

Laurie lowered her hand. She felt coldly removed from her daughter. On the stove, the egg sizzled in the pan. "I know you're not. I was just being funny."

Susan shrugged and looked down at her cereal. "Wasn't very funny to me," she said.

The front door slammed at the opposite end of the house. Ted shouted a friendly *halloo* down the hallway, his baritone voice full-bodied with reverberation. When he appeared in the kitchen doorway, he was mopping sweat off his brow with a towel. His sweaty T-shirt clung to him and his spandex shorts looked too tight. "Good morning." He seemed to be in a good mood. "It's a beautiful day out. How are my favorite ladies?"

"There's butterflies," Susan piped up from her chair.

"Yeah? Where?"

The girl pointed to the low bushes outside the bay windows. There were yellow flowers with fuzzy brown centers bristling from the bushes. "Right out there," Susan said. "I saw them earlier. They were lots of different colors."

Ted went over and kissed the top of Susan's head. "Do you know what those flowers are called?" He pointed to the yellow flowers with the brown centers.

Susan shook her head.

"Black-eyed Susans."

The girl giggled. "You're lying!"

"I'm not," Ted said, placing one hand over his heart. Beads of perspiration glistened on his forehead. "Bet you a dollar."

Susan got up from the table and stood before the windows. She peered down at the flowers that swayed calmly in the early summer breeze. "Wow," she said. "How come they're named after me?"

"Because the people who name flowers tried to think of the most beautiful name in the whole world," Ted said. "But then they realized that 'Rose' was already taken."

"Daddy!" Susan chided, laughing.

Laurie smiled and turned back to the stove. A part of her longed for the easy affection Ted and Susan shared.

"Do you want breakfast?" she asked Ted. "I'm making eggs."

"Eggs sound wonderful," he said, coming up beside her and kissing her on the cheek. "I'm gonna grab a quick shower." He turned back toward Susan as he backtracked out of the kitchen. "You shout for me if you see another butterfly, okay? I don't wanna miss 'em!"

Again, Susan beamed brightly.

Later, Laurie telephoned the estate liquidator, Stephanie Canton, and set up an appointment for her to stop by at her next available opportunity to conduct a preliminary assessment of her father's belongings. Laurie assured the woman that everything would have to go because they were selling the house. "Our place back in Hartford is very small," Laurie confided over the telephone, "and we don't have the room for anything else. I don't see me leaving here with a blessed thing."

"Nonetheless, I always advise all my clients to conduct a comprehensive inventory prior to my arrival."

Stephanie Canton spoke with the frank diction of a military officer. "Things can *hide,* Mrs. Genarro."

"Well, okay, but I'm certain we won't be keeping anything."

"The earliest I can be there is Friday afternoon."

"That's fine," Laurie said.

"If there is any paperwork for any of the items, please have that on hand."

"Paperwork?"

"For example, if you have antique furniture, some documentation as to its authenticity would prove beneficial in terms of resale. The same goes for any autographed memorabilia—books, baseball cards, paintings—and the like."

"Oh, okay. I understand. Sorry, I've never done this before."

On the other end of the phone, Stephanie Canton made a noise that could have been interpreted as either endorsement or derision. "Is there any clothing left behind?"

Left behind, Laurie thought, and shivered. "Yes. All of his clothes."

"I don't handle clothing. My recommendation would be to contact the Salvation Army or Purple Heart or any such organization and have the articles donated. It's a tax write-off."

"That's a good idea."

"You have my number. Call if you have any questions prior to my visit."

"See you Friday," Laurie said, and hung up.

She spent the remainder of the day doing just as Stephanie Canton had advised: taking inventory of all the items in the house. When she arrived in her father's study, she went through the boxes Dora Lorton had packed up, removing all the items from within and setting them down in rows on the desktop like a soldier disassembling a machine gun. Pipes, lighters, candlesticks, incense, a letter opener, sets of keys, a pewter ashtray with a faded crest engraved in the dish, and similar accoutrements. A second box held silver tie clips, two pocket watches (one gold, one silver, neither operational), old pairs of wire-rimmed glasses, yellowed and brittle stationary, a clutch of pencils punctured with teeth marks and bound together by a rubber band, and a few coffee mugs with unfamiliar emblems on the sides. The third box contained perhaps forty or so records— large vinyl LPs in timeworn sleeves that smelled musty and old. Laurie took out a number of these and examined the sleeves. Frowning, she recognized none of the names, none of the faces. Pursing one album sleeve, she reached in and pinched the LP between her thumb and index finger and slid it out. It was made of a material sturdier than vinyl. She blew a film of dust off the record and saw that the grooves looked to be in workable condition. Nary a scratch was visible. She let the record drop back into the cardboard sleeve, then replaced the album back in the box with the others.

The final box, which was the largest of all the boxes, contained two three-ring binders. The first was full of her father's paperwork, including the deed to the house, his medical information, bank records, a copy of his will, and various similar documents. The second binder was slimmer than the first and contained grainy photographs as well as a few more recent ones of Susan when she was younger. The photos of Susan were still in the envelopes in which Laurie had mailed them. The older photographs were housed in protective plastic sleeves held in place by the binder rings. She flipped through a number of them. The only people recognizable in any of them were her parents and herself as a little girl. And there were only a slim few of those. One of the photos was of a family trip they had taken to Ocean City one summer. The photo showed the three of them at the cusp of the ocean, smiling widely for the stranger whom her father had enlisted to take the picture. Laurie recalled being worried that the stranger would run off with her father's camera, but he hadn't. In the picture, her parents looked lively and healthy and happy. It was not how she remembered them at all.

The last few pages of the album were comprised mostly of photos of strangers. Some were of men working at the old steel mill. Others were of various automobiles. A few strange faces flashed smiles at her. Other photos were more esoteric—a long stretch of blacktop fading to a point at the horizon; an unidentifiable young girl smiling as she leaned out from beneath the shadow of an overpass; two dogs on their hind legs engaged in a fight in a grassy field; several photos of the mill's stately smokestacks. The next few pages were empty, the protective plastic sleeves holding no photos. She flipped past them to the back of the album. The final few photos were of Laurie, when she had been about Susan's age. There were no dates printed on the backs of the photographs, but Laurie surmised it was the year before her parents' separation.

She replaced the photograph binder back in the box,

then went upstairs with the keys she had found in the first box. One by one, she tried them on the padlock on the door that led up to the belvedere. None of them was the right key. Frustrated, she made a mental note to call Dora and then went into the bedrooms where she sifted through the drawers of the nightstands and dressers. Most of the items she came across were articles of clothing. Curiously, the top drawer of the nightstand beside her father's bed contained a silver crucifix and a Bible. The crucifix was perhaps five inches long and it felt weighty and substantial in Laurie's hand. She had never known her father to be a religious man, and the discovery of the items right there beside the old man's bed surprised her. She supposed some people became more easily accepting of a higher power the closer they got to death. Wasn't that why churches were mostly filled with the elderly? Did it become easier to believe in God the older you got or were you just hedging your bets? She set the crucifix on the nightstand, glad to be rid of it.

She proceeded to dump the clothing out onto the floors of the various rooms and then went back downstairs to retrieve a box of trash bags from the kitchen. On her way through the parlor, she found Ted on the sofa, a pen propped in the corner of his mouth, a notebook in his lap. There was the thick John Fish paperback on the table in front of him, the pages dog-eared and tabbed with countless yellow Post-it notes and index cards. She knew he was having a tough time of it. Ted was a true artist at heart, which meant he required constant encouragement and coddling. She had done her best back in Hartford, often to the detriment of her own artistic pursuits, but she just didn't have it in her at the moment. When he looked up at her despondently, the pen now clutched between his teeth, she could offer him only the most rudimentary nod of consolation. She felt bad about it a second later, but her mind was too overcome by all that now surrounded her to indulge her husband's practiced sense of humility.

There were two unopened boxes of Glad trash bags beneath the kitchen sink. She took out one box and was about to head back upstairs when she paused midway across the kitchen. Out the bay windows, the day was beginning to grow old. The color of the lawn had deepened, as had the apparent depth of its incline. The lush richness had been drained from the trees. Sodium lights at the far side of the river caused the horizon to glow a vaporous and inhospitable orange.

Two girls were kneeling in the yard, their heads bowed close together as if they were whispering secrets to each other. One was Susan, dressed in one of her long-sleeved cotton tops, her dark-skinned legs folded up under her. She had her dark brown hair pulled back into a stunted little ponytail that curled like a comma from the back of her head. The other girl's identity remained a mystery, up until Laurie approached the bay windows for a better look.

It was the girl she had seen running across the yard yesterday, the one who had watched her from behind a stand of saplings while Laurie had been examining the remains of the old greenhouse. The girl whom she had thought to be a ghost. She knew this strictly by the girl's clothes, which seemed outdated, unseasonable, and the wrong size. From her angle at the window, Laurie could not make out the girl's face.

Laurie backed away from the windows, setting the box of Glad trash bags on the kitchen table. Her feet carried her over to the screen door that led out onto the square slabs of concrete at the back of the house. A chill in the air caused gooseflesh to rise up on her arms. She thought it was awfully cold weather for the beginning of summer. At the center of the yard, the two girls remained with their heads bowed toward one another. Susan appeared to speak while the other girl listened. Then the other girl spoke while Susan cocked her head to one side like an inquisitive dog. Laurie could hear none of what they said. The other girl was dressed improbably in a muted yellow frock with puffy sleeves that reminded Laurie of the title character from *Alice in Wonderland*. The frock was too big for her and drooped down around the girl's pale, narrow shoulders, exposing the smooth white rim of her collarbone. The girl's hair was a striking auburn color, made even more remarkable in the diminishing sunlight, and spilled in waves down her back. The girl's feet were bare and dirty.

Laurie approached them. When her shadow fell over them, they both looked up at her in what appeared to be practiced unison. Laurie's eyes flitted to her daughter for just a moment before settling on the other girl.

It was Sadie Russ.

The girl's face was a moonish oval, the skin pearl-colored and unblemished except for a streak of dirt that started at the corner of her mouth and extended across her right cheek. The girl's eyes were a deep brown, almost black, beneath curling auburn bangs.

"Hi, Mom," Susan said. "This is my new friend, Abigail."

"Hello," said Abigail.

For a moment, Laurie could not move, could not say a word. She was suddenly aware of a prickling sensation along her scalp and down the nape of her neck as the hairs there bristled. When she spoke, it was as if some ventriloquist were forcing the words from her mouth.

"Hello, Abigail," Laurie said.

The girl gazed up at her with dark eyes. A few strands of her hair were slicked to the corner of her mouth.

Of course, Sadie Russ was dead. She had died a long time ago. But this girl . . . this Abigail . . . could have been Sadie's identical twin.

"How long have you been out here?" Laurie asked Susan.

"Just a little while," Susan said. "I got bored watching Daddy work."

Laurie looked down at a shallow hole that had been dug in the ground between the two girls. "What have you two been doing?"

"Looking for treasure," Susan said.

"Is that right?" Laurie's throat clicked.

"Abigail says there's treasure all over the place."

"Pirates used to bury it close to the beaches," Abigail said. "That was a long time ago, but they never came back and got all the treasure. Sometimes they forgot where they buried it."

"Is that true, Mom?" Susan asked her mother. The look on her face expressed that while she did not believe in such nonsense, she very much wanted to.

"I suppose anything is possible," Laurie said.

"I've found gold 'bloons down by the beach before," Abigail said.

"That's pirate money," Susan said, having apparently already been indoctrinated into the vernacular.

"Sounds interesting," Laurie said. "Do you live around here, Abigail?"

Abigail pointed across the yard toward the moldy fence. For one preposterous moment, Laurie thought the girl was referring to the shaggy willow tree that drooped down over the fence. But then she saw the house through the screen of trees, its back porch lights on. She could make out the rear bumper of the green sedan in the driveway again. Sadie's old house.

"How nice," said Laurie. She cocked her head at her daughter. "But now it's time to wash up for dinner."

"But what about the treasure, Mom?"

"It's been there for several hundred years," Laurie said. "I'm sure it can wait another day."

Susan planted her hands down in the grass, then popped up onto her feet. She moved with the lissome, springy sensibilities of a gymnast. Like her father, she was a natural athlete.

"Say good-bye to your friend," Laurie told her daughter.

"Good night, Abigail!"

"I'll see you tomorrow," Abigail said.

One hand against her daughter's back, Laurie ushered the girl back to the house. The kitchen lights were on and the bowing bay windows looked like the glowing cockpit of an airliner.

"How did you meet her?" Laurie asked.

"Abigail?" A strand of hair had come loose from Susan's ponytail. She brushed it absently behind one ear. "She came from the other side."

It took Laurie almost a full minute to realize her daughter had meant the other side of the fence.

CHAPTER 10

After dinner, Laurie brought out the box of LPs from her father's study and set it down on the coffee table in the parlor.

"These are great!" Ted exclaimed. He had a drink in his hands—some primordial swill from Myles Brashear's liquor cabinet—and he stood craning over the top of the box to examine the contents within like a child peering down into a box of puppies. Eventually, he set his drink down and slid out one of the albums. The sleeve was bleached to an indecipherable unintelligence. Ted let the record slip out into his hand. "It's a Diva. Lou Gold, 'On Riverside Drive.' Vocals by Irving Kaufman. This puppy is old! Where did these come from?"

"They were in my dad's study."

"I didn't realize he collected this stuff."

Laurie thought it was a strange comment, since Ted knew nothing else about the man, either.

"Put it on, Daddy," Susan said. She was perched on the loveseat, a glass of apple juice clasped in both hands in her lap.

Ted went to the Victrola and set the record down

on the phonograph's turntable. There was a crank and
handle sticking out from one side of the Victrola's maple cabinet. Ted turned the crank. "It's like starting a
Model T," he said. When he was done cranking, he set
the arm bar down on the record. A crackly whir filled
the atmosphere. Then the music played—a tinny West
End number that summoned images in Laurie's head of
Manhattan nightclubs from the 1920s.

"Oh, gross!" Susan bellowed. "That's terrible!"

Ted laughed. "So you don't want to dance?"

"No way! That music sounds like barf!"

"How is it that you are my child?"

"You *like* it, Daddy? That music?"

Ted twirled the tip of an invisible moustache. "It is
what the *cognoscenti* call *eleganza,* darling daughter."

This, of course, set Susan off into hysterics. Her hysteria only increased once Ted began waltzing around
the parlor with an invisible partner. When he came by
and swooped Laurie into his arms, Susan had to set her
glass of juice down on the coffee table to keep from
spilling it, she was laughing so hard.

Ted and Susan spent the next half hour trying out
different records on the Victrola, each one more hi-
larious (to Susan) than the previous. Leaving Ted and
Susan to their music, Laurie cleaned up the kitchen,
glancing occasionally at the bay windows and the darkened yard beyond. *Sadie.* There was a steady pulsing
at her temples. She kept seeing the girl who called herself Abigail staring up at her while digging a hole in
the ground, her oversized dress drooping off her thin
shoulders. But of course she wasn't Sadie. In fact, the
more she considered this, the more she believed Abi-

gail only shared a passing resemblance with the little girl who had lived next door during Laurie's childhood. The pale skin, the ovoid face, the dark, overlarge, soul-searing eyes . . . but Abigail's hair was lighter in color than Sadie's. Sadie had been taller, too. Just how much could she trust her memory of Sadie, anyway? Laurie had been just a child when Sadie had died.

Ridiculous, she thought. The shrill little laugh that erupted from her caused her to jump.

She took the box of Glad bags upstairs, where she went systematically through the rooms and bagged up all her father's old clothes. The clothes were all starched and laundered, though the closets themselves were haunted by the odor of old pipe tobacco and un-familiar cologne. There were many hats in the closet of the master bedroom, too—old derby hats and bowl-ers and even a straw cowboy hat—though she could not remember her father ever wearing any of them. Shoes lined one wall of the closet, everything from polished cordovans to threadbare bedroom slippers. Downstairs, the music played on.

When she had finished, the upstairs hallway was lined with several fat bags of clothing. Tomorrow, she would call the Salvation Army and set up a pickup date. *That takes care of that.* She felt a welcome sense of ac-complishment at having completed the task. It wasn't until she looked over at the padlocked door that her smile faded. It seemed to call to her.

That's silly, she thought . . . yet she went to it none-theless. On her hands and knees, she peered beneath the door. A narrow strip of darkness peered back at her. *Silliness.*

When she returned downstairs, she was overcome by an immediate sense of unease. It felt as if the walls were beginning to constrict all around her, closing in on her. She gripped the newel post at the bottom of the stairs tightly. When her eyes fell on the front door, she went to it, touched the knob—it was cool—then slid her hand up to the dead bolt. She could see by the way it was turned that it was already locked; nevertheless, she took the key from the pocket of her jeans, unlocked it . . . then locked it again. Hearing the bolt slide closed did her a lot of good. The unease slowly dissipated from her.

In the parlor, Ted and Susan were now curled up on the sofa watching a movie on Ted's laptop. Ted had already complained that he was unable to harness an Internet signal out of the air, but luckily he had packed a few DVDs.

"This place needs a TV," Susan commented to no one in particular as Laurie went on through to the kitchen.

The bay windows faced a yard as black as infinite space. The sodium glow above the trees and on the other side of the river shimmered on the horizon. She went to check the lock on the side door, too, but thought she caught movement out there in all that darkness, though she couldn't tell exactly what it had been. It had been no clearer than a dark shape wending through a labyrinth of other dark shapes.

She kicked on a pair of flip-flops that were by the screen door off the side of the kitchen and then went out. A cool breeze came off the water and over the hill, causing the trees to whisper and the bushes to shush along the fence. She peered over the fence and through the trees at the house next door. There was a light on in one of the upstairs windows and a blue flicker behind sheer curtains on the ground that probably belonged to a television set. The cars were still gone from the driveway. In the moonlight, the columns on the neighboring porch looked like polished bones and the backyard looked like a South American jungle.

Laurie crossed the yard to view the neighboring house from a different angle. Here, the trees were denser, but she could see the entire rear of the house through the partings of their branches. The yard looked overgrown and there was yet another light on upstairs at the opposite end of the house that she hadn't seen previously. As she stared at it, she thought she saw someone moving around in the window.

And then she heard movement on the other side of the fence. Close. Twigs snapped and leaves rustled.

Laurie froze. "Someone there?"

No answer . . . yet she swore she could hear *breathing*.

"Abigail? Is that you?"

She listened for a while longer, until she became convinced that the breathing she thought she heard was just the breeze shuttling through the trees, and that it could have been a squirrel trampling on those twigs.

It was when she turned around to head back to the house that she stepped right into a large hole in the ground. She twisted her ankle and dropped to her knees in the cool, damp grass.

"Goddamn it!"

She dug her fingernails into the soil. The pain was sudden and intense. Gritting her teeth, she managed to roll onto her buttocks and extract her injured limb from the shallow hole. It was the goddamned hole Susan and her new friend Abigail had been digging earlier that evening, looking for pirate treasure. Bringing her knee up to her chest, Laurie could already feel the throbbing stiffness in her ankle and the quick tightening of the skin. She had lost the flip-flop in the hole to boot.

"Shit." Her ankle was already beginning to swell. Rocking back and forth in the grass, she massaged her injury as her ankle ballooned up within her hands. The flesh felt hot. Also, she was sweating. *I'm lucky. I could have broken it.*

It was not lost on her that this hole that had hurt her had been dug—partially, at least—by a girl who so closely resembled Sadie Russ. The notion caused her skepticism to temporarily solidify into certainty regarding the girl's identity and, for a moment, she was paralyzed by fear at the prospect of what such a thing meant. But fear is a fleeting thing, and her common sense quickly filtered coolly over the smoldering red coals of her terror.

First thing tomorrow morning, Susan would be out here filling in that damned hole. Laurie would have some other chores for her to do as well, like dragging all the trash bags full of clothes down from the upstairs landing. Oh, yes, she would put the kid to work, all right.

Once the pain subsided, Laurie managed to rise and put some weight down on her foot. Fresh pain caused her to wince and she quickly lifted her foot off the ground. *I must look like a flamingo out here.* After nearly a full minute, she settled back down on her injured ankle, more carefully this time. When she found she could support herself, she managed to bend and dig her flip-flop out of that hole—*put that girlie to work tomorrow, you know it*—and that was when she noticed something else in there with her flip-flop. Catching the moonlight in just the right way, it glittered like a jewel. Laurie picked it up and examined it closely.

It was a cuff link. Gold with a black onyx at its center. The tiny object was heavy in her hand.

How the—

Her mind did the quick math. Temper rising, she hobbled back to the house and let the screen door slam.

"What happened to you?" Ted asked as she limped into the parlor. He sat up straighter on the sofa and shut the laptop's screen. Beside him on the sofa, Susan whirled around to face her.

"I twisted my ankle in a hole in the yard." She looked at Susan. "That hole you were digging earlier with your little friend from next door."

Ted set the laptop on the coffee table, got up, and went to her. "Are you okay? Let me see your foot."

"It's just sprained."

"Let me help you." He assisted her over to the loveseat, then snatched one of the decorative pillows off the sofa and set it on the coffee table. "Go on, put your foot up."

"It hurts."

"Here." He took her calf and gently raised her foot to the table. Carefully, he settled her foot down on the pillow. "Is that okay?"

"Yes."

"It's already starting to swell," he said. "I should get you some ice."

Susan stared at Laurie from the sofa. Her daughter's eyes were large and she was sucking on her lower lip, something she did unconsciously when she was upset about something. She looked very young just then, and Laurie was reminded of the fears she'd had for the girl throughout certain milestones in her life, such as when she was gone all day on her first day of school, or the first time she spent the night over at a friend's house.

"What were you doing bumbling around in the yard at night, anyway?" Ted asked. There was a hint of joviality to his tone, as if he was trying to use it to mitigate Laurie's irritation.

Laurie opened her palm and extended it toward Susan. The cuff link winked, reflecting the soft lamplight.

"Would you like to explain to me why this was in the yard?" Laurie said.

"What's that?" Ted asked.

"Why don't you tell your father what it is, Susan."

The girl looked at the cuff link, then back up at her mother. She said nothing.

"Go on," Laurie urged.

In a voice that was barely audible, Susan said, "I don't know."

"You don't? Are you sure?"

Susan continued to stare at her.

Ted took the item out of Laurie's hand and examined it. The look on his face was one of utter confusion, as if he was looking at a tooth that had just fallen from his mouth.

"It's okay," Laurie said to her daughter. "I won't be mad. Just tell me the truth."

"I don't know what it is."

"Then forget what it is. Why did you take it? You know better than to go through someone else's things and to take stuff that doesn't belong to you," Laurie said.

"I didn't take anything," Susan said.

"Where did it come from?" Ted asked, still scrutinizing the cuff link. His question seemed to be directed to no one in particular.

"It was in a box with some of my father's stuff," Laurie said.

"That stuff in the back office?"

"Yes." Laurie turned back to her daughter. "Susan, I want you to tell me the truth."

"I didn't." The girl's lower lip trembled. "I didn't take it."

"Please don't lie to me."

"I'm not lying! I didn't take it!"

"Is that so?" Laurie said. "Should we go into the study and see if those cuff links are still in the box?"

"I didn't do anything!" A tear streaked down Susan's cheek.

"All right," Ted said. He dropped the cuff link back into Laurie's hand. "First of all, you're not walking anywhere with your ankle like that," he said to Laurie.

"Those cuff links were in one of the boxes with my father's stuff," Laurie said. "I saw them the day we got here. I even picked one up and looked at it. But when I went through the boxes earlier today, they were gone. I hadn't even realized it until just now."

"Did you take them?" Ted asked Susan. His voice was much steadier than Laurie's.

Susan shook her head, though not immediately.

"I thought you knew better," Laurie said. "I thought we taught you better than that."

More sternly, Ted said, "Susan?"

"We taught you better than to lie to us like that," Laurie said.

"Okay. Enough," said Ted. To Susan, he said, "I think you should go upstairs and get ready for bed now."

"And first thing tomorrow, I want you to fill in that hole," Laurie added. "Am I understood?"

"Yes, ma'am."

So now I'm getting the "ma'am" treatment, Laurie thought.

Ted waved a hand at the girl. "Go on," he said. "Go."

Susan pivoted around and stalked across the room to her father. She hugged him around the hips and, after a moment, he bent down and kissed the top of her head. "Okay. Good night. Now get going."

A moment later, listening to the sounds of her daughter brushing her teeth in the upstairs bathroom, Laurie reclined in the chair and felt her ankle throb. Ted went into the kitchen and filled up a Ziploc bag with ice. When he returned, he placed the bag of ice carefully across her swollen ankle.

"How's that?"

"Throbs," she huffed. "You know, it's important we show a united front."

"She was playing with some cuff links. She didn't steal them."

"She knows better than to go through someone else's stuff like that."

"She was probably just bored."

"Don't make excuses for her."

"It's not an excuse."

"And it's not just the stealing. I understand that she's stuck in this house and that she's bored, and just looking for stuff to do, things to play with. But since when does she lie to us like that?"

He held up one hand and swiveled away to the liquor cabinet. He poured himself a glass of cognac. "Maybe you just caught her off guard and she didn't know what to say."

"You give her too much latitude," Laurie said.

"You're right. I should go up there and beat her unconscious with my belt. How's that?"

"Don't be an ass, Ted. You spoil her. I'm the only one doling out any discipline, and I'm starting to feel like the bad guy because of it."

"She's ten years old, Laurie—"

"And she'll be eleven next month, and an adult before we know it. She needs boundaries *now*."

There was something on the tip of his tongue, Laurie could tell. Yet he swallowed it. His lips remained firm, as if whatever words he had swallowed had tasted bitter, but he refused to give in to it.

"Is there something else?" he asked. This time, his voice was even and steady, though not without care.

"Something else what? What do you mean?"

"Is there something else bothering you?" he clarified.

All of a sudden, she thought his eyes betrayed the distrust he had of her mental stability. One look at him and she could tell he was thinking about her little episode on the highway last year. Those looks came more and more frequently, like she was slowly losing her mind, yet she was the only person oblivious to the fact.

"No," she said, turning away from him, too embarrassed to continue looking him in the eyes. "There's nothing else. I'm just exhausted."

He sighed. "I'm sorry. I'll talk with her about it tomorrow. Okay?"

"Okay. Thank you."

"How 'bout some fresh tunes?"

She smiled wanly up at him.

Ted set his drink down, then selected another album from the box. He slid the record out and was halfway to the phonograph when he paused.

"That's strange," he said.

"What's strange?"

He turned to show her. In one hand, he held the record and the cardboard sleeve. In his other hand he held a folded piece of paper, thick and yellow like parchment, the edges quite visibly frayed. He unfolded the paper and stared at it, the expression on his face pure incomprehension.

"What is it?" she repeated.

He brought it over and handed it to her.

It was an eleven-by-thirteen black-and-white photograph of three men in suits standing before a bank of steel doors. Each door had a number painted on it, and Laurie thought they looked like garage doors or large storage lockers. In the background, concrete smokestacks rose up from a multi-windowed brick building networked with catwalks and pipework. There was no date on the photo, but if she had to guess by the men's attire, it had been taken sometime in the late sixties or early seventies.

"The man in the middle is my father." She pointed as Ted leaned over her shoulder to look more closely at the photograph. "I don't recognize the other two, but my guess is they were co-owners of the steel mill with my dad. That looks like the mill in the background. There are some smaller pictures of it in a photo album in my dad's study. I'd seen it once in person when I was a little girl, too. Just before my parents got divorced, my dad drove me out to Sparrows Point—that's the industrial park along the water in Dundalk—and showed me all the buildings."

"Why do you think he stuffed it in the record album?"

"Dora Lorton said he was really out of it toward the end of his life. To try and figure out what was going through his head at the time would be . . ." She let the words trail off. Then she pointed to the liquor cabinet. "That empty frame that had been hanging on the wall the day we got here? It's behind the liquor cabinet, on the floor. Get it, will you?"

Ted went to the cabinet and crouched down. "Yeah, I see it." He reached behind it, grabbed the frame, and carried it back over to Laurie. "Looks like it's the right size frame."

"Yeah." She smoothed out the photograph, then overlaid it on top of the frame. The frayed edges of the photo were a perfect match for the tufts of thick paper still bristling from the inside edges of the frame. "That's the right picture, all right."

"But why . . ." Ted began again before letting his own voice fall away. Gently, he sighed. "I guess we could drive ourselves mad trying to figure out what was going through his head, huh?"

She handed him the frame and the photograph. "I'm tired of thinking about it," she said.

Unwilling to tackle the staircase with her sprained ankle, Laurie spent the night on the sofa. Fitfully, she slept. In her dream, she was sleeping on this very sofa when a figure came into the room and approached her. It was too dark to make out the figure's features, but she assumed by the litheness of the approach that it was a child. Susan. In her dream, she was powerless to move, though something called to her to reach out and touch the figure. Then the figure had turned and gone over to the phonograph. The handle was cranked with deliberate sluggishness. A record was placed on the spindle and the needle set into a groove. The sounds that followed were not of music but of a distant whale-like lament. Finally, she was able to sit up. The record stopped and the figure shifted out into the hall. Backlit by the moonlight falling through the front windows, Laurie could see that the figure was not Susan after all, but that of another young girl. When the girl passed beneath a panel of moonlight coming through one window, Laurie could clearly see Abigail's face looking down on her.

PART II
SPARROWS POINT:
Abigail

CHAPTER 11

In the kitchen, Ted and Susan were at the table enjoying a breakfast of waffles with maple syrup, bacon, and tall glasses of chocolate milk. They had been in the middle of some low-voiced discussion when Laurie walked in. They both looked at her and Ted offered her his winning smile. Both he and Susan sported chocolate milk moustaches.

"Sleepyhead," he said. "How's the foot?"

"Much better, thanks."

"There are waffles on the counter."

"Great."

"I hope we didn't wake you."

She went to the stove, lifted the coffeepot and found it empty. "Not at all," she said.

"Susan brought the bags of clothes down this morning and set them on the front porch," Ted said, "and I already called the Salvation Army. They're sending a truck out this afternoon."

"Well," she said, folding her arms and leaning her buttocks against the front of the stove. She smiled at them. "I feel like the shoemaker who has been visited by elves in the night." Yet this made her think of the dream she'd had, recalling Abigail's pale, moonlit face looking down on her as she lay motionless on the sofa, and the smile quickly evaporated.

"I filled in the hole in the yard, too," Susan added. Her hair, which she usually wore in a ponytail, was loose and curled just underneath the lines of her jaw. It made her look older. "First thing when I got up, just like you said."

"Thank you, sweetie."

"You should relax today," Ted said. "This whole thing has been stressful on you. Let's go into Annapolis for the afternoon. How's that sound?"

She picked apart one of the waffles from the stack on the counter. "That sounds nice but there's still too much to do. I haven't even gone down into the basement yet. The longer we put it off, the longer we're stuck here."

"Then give us chores," Ted suggested. "Let us help out."

Laurie popped the piece of waffle in her mouth. "Tell you what," Laurie said. "Why don't you two go to Annapolis together for the day and I'll stay here and wade through the stuff in the basement. If anything needs to be thrown away down there, I'll make a list for you guys and you can take care of it for me when you get back."

"That's silly. Let us help you."

"How can you help? It's my father's stuff. It'll be easier for all of us this way."

"Are you sure, hon?"

"Positive. And you guys can pick up some groceries for me, too. I'd like some fresh vegetables and fruit."

"Okay," said Ted. He turned to Susan. "What do you think? You want to go back downtown for the day?"

"Can we go see if the drawbridge will open?" There was a drawbridge that connected Eastport with historic Annapolis, which they had seen on their previous trip downtown. They had waited for nearly ten minutes to see if the bridge would open but it hadn't, and Susan had been sorely disappointed.

"Sure thing," Ted said. "If we get there early enough, maybe some of the sailboats will be going out to the bay."

Upstairs, Laurie took a hot shower. The water made her ankle feel better, and much of the swelling had gone down. She went over the incident from last night and while she didn't think she had acted unreasonably toward Susan, she was too emotionally exhausted to maintain any level of irritation over the matter. Besides, both Ted and Susan had made their peace with her. Perhaps today would be a better day.

After the shower, she dressed in a white halter top and a pair of old jeans. Beyond the bedroom windows, the day was bright and there looked to be a nice breeze running through the tops of the trees from off the water. Downstairs, she found the Volvo gone and a note on the kitchen counter written in Susan's decisive print:

I took daddy to Annapolis
We will buy fruit and veggies for you
I love you
Susan!!!

It brought a smile to Laurie's face.

* * *

The basement was an unfinished concrete crypt beneath the earth. The barren cinderblock walls would have looked more at home in a prison. Exposed beams and electrical wiring crisscrossed the low ceiling. Every few yards, naked bulbs were suspended like calcium deposits from the rafters overhead. Like the rest of the house, there wasn't much down here. Some old sheets of plywood leaned against the hot water heater. Above the plywood, hung on wall-mounted brackets, was a retractable aluminum ladder. There were some tools hanging from a pegboard beneath the stairwell. Nailed to one of the struts was a dusty plastic bag that appeared to contain paperwork for the various household appliances. A metal tool chest sat on the floor. A few other items—saws, boxes of lightbulbs, coils of extension cords, several cans of paint—lay scattered around. There was the Persian rug rolled up like a burrito and propped in one gloomy corner. It was heavy, but she was able to drag it out of the corner and drop it onto the floor with little difficulty. She unrolled it and then backed away to examine it. As she stared down at the dull rust-colored stain in the center of the rug, Dora Lorton's voice rose up in her head like vapors: *On the night of Mr. Brashear's death, the rug had been . . . damaged . . . I suppose you could say.*

The old man had evacuated his bowels onto the carpet before throwing himself out the window to his death. She remembered standing in the yard and seeing one of the windows in the belvedere blocked by something. She also remembered the lawyer mentioning a police report.

When she went back upstairs, she found a number

of men in T-shirts and jeans collecting the bags containing her father's clothing off the front porch. They loaded the bags into the back of a paneled truck with the Salvation Army shield on its side. It felt like she was ridding the house of her father's lingering presence, and she was grateful each time a bag was hoisted off the porch and tossed into the back of the truck.

From somewhere upstairs, a door slammed.

Laurie jumped. She cast her eyes up the stairwell and could see that all the doors were closed. She called out Ted's and Susan's names, and although she hadn't expected a response, she grew slightly more unnerved when none came. Gripping the banister, she ascended the steps with her head cocked, listening for any more noises. Had it been a door slamming? Had that been what she'd heard? She found she couldn't be sure.

There was no one upstairs. She checked the bedrooms, the bathroom, the hall closet. Of course, the belvedere door was still padlocked shut. Again, the urge to drop to her hands and knees and peer underneath the door accosted her, but this time she was able to fight it off and not give in to it.

She went back downstairs.

In the kitchen, she called information and got the phone number to the non-emergency dispatch for the local police department. The call went through and the man who answered identified himself as Sergeant Martinez.

"Hello, my name is Laurie Genarro. I was trying to locate a copy of a police report."

"What's the name of the reporting officer?" Martinez asked.

"I don't know."

"What's the incident?"

She told him of her father's suicide. Martinez asked her to hold, then came back on the line about a minute or so later. When he spoke, it sounded like he was reading from a teleprompter. "That would be Officer Caprisi. He's not in, but I can send you a copy of the report. Do you have a fax machine?"

"I have an e-mail address. Do people still use fax machines?"

Martinez laughed. "Good point. Go ahead with the e-mail addy when you're ready."

She recited her e-mail address for him.

"Give me fifteen minutes or so, okay?" Martinez said.

"Sounds good."

"Also, sorry about your dad."

"Thank you," she said and hung up.

Hungry, she made herself a sandwich with the lunch meat and bread Dora had stocked in the fridge. It looked nice and warm out, so Laurie opened the windows in the kitchen, then set her sandwich down on the table. She had already pulled out a container of orange juice when she remembered the liquor cabinet in the parlor. Somewhat giddy—and feeling foolish because of her giddiness—she shuffled through the dusty old bottles in the cabinet until she came across an unopened bottle of amontillado sherry. She returned to the kitchen with the bottle, where she pried the stubborn cork out of the neck with a corkscrew she discovered in one of the kitchen drawers. She filled a wineglass and took it to the table, then sat down to lunch.

She was just finishing up her sandwich and on her second glass of sherry when she saw Abigail come out from behind the fence between the two properties. Laurie paused, the corner of her mouth stuffed with food. The girl moved out onto the lawn, looked up over the crest of the hill, then retreated back toward the fence. She disappeared behind a congregation of dense foliage, though her thin little shadow lingered on the lawn. It was the insubstantial shadow of a scarecrow.

Laurie spat the last bite of her sandwich into her napkin, then stood up. The girl's shadow receded slowly into the trees . . . then appeared again, long and distorted now along the gradual incline of the lawn.

Laurie went out the screen door and broke a sweat hustling across the backyard toward the place where the girl had vanished behind the trees. On the other side of the fence, the woods were lush, verdant, and alive with a chorus of birds and insects. As she approached, the girl's shadow withdrew completely into the trees. Laurie came up to the fence, but she couldn't see anyone on the other side. Again, she thought of her dream, and tried to remember how it had ended. Had Abigail withdrawn into the darkness only to vanish? Had her pale face simply dematerialized before her eyes? She couldn't remember.

In a low voice, as if she did not actually want to be heard, Laurie said, "Abigail?"

The girl emerged just a few feet away, from behind a vibrant blind of magnolias. She hadn't been on the other side of the fence after all, but right here in the yard. The girl's proximity startled her.

"Hello," Abigail said. She wore a red-and-white

checkerboard skirt that hung just past her knees and a crimson blouse with short, scalloped sleeves. An embroidered pink rose was pinned over her heart. Abigail's face was pale and grimy and her eyes looked like they were spaced just a bit too far apart. The only thing luxurious about the girl was her hair—thick and healthy-looking, it cascaded down her shoulders in reddish-mocha waves.

"If you were looking for Susan, she's not home," Laurie said despite the dryness of her mouth. "She went out with her father for the day."

"I was just playing."

"What's your last name, Abigail?"

"Evans," said the girl.

"And you live in the house next door?"

Abigail looked over the fence, through the trees, and across the yard at the house next door. Laurie looked, too, and saw that the driveway was empty and the two cars were not in the street. Despite the fine weather, none of the windows were open.

When she looked back at Abigail, the young girl's dark black eyes reminded her of the onyx stones in the cuff links. A sudden thought shook her. "Did you tell my daughter to steal her grandfather's cuff links?" The question was out of her mouth before she even knew what she was saying.

Abigail stared up at her, the girl's thin black eyebrows slowly knitting together. Gradually, she shook her head. It seemed she shook her head because she did not know what else to do, not because she was actually answering Laurie's question.

"How old are you?"

"I'm ten and a half."

"Were you the one who put the cuff link in the hole?"

"I don't understand you."

Laurie pointed to where the hole had been in the yard before Susan had filled it back up. "The hole," she said. "The one you and Susan were digging."

"There's no hole there."

"There was before."

"We were looking for pirate treasure," said the girl.

"Yes. In that hole where you were looking for pirate treasure—did you put a cuff link in there?"

"I don't understand you. There's a bee near your head."

Indeed, a honeybee buzzed by the left side of Laurie's face. Laurie jerked backwards away from it and swatted blindly at the air. The bee trundled toward a magnolia bush, having lost interest in her.

"You didn't answer my question about the cuff link."

"What's a cuff link?"

Laurie chewed on the inside of her cheek while Abigail looked down at her own shadow. Then she looked at Laurie's shadow, which stretched up toward the crest of the hill. When she looked back up at Laurie, the girl's face was expressionless.

"Can Susan come out and play when she comes home?" Abigail asked.

"She won't be home for the rest of the day."

Abigail's eyes darted to the right. She watched the honeybee go from blossom to blossom with dutiful diligence.

"Is Abigail your real name?" Laurie asked finally. This question was followed by a slight ringing in her ears.

"Yes."

"Abigail Evans," said Laurie.

"Yes." The girl smiled: This was a game.

I don't believe you, Laurie thought. *I don't believe you and you know that I don't.*

"Are your parents at home right now?"

"No."

"You're home alone?"

"I'm not home right now." The girl's eyes were the moist black-brown eyes of a deer. "I'm here."

"Okay. Yes. But are your parents at home?"

"I'm not s'posed to tell strangers if people are home or not."

"I'm not a stranger. I'm Susan's mother."

"Anyway, they're not my parents."

"What do you mean?"

"When does Susan come home?"

Laurie shook her head. "I don't know." Her voice was almost breathless. "I told you, she'll be gone all day."

"Are you moving here for good?"

"No," said Laurie.

"Will you stay long? I like Susan."

"We're not staying long at all." Laurie's tongue felt instantly numb. It was difficult to get the words out.

"I have to go home now," Abigail said. She turned and reached out for the fence. The little door beneath the willow tree branches opened on its hinges with a squeal. "Good-bye."

Laurie didn't say a word. She watched the odd little girl meander through the trees where she was periodically blotted out by heavy foliage. When Abigail reached the back porch of her house—

(anyway, they're not my parents)

—she cast a quick glance back at Laurie before disappearing around the far side of the house.

It took the passage of several minutes before Laurie could move again. Feeling as though she had sleepwalked through her entire conversation with Abigail Evans, Laurie turned and walked back toward the house with one hand trailing along the fence in case her knees decided to grow weak and drop out from under her. When she noticed a small mound of dirt excavated from a narrow hole in the ground—the spot where Ted and Susan had buried the dead frog—she bent down and peered inside. The metallic paper covering of the cigar box with the holes punched in the lid winked at her in the sunlight. She reached in and withdrew the box. Opened it.

Empty.

She fired up Ted's laptop and tried to connect to the Internet with no luck. "Shit," she muttered. She had forgotten that Ted hadn't been able to get a signal in the house. She picked up the laptop and carried it around the house, hoping that the Internet icon in the toolbar at the bottom of the screen would light up. When she wandered into the kitchen, she became hopeful. There was a weak signal out there somewhere after all. She carried the laptop outside and onto the patio, and was finally able to make the connection.

She logged into her e-mail account. Dozens of unread e-mails cluttered the inbox. The most recent e-mail was from Sergeant Martinez, Anne Arundel County Police. Laurie clicked on the e-mail, opened the attachment, saved it to the desktop, then went back inside and reclaimed her seat on the sofa.

She had been expecting a multipaged formal report, supplemented with crime scene photographs and detailed accounts of witnesses' statements. What she found was a two-page PDF file, the first page comprised of a series of blocks in which the reporting official— Officer Joseph Caprisi—filled out his name, the date, location of the incident, and other such minutiae. The second page was the actual "report," consisting of five poorly detailed paragraphs describing the event:

On 6/3/13 at approximately 0115 hrs OFC
Caprisi was dispatched to 2109 Annapolis Road
for an apparent suicide. OFC Caprisi arrived
on scene and made contact with the witness,
Teresa Larosche. Ms. Larosche was waiting
outside the residence in her nightclothes and
in a state of panic. Ms. Larosche stated that
she was a caretaker for an elderly male, Myles
Brashear, who lived at the residence. Ms.
Larosche confirmed that she had called 911. OFC
Caprisi followed Ms. Larosche around the side of
the house and observed an unconscious elderly
male on the concrete walkway at the rear of
the residence. Ms. Larosche identified the male
as Mr. Brashear. OFC Caprisi observed that Mr.
Brashear was naked and that his body was

marked by wounds along the face, torso, arms, and thighs.

OFC Caprisi checked Mr. Brashear's pulse and determined that Mr. Brashear was deceased. At this time, another police unit and an ambulance arrived at the residence. Paramedics examined Mr. Brashear's body and confirmed that Mr. Brashear was deceased.

Ms. Larosche advised that she was employed by Mid-Atlantic Homecare Services and that she shared homecare duties for Mr. Brashear with another MAHS employee, Ms. Dora Lorton. Ms. Larosche stated she had worked nights at the residence for approximately the past two months. According to Ms. Larosche, Mr. Brashear suffered from dementia and would frequently become volatile and suffer periodic outbursts. Ms. Larosche advised that she had been awoken earlier this evening by the sounds of Mr. Brashear's voice from the hallway outside her bedroom. When she got up to check on him, she found the door leading to a small rooftop room unlocked and open. Ms. Larosche said she had put a lock on this door last month to prevent Mr. Brashear from gaining access to a rooftop room because she felt it was dangerous for him to be up there. Ms. Larosche said Mr. Brashear had gone up there, and she could hear his voice. When he stopped talking, Ms. Larosche heard the breaking of glass. Ms. Larosche went up into the rooftop room and found the window broken and saw Mr. Brashear lying down below on the pavement. It was then that Ms. Larosche called 911, she said.

OFCs Caprisi and McElroy conducted a search of the rooftop room. The door leading up to the room had been left open. One of the windows was broken, consistent with Ms. Larosche's story. There was blood on the carpet as well as what appeared to be fecal matter. The room was otherwise empty.

Ms. Larosche was provided with the appropriate contact information should she feel the need to seek counseling or speak with an officer regarding any further details she might remember about the incident.

Once she finished reading, she leaned back on the sofa and ran fingers through her hair. The details were vague, and offered hardly any more information than Mr. Claiborne had over the phone after it had happened, with one shocking exception: According to the police report, the window had apparently been *shut* when Myles Brashear had jumped out of it. Laurie supposed that if one were about to commit suicide, such things might not matter in the grand scheme of things . . . though it seemed an awfully morbid, awfully *painful* way to do it. But then she had to remind herself that her father hadn't been thinking rationally by that point. His

mind must have been a nightmarish landscape populated by demons.

Laurie got up and went to the kitchen, where she had
piled the paperwork they'd gotten from Cushing's office along with the documents she had brought down
with her from Hartford. She thumbed through the papers until she found Mr. Claiborne's phone number at
Mid-Atlantic Homecare. Pouring herself another glass
of sherry, she dialed the number and listened to it ring
several times before Claiborne's breathy yet articulate
voice came on the line.

"Hi, Mr. Claiborne, this is Laurie Genarro, Myles
Brashear's daughter."

"Oh, yes. Ms. Lorton said she turned things over to
you and your husband earlier in the week. I trust everything is satisfactory at the house?"

"The house is fine, but there is a padlock on one of
the doors upstairs. The caretaker who stayed nights at
the house, Teresa Larosche, has the key, but I don't have
a number for her. I was hoping she was available so I
could speak with her?"

"Goodness. All keys were supposed to be turned
over to you upon your arrival. Are you certain your
husband hadn't received it, Mrs. Genarro?"

"No, he hasn't. Is Ms. Larosche available?"

"She isn't, no."

"Has she been reassigned? Perhaps there's a phone
number where—"

"She turned in her resignation, I'm afraid."

"She quit? So recently?"

"Immediately following the . . . incident . . . with

your father. She was rather troubled by the whole thing, as I'm sure you can imagine."

Laurie wondered if, in fact, Claiborne had fired the poor woman in an effort to show good faith in case Laurie decided to file a lawsuit. She decided not to ask him about it. "Is there a forwarding number? Some way I can reach her?"

"There is probably a home phone or cell number in her file."

"That would be great. Could you check, please?"

"You see, Mrs. Genarro, it's against policy to give out that information to people outside the organization. I'm sure you can understand the position I'm in."

"My lawyer didn't seem to think you'd have a problem providing any information on request," she said, and although she had no idea what Charles Claiborne looked like, she could imagine his eyes growing comically wide on the other end of the telephone following the sharp intake of breath she heard. "*Is* there a problem, Mr. Claiborne?"

"Ah, there's . . . ah, no, there's no problem," Claiborne stammered. He cleared his throat, the sound alarmingly similar to the report of a small-caliber pistol, and Laurie could suddenly hear the man's fingers rapidly clacking away on a keyboard. "These records," he grumbled, though he did not complete the sentiment. "Ah, yes. Here we are. No cell phone, but there is a home phone number."

"That'll do."

Claiborne prattled off the number and she jotted it down on the pad beside the phone. Before she even set the pen down, the breathy little voice was already back in her ear. "If there is anything you or your lawyer need during this time—an understandably *stressful* time, I am sure, and how horrible this whole thing is—please do not hesitate to get back in touch with me. The whole staff here at Mid-Atlantic Homecare feel awful about the—"

"Thank you," she said, and killed the line. Once the dial tone returned, she punched in Teresa Larosche's telephone number. It rang only twice before a paper-thin voice answered. "Is this Teresa Larosche?"

"Yes." She sounded very young.

"My name is Laurie Genarro. My father was Myles Brashear." Laurie paused to allow the girl time to digest the information. When no response came, Laurie said, "Hello? Are you still there?"

"I'm here. I'm sorry about what happened."

"It was just a terrible accident," she said, hoping this would help relieve Teresa Larosche of any concern she might have that Laurie held her accountable. "I'm sorry you had to be there the night it happened."

Silence on the other end of the telephone.

"Ms. Larosche, there's a padlock on the door upstairs that leads to the belvedere and I don't have a key—"

"The belvedere?"

"The little room on the roof. The room where . . . where my father . . ."

"Oh. Yes."

"I don't have a key for the lock, Ms. Larosche."

"Call me Teresa."

"Thank you, Teresa. You know the lock I'm talking about? I was told you might still have the key."

Another beat of silence on the other end of the line.

Just when she thought Teresa would have to be prodded again, the woman said, "Yes, I have the key. I apologize. I thought I'd turned everything over to Dora after I left."

"It's no big deal, though I'd like to have it back."

"I can drop it in the mail for you first thing tomorrow."

"If it's not too much trouble, I'd prefer we meet and you could give it to me directly. If it got lost in the mail, I'd have to tear the molding off the door just to get the lock off." This wasn't exactly the truth, but it was good enough.

"Are you at the house now?"

"Yes."

"I don't want to go to that house," said the woman.

"Oh. Okay. Well, that's not a problem. I'd be more than happy to meet you someplace that's convenient for you."

A dog yipped on the other end of the line. Teresa mumbled something to it, then returned to the receiver, her voice breathy and sleepy-sounding. "Okay. I can meet you around noon on Saturday. There's a place downtown on Main Street called The Brickfront. It's a coffee shop. Can you find it?"

"Yes. And thank you for—"

"No problem," Teresa Larosche said and immediately hung up.

CHAPTER 12

Stephanie Canton was a meticulous little woman who arrived Friday afternoon dressed in a lime-green knit pantsuit, her cadaverous complexion offset by bright red lipstick and a shock of orange hair more befitting of a circus clown than an estate liquidator. With a black loose leaf binder tucked under one arm, she marched through the house with Laurie at her elbow, examining the furniture as well as the overall condition of the house itself. When she paused to swipe a pointy little finger through the dust on the top of the piano in the parlor, Laurie imagined herself clubbing the woman over the head with the brass candelabrum, then dragging her dwarfish body down into the sanctum of the dungeonlike basement.

"When was the house built?" Ms. Canton quipped.

"You know, I have no idea. Maybe sometime in the sixties?"

"The woodwork is handmade. Do you see the detailing in the balustrade?" They were in the foyer now, with Ms. Canton pointing at the stairwell banister. This was their second lap around the house and the woman had yet to make any notes in her little black binder. "The spindles look hand-carved. Do you see the variants in each spindle? Do you?"

Laurie leaned close and squinted at the balusters. "I guess so. . . ."

"Did your father do any woodworking himself, Mrs. Genarro?"

"Not that I know of. He was a businessman. And a gardener."

Ms. Canton made a noise that suggested her disapproval of either businessmen or gardeners. Or both.

"The floors are in abhorrent condition," the woman went on. "Often, wood like this can be rejuvenated with some polish and buffing, but these appear to be beyond repair."

"Forgive me, but I thought you were here just to look at the furniture."

"I'm fearful to learn that the items I may have interest in will be in a similar state."

In the parlor, Ms. Canton scrutinized the Victor Victrola for a decent amount of time. She opened the cabinet doors and inspected the wood grain within. She examined the felt of the turntable and the condition of the arm. She finally opened the black binder and took down notes. "May I?" she inquired, nodding sharply at the crank on the side of the cabinet.

"Go right ahead," Laurie said. She watched while the smallish woman wound the crank and then stood on her toes while positioning the needled arm onto the record that had begun to spin on the turntable. A shushing sound radiated from the machine—a lilting waltz adorned with pops and hisses. Laurie was reminded of her dream, the one where the phonograph started playing as Abigail hovered above her in the darkness.

"Do you see this?" Ms. Canton said as she pointed to a label on the underside of the Victrola's hood. It showed a dog listening to a phonograph with its head cocked at a curious angle. "That's the authentic trademark of the Victor Talking Machine Company. See? It even says so beneath the picture. The first of these machines was built in 1901."

"When was this one built?"

"This is a Victrola model. The date is worn away, but if I had to guess, I'd say it was built around 1909 or 1910."

"Wow."

"Is this a family heirloom?"

"No. When my father was young, he worked in the steel industry and eventually owned a factory in Sparrows Point. There was stuff left behind in storage from the original owners of the factory, and my father spent some time going through the place and cleaning it up. I can't be sure, but I think this was one of the things my father had salvaged from the factory's storage sheds."

Ms. Canton stepped to the left of the Victrola and peered down into the boxful of record albums. One curious eyebrow raised, she jotted another note in her binder, then snapped it shut with an audible clap.

Next, Laurie took the woman into her father's study. Ms. Canton paused, cocking an eyebrow at the crosses carved into the paneled walls, before zeroing in on the old rolltop desk. She ran a hand along its surface and commented, "Nice piece." In the master bedroom, Ms.

Canton committed more notes to her binder while she examined the four-poster bed and the matching nightstand. However, unlike with the Victrola and the rolltop desk, she made no verbal comments about the items. Once they were finished, Laurie offered the woman a cup of coffee. Ms. Canton seemed pleased and they went into the kitchen together. Ted and Susan had gone for a walk through the woods and down to the river, so the house was quiet.

Ms. Canton sat down at the kitchen table while Laurie poured the coffee into big mugs. The woman set her bulky purse and her sleek black binder on the tabletop, then gazed out the bay windows at the yard. It was a slightly overcast afternoon, and intermittent shadows webbed across the lawn.

"Cream and sugar?"

"Yes, please. Both."

Laurie added the cream and sugar to the mugs and then carried them over to the table and sat down.

"You said you grew up here?"

"I did, yes," said Laurie, sliding the woman's coffee over to her.

Ms. Canton nodded primly. "Thank you."

"Do you think there's any money in any of the stuff?"

"I should say there is." Ms. Canton lifted her coffee and slurped noisily, though she kept her pinky finger out the entire time. "Typically, I would recommend an estate auction at this phase, but you've got so few items that it would be more hassle than benefit. For you and your family, a tag sale would be more convenient. You've been to yard sales before, I presume?"

"Of course."

"In practicality, an estate sale is no different. Given your limited items, I would recommend you authorize me to contact a few acquaintances of mine who deal in antiquities. There may be interest right out of the gate, to use the expression, and you'll find there's no need for some drawn-out event, or to prolong the process any more than necessary."

"You really think someone will be interested in all this stuff?"

"The rolltop desk and the furniture in the master bedroom in particular."

"That would be fantastic. Yes, please contact whomever you need to. The sooner the better. We're sort of here under some duress until we get all this squared away."

One of Ms. Canton's slender black eyebrows arched. "Duress?"

"Well, it's keeping my husband away from work and my daughter away from her friends." She smiled tiredly at the woman across from her. "And to be frank, Ms. Canton, I don't like being here in this house."

"Yes. David Cushing advised me of what happened to your father. I'm very sorry to hear it."

It's not just that, she wanted to add. *I feel a cold suffocation slowly coming over me here, as if the walls were alive and slowly closing in on me. I can't be sure, but I don't think all is right in this place. I don't think my family and I are one hundred percent completely alone here, either. Also, there is a troubling little girl who lives next door. She reminds me of another girl, a horrible girl who died. . . .*

But she couldn't say those things. Instead, she smiled

wanly at the woman, then covered up her fear behind her coffee mug.

"You mentioned some . . . business properties . . . that had belonged to your father—factories, warehouses?"

"What about them?"

"Since his death, does that mean you are now in possession of them?"

"Oh, no! He had his partners buy him out long ago, and I think Bethlehem Steel eventually came in and absorbed the whole company. From what I gathered from my father's financial statements, he hadn't been involved with the business in many years."

"He sounds like he was an interesting man," said Ms. Canton.

After Stephanie Canton left, Laurie placed the empty mugs in the kitchen sink and was bagging up the trash when she caught movement in her periphery vision. She turned toward the bay windows just as thunder rolled in the distance. At first, she thought the girl she saw streaming quickly across the yard was Susan. But then she saw the luxuriant bouncing hair. Today, the girl was dressed in the same faded blue dress she had worn the first time Laurie had glimpsed her, rushing across the yard and into the trees in a similar fashion. She recalled the strange dream where Abigail hovered above her in the darkness, watching her sleep. Or had it been Sadie in the dream? She found now that she couldn't remember, and wondered if the difference truly mattered. She finished with the trash and quickly carried it out back, where a rank of trashcans soldiered up against the side of the house. She dumped the trash into the nearest receptacle, then cut across the yard.

There was no sign of the girl anywhere.

She had come from the corner of the fence and had crossed the property at the back of the house. It was possible that the girl had disappeared over the hill and continued on through the woods. Laurie climbed the hill. Sunlight broke through the black clouds over the treetops and knifed her eyes. At the cusp of the woods, she looked around but could find no sign of the girl. Had Abigail come down this way, she had truly vanished. Ghostlike.

CHAPTER 13

For dinner the three of them ate steak, baked potatoes, and green beans. Afterwards, Ted poured himself a few fingers of scotch from Myles Brashear's liquor cabinet, and it kept him in a good place for the rest of the evening. After watching a DVD on the laptop, he and Susan adjourned to the kitchen to load the dishwasher while Laurie sat in the parlor going through some of her father's stuff.

"Mommy seems sad," Susan said, stacking plates into the dishwasher.

"Well, it's been a pretty stressful week for her."

"Because her daddy died?"

"Yes."

Out of nowhere, Susan wrapped her arms around Ted's waist and squeezed him hard. "I would be very stressful if you died, Daddy."

He felt a swelling of emotion inside him. "Thank you. Do you know what 'stressful' means, sugar-booger?"

"Does it mean sad?"

"Not really. It means you have a lot of things to worry about."

"Well, I would be sad if you died, Daddy."

"I'm not going to die."

"Not ever?"

He rubbed the top of her head and then gently separated her from him. "Everyone dies eventually. You know that."

"I do. But it doesn't have to be for a very long time, does it?"

"No," he said. "It doesn't."

"Good. Because I want you to not die for a very long time. Not for a very, *very* long time!"

He couldn't help but smile. "I'll do my best," he told her. "Now why don't you hop upstairs and take a bath? You've made quite a mess of yourself from playing in the dirt all day. Look how gross and grubby you are."

Susan crossed her eyes and stuck her tongue out. Ted laughed and feigned a grab for the tip of her tongue. Giggling, Susan raced through the kitchen and darted out into the parlor. He finished rinsing the plates, then loaded the rest into the dishwasher. Just as he finished, he heard the faucet come on in the bathroom upstairs.

In the parlor, Laurie sat on the loveseat staring out the darkened windows across the room. On her lap was one of her father's photo albums.

"What're you up to?"

Laurie sighed and looked wearily over at him. "Just going through some old photos."

"There are a few good shots of you and your mom in there. I hope you don't mind, but I went through it the other day. You might want to keep some of those."

"I suppose."

"What is it, Laurie?"

"It looks like some photos are missing. They're in

perfect order otherwise." She closed the album. "Or maybe I'm just looking too deeply into things. I don't know."

"Are you doing all right? Hanging in there?" he asked.

"Yes. Just like the little cat in those inspirational posters. What about you? You've seemed stressed since you came back from Annapolis yesterday."

"It's nothing huge." He sighed. "Got a call from Steve Markham while Susan and I were out. He says the high and mighty John Fish isn't happy with the outline I submitted. I've just wasted months of my time writing pages of a play while all along Fish the *wunderkind* wasn't happy with the lousy outline to begin with."

"I thought you said the outline was approved?"

"By the production office, yes," Ted said. "Per his contract, Fish gets final say."

"Seems awfully negligent of him."

"Ha. To say the least."

"Isn't there a way you can salvage the pages you've already written? Maybe you won't have to change any of it."

"I don't know. Markham is going to talk with Fish's agent, see if we can reach a compromise." He went to the liquor cabinet, decided against more scotch, and poured himself a glass of wine. "This house feels very cold."

"It's been a mild summer so far," she said absently.

"That's not what I mean." He sat down on the sofa and faced her. "This house holds some power over you."

"It's not that." She ran a finger along the edge of

the photo album. "Have you been hearing any strange noises in the house?" she asked.

"What kind of strange noises?"

"Noises upstairs. Like someone moving around. Twice I thought I heard a door slam when there was no one up there."

"I'm sure it's just Susan."

"Susan wasn't up there. And it's not in the bedrooms." She pointed straight at the ceiling. "I think it's coming from the belvedere."

"That door's locked."

"I know. It's stupid." She seemed to consider something for a long time. "Susan's frog," she said eventually. "The one in the cigar box. It looked like someone squeezed it to death."

"What are you saying? That Susan did it?"

"No, of course not. I know she wouldn't do a thing like that. And she was so upset . . ."

He got up, went over to her, and squeezed her shoulder. "It's stress. This whole thing is grating on you."

"You're probably right."

"There are unresolved issues with your father. It's going to take some time for you to learn how to deal with them. In the meantime, I'm worried about you."

"Don't worry," she said. "I'm keeping myself together."

She's talking about the highway incident. Because, yes, she seems as peculiar as she had back then, right after that whole thing had happened. A shiver took him at the base of his spine and traveled up toward his shoulder blades.

"I could take you and Susan back to Hartford, you know. You don't need to stay here if it makes you uncomfortable. It isn't necessary."

"Stephanie Canton's expecting to bring buyers to the house throughout the week."

"I can stay here and take care of Stephanie Canton and her buyers."

"I don't want us to split up like that." Laurie frowned and then sat up straighter. "I almost forgot. There's a rug in the basement that needs to be taken to the trash. It's big, so it will need to be cut up."

"All right." He stood, kissed her on the forehead, and carried his wine out into the hallway. Through the walls he could hear the water pipes chugging. He had yet to descend into the basement, and it took him a couple of seconds of wending through the labyrinthine hallways—and the opening of two hall closet doors—before he located the basement door.

It was cool and damp belowground. There were minimal items down here, much like the rest of the house. The rug was unrolled in the center of the floor. A disconcerting copper stain blotted its center.

There was a tool chest beneath a pegboard under the stairs. He knelt before it, unlatched the lid, and peered inside. Various tools lay in a rusted jumble. Carefully, he sifted through the tools until he located a razor housed in a plastic sleeve. The blade was rusty but still looked sharp enough to do its job. Sliding the toolbox back in place, he went about his business, slicing the stained Persian rug up into ribbons.

Once he had finished, he was sweaty and the muscles in his arm hurt. He filled two larger trash bags with pieces of the rug. He swept up the fibers with a dustpan and brush, dumped the fibers into one of the big bags, then tied both bags closed. Grunting, he lugged them upstairs, down the main hall toward the foyer, and out the front door.

It was cool and windy outside, but the rain had held off. Still, the air smelled of ozone as he traipsed along the lawn and down the long and winding driveway toward the street. Vapor street lamps glowed along the curve of Annapolis Road. Somewhere in the distance, a lone dog barked. On his walk back up to the house, he heard the flat heartbeat of thunder. It sounded very close. When he heard it a second time, he realized it wasn't actually thunder, but something else.

There was movement by the side of the house. Ted squinted through the darkness. A person stood on the front lawn between the fence and the driveway, small of frame but strangely tall. As he approached, the figure hopped up into the air. Upon landing, the sound the person made was the sound Ted had originally mistaken for thunder.

"Who's there?" he called.

It was a young girl. The reason she looked so tall was because she was standing on the plank of wood that covered the well. As he watched, the girl jumped up again, the board groaning beneath her feet as she came back down on it.

"Jesus, kid, you shouldn't be doing that." He rushed over and extended a hand to her. "Come on down. It's dangerous."

She didn't reach for his hand. Beneath her feet, the old plank made a straining, moaning sound.

"Honey," he said, his hand still extended.

The girl took his hand and hopped down off the well. She looked to be no older than Susan.

"Are you Abigail?" he asked. "The girl who lives next door?"

"Are you Susan's daddy?"

"I am. Do your parents know you're out here?"

"Probably not."

"Honey, what you were doing . . . you know that's really dangerous, don't you?"

"It bounces like a trampoline."

"I'll bet it does," he said, "but if it breaks, you'll be in a world of trouble. *Capisci?*"

"You talk funny," said the girl.

"Yeah, well, you should probably get on home. It's late."

"I used to throw rocks down there," said the girl, pointing to the well, "before it was covered up. They covered it up after the old man died."

"It's safer that way."

"Can we take the cover off so I can throw more rocks down there?"

"I don't think that's a good idea."

"I'll just take the cover off when you leave."

Her impudence shocked him. "Do you know what *trespassing* means, little darling?"

"No."

He laughed. "Get on home, will you?"

The girl turned and ran along the fence-line at the side of the house. Ted called after her again, but she ignored him this time. After the darkness swallowed her up, the only evidence of her was the sound of her quick little feet whipping through the overgrown grass. He heard something that sounded like the wooden gate slam shut on the fence. The girl's footfalls were now on the other side of the fence, shushing through the underbrush at a quick clip. For a second the footsteps paused. Ted listened. He could hear the little girl breathing on the other side of the fence. He considered scaring her—perhaps popping up over the fence and roaring at her, as he had once done to some rowdy kids sitting behind him and Laurie in a movie theater—but then he thought he'd feel bad if he actually frightened her. Instead, he turned and walked back toward the house. He was halfway up the porch steps when he felt something small strike his right shoulder blade. He whirled around in time to see a stone the size of a quarter bounce down the porch steps and vanish in the darkness.

The house was quiet upon his return.

Upstairs, Laurie was asleep in the master bedroom. In the dark, Ted stripped off his clothes, considered a shower, then decided against it. He crawled into bed beside Laurie. She stirred and murmured something unintelligible as he draped an arm around her shoulder and started to kiss her neck through the web of her hair.

"Please," she said quietly.

He rolled on top of her and sought out her mouth with his in the darkness. He kissed her and she kissed him back before turning her head away from him. She smelled warm and like sex. It made his groin ache.

"I can't," she whispered, not facing him. "Not in this house. Not in this bed."

It had been weeks since they'd had sex. Ted groaned and continued kissing down her neck. She was wearing a T-shirt to bed, something she had started doing since the highway incident last year, and again he was struck by a flicker of certainty that she knew about what had happened between him and Marney. If she really did know, would it be better for him to confess it to her? Or was it one of those things that, once spoken aloud, would corrupt everything? Perhaps she could feign ignorance as long as he enabled her to.

"Please," she said one last time, and set a cold palm against the side of his face.

He rolled over onto his side of the bed, his erection thrusting up beneath the bedsheet like the mast of a sailboat. Sighing, he laced his hands behind his head and stared at the shimmery blue light that came through the side windows and played along the ceiling in geometric surrealism. Shadows of tree limbs danced in the ghostly blue panels.

He hadn't even realized he had fallen asleep until he awoke sometime later. The house was tomblike in its silence. Rolling over, he found Laurie's side of the bed empty. He rubbed one hand along the mattress and found that it was cold.

She wasn't in the bathroom; the door stood open and the light was off. Listening, he could hear not a single sound throughout the house. *It's like floating through space*. And on the heels of that thought: *Maybe I'm still dreaming*.

Naked, he climbed out of bed and went out onto the landing. Peering over the railing, he could see no lights on in any of the rooms downstairs. Around him, the big house creaked like an old whaling ship.

When he had been just a boy, he had suffered from a recurring nightmare where he would wake up in the middle of the night to find the small brownstone where he lived with his family empty. He would scamper to his parents' bedroom, but there would be no sleeping bodies spooning each other in the bed. Similarly, the family dog—a sloppy-eyed bulldog named Stooge—was gone from his nighttime crate they kept in the kitchen. Young Ted was alone, and in these dreams he would begin screaming for the parents that were no longer in the house, the sloppy-eyed dog that was no longer in his crate. In the real world, the screams would alert his mother, who would rush to his bedside and wake him, then console him against her warm breast. The nightmare had come with unsettling frequency for several months before it simply stopped altogether. (The nightmare would not return to him until years later, when his parents were both killed in an automobile accident, allowing the horrors of the dream to become a waking reality.)

That nightmare returned to him now with all the strength and terror he remembered from his childhood. The power of its resurgence was like a shockwave. His palms were sticky with sweat on the railing.

He took a step back and saw Laurie curled up in a ball on the floor of the landing. The sight of her first startled, then terrified him.

"Laurie?"

She jerked her head up from the floor, the movement so quick it caused his heart to leap.

"What are you doing?" he said.

She sat up on her knees and propped one hand against the belvedere door. "I thought I heard something."

"The noises again?"

"I don't know."

"What did it sound like?"

"Like someone trying to get in." She touched the doorknob. "Someone turning the knob from the other side. And then . . ." Her voice trailed off as she looked at the door.

"And then what?" he prompted.

She pointed toward the ceiling. "Footsteps," she said. "Up there."

The distance between them made her face look like a white mask. "It's an old house. There's noises," he told her. "Come back to bed."

"I'm listening."

He watched her for perhaps fifteen or twenty seconds before his skin began to tighten in to gooseflesh. He listened, too, but could hear nothing. All of a sudden, his face felt too small for his skull. "You're freaking me out," he said. "There's no one up there. Come back to bed."

She came.

CHAPTER 14

The Brickfront was tucked discreetly between two larger shops and was nearly invisible. Laurie drove past it twice before she finally saw it. At noon on a Saturday, it was difficult to find street parking, so she opted for one of the parking garages, parked at the top, took the elevator down, then hustled across the street to the inconspicuous little coffee shop.

It was larger on the inside than Laurie had expected. There were maybe four or five circular tables on the floor, with additional booth seating on a raised platform against one wall that ran the length of the shop. Leather-bound books stood on high shelves and a brick hearth, which looked like it hadn't been cleaned in ages, took up much of the wall at the back of the coffee shop. Young girls in green aprons rotated between tables to serve lunch orders and refill drinks. Laurie claimed a small booth near the windows and set her purse down on the table. Although the food smelled delicious, when one of the young waitresses came over to the booth, Laurie ordered a cup of coffee and nothing else.

For a time, she thought about Susan. Returning to the house weighed on Laurie, but it distressed her in some inexplicable fashion to have Susan there. It wasn't a revelation that had dawned on her all at once; rather, it had happened—and was still happening—incrementally, bit by bit. Last night she had awoken to sounds in the house. Low talking, it had sounded like—the whispers of little girls. It had reminded her of sleepovers at friends' houses in her own youth, and all that hushed giggling behind cupped hands in the dark. But there had been a darker component to that sound last night. She had climbed out of bed and tread out onto the landing for a better listen. She first checked Susan's room, but she was sound asleep. Then she went downstairs and made sure all the doors were locked and the windows were latched. They were, but it didn't help quell her anxiety. When Ted had found her five minutes later in the upstairs hallway, she had been convinced she had heard footsteps on the other side of the belvedere door.

It occurred to her now that she harbored an imprecise concern for her daughter being in that house. This notion reminded her of all the fears she'd suffered at the onset of motherhood, when she worried about all the dangers of the world out there, ready to take a bite out of her helpless daughter. Strange noises in an old house were nothing compared to the brutality of the real world.

Now, in the bright light of a new day, it was easy enough to believe those noises she had heard last night had been nothing more than sounds carried over from some forgotten dream.

She was on her third refill when a bleached blonde came into the shop. She was young, perhaps in her late-twenties, and possessed the aquiline profile of a Greek bust. The heavy costume jewelry around her neck and wrists jangled as she approached Laurie's booth. The girl's smile was surprisingly earnest despite her sharp features.

"Mrs. Genarro? I'm Teresa Larosche."

"Hi. Please sit down."

The girl sat across from her on the opposite side of the table. She had iPod earbuds in her ears, which she popped out now. Her ears were adorned with cheap studs and hoops. A diamond stud twinkled on the left side of her nose.

The girl must have sensed something wrong with Laurie. "You're Mrs. Genarro, right? We spoke over the phone?"

"Yes. I'm sorry, I was just expecting someone much older. Someone more like—"

"Dora Lorton, right?"

"Exactly."

Teresa Larosche smiled again. Laurie decided she was very pretty.

"The truth is, I haven't been doing the whole home-care thing very long. I got my nursing license a few years back and was working shifts at North Arundel up until about a year ago when they laid a bunch of us off. There are other jobs to be had, but I didn't want to just pack up and move someplace." She exhaled a soft laugh. She possessed the sensual rasp of a phone-sex operator. "Hell, I didn't have the money to move nowhere, so I figured I'd see what else was out there."

"How long had you worked for Mid-Atlantic?"

"Just about seven months or so."

"Did you quit because of what happened or were you fired?"

Teresa exhaled again. Laurie could smell cigarettes on her breath. "You know, my boyfriend warned me not to get into too much of this stuff. About what happened that night, I mean. Mr. Claiborne did, too." She began fidgeting with the cluster of silver rings on her left hand. "Everybody thinks you're gonna sue."

"I'm not suing anybody. I'm just curious about what happened to my father. I've got some questions and I was hoping you might be able to answer some. If you're uncomfortable with any of it, you don't have to say a word."

Teresa nodded and looked suddenly sad.

"Would you like a coffee?" Laurie offered. She waved over the young waitress.

"Café Milan," Teresa told the waitress.

"Back in a jiff," said the waitress before moving on to another table.

"Just so you're aware, I saw the police report concerning my father's suicide. Any information I might bring up while we talk today, I got from that report. Admittedly, there wasn't much to the report, but I want you to know that upfront, and not assume that I had been asking Ms. Lorton or Mr. Claiborne about you behind your back. Because I haven't, and I wouldn't do that. Okay?"

Again, Teresa nodded. "Okay."

"And if you want me to sign something saying I won't sue you, I'll be glad to, if that puts your mind at ease."

Relief came readily to the young woman's face. She stopped fidgeting with her rings. "Okay. I believe you."

"Good." She offered the girl a warm smile before proceeding. "The police report said you started working the night shift at my father's house approximately two months prior to his death. Is that correct?"

"Yes. My previous patient was daycare only—cooking meals, doing laundry, making sure she was able to take a shower without slipping and breaking her hip. Easy enough. Just after Christmas, her family decided she would be better off in one of those assisted living facilities. From there, I was basically a floater until the night shift gig opened up with your dad."

"What's a floater?"

"It's what we call someone just picking up other jobs until a steady one comes through. There's always a window of downtime when a patient . . . well, moves on before we get reassigned to someone else. I would fill in for permanent caretakers if they took vacation days or were sick or something. Mr. Claiborne had me doing some clerical stuff at the office, too, but I was going bored out of my skull with that, you know? I didn't go to nursing school to sit around and file office papers and sharpen pencils."

The waitress brought over Teresa's coffee. Laurie could smell the alcohol in it.

"How bad was my father when you started working the night shift at the house?" Laurie asked after the waitress had left.

"Like, how . . . gone . . . was he?" She pointed to her temple to illustrate that she meant *gone mentally*. "To be honest, he was fine at first. He went to bed early and by the time he woke up in the morning, Dora was already coming in for her shift. I was really there in case something happened—an emergency or something, you know? It was really a no-brainer for the first few weeks. I mean, I read books, listened to my headphones, stuff like that. The only bummer was that there were no TVs in the house, but I got a lot of reading done those first few weeks."

"So what happened after the first few weeks?"

Teresa's hands wound around her coffee. She hadn't tasted it yet, but looked like she wanted to—like she needed to.

"Well, see, before I got there, Dora had the locks changed. They used to be regular old crank deads on the doors—"

"'Crank deads'?" Laurie asked.

"Sorry. Dead bolts—you know, the kinds with the knob on the inside that you turn instead of having to use a key, which Mr. Brashear could unlock easily enough. Dora had them changed so that you needed a key to unlock them. She said this was because he had tried on a few occasions to sneak out of the house. Folks with dementia sometimes do that."

"Sure," said Laurie, nodding.

"I was worried about what might happen if he tried to get out. Like, what if he became violent, you know, and I couldn't stop him from leaving? Your dad, he was a pretty big guy."

Laurie remembered him being huge, but of course she had been a much younger and smaller person at the time.

"Did he ever get violent with you?" Laurie asked.

Teresa's eyes narrowed and grew distant. Laurie couldn't tell if she was trying to remember a specific event or if she were just trying to figure out the best way to relay it.

"No," she said eventually, though she stretched the word out which raised more questions than it answered—*noooo.* "Sometimes with himself, but never with me."

"Good. I'm glad to hear it."

Teresa sipped at her alcohol-infused coffee, sucked at her lips, then continued. "He never tried to get out of the house while I was there. By then, he was more concerned with people getting *in*."

"Dora said the same thing to me. I asked her to explain what she meant, but she brushed it off as a symptom of my father's dementia. It bothers me that I don't know what he was afraid of."

Teresa took another drink, then asked if Laurie had ever spent any time with someone suffering from dementia.

"No, I haven't. I hadn't even seen my father in . . . well, in many, many years."

"They're sort of like children trapped in the bodies of grownups," Teresa said. "They sometimes say and do things a spoiled child might do." She lowered her voice. "But sometimes, you know, there's . . . something else there in their eyes, *behind* their eyes. It's like they're actually prisoners inside themselves, peering out windows, and watching helplessly as their body and mind betray them. That part scares me to death."

"Scares you how?"

"Like, what if that's me someday? You know what I mean?"

"Yes."

"Your father was like that sometimes. Not always, but sometimes. He would come in and out of it. It was like there were two people inside him—this evil devil and this helpless old man. I felt pity for him."

Laurie brought her own coffee to her mouth. All of a sudden it tasted bitter and she quickly set it aside.

"You asked about the locks on the doors," Teresa went on. "I had a copy of the key, of course, just as Dora did. After I'd been there a few weeks, your father would wake up in the middle of the night and insist I go around and relock the doors. He insisted on watching me do it, too. Some nights, I had to do it three or four times."

"Did he ever say why he thought people were trying to get into the house?"

"He didn't know why. But he was certain of it. Terrified of it, really. And do you want to hear something ridiculous?" The young woman laughed nervously. "After a while, he started to convince *me* of it. And I started to think, shit, what if he's right? He seems so certain, *what if he's right?* Soon, I started waking *myself* up just to go around the house and make sure the doors were all locked. And, see, that freaked me out even more because, you know, just like I said—what if his dementia was contagious? What if it had somehow seeped into me?"

Laurie offered the young woman a pained smile. Inside, however, her stomach felt like it was beginning to boil. She couldn't help but recall her own recent obsession with checking the locks in the house, fearful that someone could get in . . . or possibly already had. To think that she shared this identical psychosis with her demented and suicidal father alarmed her.

"Yeah, I know, it sounds crazy," Teresa said quickly, no doubt discomfited by the look of distress on Laurie's face. "I'd think I was crazy if I was in your place."

"I don't think you're crazy at all."

"I mean, I know it isn't possible—I'm not a dummy— but when you're there alone in a strange house with nothing but time on your hands to think of all these ridiculous things . . ."

"There's no need to explain yourself," said Laurie. "Please go on."

Teresa drank down half her coffee in two large gulps. When she set it down, Laurie could see that her hands were shaking.

"I once saw this movie about a psychiatrist who has these sessions with this mental patient. Only instead of, like, making the patient better, by the end of the movie the patient made the psychiatrist insane. It sort of felt like that, Mrs. Genarro."

"Call me Laurie."

"Okay." She pressed her hands flat on the table, presumably to stop them from shaking. "You know, it's hard to explain. His concern about the doors being unlocked, I mean."

"How so?"

"Well, at first it was no different than how you or I would check to see if the doors are locked before going to bed. He'd follow me around the house and watch as

I turned the key in each lock. He had to actually see the key *turn* before he was satisfied. Then we would check the windows." The corner of her mouth turned up in a lopsided grin. "There are a lot of windows in that house. And he kept saying they were too easy."

"Too easy for what?"

"For someone to get in."

"Is that why they're all nailed shut?"

"Jesus, yes. I'd forgotten about that. But he'd nailed them shut before I came on board. I wouldn't have allowed him to have a hammer and nails."

"Of course," said Laurie.

"But even with them nailed shut, he didn't trust them. So we checked the windows. This was fine with him for maybe about an hour or so, when he would forget that we had locked everything up already and he wanted to go through the house again. Like I said, we sometimes did this a couple times every night."

Laurie shook her head. "I can't imagine. . . ."

Teresa shrugged. It was obvious that whatever had happened after things got worse made this part seem trivial. Whatever it was, it still nested inside Teresa Larosche. She was still afraid of it.

"After a while, he became focused on one door in particular."

"The front door?" Laurie guessed.

"No. The door off the kitchen. The one that leads out into the side yard. I thought maybe because it was dark and hidden from the road, and if you were a burglar, breaking in through that door would make the most sense."

"But my father wasn't thinking logically by then. He had no sense left in him."

"Yeah, that's what I thought, too."

"Did you ever ask him why he had become obsessed about that particular door?"

"Yeah, I did. But his answers never made any sense to me."

"What were his answers?"

"Something about locking up the passageways, that passageways let it in and out like a turnstile. He actually said that—like a turnstile."

"It lets *who* in?"

"Sometimes he called it the Hateful Beast," Teresa said. "Other times, it was the Vengeance. Most times, though, he didn't *have* a name for it, or at least didn't give me one. God, it sounds so silly now, sitting here in a coffee shop telling you about it—and look at that, my hands are shaking—but it used to spook the hell out of me when he'd say it."

"What exactly did he mean? What was 'the Vengeance'?"

"Beats me. All I know is it scared the shit out of him and it started scaring the shit out of me, too. I assumed he got it from the Bible. He read the Bible most nights. When he was able to, anyway."

"I never realized he had become religious."

"You didn't know him very well, did you?"

"Not since I was a little girl. And even then I don't think I really *knew* him."

Teresa nodded. The look on her face was one of understanding. Perhaps she had issues with her own father. "Anyway," she went on, "I humored him, and that seemed to make us both feel better. Sometimes he'd have me lock that door five or six times. Once, he watched me lock it and when we were headed back out into the parlor, he paused in the kitchen doorway, turned around, and insisted I *relock* the door. Of course, for him it wasn't *relocking*, because he'd forgotten we had already locked it the first time. Times like that, when the forgetting came on him so quickly, I could almost see the memories draining out of his face.

"He only really became upset when he thought someone had actually gotten into the house. He said he could hear someone, and that they were hiding from him. Sometimes he would go looking for them, shouting and stomping around the house and checking all the rooms. Other times, the poor guy would cower in his bedroom and not come out. It really freaked me out when he would get like that. I mean, it sounds so incredibly naïve, but he started to . . . I mean, there were a few times when he had . . ."

"Yes?"

"He had started to convince me."

"That someone was in the house?"

"Sometimes I thought I could hear someone talking softly in the next room, or that there'd be footsteps at the far end of the house. A few times I thought I caught movement out of the corner of my eye when no one was there. That sort of thing. Yeah, yeah, I know—jumping at shadows, right? I believe it now, but it was plenty real in that house when it's the middle of the night and you're starting to let your imagination run wild. It was like I could hear everything *he* could hear, and it didn't matter if you were sane or crazy to hear it."

The waitress came over to refill their coffees. Laurie found she was thankful for the brief interruption. She had begun to sweat under her arms.

"After he was content with the doors being locked," Teresa went on after a while, "he would sometimes stare at the ceiling. Just randomly, you know? He reminded me of my father when he would do that. I grew up in Havre de Grace, in a big old farmhouse, and one fall a family of raccoons took up residence in our attic. The noises they made were tremendous—you wouldn't think raccoons could make so much noise—and we didn't know what was going on at first. Finally, my dad went up there and chased them out. He found the hole they'd come in through and boarded that up, too. That kept them out for good, but my dad spent the rest of that year periodically peering up at the ceiling, his head cocked like an old hunting dog, as if in anticipation of some noise the rest of us couldn't hear."

"Did my father ever say what noises he was hearing?"

"Dry creaking noises. Like attic beams settling."

"That's how he described them?"

"No, he never told me what they sounded like to him. I never asked."

"Then how do you know what they sounded like?"

"Because I heard them, too," Teresa said.

"Oh." Laurie blinked. "So . . . then they were real noises. . . ."

"Yeah. I mean, I thought it was just the house set-

tling . . . but the way your father looked up at the ceiling
when he heard it . . ." She shook her head, as if to rid it
of the memory. "Like I said before, I was beginning to
wonder if I wasn't losing my mind in that place. I figured if he stayed just one step ahead of me—forgive me
for how I say this, but I kept thinking that if he stayed
just one step ahead of me on the crazy scale—then I
might be able to see the full-fledged insanity coming
before it got me." She hung her head. "I'm sorry. That
sounds horrible. I didn't mean it like that."

"You did, but that's okay. You're being honest with
me and I appreciate it. Please go on."

"Then one night he lost all interest in the side door,
and turned all his focus on that narrow little door in the
upstairs hallway. It leads to that strange little room upstairs on the roof. You know what I'm talking about?"

Laurie didn't answer. Suddenly, she was looking at
Teresa Larosche from the wrong end of a telescope. Her
flesh prickled.

"Mrs. Genarro? You okay?"

"Yes." Her mouth was dry. "Please, go on."

"Well, he became paranoid that someone was up
there, or maybe trying to get into the house from up
there. A few times I wanted to take him up there and
show him that wasn't the case, but he refused to go. I
went up there by myself a couple of times just to show
him there was nothing there."

"Did you . . . did you ever find anything up there?"

"No. Of course, I didn't. It was just an empty room.
Very creepy, but there was nothing there."

Some teenagers burst into the coffee shop on a wave
of raucous laughter, startling Laurie. She hadn't real-

ized how low they had been talking until just then. Laurie watched the teenagers—there were four of them—go to the counter and take a long time placing their orders. Even the young waitresses in the green aprons looked irritated.

"Downtown sucks in the summer," Teresa commented. "Every idiot and their mother comes down here and ruins the place."

One of the teenagers was handed a paper cup. He took it over to a counter on which stood several insulated drums of flavored coffee. He hummed loudly as he peered at all the labels on the pots, then spilled some coffee on the floor when he went to fill his paper cup.

"Anyway," Teresa continued, digging around in her purse now, "that's how that door came to be locked." She set a small silver key on the table and slid it over to Laurie.

"So the lock wasn't put on the door to prevent my father from going up there . . ."

Teresa shook her head. Her expression was grave. "It was to prevent someone from coming *down*," she said. "To stop them from getting into the house. Your father was convinced someone would get in if the door wasn't locked—that someone was *trying* to get in."

"But the police report said—"

"I tried explaining it to the police, but they didn't understand. Police don't like things like dementia or Alzheimer's or schizophrenia—anything that muddies up the waters of logical thought. They can't make sense of things that aren't logical."

Laurie let this sink in. At the coffee station, the coffee-spiller was joined by his three friends, each of who seemed incapable of reading the labels on the coffee drums quietly and to themselves. Behind the counter, someone dropped a plate and the teenagers cheered. Heads throughout the place swiveled in their direction. Once the four teenagers left and the place quieted down, Laurie turned her attention back to Teresa Larosche.

"What did my father think would happen to him if this . . . person . . . actually got in?"

Teresa's mouth unhinged the slightest bit, though for a moment she didn't speak. "I don't know," she said finally. "I have no idea. I don't even know if he believed it *was* a person." Teresa seemed to consider this last point.

"Tell me about what happened the night he died."

Teresa shifted uncomfortably in her seat. Her eyes darted across the room, as if drawn to the large chalkboard scrawled with the day's specials at the opposite end of the coffee shop. When she spoke again, she sounded as if something were caught in her throat.

"It was sometime after midnight. I was asleep in the guestroom upstairs, at the opposite end of the hall from where your father slept. He had gone to bed around nine and hadn't gotten up at all, so I was thinking— well, hoping—that it might be an easy night.

"I was lying in bed reading a book. I had one earbud in so I could listen to my iPod, but I always kept one out so I could hear if he made any noises in the night. Just before midnight, I went down the hall and checked in on your father. I could hear him snoring, so I knew he was okay. So I went back to my room and went to sleep.

"Sometime later I woke up. Or maybe I thought I

did. I don't remember. I heard low voices talking in whispers, or maybe that part was in my dream."

"Voices? More than one, you mean?"

Teresa appeared to consider this for a while before answering. "I think maybe it was one voice, though it sounded like one end of a conversation."

"Meaning my father had been talking to himself."

"I guess. I mean, something like that. I can't really be sure. I never heard the door open—that door that goes to the room upstairs." Again, she paused to consider this. "I think I *dreamt* I heard the door open, but maybe I never did. All I know is I didn't get out of bed until I heard him shouting. I got up, went into the hall, and saw the door standing open. I was shocked at this, you know, because it was *always* locked."

"But was it that night?"

"It was *always* locked," Teresa repeated. "We checked it every night."

"And I assume my father didn't have access to the key?"

"Of course not. I kept it on my keychain with my car keys, and those were in my purse."

"Okay. So the door is open . . . ?"

"By the time I reached the door and looked up the stairs, your father had stopped shouting. The whole house went eerily quiet. Then I heard the window smash. I ran up the stairs to the room and saw the window broken. When I looked out, I saw him on the pavement below. He was cut up from jumping out the window—he hadn't opened it first, just jumped through the glass— and I could tell by the way he was lying down there that he was dead."

"Did you see anyone else out there in the yard when you looked down?"

"No. Who would I see? It was after midnight."

Laurie picked up the silver key. "Why was the lock put back on the door after my father's death? There would have been no reason to prevent him from going up there anymore."

Again, Teresa Larosche glanced down at her hands. Her unpainted fingernails had been gnawed down to nubs, the cuticles stained to the color of mercurochrome from nicotine. There was a small tattoo of a butterfly in the fleshy webbing between the thumb and index finger of her left hand.

"Teresa?" Laurie prompted when it didn't appear that the girl would respond.

"It's silly," Teresa said. Laurie couldn't tell if she was about to laugh or cry. "Mr. Claiborne insisted we clean the house up, get it ready for your arrival. I guess your father just got to me. Scared me, you know? Like that movie about the crazy guy who turns the psychiatrist crazy, too. I just felt . . . *safer* . . . being back in that house with the door locked." When she finally looked up, Laurie saw that her eyes were moist. "Stupid, right?"

Laurie reached out and touched one of the young woman's hands. "Not at all," she told her.

"I quit the next day. I just couldn't be in that house. I was hearing things by then, too . . . or at least convincing myself that I was. I kept thinking that Mr. Brashear was dead but his phobias were not. Toby said it could be ghosts. He believes in life after death and all that weird stuff. Even if I don't—and I *don't, I don't* believe in that stuff—Toby might still have a point." She laughed uncomfortably. "I don't know. I guess I sound like an idiot." Almost apologetically, she added, "Toby's my boyfriend."

Laurie's smile felt like a grimace on her face. "You were there that night, so I want to ask you a question, and I want you to be perfectly honest with me in your answer. I don't want you to be embarrassed or think I'm judging you or anything. Okay?"

Teresa's silver rings made knocking sounds against the tabletop as her hands started to vibrate again. She smiled painstakingly at Laurie. There was sadness in her smile, a tired resignation. "Yeah, okay."

"Do you believe there was someone else in the house with you the night my father died?"

"Now you're just freaking me out," Teresa said.

"That's not my intention. I just want to know what you think."

Teresa Larosche stared at her for an indeterminate amount of time, not blinking. "Listen," she said after a time, "do you mind if I grab a smoke real quick?" She stood and slung her purse over one shoulder.

"Be my guest."

Already shaking a cigarette from the pack, Teresa crossed the coffee shop and stepped outside. Through the narrow window beside the door, Laurie watched her lean against the building and light the cigarette.

"Did you want another refill, ma'am?" said the young waitress as she appeared beside the table. She held a stainless-steel carafe in one hand.

"Yes, please. Thank you."

The girl refilled the coffee and Laurie asked for a lunch menu. By the time the girl returned with the menu, several minutes had passed. Laurie looked up and out the window to the street. She could no longer see Teresa Larosche leaning against the building, smoking. Laurie got up and went out the front door. She looked up and down Main Street, but it was a futile search. Teresa Larosche was gone.

CHAPTER 15

Ted was in the parlor scribbling notes in the margins of the John Fish novel when Laurie returned home. A bottle of Cherry Heering liqueur stood on the table beside a stack of Ted's papers. *Pagliacci* played on the Victrola.

"Where's Susan?" she asked.

"Upstairs." He dragged a hand through his hair. "Goddamn it, I'd say this is like trying to condense the Bible down to one hundred pages, but I wouldn't want to gift John Fish with the literary comparison."

"Do you smell something funny?"

"Funny like what?" he said, not looking up at her.

"I don't know. It just smells bad in here."

"So open some windows and air the place out."

She went upstairs and found Susan lying on her bed reading *Harry Potter and the Chamber of Secrets*.

"Everything okay, pumpkin seed?"

Susan eyed her from over the top of her book. "Hi."

"Did you want lunch?"

"I already ate."

"What'd you eat?"

"Peanut butter and jelly."

"Did Daddy make it for you?"

"I made it myself."

Laurie smiled at the girl but Susan's concentration was wholly on her book. For a moment, Laurie was reminded of Susan's first day of preschool, and how Laurie had walked her into the classroom while tightly gripping the girl's hand, reluctant to relinquish her into the throng of children. It had taken more strength to let her go than to hold on to her.

"I saw your little friend Abigail the other day," Laurie said.

"Oh."

"Have you ever been over to her house?"

"No."

"Have you ever met her parents?"

"No."

Laurie felt her left eyelid twitch. "Do you like Abigail?"

Susan shrugged. "She's okay."

"What kind of games do you play?"

"I don't know."

"Did she tell you to take granddad's cuff links from the study?"

Susan's eyes swept up to meet Laurie's from over the top of her book. Laurie didn't like the sudden change of expression on her daughter's face.

Smoothing Susan's hair out of her eyes, Laurie said, "Does she sometimes tell you to take things out of the house and bring them to her?"

"I didn't take anything out of the house." Susan's soulful eyes hung on her mother's. They were Ted's eyes now.

Then who did? Who came into this house and took them? And where is the missing one?

Hurt, Laurie sighed. She couldn't help but feel that if it had been Ted who had initially confronted Susan, she wouldn't have lied to him. Because Laurie was the disciplinarian, she had earned herself a modicum of distrust in her daughter's eyes. Not for the first time, Laurie wished she could just shirk the responsibility of parenthood and simply embrace her daughter, love and laugh with her, and not get caught up in worrying about her.

"Okay," Laurie said at last. "Never mind." She leaned in and kissed the girl's forehead.

Out in the hall, she slipped the silver key Teresa Larosche had given her from her pocket and approached the locked belvedere door. It was silly, but she suddenly heard Teresa speak up in her head: *I guess your father just got to me. Scared me, you know? Like that movie about the crazy guy who turns the psychiatrist crazy, too.*

The little silver key fit the padlock perfectly. She turned it and the lock popped open. The door squeaked and inched toward her, as if some presence on the other side was gently pushing on it. Laurie removed the padlock from the eyelet, flipped over the clasp, and pulled the door open. A set of unpainted wooden stairs—steeper than regular stairs—appeared before her. There had once been a handrail, but that was gone now. The walls were paneled in dark wood, just as they had been when she was a child and had lived here. As a young girl, she had been forbidden to enter the belvedere. Her father had said it was unsafe and her mother had silently agreed. Now, climbing those stairs, she was overcome by a strange sense of rebellion even after all these years.

The staircase entered the belvedere through a rectangular cutout in the floor. There was a half-wall here, to which the upper part of the banister had once been bolted. As Laurie came up through the floor, her first thought was that the room was much smaller than she had remembered it. Despite being forbidden to tread up here in her youth, she had still on occasion snuck up. A few times she had even taken Sadie up here, though those instances were usually at Sadie's behest. Sadie had thought of the room as a crow's nest, like on an old pirate ship, and she had taken sinister pleasure in surveying the neighborhood from such a vantage, unobserved. Laurie's memory of the room was of an expansive four-sided chamber with a large pane of glass on every wall, nearly floor-to-ceiling. From this vantage, one was able to achieve a full 360-degree view of the surrounding area. Facing front, it was possible to follow the curving driveway down to the ribbon of blacktop that was Annapolis Road. At the rear, the tree line looked stunted and it was possible to make out the tree-studded bank on the opposite side of the Severn River.

Now, the room was no more than a narrow shaft with bits of broken glass on the floor and what looked like splotches of dried brown blood on the wood paneling. The window her father had gone through had not been replaced. There was a board nailed over the broken window, not dissimilar to the one used as a covering for the well in the front yard.

Dora and Felix had cleaned the whole house after his death, but they hadn't cleaned up here. She wondered if it had been left as a crime scene, if the police had forbidden Dora and Teresa from coming up here. But then she thought about what Teresa had said—about putting the lock back in place upon returning to the house so that she would feel safer—and wondered if they had all just forgotten about the room. Maybe on purpose. Or perhaps Dora had no way to access this room once Teresa quit and took off with the padlock key.

Those brownish bloodstains on the floor. . . .The fact that the window looks like it had been broken from the outside instead of on the inside . . .

Had this had happened to someone not suffering from dementia, would the police have investigated further? Could it be that there *had* been someone else in—

No. She wasn't prepared to go that far.

She looked out the nearest window and beyond the interlocking branches of the trees to the house next door. An image leapt to her mind then—of standing beneath the portico of the old well on the front lawn with Sadie Russ beside her, both girls peering down. The water was black and sightless. Laurie told her it was a wishing well, and if you threw riches into it, the well would grant you any wish you liked. Sadie said she was wrong, and told her it was an evil well, that if you fell down into it you were sucked off to another dimension where there were evil trolls and dogs with many heads. *And if you throw someone's riches down there,* Sadie had insisted, grinning as she said it, *you can make horrible things happen to them.* The memory made Laurie's skin crawl. She had never again thrown anything down into the well after that day.

From this height, the tops of the large trees that grew

up from the old Russ property and leaned over the fence were at eye-level. A few of the thick branches twisted like helixes across the span of space between the fence and the house, and a few of the branches extended out over the roof. None of them reached as far as the belve-dere itself, but a good number of sturdy branches hung out over the roof.

She was about to turn and leave when she noticed something on the floor. She went over to it, bent down, and picked it up. It was a carpenter's nail. She glanced around the floor and saw several more scattered about. She went to the boarded-up window and ran her hand along one edge. Nail heads speed bumped against the tips of her fingers. But there were no bumps along the bottom of the board. She got down on her knees and could see that there were nail *holes* but no nails. Some-one had pried them out and left them scattered about the floor.

She stuck her hand up underneath the bottom section of the board and could feel the ridged sill on the other side. Bits of jagged glass, sharp as guillotine blades, poked up from the frame on the other side of the board. With both hands, she was able to pry the lower half of the board away from the window frame several inches—enough, she realized, for someone small to slip through. Peering behind the board, she could see the triangular teeth of glass jutting up from the windowsill on the other side. When she let the board slap back into place, it made a sharp report that sounded very much like someone slamming a door.

* * *

Back in the kitchen, Laurie located Dora Lorton's phone number on the pad beside the phone and dialed it. It rang several times without answer, and Laurie was just about to hang up when the ringing stopped. Silence simmered in her ear but no one said a word.

"Hello?" said Laurie. She thought she heard someone breathing.

"Who's this?" It was Dora Lorton's clipped, businesslike voice.

"Ms. Lorton, this is Laurie Genarro. I hope I'm not disturbing you. Do you have a moment to talk?"

The woman exhaled loudly on the other end of the phone. Laurie thought she heard a TV on in the background. "What is it?"

"I wanted to ask you about the little girl who lives next door," Laurie said, searching now for a sign of Abigail through the bay windows as she spoke. "Do you know her?"

"There is no little girl who lives next door."

Laurie thought she had misheard the woman. "The little girl with the long reddish-brown hair. Surely you've seen her. She plays in the yard."

"There is no girl who lives next door," Dora repeated. "The Rosewoods live next door and they do not have any children."

"Their last name isn't Evans?"

"No. There are no families named Evans that I am aware of on Annapolis Road, or anywhere else in the neighborhood, for that matter."

"Ms. Lorton, a little girl named Abigail Evans—"

"Some months ago there was some trouble with vandals," Dora said. In the background, the sound of the

TV had vanished. Perhaps she had muted it or turned
it off. "People's mailboxes were stolen, windows were
broken, and cars were vandalized. It turned out to be
teenagers from a few streets over. Perhaps this girl is
one of them."

"No, no, she's much too young. The girl is Susan's
age, and she—"

"Susan?"

"Yes. My daughter. The girl is ten years old. You're
telling me you know of no such girl?"

"I have never seen a young girl at that house. I don't
know any family by the name Evans."

Laurie stood there with the phone to her ear, unable
to think of anything else to say.

"Mrs. Genarro? Are you still there?"

"I'm here."

"Is there a problem at the house?"

"No," she said, but her voice was small now, nearly
nonexistent. "No problem."

"I'm glad to hear it. Was there anything further?"

Laurie shook her head. She thought she saw someone's silhouette move between the trees on the other
side of the fence, but then realized it was just a leafy
bough swaying in the breeze.

"Mrs. Genarro? Hello?"

"Sorry. No, I'm okay. Thank you. Good-bye."

She hung up the phone.

CHAPTER 16

Ted was cursing to himself while hunched over his laptop in the parlor when Laurie came through on her way to the front hall. He didn't even seem aware of her presence. She went out the front door and walked down the driveway. Annapolis Road was a curving band of asphalt that ran a rough parallel to the Severn River, heavily wooded and dotted with lampposts and the occasional parked car. Laurie walked next door to the rundown house on the other side of the fence. Unlike her father's well-kept property, the front yard here was wildly overgrown and populated by a multitude of ceramic garden gnomes. The driveway was comprised of unpaved concrete slabs that had been reduced to rubble in places. The green sedan was back in the driveway, its bumper dented, its tires bald enough to let the steel bands poke through. The white car with the BGE emblem on the door was gone.

Years ago, when Laurie Genarro had been Laurie Brashear, this house had belonged to Sadie Russ and her parents. In Laurie's youth, she had been in the house on a handful of occasions, and she recalled the dark rooms and the smell of bad meat coming from the kitchen. The Russes had been liberal and inattentive parents who would let the girls do as they pleased whenever Laurie came over to play. She recalled Sadie leaving empty dishes all over the house, clothes in every corner of her bedroom, socks and shoes left out overnight on the back porch. It looked like the same house now—even more so in its disrepair and neglect—and as she walked up the front porch and knocked on the door, she wouldn't have been surprised if Mr. or Mrs. Russ answered her knock, though she knew they had moved away soon after their daughter had died.

The woman who answered was not Mrs. Russ, but a woman who might have proven a suitable counterpart. With short, choppy blond hair, a clear complexion, and startling green eyes, she was good-looking in a pleasant, carefree sort of way. She wore an open chambray shirt over a ribbed undershirt, loose-fitting Capri pants, and sandals. With a partial smile, the woman offered her a breathy hello. She looked to be about Laurie's own age.

Laurie smiled and tried to appear harmless. "Hello. My name's Laurie Genarro. My father was Myles Brashear. He lived next door."

The woman's mouth came together in an *O* while her thin yellow eyebrows drew together. "Oh, shoot. Oh, no. I'm so sorry to hear of your father's passing. Please, come in." She stepped aside and allowed Laurie to enter. "I didn't know your father very well, except to say hello when I saw him sitting out in the yard. That was so long ago now. He seemed like a nice man. I'm sorry for your loss."

"Thank you."

The house was dim, the windows in the adjoining rooms overrun with foliage that blotted out the daylight and left the hallway as dark as an undersea chasm. The air itself tasted of some nonspecific uncleanliness. Amazingly, it was just as Laurie remembered it.

"I'm Liz Rosewood." The woman offered her hand to Laurie and Laurie shook it. The woman had small pointy breasts beneath her ribbed undershirt and the figure of a teenaged boy. "Let's sit inside. Do you drink tea? I'm just about to have some."

"That would be wonderful. Thank you."

Liz Rosewood led her into a small kitchen at the back of the house. The walls and floor were done in muted earth tones and there were many papers, magazines, and unopened envelopes scattered about the counter and a nearby hutch. A wall of windows looked out on a weather-grayed deck and an untidy backyard. It was all distantly familiar. Liz Rosewood waved a hand at the small kitchen table and beckoned Laurie to sit. Laurie pulled out a chair and dropped down in it before her knees could give out. Liz went to the stove and poured two cups of hot tea.

"This is an omen," Liz Rosewood said. "I was just telling Derrick last night that I should bake some brownies or cupcakes or something and come by your house. I felt horrible about not coming by sooner but Derrick said it would be too intrusive, considering what you poor folks are dealing with at the moment. I mean, we saw the ambulance and the police cars that night. Derrick went over to see if he could help in any way. Such a terrible thing." She stepped to the table and set down the two steaming mugs. "Derrick is my husband."

"Don't worry about it," Laurie said, pulling her hot mug in front of her. "It's been a circus over there. We're from Hartford, Connecticut, and we had to pick up and come down here at the last minute. It's my husband, Ted, and our daughter, Susan. She's ten, and was pretty upset about coming down this way for the summer."

"Yes, I've seen her playing in the yard," Liz confessed, sitting down in a chair opposite Laurie at the table.

"Well, I figured I'd introduce myself, seeing how our daughters have apparently been hanging out together."

Liz smiled, shook her head, and looked down at her tea. "Abigail's not my daughter."

"No?"

"She's my niece. My sister and her husband went to Greece for the summer. Derrick and I said we'd keep an eye on her. We don't have any kids of our own."

Relief hit her like a tidal wave. Only then did it occur to her that she had been expecting Liz Rosewood to say she didn't know what the heck Laurie was talking about, and that no girl by the name of Abigail Evans lived here.

"Oh," Laurie said. The word was borne on a shuddery exhalation. "Well, that's good of you. To do that for your sister, I mean."

"Oh, Abigail's no trouble. And my poor sister and her husband never get any time to themselves. Derrick and I were happy to do it."

"Does your sister live in this neighborhood?"

"They live in Ellicott City. It's not far, maybe half an hour or so. Are you familiar with the area?"

"Actually, I grew up in the house next door."

"No kidding?" Liz Rosewood brightened. "A Nap-town girl!"

"Barely. My parents got divorced when I was ten and my mother and I moved to Virginia. I feel like a bit of an outsider, to tell you the truth."

"That's the beauty of this area. It's a brilliant mix of locals and refugees."

"Refugees?"

"Interlopers. Imposters." Liz smiled warmly. "Folks from out of town. With the Naval Academy downtown, we've always got tourists and out-of-towners coming in and out of the city. You may feel more welcome than most."

"Did you know the Russes? They lived in this house when I was a little girl. It was a long time ago."

"The Russes? No, I'm afraid not. We've only been in the house a few years, and we bought it from a fam ily named Cappestrandt. Derrick and I are originally from the Eastern Shore, but he took a job with BGE and the commute over the Bay Bridge was murder on him, so we started looking around on this side of the bridge. We looked at a number of places in Baltimore—it would have been much cheaper out that way—but it's so much nicer out here by the water, don't you think?"

"It's lovely," Laurie agreed. "So how long will Abigail be staying with you?"

"Until the end of the summer. We've been having fun."

"When did she get here?"

"A few weeks ago, just after school let out for summer vacation."

"So then she was here when my father had his . . .

his accident. I'd hate to think she was troubled by what happened."

"To be honest, I don't think she even knows what happened. The sirens woke Derrick and me up, but I think she slept straight through it all."

At first, the word *sirens* summoned images of mermaids in Laurie's addled brain. She struggled to keep a smile on her face. "Well, it's nice of you to take her for the summer. Your sister and her husband are lucky to have you."

"My brother-in-law is an architect, so this Greece trip is half pleasure and half business. They kept putting it off until Derrick and I finally said go, go, go. Have you ever been to Greece?"

"No."

"What do you do?"

"I used to teach, but I've been home now with Susan for about a year. Ted, my husband, he's a playwright. He's working on an off-Broadway adaptation of a John Fish novel right now."

"Is that right? Wow, that's spectacular. I've read a bunch of Fish's novels. I love him. Have you met him?"

"No, but my husband has."

"That must be very exciting. So he's writing a theatrical version of one of the books?"

"Yes. It's called *The Skin of Her Teeth*."

"I've read that one! How fantastic! Will you get special seats for the opening night, seeing how you're the wife of the playwright?"

"I suppose so." She recalled opening night for Ted's play *Whippoorwill* a number of years ago now. There hadn't been any special seating in the tiny Greenwich theater, unless you counted the metal folding chairs lined up in the walkways.

"Derrick and I saw *Wicked* in DC last year; it was wonderful. It must be such a rewarding profession."

Laurie thought of Ted cursing to himself on the sofa as she slipped out of the house just moments ago, and she smirked ironically. "It's a lot of work," was all she said.

"Well, it's nice that Abigail has found a friend for the summer. There are so few kids on this block for her to play with, and of course she doesn't know any of them, anyway. She can be a bit shy, the poor thing. Will you be here much longer?"

"We're liquidating my father's estate, so we'll be here until that's done. I'm not really sure how long it will take."

"And then it's back to—Connecticut, did you say?" She sipped her tea with both hands around her mug. She looked like a squirrel eating a nut.

"Yes. Hartford."

Liz reached across the table and touched the top of Laurie's hand, startling her. "Do you mind if I smoke?"

"Go right ahead."

Liz sprang up and went to a credenza where she rifled through paperwork and checkbooks until she located a carton of Marlboros. "Want one?"

"I don't smoke, thanks."

Down the hall, the front door slammed.

"Well," Liz said, sitting back down at the table. "Speak of the devil." A cigarette bouncing from her mouth, she called down the hall, "Abigail! Come here for a minute, love."

Laurie held her breath as she heard the girl's approaching footsteps. A moment later, Abigail appeared in the kitchen doorway.

"Hey, peaches," said Liz Rosewood. "Your friend Susan's mom stopped by to say hello."

"Hi," Abigail said. Her faded blue dress looked too big on her. Harsh black shoes reflected the paneled lights in the ceiling.

Laurie said, "Hello."

She watched Abigail go to the refrigerator, pop open the door, and scrounge around within. There was artwork on the refrigerator door, if the repetitious drawing of circles could be called "artwork." Circles of varying sizes in a multitude of colors. They looked like something a kid with Asperger's might draw. The girl came out of the fridge with a carton of apple juice, which she set on the counter. Laurie saw that her fingernails were black with grit, and there was just the faintest smudge of dirt or grease beneath her chin. There was a stepstool beside the cabinets, which Abigail used to get a glass out of one of the high cupboards.

"I was thinking tacos tonight," Liz told Abigail. "How's that strike you, hon?"

"Hooray!" The girl beamed. "Can Susan eat over?"

"Well," said Liz, turning to Laurie, "that's up to Susan's mom."

Laurie smiled wearily. Her face was beginning to hurt.

"Derrick and I, we sometimes regret not having children." Puffing on her cigarette, Liz Rosewood looked down longingly at her tea, as if to divine some comfort from its steaming surface. "It's so much work, but then again, I don't think you truly *live* until you raise a child of your own. It must be so rewarding."

It was the sort of thing people without kids seemed obliged to say to people who had them, as if attempting to commiserate over an illness they did not have. She nodded in a simulacrum of agreement while she watched Abigail replace the apple juice in the refrigerator. Then she watched as Abigail chugged down half her glass of juice, her grimy little fingers leaving smudges on the glass.

"It's no trouble, of course," Liz said as Abigail put her empty glass in the sink. It clanked against a stack of dishes. "If Susan wants to have dinner here, I mean. It would be nice for the girls to spend some more time together. They're both refugees this summer."

Abigail ran a pointy little tongue over her lips.

"I'll check with Susan," Laurie said, though the thought of her daughter spending any time in Sadie's old house—with a little girl who looked disconcertingly *like* Sadie—caused a fist to shove up through Laurie's guts. Suddenly, she wanted to get the hell out of here.

"We drew pictures of dinosaurs the other day," Abigail said. She had taken a napkin from one of the kitchen drawers and was running it back and forth across her mouth. "I did a stegosaurus and Susan did a tyrannosaurus." She balled up the napkin and placed it in the trash. "Tyrannosaurus was the king of the dinosaurs. Its name means . . . something . . . lizard."

"Tyrant lizard," commented Liz Rosewood.

"That's right," Abigail said gloomily.

Get me out of here, Laurie wanted to scream.

"I like tacos," Abigail told no one in particular.

Abruptly, Laurie stood. "I need to get back to the house now."

"Oh." Liz stood as well, though with less fervor. The cigarette hung limply from her lips. "Well, it was wonderful meeting you. Won't you let me know if you need anything from us?"

"I will."

"And again, I feel horrible for not stopping by earlier—"

"Don't be silly. Thank you for the tea."

Laurie moved quickly down the hallway to the front door. Liz set her tea down and rushed to catch up.

"So can Susan come for dinner?" Abigail asked from the far end of the hallway. Her slight silhouette in the oversized dress was framed in the kitchen doorway. "Please?"

"Really," Liz said to Laurie, her voice dropped to a half-whisper now. "It's not a problem."

"I'll have to check with Ted," Laurie said. "I'll let you know." She gripped the doorknob more tightly than necessary. "Thank you again for the tea. It was nice meeting you. Good-bye."

Chapter 17

"Let her go," Ted said. "It'll be good to have a night to ourselves."

She had been foolish to tell Ted about going over to the Rosewoods', and about the invite Susan had received for dinner. She wished she could rewind time and take it back. The thought of her daughter in that house with that girl troubled her. Every time she thought of those drawings of circles hanging on the refrigerator door, she shivered.

"I don't know," she said. They were in the kitchen and she was digging out pots and pans from the cabinets. "She can be a handful."

"A handful? Susan? The kid's an angel. Seriously, Laurie, what harm can it do? You and I can go out and eat a nice meal, maybe catch a movie. We haven't had any time for ourselves lately. And frankly, I think it would do you good to get out of this house for a while."

"That's irresponsible."

"What? Don't be ridiculous."

"Ted, we don't even *know* those people. And you just want to leave our daughter with them for an evening so we can go to dinner and a movie?"

He ran his hands through his hair. "Jesus Christ. They're not serial killers. You met the mother—"

"The aunt," Laurie corrected.

"—and Susan likes hanging out with the girl, so what's the big deal? I swear, you make things bigger than they need to be."

"Is that what I do?"

"What you do is have situations dictate your life instead of having your life dictate your situations."

"Is that one of your arty amendments?"

He frowned. His nostrils flared. More calmly than she would have suspected, he said, "Why is it you always have to take a jab at my career? Is it because I don't make enough money to suit you? That you think I'm wasting my time with all this?"

"You know that's not true."

"I'm proud of what I do, Laurie. Lately, you've been trying to downplay all of my accomplishments. Don't think I haven't noticed."

"This has nothing to do with your accomplishments."

"Then what does it have to do with? Tell me, because I'm dying to know."

Susan appeared in the doorway. They both fell silent.

"What's for dinner?" the girl asked.

"Would you like to go over to your friend Abigail's for some tacos tonight?" Ted asked her before Laurie could say anything.

Susan's face lit up. "Can I? That would be great!"

"Go on up and put your shoes on," Ted said. "I'll walk you over."

Susan turned and bolted down the hallway, then thundered up the stairs.

"Well, that was just wonderful," Laurie said. "Thanks so much."

"We'll have a nice time." His smile glowed. "You'll thank me for it."

Fifteen minutes later, as Ted walked Susan next door to the Rosewoods', Laurie watched them from one of the dining room windows. The two of them paused for a few moments at the foot of the driveway and Ted dropped to one knee before the girl like someone proposing marriage. He talked for a while and then Susan nodded and said some things, too. At one point Susan pointed toward the house and both she and Ted glanced up. Laurie's heart leapt; she thought they had spotted her spying on them. But then Ted stood and squeezed Susan's shoulder. Susan snaked a thin arm around Ted's waist as they continued into the street. Laurie wrung her hands the moment they disappeared from view on the other side of the fence.

She had been twenty-eight when she learned she was pregnant with Susan. The knowledge struck cold fear into her heart—fear at the prospect of being a parent. Previously, both she and Ted had confessed a passing disinterest in being parents, and her pregnancy was what some people termed "an accident." But accidents made her think of fender-benders and broken drinking glasses in the kitchen trash. Laurie thought it was more tragic than accidental. When she informed Ted of her condition, she had expected reciprocal despair. Yet his elation astounded her. Ted had scooped her into his arms and twirled her around the kitchenette of their small apartment in Newington.

She had progressed through her pregnancy like someone preparing for an exam. She attended the requisite visits to the OB/GYN, was responsible about her diet, and ingested the prescribed bouquet of prenatal vitamins. She attended classes for new mothers-to-be, and she checked out countless books from the library on what to expect from a first pregnancy. And while all these totems were certainly informative, she realized that none of them promised her any success at her impending new career as a parent. She became convinced that no matter how many books she read and how many classes she attended, she was destined for failure. This certainty terrified her. Her own mother had still been alive back then, and she found herself speaking to the woman several times a week during her third trimester, as if to siphon some motherly wisdom from the woman over the telephone. But those phone conversations, while pleasant, did little to assuage her fear. Toward the end of her third trimester, she began frequenting the neighborhood playgrounds and parks, where she would sit on a bench and feign interest in some paperback novel. In actuality, she was there to observe. Mothers chased children around the playground, pushed them on swings, wiped snot from their noses and brushed dirt off their Oshkosh overalls. These mothers were curious creatures. Their hair looked uniformly choppy and serviceable at best. They wore horrendous jeans with high elastic waistbands and drab blouses that looked like they hadn't seen an iron since the previous presidency. It was when Laurie began to feel like Dian Fossey among the apes that she finally abandoned this morbid little enterprise.

Ted had turned the extra bedroom of their miniscule apartment into a nursery. He did this of his own accord, without any prompting from Laurie, and she found his behavior endearing. She tried to absorb some of his confidence, but it was a futile exercise.

And then there she was—Susan Leah Genarro. Laurie became a mother not in learned and practiced increments, but instantly and all at once. Maybe that was how it was done. And she found that she had been *good* at it, and that she loved her little girl, and maybe she wouldn't turn out to be a failure as a mother after all. Maybe she could, in fact, keep her daughter safeguarded against the evils of the world. . . .

As she watched Ted and Susan disappear over the fence into the Rosewoods' yard, she felt that old familiar fear begin to tremble at the core of her being. It was no different than watching her daughter slip away into that crowd of children on the first day of preschool, just another face blending among the crowd. The fear had been gone so long its sudden presence now—albeit a faint presence—was nearly alien. Yet she recognized it, and the recognition chilled her.

Before she could turn from the window, she saw a dark brown sedan pull up the driveway. Its windshield was cracked and there was an ugly ding in the hood. When a tall man in a dark suit and necktie got out, she went to the front door and opened it.

"Hiya," the man said amiably enough. His smile was genuine and pleasant—cheerful, almost—and he walked with the casual swagger reminiscent of John Wayne Westerns. He carried with him a nylon case that might have held a laptop computer.

Cop, Laurie thought.

The man climbed the porch steps and extended a smooth, clean palm. The smile never faltered. "Mrs. Genarro?"

"Yes." Laurie shook his hand.

"I'm Detective Brian Freeling." A badge and credentials made a brief appearance before disappearing back into the inside pocket of his suit jacket. Detective Freeling looked to be in his mid-forties, though the only reason Laurie estimated him that old was because his sensibly cut dark hair had started to gray at the temples. Otherwise, his features were youthful and there was a roguish handsomeness to him. He gave off a relaxed air that might have put most people at ease but only seemed to heighten Laurie's apprehension. "This is completely embarrassing, but I feel I owe you an apology."

"A—what?" She thought she had misheard him.

"There was some miscommunication at the office. I was under the impression that fingerprints had been taken when in fact they weren't, and now I'm tasked with showing up here looking like a . . . well, a fool, Mrs. Genarro." As if the mention of her name triggered some memory inside him, Detective Freeling's cool, unperturbed countenance switched instantly to one of vexation. "Christ, how callous. I'm standing here blabbing and—" He cut himself off, then extended his hand to her again.

With a bit more trepidation than she had felt the first time, Laurie shook it once more.

"My condolences about your father," he said. His voice had dropped nearly a full octave, rising up from deeper in his chest now.

"Thank you. Did you want to come inside?"

"If it's no trouble, ma'am."

She widened the door and he passed through it, the John Wayne swagger now somewhat diminished. A quick appraisal of the house was followed by a muted whistle.

"Nice place," he said.

"I grew up here."

"Did you? How nice."

"What was it that you said you needed, detective? Something about fingerprints?"

He folded one arm beneath the other, and Laurie could see the bulge of his pistol beneath the fabric of his suit jacket. "The guys were supposed to get fingerprints of the room upstairs. I thought they'd done it, but they hadn't. Now I'm late to the party." The sigh he unleashed made him sound infernally bored. "It's probably a moot point by now, but I should still see what's there."

"Fingerprints from the room upstairs? The room where my father . . ."

"Yes, ma'am. If it isn't too much trouble."

"Not at all. I'll take you up, but I need to get the key first."

His smile widened. "Of course," he said, as if he knew what the key was for. Perhaps he did.

She returned thirty seconds later and led him upstairs. While he knelt on the floor and opened his nylon case, Laurie slid the key into the padlock and turned it. The lock popped open.

"To be fair," she told him, "you wouldn't have had much luck had you come a day earlier. I just got the key from one of my father's caretakers this afternoon."

"That would be Ms. Lorton or Ms. Larosche?" he said as he slipped on a pair of latex gloves.

"Teresa Larosche. Do you know her?"

"I've spoken with both women. Routine questioning."

"I didn't realize they had a detective on the case. Do you suspect something happened to my father other than what's in the police report?"

Detective Freeling shrugged disinterestedly and his lower lip protruded just a bit. "Nah, not really. Your father was sick, wasn't he? Alzheimer's?"

"Dementia."

"I've seen stuff like it before." He rose up off his knees.

"Have you really? Old people throwing themselves out of windows?"

"The elderly and confused hurting themselves," he said. He went to the door, pushed it open with the toe of his shoe, and then addressed the doorknob on the inside with what looked like a makeup brush. He proceeded to brush powdered ink onto the doorknob. "Are you here alone?"

"Yes." She made a distant wheezing sound. "Oh, you mean—no, no, I'm not. My husband and daughter are here with me."

"Have any of you been up in this room?"

"I have."

"No one else?"

"No. I've kept the door locked."

"Did you touch this doorknob?"

"Well, yes. To open the door."

"No, not the outside knob." He pointed at the knob

he was dusting and looked up at her. His eyes were blue flecks of ice. "This one."

She tried to remember. "No, I don't think so. I left the door open when I went up. When I came back down, I shut it from out here."

"Okay. Good."

"Do you suspect someone murdered my father?"

That roguish smile reappeared. It made him look even younger. She thought of her own husband, the man who never aged.

"Nah," he said. When he stood, the creases in his dark pants were suddenly very noticeable. He turned and glanced up the tight stairwell. "I'm gonna go on up."

"Okay. I'll keep out of your way. Can I get you anything?"

"Coffee would be great," he said, climbing up the steps to the tiny room.

Twenty minutes later, when Ted returned from next door, he encountered Detective Freeling in the driveway. Through the front windows, Laurie watched the men converse, the driver's door of Detective Freeling's sedan standing open. Then they shook hands and Freeling climbed into his car and drove away. Ted came in through the front door and went directly upstairs. A moment later, she heard the shower clank on.

In the parlor, Laurie went to her father's liquor cabinet and opened it. The bottles seemed to soldier right up to the edge of the shelves. All of them had been opened and many of them were now only half full. Ted had been getting some work done, all right. She was halfway through a glass of sherry when Ted came into the room.

"That guy seemed more like a game show host than a cop," he commented, folding his arms and leaning against the wall. He had changed into an American Eagle polo shirt, khakis, and thatched loafers without socks. His hair was combed back off his forehead and still damp from the shower. "I don't buy his peaceable demeanor. Pour me a glass of that, would you, please?"

She poured a second glass as he went to the piano and sat down. He played a soothing melody on the high keys, one-handed. He was a fine pianist.

"Liz and Derrick Rosewood seem nice enough," he said. When Laurie didn't answer, he said, "Are you still mad?"

She set his glass of sherry on top of the piano. He still tinkled the high keys playfully.

"Is it such a terrible thing," he continued, "that we should spend some time together?"

No, it wasn't such a terrible thing. No, she wasn't still mad. Even now, she realized her anger had actually been anxiety, had been fear. She didn't like the noises she had been hearing, and the loose board over the window upstairs troubled her. Even worse, she didn't like Abigail's resemblance to Sadie Russ, worsened by the fact that she was staying with her aunt in Sadie's old house. Of course, she couldn't quite verbalize this to Ted without sounding like a head case. Since the highway incident, she had become heedful of the things she told her husband.

She bent and kissed the side of Ted's face. "I'm not mad."

"Does that mean we can go out and have a nice time?"

Her blood cooled at the idea of leaving the house while Susan was next door. But really, wasn't she being foolish? Maybe Ted was right after all—maybe it was all just stress and nothing more.

"Yes," she said. "That sounds nice."

"Derrick Rosewood told me of a great wine bar downtown. Run upstairs and get dressed?"

Laurie showered and dressed in a pair of sleek black slacks and a beige halter top. They were the best clothes she had packed, since she hadn't anticipated a night on the town while packing her suitcase back in Hartford. As they climbed into the Volvo, Laurie's anxiety over leaving Susan with the Rosewoods had subsided to a remote disquiet, like the solitary light shining in the window of a house that was supposed to be vacant.

"Derrick Rosewood says it's the best spot in town," Ted said as he backed the car down the winding driveway.

As it turned out, it was a nice spot. They sampled different kinds of wine and instead of ordering meals, they snacked on assorted cheese platters, toasted breads, caviar and crackers, escargot, and plates of Italian olives throughout the evening. Ted talked a lot about the play he was working on. After some wine, his complaints about John Fish transitioned to a more diplomatic opinion of what a successful adaptation of Fish's work could mean for Ted's career. "Even if we don't open on Broadway," he said through a mouthful of escargot, "Fish's name will bring A-list talent to the production. It could change things for us, Laurie. It could change a lot of things."

"What about the outline?"

"I've decided not to worry about it until I hear back from Steve. I'm hoping this can get squared away as painlessly as possible. And besides, what Fish is asking for is virtually impossible, so it's not like they can replace me with some other writer."

She smiled.

"You know," he said at one point, "you should really start painting again."

"I've thought about it."

"Have you?"

"It's probably no different than your writing. A seed is planted in the center of your brain and something inside you just . . . well, it turns it into something. It wants to come out, wants to break free. It's like growing a plant." She thought about her father's greenhouse, now a desolate tomb hidden deep in the woods beyond the house. This made her think of Sadie Russ, and what happened to her.

"What?" said Ted. "What is it?"

"It's nothing. My mind's just wandering, that's all."

"How'd that cop get up into that room today? I thought we didn't have a key for the padlock on the door."

"We do now. I picked it up earlier today."

Ted frowned. "Picked it up from whom?"

"Teresa Larosche. She met me in Annapolis this afternoon. You were busy working and I didn't want to disturb you."

"This woman was your father's night nurse, right?"

"Yes." She drank some wine and then added, "I also read the police report filed by the officer who responded to my dad's death. Turned out it was in with some of David Cushing's papers after all." She fabricated this last part because she feared she would sound too paranoid admitting to him that she had contacted the county police and requested the report. It hadn't seemed paranoid to her at the time—in fact, it had seemed perfectly natural—but now she wasn't quite sure. "Ted, my father didn't open the window before he jumped out."

Based on the expression that came across Ted's face, she didn't think he had properly heard her.

"He jumped right through the glass," she restated. "One of the windows up there is shattered and there's a big piece of wood covering it up."

"That's just horrible," he said, his voice small. All of a sudden, his eyes had become these furtive little beads that she didn't quite trust. They looked wholly unfamiliar to her.

"Teresa Larosche said he had been concerned that someone was trying to break into the house at night, that someone was trying to come after him."

"The guy was probably paranoid about a lot of things."

"And now that police detective who came by, he took some fingerprints. . . ."

"What are you saying?"

"I'm wondering if my father jumped at all," she said, "or if maybe someone pushed him."

Ted leaned back in his chair. He dabbed the corners of his mouth with a cloth napkin, then tossed the napkin on the table. "Someone? You think this Larosche lady pushed him?"

"No."

"Then who? No one else was in the house."

"Maybe someone *got* in."

"You're getting that based on what this Larosche woman told you? That your father—who suffered from dementia, don't forget—thought someone was trying to get him?"

I think the Larosche woman believed it, too, she thought. *Toward the end, anyway. He had convinced her of it, I think. Or perhaps poisoned her with the notion of it.*

"Maybe it wasn't the dementia," she said. "Maybe he was actually aware of something."

"Aware that someone was trying to kill him," Ted said flatly. "Honey, that's silly. Listen to yourself. Don't you hear how silly that is?"

"If you're going to jump out of a window, wouldn't you open it first?"

"Laurie, I *wouldn't* jump out a window. See? That's the difference. Your father wasn't rational. You can't infuse logic to an illogical situation. You'll make *yourself* mad."

His words were close enough to what Teresa Larosche had said back at the coffee shop—about being afraid that Myles Brashear's dementia might seep into her and cause her to go crazy—to cause Laurie's flesh to grow instantly cold.

"The board over the window is loose," she went on. "There were nails on the floor, like someone pried them out."

"See?" Ted beamed. "That explains your noises."

"Does it? How?"

"It's the wind blowing against the board. You said yourself it sounded like a door slamming up there."

It seemed like an impossibly plausible explanation. Yet it didn't make her feel any better.

"Isn't it possible that someone could climb onto the roof and get up into that room?" she suggested. She was thinking of the way the tree branches crept out over the roof. All someone would need to do was climb the tree, get on the roof, and push open the loose board—

"No," he said flatly. "It isn't possible. And even if someone *could* do that, the door's locked. Where would they go? They couldn't get into the rest of the house."

"But it's *possible*. . . ."

"Darling, no one has been getting into the house. I'll hammer down that board when we get back to the house tonight," Ted assured her. He took a sip of his wine and ran his tongue along his teeth. "You know, when my parents died, I thought, wow, I'm a goddamn orphan. I'm just like one of those little street urchins with fingerless gloves and hats that are too big for their heads, like in a Dickens novel. I had no brothers and sisters and I thought, damn, I'm alone. And maybe for a while I really was. But now I'm not. I've got you and I've got Susan." He touched her hand across the table— strangely similar to how Liz Rosewood had done when she asked if Laurie minded if she smoked. "You've got us, too, Laurie."

"Thank you."

"I mean it. Don't forget that. Don't lose sight of it and run off chasing things that aren't there."

She believed him. There had been a time recently in their marriage when Ted had grown distant and incommunicative, spending more hours than necessary working outside the house. She knew he had been unfulfilled in his career, overly stressed about what the future held for him and his writing, so she had allowed him to remain for a time in his self-pitying cocoon. During this period she wondered if he would ever return to her, the man she had married, or if his emotional distancing signaled the eventuality of divorce. But he was here now, and she found that she trusted him.

After dinner, they walked down Main Street, peering in at the crowded bars and watching middle-aged couples stroll up and down the cobblestones. Midshipmen in their starched whites flocked together outside bars, their faces impossibly young, square, hairless. Down along the water, boats clanged in their moorings. People in shorts and crewneck shirts lounged on the decks of large yachts, their radios tuned low while their conversations were lively and inebriated. Ted laughed and waved to a boat deck of young men and women passing around a bottle of tequila, and some of the women and one of the men waved back.

There was a cigar shop with a wooden Indian on the curb across the street from the outdoor restaurant where they had eaten the day after visiting David Cushing's office. Ted squeezed Laurie around the waist and said he had the strange urge to buy a cigar.

"Go on," she told him.

Like an excited child, he scampered across the cobblestone street and disappeared into the small smoke shop. A young woman in spandex running gear paused beside the wooden Indian to let her Pomeranian lap water from a great silver bowl someone had set out for just such a purpose. Laurie smiled to herself.

She turned and found herself facing the neon handprint in the window of the palmist's reading room. She recalled Susan running up to the glass on their previous trek downtown together, touching her small hand to the lighted one, and saying, *Ooh. It's warm.*

There were memories—distant ones—of coming down here as a young child with her parents. She could recall these memories only in brief snapshots. One particular memory had her family framed along the bulkhead that overlooked the inlet. It was around Christmastime and the parade of boats came down the inlet, one by one, their masts spiraled with colored lights, their bows decked out with small decorated pine trees and holly wreaths hanging where the life preserver should have been. Some of the boats had small speakers affixed to the tops of the masts where tinny Christmas music would trickle out and echo across the inlet and out into the Chesapeake Bay.

It could have been someone else's memory for all it mattered now.

"Curious what the future holds?" Ted said, coming up behind her. He had an unlit cigar in his mouth. She thought he looked ridiculous.

"What?"

"Palm readings." Just as Susan had done, he placed

his palm against the neon hand behind the glass. "It's warm," he said.

Laurie was silent for much of the car ride back to the house. Ted smoked his cigar with the windows down, the smell of the smoke making Laurie woozy. It reminded her of the way her father's clothes had smelled, and how the closets in the house still smelled. With some disillusionment, she wondered if she were trapped in some time warp, where things reflected other things, and new people took on the personifications of old ones.

After they pulled into the driveway, Ted turned off the ignition and squeezed her left knee. "I had a nice time tonight. I'm glad we went out. We both needed it."

She hugged herself and stared out the passenger window. It was fully dark now. The trees were black pikes rising out of the earth.

"What?" he said. "What is it? Are you cold?"

"I'm not cold."

"Then tell me. We had a good time, didn't we? What is it, Laurie?"

She remained silent.

"Please," he insisted.

"There's something you don't know," she said. "Something I've never told you. I never thought I would, to be honest, because I never thought I would have to. But I'm back in that house now, and . . . well, maybe it'll help you understand what's been bothering me lately."

"Jesus, babe, what is it?"

"When I was a little girl living in that house, I was

friends with the girl who lived next door. Her name was Sadie Russ. We were friends at first, but as we got older, she started to . . . I guess . . . *change*. Out of nowhere she would have these fits. Tantrums. She would scream and pull at her hair. A few times when this happened and I was there, she would rush at me, hit and pinch me, or try to knock me down. She would always apologize later, but she started to scare me. We were just little girls. I tried not to play with her after a while, but she would always come to the house calling for me, and my folks would always let her in.

"Then she got worse. She would still hit me and pinch me . . . but then she would laugh, like it was all a big joke. She stopped apologizing. Sometimes she would go down to the water and catch frogs, and squeeze them to death. Or she would catch minnows in a net, then smash them on the rocks. Once, she took one right out of the net and bit it in two. Blood spurted down her chin."

"Jesus Christ, hon."

"It made me feel bad, and I would sometimes dig a hole and bury the dead animals that she killed. But Sadie, she would dig them up just to spite me, leaving all these little holes in the yard. It was all part of her twisted game."

Ted said nothing; he stared straight ahead at the darkened house, his mouth firm.

"There were times when I would come downstairs to breakfast to find Sadie already in the house, waiting for me. My parents had let her in. She was good at fooling parents. She put on a mask, a different face. Lots of people do that, sure, but Sadie was different than other people. My father used to grow these harmless-looking flowers that were actually poisonous, and Sadie was like that. By the time she died, she had become a monster."

"Died?"

"Hold on. I'm getting there."

He squeezed her knee, urging her to go on.

"She made me steal stuff from my parents," Laurie said. "She would see a wristwatch my father wore or some jewelry my mother had on, and she would tell me to steal it and bring it to her. And if I didn't bring it to her, she would be . . . well, she would be just *horrible* to me. There were times when I refused to do the things she asked, and she would hurt me. Other times she would make me eat dirt, bugs, other things.

"One afternoon, after I had refused to steal a pair of my mother's diamond earrings, Sadie approached me in the yard with a shoe box tucked under one arm. Sadie always wore hand-me-down dresses that were too big for her, and this day was no different—one bare shoulder poked up from the wide neckline of an ugly pleated sundress. God, I remember it so clearly. I told her to go away, that we weren't friends anymore, but she refused."

"Why didn't you just tell your parents?"

"Because by that point I had already stolen some stuff for her and she threatened to tell my parents what I'd done if I stopped being her friend and told on her."

"How *old* was this kid?"

"Susan's age."

"Jesus. What was in the shoe box?"

"When she opened the shoe box, I didn't know what I was looking at, and I wouldn't truly know until I was older and had my first period. To me, it was just some cylindrical cotton tube that had been saturated in a dark clotted fluid. But I knew what that fluid was, even then, and the idea of it horrified me."

"God," Ted said. "You mean . . . was it . . . ?"

"A tampon. Used. Her mother's, I suppose, fished out of the bathroom trash or wherever. I don't think Sadie had started having periods by that point." Laurie swallowed and her throat felt raw and abraded. "She made me put it in my mouth. Suck on it."

Ted said nothing; he stared blankly out the black windshield.

"If I didn't do it, she'd hurt me. She kept threatening to tell my parents about all the stuff I stole from them, the stuff she told me to take. Somehow she got me believing that I was the one who'd done wrong." Laurie placed her hand atop Ted's own. "I know it's uncomfortable for you to hear, but I feel I have to say it," she said.

"Then say it."

"She was eleven years old when she died," Laurie said. "I was there. I saw it happen."

"Jesus."

"You and Susan saw the remains of that old greenhouse in the woods?"

"Yes, we saw it," Ted said. "It was the first day we got here. There's a path that leads to it."

"It was my father's. When I was a little girl, he would spend hours in that greenhouse tending to his flowers, his plants. Sometimes it seemed like his plants were the only thing he truly loved. He had taken me in there on a few occasions, and even now I can remember the great bursts of flowers and the thick, rubbery leaves of the plants. The air was always humid and rich with the scent of vegetation and soil. I remember the black soil in little heaps on the floor, dotted with white foamy specks, and the terracotta pottery stacked underneath tables. Vines crisscrossed the glass ceiling. There is something wondrous and transcendent about a structure made entirely of glass and filled with flowers.

"There were shades that hung from the windows, similar to the kinds of plastic pull-down shades you see in classrooms. When my father wasn't working in there, he would pull the shades down. The only way you could see inside was by climbing a nearby tree, crawling out on a limb, and peering down through the greenhouse's glass ceiling.

"One afternoon, Sadie wanted to see inside. She climbed up into the tree and crawled out on the limb that extended over the roof of the greenhouse. I climbed the tree, too, but Sadie lost her balance and fell before I crawled out onto the branch."

"She fell through the roof?" Ted whispered.

"Yes."

And she could see it even now: the girl's oversized dress billowing out as she dropped . . . the crashing glass as she went through the peaked roof . . . the shower of crystal shards that rained down, both inside and outside the greenhouse . . . the awful, bone-crunching thump as Sadie struck the ground.

"I ran to my house and told my parents. My mother called for an ambulance while my father ran out to the greenhouse to see what had happened. I wanted to go with him, but he wouldn't take me."

"Of course, he wouldn't."

"I sat in the backyard and waited for him to come back. The next thing I remember was Mrs. Russ screaming and running through the yard toward the woods. Sadie's father ran with her, his face ghostly white and expressionless as he hurried along the fence and ran down the wooded path to the greenhouse. Then I heard sirens coming up the block." She blinked and found her eyes wet with tears. "I don't remember much of what happened after that. It's all jumbled in my head."

Ted shook his head. "I can't imagine what that was like."

"She was cut to ribbons, Ted."

Ted said nothing. The sudden silence was like heavy wool draped around them both.

"So that's what's been going on with you?" Ted said after a while. He turned to her. Half his face was masked in shadow. "That's why you've seemed so on edge? Because of what happened all those years ago, and having to come back here and relive it all over again in your head?"

"It haunts me," she said.

"It's in the past, Laurie. That all happened a long time ago." He reached out and rubbed the back of her neck. She was surprised by his tenderness.

"My father was cut up by the glass when he fell through that window," she said. "Just like Sadie had been. And just before it happened, he fouled the rug just like a scared little kid might do. Like someone had frightened him."

"I noticed you said he *fell* as opposed to he *jumped*," he said. "You want to tell me what that's about?"

"I don't know, Ted."

"Do you want to hear what I think?"

"All right."

"I think you're overstressed and thinking about all this too much. You had a lot of unresolved issues with your father—and I'm sorry about that, I really am—but now you're trying to find some understanding in the messy pieces of his death." Gently, Ted squeezed the back of her neck.

"You're right," she said. "It makes sense." Yet in her head, all she could hear was Teresa Larosche saying, *Sometimes he called it the Hateful Beast. Other times, it was the Vengeance.*

"First thing tomorrow," he said, "we'll pack some bags and grab a hotel in town. You don't need to spend another day here in this place."

"No. I don't want to do that. I don't want to run from it."

"It wouldn't be running."

"Of course, it would." Gently, she touched his arm. "Thank you, but no. I need to stay until we're done here."

Ted leaned in and kissed the side of her face. "If you think that's best."

"I do."

He opened his door. "You go on inside. I'll grab the kiddo from next door."

They got out of the car, Laurie going up the walk while Ted cut across the yard to the Rosewood house. Laurie watched him go, hugging herself in the chilly summer air. Then her gaze cut to one of the upstairs windows of the Rosewoods' house, where a light shone brightly, bracketed by sheer curtains. The silhouette of a young girl stood there, both palms splayed against the glass.

Staring.

CHAPTER 18

O f course, there had been things about Sadie that she simply couldn't tell her husband. *Her dirty little hands all over me, tugging at my pants, pulling up my skirts*. One afternoon while they were playing in the woods, completely out of the blue, Sadie hiked her own skirt up over her head and showed young Laurie Brashear her nakedness. The girl wore no panties and the sight of her smooth cleft between her legs caused Laurie to cry out. Sadie had laughed and called her a big sissy baby.

But Sadie Russ hadn't always been that way. The change had come on gradually, manifesting itself at first in an introverted sullenness. She would become easily angered—perhaps if something didn't go her way or she was reprimanded by a schoolteacher—and this anger would arrive on a sudden, shocking tide of obdurate cries. She began printing dirty words on her school papers; she whispered them to Laurie when they passed each other in the hallways or on the playground; she carved them in the trunks of trees. At recess, other kids stopped playing with Sadie. Some kids teased her mercilessly, and there had been one boy who seemed to enjoy firing phlegm onto her scuffed black Mary Janes. But Laurie knew that deep down they were scared of her, too. Sadie began to frighten a lot of people. Even some of the teachers.

Sadie the sadist. Sadie's twisted wretchedness. She had grown gaunt. A thin blue vein descended from each corner of her mouth, making it appear as though her mouth worked on a hinge, much like a ventriloquist's dummy, and might at any moment drop open. Those self-inflicted bruises, the gashed knees with their tortoiseshell scabs. The creases of Sadie's palms had always been black with grit.

Look—see here? Let me touch you here. Then you do it. Do it to me. See that? You see? How do you like that? Moisture crowded the corners of Sadie's small mouth.

And still—

How much were genuine memories and how much had Laurie's mind unconsciously altered after all these years?

Toward the end, I hated you, Sadie. I was afraid of you, yes, but I hated you even more. After I got over the initial shock of what I saw happen to you, I found that I was relieved. I was glad.

CHAPTER 19

Stephanie Canton called early Monday morning and advised Laurie that she had begun compiling a list of interested buyers to come to the house and look over the items. This would begin later that afternoon, as Stephanie had someone very interested in the office furniture in her father's study. Laurie agreed to the time and hung up, feeling somewhat lightheaded from Stephanie Canton's efficient and businesslike approach to conversation.

A few minutes later, as Laurie began making breakfast, she heard the shower turn on upstairs. A moment after that, a resounding clang reverberated down through the ceiling. Ted's curses were muted, but the rage in his voice was not. In the upstairs hallway, Laurie found Susan standing in her sleepwear in the doorway of the master bedroom. Laurie moved past the girl, grazing her small shoulder with a soft hand, before rushing into the bathroom.

Naked and wet, Ted stood with one foot inside the shower and one planted firmly on the ecru tile floor. Something metallic roughly the size of a softball was in his hands. When he looked up at Laurie, there was a bemused expression on his face. A reddish knot swelled at the center of his forehead.

"What happened?"

He showed her the metallic softball-sized object. "Goddamn showerhead shot right off the spigot. Cracked me in the cranium."

"Oh, my God, are you okay?"

"I'll live. The bitching thing could have taken my head off, though." He thrust the showerhead at her, then turned off the water. It dribbled from the broken nozzle jutting bent-elbowed from the shower wall.

At that moment, the smoke alarm went off.

"Oh, damn!" Still clutching the showerhead, she rushed back out into the hall (Susan still stood mesmerized in the doorway, shocked into speechlessness at her father's barrage of curse words) and down the stairs. In the kitchen, smoke roiled from the slices of French toast that burned in the pan. She scooped the pan up off the burner and rushed it over to the kitchen sink where she dropped it, along with the broken showerhead, unceremoniously. Snatching a dishtowel off the counter, she hurried to where the little white disc beeped in the ceiling. She climbed onto a chair and flapped the dishtowel like a matador's cape until the smoke dissipated and the alarm went silent.

At two o'clock, Stephanie Canton arrived with a companion—a fastidious little man with a droll smile and the flattened nose of a prizefighter. He wore circular glasses with wire rims. The top of the man's head was completely bald while the sides and back were in full bloom with wiry corkscrews of hair so dense it more closely resembled the fur of some woodland creature. He wore a forest green sport coat of a material that looked suspiciously like velvet and pants whose cuffs had been hemmed too high over the tops of his suede loafers and seaweed-colored socks.

His name was Smoot and he was a self-proclaimed collector of antiquities. He was the proprietor of a boutique on West Street that sold refurbished pieces from the turn of the century. In the study, Smoot ran stumpy hands with abbreviated though well-manicured fingers along the aged wood with a lover's caress. Laurie watched him with curiosity, the way one might watch a small but colorful beetle thudding around inside a mason jar.

"Would you like some coffee?" Laurie offered him when it seemed he was permanently lost in a trance while staring at the piece.

"Never, never," chirped Smoot. "Gives me angina."

Susan, who had been in the hallway eavesdropping, broke into a fit of giggles and scampered away. Laurie smiled apologetically at both Smoot and Stephanie Canton.

"Very nice," Smoot said, returning his concentration back to the desk. He spoke with an effeminate lisp. "This is a Cutler, you know. A handsome model, too. There is no date-stamping, but I would guess it's circa 1910 or thereabouts."

"Wow," Laurie said.

"Wow, indeed," said Smoot. He opened and closed the desk's flexible tambour, then stood upright while straightening his sport coat. "Do you have any of the original paperwork?"

"I wouldn't know. My father's old housekeeper might know where it is, if it's still around."

Smoot nodded perfunctorily. "I'll give you eighteen hundred for it. And an extra two hundred for the book-case."

Laurie blinked. "Dollars?"

"Do you prefer francs? Pesos? Indian rupees, perhaps?" He smiled wryly and Laurie could see that this was as close to humor as this punctilious little man probably came. He withdrew a slender checkbook from the inside pocket of his coat.

"Sold," Laurie said, still in disbelief.

Smoot leaned over the desk and meticulously printed out the check, which he then tore from the checkbook and handed over to Laurie.

"I'll have some men come for it later this evening," he said.

As Smoot left, another fellow arrived. Slender and well-dressed, and with an approachable demeanor, McCall was the antithesis to the Dickensian Mr. Smoot. McCall's interests lay in the ornate bedroom furniture in the master bedroom. Ted was in the bathroom fixing the showerhead when McCall made his circuitous passes around the bed and nightstand; at what was probably the most inopportune time, Ted poked his head out into the bedroom just as McCall bent down to inhale the scent of the wooden headboard. McCall made an offer just slightly less generous than Smoot's, though still quite impressive, and Laurie accepted it without hesitation.

"I'll need a truck for the bed," McCall said, "but if your husband would be kind enough to assist me in transporting it, I can fit the nightstand in my car."

Together, Ted and Mr. McCall lifted the nightstand and duck-walked it out of the bedroom. Out in the hall, one of the drawers slid open. Her father's Bible tumbled out and struck the floor.

"That's seven years bad luck," Ted commented.

"I believe you're thinking of breaking a mirror," McCall retorted.

Laurie scooped up the Bible, then watched as the men slowly navigated the nightstand down the stairs, across the foyer, and out the door. Stephanie Canton followed them out, scribbling diligent notes in her binder.

Laurie looked down. There was something poking out between the pages of the Bible. She opened the book and saw there was a photograph inside. She turned it over to view it and her skin prickled.

It was a photograph of two young girls. One of them was Laurie, around age eight or so. In the photo, she wore a ribbon in her hair, a cream-colored knit sweater, and boyish corduroy pants. Beside her in the photo was Sadie Russ. Sadie was the same age as Laurie, but she looked much taller in the photograph. Sadie's face was narrow and pale, framed in a cascade of russet hair. She wore a hand-me-down print dress that was too big on her; the hem hung almost to the tops of her feet and only a hint of a few fingertips poked from the long blousy sleeves. At first glance, it appeared that both girls were smiling at the photographer . . . but on closer inspection, she could see that Sadie's smile looked more like a grimace.

It was irrefutable. Abigail Evans was the identical twin of the girl in the photo.

Smoot's men showed up around five in a paneled truck with no writing on the sides. They were gruff-faced and silent as mimes, and wore little patches on the breasts of their uniforms that read w.w. smoot, antiquities. They hauled both the desk and the bookcase into the back of the truck without as much as a grunt, then left before Laurie could offer them a glass of water or the folded singles she had pressed into her palm as a tip.

The following day, a middle-aged couple came by and, much to Ted's dismay, relieved them of the old Victrola. Ted even helped them load it into the back of their truck. To Laurie, who watched him from the front windows, he looked like a pallbearer loading a coffin into the back of a hearse.

Recalling Smoot's request of the Cutler desk's paperwork, Laurie went into the basement to see if she could find anything in the plastic sleeve that hung from one of the wooden struts beneath the stairs. Inside the sleeve were the papers for the kitchen appliances, as well as for the water heater and furnace. There was nothing for the Cutler desk. With some reluctance, she telephoned Dora Lorton. A part of her hoped the woman wouldn't answer.

"Yes," came the woman's stern, practical voice.

"Hello, Ms. Lorton, this is Laurie Genarro again, Myles Brashear's—"

"I know who you are."

"Sorry to disturb you, but I was wondering if you might know if my father had kept any original paperwork for the rolltop desk in his study. A buyer was interested in—"

"If it's not in with his personal papers, I wouldn't know where it would be."

"I see." It wasn't until that moment that she realized she had an ulterior motive for calling Dora Lorton, and it had nothing to do with the desk. Since Teresa Larosche's sudden disappearance from the coffee shop Saturday, Laurie had tried a few times to reach the woman again by telephone. The calls usually went straight to voice mail, with the exception of one time when someone picked up the phone just to slam it back down again. "Perhaps Teresa Larosche might know? Have you spoken with her lately?"

Dora's voice seemed to creak through the phone lines. "What is it you're doing, Mrs. Genarro?"

"I beg your pardon?"

"Ms. Larosche told me about your . . . meeting. She also told me you've been calling her nonstop, harassing her. She said you wouldn't leave her alone."

"Now that's not exactly true. . . ."

"No? I don't see why the poor dear would have any reason to lie to me, Mrs. Genarro. *Have* you been calling her?"

"I tried a few times, but I wasn't harassing her. I just wanted her to clarify some things she told me the other day, that's all."

"She is *afraid,* Mrs. Genarro. Can't you see that?"

"I've already promised her there would be no lawsuit."

"This has nothing to do with lawsuits."

"Then what does it have to do with?"

"Leave Teresa Larosche—and me—alone," Dora said, and hung up the phone.

Ted was talking to someone on the front porch with the door wide open. Laurie came up behind him . . . then paused when she saw that the person to whom Ted was talking was Liz Rosewood. The woman wore a thin cotton tee that looked like a man's undershirt and faded blue jeans. She smiled at Laurie from over Ted's shoulder.

Ted squeezed Laurie's forearm and pulled her out onto the porch beside him. "Liz has offered to take the little bugger off our hands for a while," he said.

"What?" Just then, Laurie saw the two girls, Susan and Abigail, streak across the front lawn, laughing and shouting.

"There's a cute little park just up the road," Liz Rosewood said. "Abigail and I were going to go for an hour or so, and I thought Susan might like to join us."

"That would be great," Ted said. "Thank you so much."

Susan and Abigail now stood within a wedge of spindly trees on the front lawn. They spoke in quiet voices while Abigail pointed at something on the ground. When Abigail looked up, Laurie swore the girl looked straight at her.

"That does sound wonderful," Laurie said. "In fact, would you mind if I tagged along? This house is becoming oppressive."

Liz Rosewood's smile widened. "Oh, please do. I'd love that."

Ted rubbed Laurie's back. "Great. Then I can get some work done while I'm alone."

"Just let me put on some shoes," Laurie said, and hurried back inside the house. Her shoes were in the laundry room where she'd left them, but she went upstairs first and went through her suitcase until she located the bottle of Excedrin she'd packed. She popped the cap and dry-swallowed two tablets. Her temples pulsed. Then she took the photo of her and Sadie and tucked it in the rear pocket of her jeans. Downstairs, she laced up her Keds and went back out onto the porch.

Ted kissed the side of her face. "You girls have fun," he said. He leaned over the porch rail and shouted to Susan, "Have fun, pumpkin pie!"

Susan laughed and executed a fairly impressive cartwheel. Abigail just watched Susan from between the trees.

"Let's go!" Liz called to the girls as she climbed down the porch steps. "The train's movin' out!"

The park was roughly a mile from the house on Annapolis Road. Back when Laurie had lived here it had just been woods, but it was now a sizeable clearing in which swings, seesaws, monkey bars, and tetherball poles had been erected. A paved parking lot shouldered the road and there were cars in a few of the spaces. Kids raced about while parents, perched on uncomfortable-looking benches, supervised from overtop the paperbacks and Kindles they were reading. In the distance beyond the park, the smooth green lawns of a cemetery rose up, the tombstones nothing but tiny specks behind a black wrought-iron fence.

"Neat!" Susan said as she surveyed the park grounds. Back home, the playgrounds were little more than concrete basketball courts sprayed with broken glass.

Abigail snatched up Susan's hand. "Come on," she said, and tugged Susan toward the monkey bars.

Panic rose up in Laurie. "Be careful, Susan!"

"They'll be fine," Liz assured her. She shook a cigarette out of its pack as they walked to an empty picnic table. "I'm glad you folks showed up this summer. Abigail was growing bored without someone to play with." They sat together on the same bench at the picnic table. "It's only been a few weeks, but it must seem like a lifetime to a little girl when you're away from your friends. Susan must feel the same way."

"Yes. She was upset when she found out we were coming down here," Laurie said . . . though she was hardly thinking about it now. Instead, she was considering the coincidental time frame of Abigail's arrival in town and her father's sudden death.

"Have you and your husband decided what you're going to do with the house?"

"Sell it, I suppose."

"It's a lousy market right now. I used to be a realtor. Are you working with anyone yet?"

"A realtor? No. We haven't gotten that far."

"Well, you let me know when you're ready. I can put you in touch with someone who can help you out."

"Thank you."

"I'm happy to do it." Liz puffed on her cigarette.

Across the playground, Susan and Abigail hopped down from the monkey bars and ran toward the only empty seesaw. Two other little girls made a move for the seesaw but they stopped, perhaps intimidated by Susan's and Abigail's fortitude. Susan claimed the downed seat, then shoved up off the ground so that the opposite end went low enough for Abigail to climb aboard.

"Had Abigail ever met my father?"

If Liz Rosewood found the question unusual, she didn't show it. "Abigail? I don't believe so. Derrick and I only spoke with him on a handful of occasions. He used to sit outside when the weather was nice, but I hadn't seen him out there since summer started." Liz sucked the cigarette down to the filter, then tossed it on the ground. "It was Alzheimer's or something, wasn't it?"

"Dementia."

"I got to know Dora Lorton a little," Liz said. "As well as you can know someone like her, I guess. She was a bit standoffish. Do you know her very well?"

"I just met her when we got here."

"I'd sometimes pick up things at the supermarket for her if I was on my way, seeing how she never left your father unattended."

"What about the other nurse?" Laurie asked. "Teresa Larosche. Did you know her as well?"

"The one and only time I saw her was the night your father . . . the night he had his accident. Derrick and I heard the sirens and Derrick went over to see what had happened. When Derrick didn't come back right away,

I went out myself, just as the ambulance was pulling up the driveway. The woman—Teresa, you said?—she was talking to police. She looked petrified."

"Did you speak with her?"

"I think Derrick did, once the police left. Just checking to see if she was okay, if she needed anything, that sort of thing."

Across the park, the two girls who had been making their way to the seesaw at the same time as Susan and Abigail now stood beside it, on Abigail's side. Each time Abigail descended, one of the girls said something to her. Laurie could see the exchange even if she couldn't hear what was said.

"Is your mother still alive?" Liz asked. Her voice sounded very far away now.

"No. She died a few years ago."

One of the two girls who had wanted the seesaw picked something up off the ground. As Laurie watched, the girl cranked her arm back and chucked the object at Abigail. The thing—it looked like a pinecone— whizzed past Abigail's head. The pinecone-chucker's friend laughed and pointed.

"Ted seems very nice," Liz said, perhaps desperate to change to a less morbid conversation. "We talked briefly about the John Fish novel he's adapting. He seems like a very talented man."

"Thank you."

The seesaw stopped sawing. As Abigail's feet planted on the ground, she leaned over and dug her own object out of the dirt. It was a rock roughly the size of a golf ball. The two girls backed away from the seesaw. Abigail hurled the rock at the pinecone-chucker. It struck the girl, who was a bit red-faced and chunky, high on the forearm.

Laurie sprang up from the table. "Hey! Don't do that!"

The outburst caused Liz to jump. She elbowed her pack of cigarettes off the table and into the grass.

Laurie pointed. "Abigail just threw a rock at that little girl."

Tears burst from the eyes of the chunky red-faced girl. She whirled around and darted toward one of the benches where, presumably, her mother sat not watching her. The chunky girl's companion, a stick-thin redhead with frizzy curls, just stared in amazement at Abigail, who was now climbing down off the seesaw. The girl looked paralyzed by terror.

Liz cupped her hands around her mouth and shouted, "Abigail! Get over here!"

Laurie was just about to shout Susan's name when the seesaw dropped out from under her, thudding hard against the earth. The expression on Susan's face was one of shock.

Liz stalked over to Abigail, who stood blocking the redhead girl's path to the seesaw. The girl who had been struck with the rock was still moaning while her mother, an equally red-faced and chunky individual, mopped at her daughter's leaky eyes. Liz hooked a hand under Abigail's arm and turned the girl around. Abigail's face was eerily serene. When Liz bent over to address her, Laurie thought Abigail's eyes were, in fact, focused on her and not Liz.

Laurie jerked her gaze away. She searched for Susan at the seesaw, but Susan was gone. Panic was like a switch that had been instantly flipped inside her . . . but then she caught sight of her daughter racing over to the swings. Wiping sweat from the side of her face, Laurie forced herself to calm down.

The crying girl's mother approached Liz. The women seemed to know each other. Liz said something to Abigail and then pointed at the picnic table where Laurie was slowly sitting back down. Abigail was already looking at the table and, Laurie thought, at her. As Liz turned back to the other girl's mother, Abigail strode toward the picnic table and Laurie. This day, the girl was dressed in a boy's striped polo shirt and threadbare corduroys. Her long dark hair was done up in pigtails. Laurie said nothing as the girl sat down on the opposite side of the picnic table, directly across from her. Abigail said nothing, either; her lips were clenched firmly together and her head was slightly downturned so that she had to look up at Laurie from beneath her brow. Her irises were like two globs of oil. When Abigail set her hands on top of the picnic table, Laurie could see that the fingers were grimy, the fingernails gritty black crescents.

In a small voice, Abigail said, "That other girl started it. She threw something first."

"Yes. I saw it."

Abigail's eyes hung on her. They seemed to burn through her.

"I have something I want to show you," Laurie went on. She was determined to keep her voice composed.

Abigail said, "What?"

Laurie took the photograph out of her pocket and set it before Abigail on the table. Abigail looked at it, but didn't touch it; in fact, she slid her hands away from it. When she looked back up at Laurie, her expression was unchanged. "Little girls," she said.

"Yes. Do you recognize anyone in that picture?" Laurie asked.

Abigail shook her head.

"Are you sure?"

The girl's head rotated slightly to the right. Those black eyes were muddy with thought. One of Abigail's hands dropped off the table while the other hand inched closer to the photograph. She didn't look at it as she picked it up.

"The taller girl," said Laurie. "The one in the dress."

"It's pretty," the girl said. "I like that dress."

"Is it yours?"

"Mine?"

"Yes. Is it?"

"No. That's silly."

"Are you telling the truth?"

"Yes."

"Have you ever seen it before?"

"No."

"What's your name?"

"You know my name."

"Tell me again. What is it?"

"Abigail Evans."

"Where do you live?"

"At home."

"Where is that?"

"With my parents. They're in Greece. Aunt Liz is my aunt."

"Yes, I know that." She took the photograph from Abigail's hand and pointed to Sadie. "Do you know this girl?"

"No."

"What's your *real* name? I want to hear you say it."

"Abigail *is* my real name," Abigail said. Her thin black eyebrows moved a bit closer together. "You're being weird."

Briefly, the world swam out of focus. The children on the playground pixelated and consciousness threatened to slip away from her. A flush of heat welled up out of the open collar of her shirt.

"Do you know who my father was?" Laurie said.

Abigail nodded slowly. "He died."

"How did he die?"

"He fell out a window."

"Did Aunt Liz tell you that?"

"No."

"How do you know that?"

"He fell," said Abigail. "Out."

Her voice just above a whisper, Laurie said, "Did you do something to him?"

Abigail's lips parted, then curled upward in the suggestion of a grin, as if she thought Laurie was playing some sort of game with her. The girl's throat constricted as a laugh juddered out. Its sound was not unlike something a goat might make. One of her hands slipped down beneath the table. Slowly, Abigail brought her chin down to rest on the tabletop. Her eyes continued to drill into Laurie's.

"I have a secret," Abigail said. "A good one." And then, just like that, Abigail's eyes softened. Her mouth worked itself shut.

All around Laurie, the world seemed to swim back into focus. Even her breathing began to regulate. She was acutely aware of the sweat that coated her flesh.

Across the playground, Susan hopped down off the swing and hurried over. She was smiling and her hair was in her face.

"Did you see me on the swing, Mommy?"

"I sure did."

"You were great," Abigail said.

This was the icing on the cake. "Thanks!" Susan crowed. Then she saw the photo in Laurie's hand. "What's that?"

"It's nothing," Laurie said, tucking the photo back into her pocket.

Liz Rosewood appeared, some sort of embarrassed half-smile on her face. "It's always something with that girl," she said, already digging another cigarette from the pack. "I've known the Laws for some time now. Their daughter is a bit of a troublemaker." She turned to Abigail. "But that doesn't give you permission to sink to her level. Do you get what I'm saying, Buster Brown?"

"No," Abigail said.

"It means you don't have to be mean just because someone else is."

"Oh."

"Now go over and apologize to that girl."

Abigail narrowed her eyes and stuck out her lower lip. "I don't want to."

"It's the nice thing to do."

"But she started it! Susan's mom saw!"

Laurie shrugged. "The other girl threw something, too, I think."

Liz waved a hand in front of Abigail's face, as if swatting away invisible flies. "I don't care. I have to live in this neighborhood with these people. Get off your rump and go apologize, Abigail."

Pouting, Abigail swung her legs over the bench seat and got up from the table. Her fists were clenched as she stormed across the playground to where the chunky red-faced Law girl stood with her mother and some other women. The chunky girl flinched when she saw her coming. Laurie wondered if it gave Abigail some satisfaction.

"Can I go, too?" Susan said, tugging gently on Laurie's arm.

"No. You stay here."

Liz sat on the bench and puffed her smoke. "Girls will be girls," she said.

"I suppose," said Laurie.

"You and your husband should come by for dinner one night," Liz suggested. "You haven't even met Derrick yet."

"We're terribly busy at the house. . . ."

"It'll do you good to get out."

"Yes," said Laurie. "Everyone keeps telling me that."

Susan jabbed a finger at Liz Rosewood's cigarette. "That gives you cancer!"

"Yes, they do," Liz agreed, still puffing.

Laurie swatted Susan's arm down. "That's impolite."

"But those things *kill* people, Mom."

Liz laughed. She was unattractive when she laughed—too brutish and loud, and she opened her mouth too wide. "Very smart little girl."

At the other end of the playground, Laurie watched as Abigail spoke to the red-faced chunky girl and her mother. The girl's mother smiled at Abigail and went to pat her head or her shoulder, but Abigail sidestepped the pat with such agility that, for a moment, the woman's hand hung in midair, a confused and somewhat startled expression on her face.

"Please," Liz said, though there wasn't much pleading to her tone. "Tonight. We can grill up some steaks. It'll be nice."

"I want to eat over at Abigail's house again," Susan said.

Once more, Liz Rosewood laughed. She had an elbow propped on one knee, smoke trailing from the cigarette held loosely between two fingers. She looked like a magazine advertisement. "It's really no trouble," she said.

"I'll have to check with my husband. He's been trying to get some work done while we're here. It hasn't been going very well for him. "

Like a small wooden soldier, Abigail marched back over to the picnic table. She was unsmiling. One of her pigtails was coming undone and there were loose strands of dark brown hair swiped across her sweaty forehead. A greasy smudge stood out sharply on her left cheek. "There. Are you happy?" she said as she sat down.

"Yes," said Liz. "Thank you. And what do you have in your hand?"

Glancing at Laurie, Abigail held up what looked like a pink barrette for Liz's inspection. It looked like one of the barrettes that had been in the hair of the chunky red-faced girl.

"Where did you get that?"

"I found it."

"Stop picking up trash," Liz scolded her. "Go throw that in the garbage can."

"We're eating dinner at your house tonight!" Susan informed her friend.

Still pouting, Abigail said, "That's not my *real* house."

CHAPTER 20

At an easy two-hundred-twenty pounds and a gruff, workmanlike appearance, Derrick Rosewood seemed a poor match for Liz's easygoing liberalism. He possessed a large, angular, red face that reminded Laurie of a stop sign, and there was dark grease in the creases of his neck and smears of it along his sunburned forearms. His hands were big paws and his eyes were the dim brownish-yellow eyes of a jungle cat. He ate in his work clothes, which consisted of a matching white-and-green jumpsuit which he unzipped down the front so that his stomach could protrude over the elastic waistband, and he exuded a smell that was ambiguously mechanical in nature, though not necessarily offensive. He was also very friendly.

The Genarros arrived at the Rosewoods' around seven. Ted brought a bottle of Da Vinci Chianti Reserva and Susan had made a friendship bracelet out of colored string and plastic beads for Abigail. Derrick was already out on the deck warming up the barbeque when they arrived; he waved one of his big paws at them through the kitchen windows. Liz greeted them with a smile and commented about how nice it was for them to bring a bottle of wine.

"Where's Abigail?" Susan asked Liz. Then she held up the friendship bracelet. "Look at what I made for her!"

Liz bent down, planting both hands on her knees. "Well, that is a particularly exquisite piece of jewelry. I think Abigail will like it very much. I also happen to know she made you something, too. She's upstairs in her room. Go on and fetch her."

"Can I, Daddy?"

"Sure, pumpkin pie."

"Yay!" She raced off down the hall and tramped hard upon the stairwell.

Outside on the deck, Derrick introduced himself to Laurie with a meaty handshake and a broad smile. Then he went instantly somber. "I'm so sorry to hear about your dad. He seemed like a nice old fellow."

"Did you know him very well?"

"I would sometimes see him sitting out in the yard before he got sick. We used to say a few words to each other and he was always very friendly. It was terrible what happened."

Liz put a hand on Laurie's shoulder and offered her a seat at the picnic table that stood on the slouching deck. Once Laurie sat down, Liz took everyone's drink order. Ted said he'd have some of the wine he brought while Laurie just asked for an ice water. At the table, Laurie positioned herself so that she could see the light on in the window upstairs—what she assumed was Abigail's bedroom, since it was the only light on up there. She couldn't hear the girls, couldn't see them. There was a stubborn lump in her throat.

"Anyone want something other than medium rare?" Derrick asked when Liz arrived with the drinks and a platter of raw sirloins for the grill.

"Susan will have hers well done," Laurie offered. "Where are the girls, anyway?"

"Playing upstairs," Liz said. She was having a beer and leaning against the deck railing. "Don't worry about them, they're fine."

"I'd hate to think my daughter is getting into anything up there."

Without looking at her, Derrick waved a hand. "Kids get in trouble anywhere. Better they're keeping each other busy."

Ted lifted his glass of wine. "Agreed."

"There's nothing they can get into," Liz confided, winking at Laurie.

The sun sank low in the west, toward the front of the Rosewoods' house; toward the east, the pulsing sodium lights on the other side of the river radiated up over the trees.

"You know, Laurie, I had no idea your father had been a big-time steel mogul until I read his obituary," Derrick commented. "He was part owner of one of those old complexes down at Sparrows Point back in the seventies, wasn't he?"

"That's right."

"I work for BGE and service Sparrows Point as part of my route."

"What's BGE?" Ted asked.

"Baltimore Gas and Electric. We've been taking a

lot of heat from Sparrows Point the past few years over the size of the mills' utility costs. Armor Steel pays just over twenty thousand dollars a day for natural gas and electric services—"

"A *day?*" said Ted.

"—with an annual bill of around eight million bucks."

"That's unfathomable," Ted stated.

Derrick pumped one big shoulder and said, "Let's not forget how much money these companies actually *make*. Your father made out all right, didn't he, Laurie?"

"Yes, he did very well."

"Where *is* this Sparrows Point?" Ted asked.

Derrick pointed out across the yard and over the trees at the eerie light on the horizon. The color was an indistinct electrical hue, not quite white, not quite pink, not quite orange. "Dundalk, which is maybe forty minutes by car, although it's quicker if you cut through the channels. The waterways, I mean. But you can see the factory lights straight across the river when it starts to get dark. Makes it look like Roswell over there, don't it?"

"Industrial pollution is what it is," Ted commented.

"All kinds of pollution," Derrick said. "Not just in the air, I mean. There's pollutants in the sediment, in the oyster beds, all throughout the wildlife that feed off the waterway. Water got so bad the past few years, Maryland crabs were being shipped in from North Carolina and Louisiana, though the locals don't really like the tourists to know. There's methods for cleaning it up, but the big question is who's gonna pay for it?"

"When I was a girl, I used to think it sounded so pretty," Laurie said. "Sparrows Point. Then one day my father drove me out across the Key Bridge. It was a wasteland of factories and shipyards—smokestacks, industrial pumps, hazard lights."

"It's mostly a ghost town now," Derrick assured her. Meat sizzled on the grill, the smell of it strong and smoky. "Half the factories have closed down. Now they just sit there like giant castles that have been evacuated because of some deadly plague. I guess industry itself was the plague, killing off the old steel mills and replacing them with liquefied natural gas terminals. Back in the seventies, Bethlehem Steel invested millions of dollars in the shipyards, and for a while it was profitable. But it's changed hands about half a dozen times since then, maybe more. Baltimore Marine owned much of it at one point back in the nineties, and maybe they still do, though you don't hear much about it anymore, unless it's chatter about the pollution and the dead critters that wash up on shore after a heavy rain."

"That's terrible," said Laurie. "It's better that the steel mills and factories have shut down."

Derrick nodded eagerly, but there was disagreement in his eyes. "But, see, that's the problem—most of those companies who polluted the watershed have shriveled up and died, so who's responsible for it now?"

"The factories might be shut down but the companies must still be around," Ted said. "In some form or another. Companies that big never go away completely."

"The property is all tied up with your basic multinational conglomerate corporations," Derrick continued, "but they wave their hands and say, hey, we just bought these big buildings, broke them apart, and reconstructed the pieces. They own the lots, but they don't own the claim to the pollution and to what those factories did before they came on the scene and bought them up."

"No accountability," Ted confirmed.

"They fling some money at charitable organizations, Save the Bay, those types of things, and it's like they're buying their own absolution. Meanwhile, honest men can't make a living anymore out on the bay."

"Both of Derrick's grandfathers were watermen," Liz explained. "He's very emotionally invested in the issue."

Derrick frowned. "It's important." It was the voice of a petulant child.

"I know, hon."

The deck door slid open and Susan and Abigail came out. Susan bounced over to Ted and climbed up into his lap. She wore a wreath of flowers like a crown on her head—a daisy chain made from black-eyed Susans.

"Cool headgear, babe," Ted said, grinning at Susan.

"Abigail made it for me." Susan beamed as she reached up and gently touched one of the flowers.

Abigail surveyed the people on the deck, and Laurie thought the girl's eyes lingered longest on her. Then she went over to Liz and showed her the bracelet she wore on her wrist. "Look what Susan made."

"That's very pretty. Did you thank her?"

"I did. Upstairs."

"Good work, kiddo."

"Okay, everybody wash up!" Derrick bellowed. "Food's on!"

Susan bolted for the door. Abigail walked more serenely, glancing again at Laurie as she went into the house.

The food was good but Laurie didn't have much of an appetite. She ate only half her steak, and was silently grateful when Ted finished it for her. The girls sat together at a plastic table and chair set Derrick had brought up from the basement, whispering and tittering behind cupped hands. (Though the girls had presumably washed their hands prior to eating, Laurie noted with mounting disquiet that Abigail's hands remained filthy; she ate with her fingers, too, and the sight of those grubby meat-slickened digits sliding in and out of the girl's mouth was slowly making Laurie ill.)

After dinner, Laurie waited for some coffee to be served, but Liz Rosewood only brought out another clutch of beers onto the deck. Ted finished off the wine he'd brought with him and Laurie stuck to ice water. She didn't think she could stomach alcohol at the moment. When the girls went into the house to play, Laurie was glad to have Abigail's eyes off her for a while, although she was fearful of having Susan out of her line of sight for too long.

"Lizzie says you folks are planning to sell the house," Derrick said, cranking the cap off a bottle of Flying Dog. "Market's a bear right now. You might want to hang on to it, rent it out or something, until things get better."

"If they ever do," Ted added.

Derrick tipped his beer in Ted's direction. "You know it, my friend."

"Derrick's brother Pete used to have a nice little place in Elkridge," Liz said, "but then he lost his job and then he lost his house sometime after that."

"The place wound up being worth less than he owed on it. It was like pouring water into a bucket with a hole in it," Derrick said.

"Listen," Liz said. "Before you folks leave tonight, I'll give you my friend Harmony's card. She's a realtor and she'll help you guys out. It'll be good to have someone help take some of the burden off your shoulders."

Ted smiled and thanked her.

The patio door swooshed open again and Susan wandered out onto the deck. She looked flushed and tired, and went directly to her father where she climbed up onto his lap and rested her head on his shoulder. Ted stroked her hair. "Getting sleepy, Snoozin?"

"Not really."

"Where's Abigail?" Liz asked.

"Watching TV. I got bored."

"Maybe we should leave," Laurie suggested.

Ted examined his wristwatch while Derrick said, "It's still early yet."

Laurie stood and collected some of the plates off the table. Liz told her not to worry about them, but Laurie said it was no problem. She carried them into the kitchen and stacked them in the sink, then ran water over the coagulated patches of grease.

The living room was off the kitchen. It was small and drably furnished, with walls the color of burnt umber and a sofa and loveseat combination that looked like it had been salvaged from a yard sale. Ugly prints of hunting dogs and mallards collected dust on the walls.

Laurie lingered in the doorway and stared at the back of Abigail's head. The girl was planted cross-legged on the floor in front of the TV. With the remote, she flipped through the channels at random and did not settle on a particular program.

Back in the kitchen, Laurie could hear the murmurs of conversation out on the porch. She peeked through the partially curtained window over the sink and saw Susan still curled up on her father's lap. Laurie crossed into the hallway and paused at the bottom of the stairwell. The stairs were covered in a woven runner of oriental design and there were crooked little picture frames going up the wall. The house was smaller than her father's, and there were only two bedrooms at the top of the stairs. Only one of the bedroom doors stood open. Laurie peered in, saw the queen bed outfitted in a hideous floral spread, and knew it was the master bedroom. She turned and approached the closed bedroom door at the opposite end of the hall, peering into a darkened bathroom along the way. Clutching the knob, she expected to find it locked, but it wasn't. She turned the knob and went inside.

The Rosewoods had done their best to make the room homey: There were dolls and stuffed animals on the bed, toys on the floor, a small television on a refurbished dresser, drawings taped to one wall, and various arts and crafts atop a cramped little desk in one corner of the room. Laurie took a deep breath and could smell cleaning products and faint perfume. Was there the scent of dirt hidden beneath those other smells? She thought that there was.

That's because this used to be Sadie's bedroom, she

thought. *I can still smell that girl beneath all this newness.*

She went to the desk and picked up various art projects. At first glance, there was nothing unusual about any of them—a shoe-box diorama, a few crayon drawings, a sock puppet with Ping-Pong balls for eyes and bright yellow yarn for hair, what appeared to be stories or poems printed out in a child's swollen, bubbly handwriting. Had she not been searching for deeper meaning in the items themselves, she might have missed it, passing off the art projects and looping vowels as a preadolescent's unremarkable juvenilia. But it wasn't. The swollen loops of her handwriting made it look like each individual letter was a cell engorged with disease. Smudgy fingerprints had been embossed like wax stamps at the corners of each page. The shoe-box diorama depicted a crudely drawn family, their clothing colorful and done in great detail while none of them had any faces. Laurie picked up one of the drawings. It was of trees, done in crayon, with green curlicues for leaves and forked trunks like upside-down peace signs. Printed in pencil across the trunk of one tree, in all capitals, was the word FUCK. Laurie let the paper flutter to the desktop. She picked up the sock puppet. A bright red crayon had been used to emboss pupils on the sock puppet's Ping-Pong ball eyes. Laurie brushed a thumb across one eyeball and flakes of red wax rained down on the desktop. The sock itself smelled awful, like industrial cleanser. It stung her eyes and she quickly dropped it.

"What are you doing in here?"

Laurie whirled around, a scream ratcheted midway

up her throat. Abigail stood in the doorway, her small white face expressionless except for a fiery simmer behind her eyes. She took two steps into the room, her gaze still locked on Laurie. "This is where I sleep," said the girl. "But this isn't really my room. It's just where they let me stay."

Laurie realized her hands had involuntarily clenched into fists, and she slowly relaxed them now.

"This is just where they put me down," Abigail went on. She sat on the edge of the bed and rattled her friendship bracelet—the one that Susan had made for her.

"Earlier today, you said you had a secret," Laurie said. "Tell me what it is."

"You should guess," said Abigail. "I think you know it."

"We need to stop playing these games now," Laurie said.

Abigail's mouth unhinged and a small pink tongue darted out and moistened her lower lip. The plastic beads of the friendship bracelet sparkled. "Did you see my drawings?"

"You're not Abigail Evans at all," Laurie said. She felt herself trembling. "Your name's Sadie Russ."

"Who do you want to be?"

"This isn't a game," Laurie said. "I'm not playing a game with you. I know who you are."

Abigail swung her feet back and forth. There were socks and a single black shoe under the bed. "What games do you like?"

"I don't like games."

"No games?"

"No. You did something to my father, didn't you?

You were in his house. You've been in there recently, too, haven't you?"

"My favorite is hide-and-go-seek. Do you know that one?"

"I don't want to talk about games. We're done pretending now."

"Sure. Do you like my drawings?"

"Please stop."

Abigail frowned, but there was a devil's trickery embedded within the expression. "You didn't even look at them."

Not wanting to turn her back on the girl, Laurie backed up against one wall so she could look at the drawings while keeping Abigail in her periphery. The drawings were rudimentary renditions of horses with too many legs, people with the wrong number of eyes in their eggplant-shaped heads, houses that looked like pyramids with windows.

"No," said Abigail. "You're looking at the wrong ones."

"Which ones?"

"Lower. The ones on the bottom. Those are the good ones."

"These are—"

Her voice died in her throat. She was looking now at the bottom row of drawings, and noticed that half of these drawings were of the same multiwindowed breadbox surrounded by some hastily drawn trees. The other drawings were of great looping gyres done up in many colors—circles, spheres, funnels that spiraled off into infinity.

"Do you like them?" Abigail's voice was suddenly

right behind her. Laurie turned to find that the girl had crept up on her and now stood less than two feet away. "That's the little house in the woods."

"The greenhouse," Laurie whispered.

"It's not a green house. It's a *glass* house. But it's very dirty."

Laurie swallowed a lump that seemed to burn her throat. "What do you want from me?" The words croaked out of her.

Abigail went back to the bed, sat down, crossed one ankle over the other, and proceeded to swing her legs.

"I want you to leave me alone," Laurie seethed through her teeth. "I want you to leave my daughter alone."

Abigail's legs stopped swinging. "Haven't you missed me, Laurie?" she said. "After all these years, haven't you missed me?"

Laurie merely stared at her. She could no longer formulate words. Again, as it had done earlier at the park, her vision threatened to splinter apart. She felt instantly hot and her entire body tingled. A high-pitched keening filtered into her ears. Around her, the walls began to balloon inward. On the bed, Abigail's face seemed to inflate as well . . . and then her features rearranged themselves, sliding and melting wetly into one another. One of her eyes bled down her cheek in a dark greasy ribbon while her left nostril widened and widened until it was no longer a nostril at all but a massive sinkhole in the center of her face. Only the girl's hideous smile remained unchanged.

CHAPTER 21

"Hon? Honey?" It was Ted's voice, swimming back to her through the ether.

She blinked open her eyes. Faces congealed before her. Ted's was closest, concern stitched across his face. He rubbed her cheek with one smooth hand.

"Where am I?" Her throat was sore. "What happened?" When she tried to sit up, Ted held her back down.

"Don't," he said. "Just give it a minute."

There was a faint vibration, like the strumming of guitar strings, in the center of her head. Her entire body was clammy with perspiration. "Did I pass out?"

"Not exactly." Ted slipped a hand under her neck and helped her sit up.

She found she was in a strange room, on a strange bed crowded with stuffed animals. People she did not recognize stood just behind Ted, staring down at her in concern. After a moment, she recognized the couple as Derrick and Liz Rosewood. Then she recognized the room as Abigail's bedroom. When she looked across the room, she could see the drawings of the greenhouse and all those concentric circles on the wall.

"Mom?" Susan appeared beside her father, her eyes moist with tears. The girl looked frightened. "Are you okay, Mom?"

"Yes, love."

Abigail approached the bed, peering at Laurie from between Susan and Ted. The girl's face was hollow.

"How long was I out?"

"Only a few minutes," Ted said.

From the doorway, Derrick said, "Should I call an ambulance or something?"

"No," Laurie said quickly. Then she softened her voice. "I'm okay. Extremely embarrassed, but okay."

Liz came up behind Abigail and put a hand on the girl's shoulder. "Go on downstairs and get Mrs. Genarro a glass of water."

Abigail's eyes hung on Laurie for a moment longer. Then the girl spun away and hurried out into the hall and down the stairs.

Laurie eased her legs over the side of the bed. Her clothes were drenched in sweat and the strumming at the center of her head had reduced to a light buzzing. *It happened again.*

"Are you sure you should get up?" Ted said. "There's no rush."

"I'm fine, Ted." Nonetheless, she braced herself against his shoulder in order to stand. Her legs felt as unreliable as toothpicks.

In the doorway, Derrick stood with a portable telephone in one hefty paw. His big octagonal face was mottled red in his confusion. He kept looking down at the telephone, as if he was unsure how it had gotten in his hand.

Abigail returned with a glass of water. She crept through the small crowd and arrived before Laurie, holding the glass out to her in both hands. There was a dark shine in her black eyes. Her hand shaking, Laurie reached out and took the glass from the girl, brought it to her lips. She did not take her eyes off Abigail as she gulped half of it down.

Back down the street, Ted helped her into bed. While she lay there, he peeled off her shoes, then tugged off her pants as Susan, still looking frightened, stood watch in the doorway. Laurie kept promising Susan that she was fine but her words didn't seem to allay the girl's fears.

"My head hurts," she said. "Did I bump it when I passed out?"

"You didn't pass out. When I came into Abigail's room, you were just standing there staring at the wall. You were awake, but when I called your name, you didn't answer. Your pupils were dilated."

"Oh." Chilled by the image this put into her head, she was glad when Ted piled the blankets on top of her. "How did I get on Abigail's bed?"

"I put you there."

"Did it take me long to come back around?"

"A couple of minutes, I guess."

"I'm not even tired." But her voice was already someone else's, floating through darkened corridors and across the vast recesses of space.

Ted went to the door, a grim expression on his face. Out in the hall, Susan hovered like a shadow.

"Yes, you are," he told her, and turned out the light.

* * *

She lay in the dark, accompanied by night sounds. A muted thump above the bedroom ceiling. A muffled sliding sound, like bare feet gliding against hardwood floors. She came fully awake, a scream caught in her throat, and realized she had been dreaming.

CHAPTER 22

She spent the next day and a half in bed, resigned to have Susan or Ted bring her food and water. Of course, she insisted that she was perfectly fine and that there was no need to wait on her, but she would be lying to herself if she said she didn't like the attention. Ted even brought up his laptop so she could watch DVDs. For dinner, Ted went out and picked up Chinese food, and the three of them ate in the big bed in the master bedroom while they watched a Jim Carrey movie on Ted's computer.

She was aware that at one point Liz Rosewood came over, presumably to ask about her condition. Laurie had heard Ted speaking with Liz downstairs in the parlor, their voices carrying up the stairwell and into the bedroom. Though she couldn't make out what was said, she could sense a conspiratorial undercurrent to their hushed tone. Was Liz suggesting she see a doctor, much as she had suggested the realtor to help sell the house? It seemed likely. It was only a matter of time before Ted would suggest she see a doctor, just as he had after the highway incident last year. That horrid little intermission. One of the doctors whom she had seen had stated concisely, *When you're dealing with the brain, even the smallest thing could be a reason for concern. Imaginary odors, seeing or hearing things that aren't there, unprovoked blackouts—these are all things that might seem harmless but could actually be a symptom of something quite dangerous.* But he hadn't found anything dangerous. He hadn't found anything at all. None of the doctors had found anything. At the time, she had joked that it was probably nothing more than plain old crazy . . . but now, in the wake of this second incident—another horrid intermission—it didn't seem so funny. Probably because she was starting to wonder if it wasn't actually the case. . . .

That night, when Ted came to bed, she feigned ignorance and asked if someone had stopped by the house earlier that day because she had thought she had heard him talking with someone.

"Liz came by to see how you were feeling," he said. "She dropped off her friend's business card, too. You know—the realtor? Harmony somebody. We should give her a call when you're feeling better."

Laurie said nothing, just continuing to stare at the ceiling.

"Despite how crummy the housing market is, I think we should put the house up," he went on. "Do you feel okay about that?" He cleared his throat. "Laurie?"

"I guess so."

"This place is haunting you," he told her.

You just want the money, she thought.

"I think maybe it's haunting me, too." It was easy to tell he was smiling to himself in the darkness. "Isn't that funny?"

Laurie made a *hmmm* sound, rolled over, and went
to sleep.

On the second day, she realized her wedding band
was no longer on her finger. She tried to remember the
last time she saw it, but she had never been consciously
aware of it and couldn't remember. She tore the sheets
off the bed, the pillow cases from the pillows, and
looked under the bed itself. The ring wasn't there. She
checked the bathroom—the sink, the tub, the toilet. A
friend of hers back in Hartford had once set her wedding
ring down in a Kleenex after cleaning it, then accidentally chucked the Kleenex along with some other trash
into the toilet. She hadn't realized what she'd done until
she had already depressed the flusher. Laurie thought
of that now. Had she carelessly dropped it in the toilet
and flushed it down into the sewers, out into the bay?
No, she didn't think that was possible . . . although she
had taken it off a few times while cleaning up around
the house. Had she mistakenly left it somewhere else?
It seemed likely, and she had been similarly careless in
the past. Once, she had lost it for a whole week—never
telling Ted—until she finally found it in her purse, in
the little nylon case that held her sunglasses. So yes,
it was most likely in the house somewhere. Yet panic
shook her. She felt like she was underwater, breathing
through a tube.

At one point, she went downstairs to find Abigail
standing in the parlor. For a moment, Laurie believed

she was actually still in bed and dreaming. It was all one big dream—the missing wedding band and Abigail Evans standing in her childhood home. Abigail smiled at her and Laurie felt her entire body surge with an icy numbness. The girl was dressed in an adult's chambray shirt, the sleeves coming down past her fingertips, and a pair of faded jean shorts tasseled with string at the hemline. Brown sandals were on her feet. And then the girl blinked out of existence and Laurie realized she *had* been dreaming.

Ted was in the kitchen cleaning up from lunch. When he looked up and found her in the kitchen doorway, he toyed with a crooked smile, though she could tell he wasn't completely happy to see her out of bed. She was determined to buck any suggestion from him that she consult a doctor.

"Can I get you something to eat?" he asked.

"I want to show you something," she said, and handed him the photo of her and Sadie.

Ted looked at the photo and smiled offhandedly. "Look at you. You're a little cutie," he said.

"Do you recognize the other girl?"

Ted brought the photograph closer to his face. "No," he said eventually. "Should I? Who is it?"

"It's *her*," she said, meaning Abigail.

"Her," Ted repeated, still staring at the photo. Then he said, "Oh. That girl Sadie. The one who did all those . . . those horrible things."

"You don't think she looks like the girl next door?"

"Abigail?" He scrutinized the photo again. Slowly, his head began to shake. "No. Not really."

"You're sure?"

"Well, I mean, they've both got dark hair and fair complexions, I guess, but I don't think they look too similar beyond that. Why?"

She took the picture from him and looked at it more closely herself. Similarities or not, there was no denying what Abigail had said to her in her bedroom that had brought on her trance. *Haven't you missed me, Laurie? After all these years, haven't you missed me?* There was no denying it . . . unless she allowed herself to believe that she had imagined the whole thing, that she had already been slipping out of consciousness and had dreamed it.

"Maybe you should go back upstairs and lie down," Ted recommended.

Instead, she got herself a glass of water from the tap. She decided she wouldn't say anything more about this to Ted. She didn't like the way he had been looking at her lately, and didn't want to add fuel to that fire. "Really, Ted, I'm fine. I just got dehydrated the other night. I'm feeling much better now."

He cleaned his hands on a dishtowel as she went to the kitchen table and sat down.

"I think I just needed the rest," she added, thinking she sounded false to her own ears.

"Good to hear." He folded his arms as he watched her from across the room.

"What?" she said. "What is it?"

"Steve Markham called this morning. Looks like

I'm going to get that face-to-face with John Fish after all."

"That's great. That's what you've wanted from the beginning."

"It means I have to be in the city for the meeting."

"New York?"

"It'll just be for the day. I could drive up in the morning and come back that evening."

"That's a lot of driving all in one day."

"I don't like the idea of leaving you and Susan here alone."

"We'll be fine." When she saw his eyes slide sideways, she knew there was something else. "Tell me," she said. "Spit it out, bub."

"I don't think being in this house is good for you."

"That's silly."

"Is it?"

"It was your idea in the first place, remember? It was what you wanted."

"Yeah, well, I was wrong."

"When do you have to go to New York?"

"Steve said he'd get back to me once they finalize a time. Most likely it'll be sometime in the next couple of days." He pulled out one of the kitchen chairs, but didn't sit in it. "Why don't you and Susan come to the city with me? I could drop you back in Hartford and you can stay at the house. Susan can see her friends."

As much as she liked the idea of taking Susan away from Abigail, Laurie now had something else she felt she needed to do, something she couldn't do back in Hartford. "I'll think about it," she said.

"Yes. Please do. I'm being serious."

"So am I," she told him. "I promise."

"Good." He clapped his hands together, then ran them both through his hair. "I'm going to try and get some work done."

"I'm going to get a shower, then maybe go for a walk."

"Okay, but don't go too far from the house."

"Okay, boss."

He kissed the top of her head. "Yeah," he said, playfully wrinkling his nose. "Take that shower."

Before heading to the bathroom for a shower, she found herself back in her father's study, the dead man's photo album opened before her while she sat cross-legged on the floor. She progressed slowly through each of the photos. She took her time, studying the alien faces of the people in the photos, the unfamiliar locales. When she came to the last few pages with the empty panels, she slipped the photograph she had found in her father's Bible into one of them. When she was done, she looked down at the line of white flesh on her ring finger. The absence of her ring made her whole hand look naked. She thought of Sadie Russ, making evil wishes by throwing things down into the well. Things that belonged to other people.

After her shower, she walked north along Annapolis Road. The day was cool and the sun felt good on her face and shoulders. She heard the shouts and laughter of children before she actually saw them, crossing the street and standing in the parking lot which over-looked the park grounds. Little girls hung upside-down from the monkey bars. A young boy rolled toy cars through the patchy grass. There were some women talking by one of the picnic tables, but they looked old enough to be grandmothers.

Laurie went over to one of the benches and sat down. Absently, she wished she'd possessed the fore-sight to bring a book, as she had done in the days of her pregnancy with Susan when she would go down to the neighborhood parks to watch as the children con-gregated at playgrounds and flocked to ball fields and cul-de-sacs like creatures sharing a single brain. Liz Rosewood had mentioned that there weren't many kids in town for Abigail to play with. To Laurie, it seemed like there were plenty of kids around. They were like stunted wild men rooting through the debris of some fallen civilization. *Maybe they just don't want to play with Abigail Evans.*

This scenario was so much like what she had done during her pregnancy that it was nearly like déjà vu. Yet she thought she was able to see her motivations more clearly now, without the lies she had told her-self early on. Had it been fear of motherhood that had caused her to seek unspoken counsel from the women on the playground and the consolation of the church on King Street, or had she feared something else, something darker? *Children change,* she knew. *Girls change.* It had been Sadie who had taught her that les-son, and that lesson had been at the heart of it. *Children* were the problem, *little girls* were what terrified her. They constantly stared with the slack, insensate faces of dullards. Dried food on their cheeks and mouths, mealy crust in their eyes, rogue bulbs of snot yo-yoing in and out of narrow little nostrils, bright orange vegetation sprouting sporelike from ear canals. . . . It was children she feared, with their thin, probing paws, fingernails ground to nubby scales tinged in dried blood. The notion of motherhood had left her feeling helpless and imprisoned, like a chunk of pineapple suspended in Jell-O.

Had she been frightened *for* Susan . . . or frightened *of* her? Scared of her potential, of what she could become?

She was loathe to admit this to herself now, as if the revelation siphoned something vital from her relationship with her daughter, her beautiful daughter. But there could be no denying it. The horrible things Sadie had done to her made her fearful of the dark and hidden potential within her own daughter.

I won't let that happen to her.

It was around three in the afternoon when a soccer ball rolled over near Laurie's bench. A little girl of about seven or eight chased after it, little auburn pigtails bouncing, her shirt decorated with smiling Elmo faces. The girl's eyes were bright as headlamps and she had a pointy little tongue cocked in one corner of her mouth.

"Hello," Laurie said to the girl as she watched her gather up the soccer ball. "What's your name?"

"Meagan."

"Hi. I'm Laurie. I like your shirt."

"Elmo," said Meagan.

"Is your mother here?"

"Elmo. Elmo." The girl pointed to the gaggle of women by the picnic tables. "Over there." Meagan had a tough time pronouncing the *r*'s.

"Do you know a girl named Abigail Evans? She lives just down the street here."

Clutching the soccer ball to her chest, Meagan shook her head. A snail-trail leaked out of her right nostril and that pointy little tongue darted up and lapped at it, much like a frog would slurp up a particularly tasty dragonfly.

"Have you ever heard of her?" Laurie asked.

"I have to go now."

"What about your friends?"

"Good-bye," said Meagan. She spun around and ran back toward her friends, her stubby little legs pumping furiously.

Laurie looked up and saw that none of the women by the picnic tables were paying her any attention. *If I were a man, they would notice.* She got up to head back home. It had been her intention to come down here and ask a few of the neighborhood kids about Abigail. Instead, she had lost her nerve after speaking with Meagan, realizing how ludicrous it all was, and she had wound up wasting two hours on a park bench. At least the weather held up.

Instead of going back to the house right away, she walked around the swings and seesaws and over to a woodchip pathway that wound around the circumference of the park. Two joggers in brightly colored spandex ran past her. At the farthest point of the playground area, the path diverged, one pathway continuing back around to complete the circle while the divergent path graduated up the slight hill toward the wrought-iron fence of the cemetery. It was the cemetery on Howard Avenue, visible now only because the neighborhood had conspired to raze this section of the woods and build a playground. As a child, she had known of the cemetery, but hadn't realized it had been just on the other side of the street she'd lived on. Roads made things seem farther away than they actually were.

She expected to find the cemetery gates locked, but they weren't. The footpath continued onto the cemetery grounds and Laurie followed it. A single glance at the nearest headstones informed her that this was the newer section of the cemetery. The stones were smoothly polished, low to the ground, and shaped like the type of nameplate you might find on a banker's desk. The dates on some of the graves were as recent as this year.

She was careful crossing over the plots toward the older section of the graveyard. There had been a few people back at the newer section—mostly children who had gotten bored playing on the swings and now searched for more stimulating adventures—but the older section of the cemetery was a ghost town. Here, the headstones were as gray and craggy as rotting teeth, disconsolate beneath the shade of stately pines, elms, and maples. Birds tittered and a lone squirrel loped from headstone to headstone a few rows away, seemingly oblivious to her presence.

It took her about fifteen minutes to locate the stone. It was a simple marble marker wedged between two larger headstones on a parcel of ground that, judging by the height of the weeds, probably hadn't been attended to since last fall. Dead brown leaves were bunched at its base and there was the milky spatter of dried bird shit on the marker's face. Still, she could make out Sadie's name along with the dates of her birth and her death. There was no kitschy epitaph, no saccharine poetry— just the name and the dates. At the top of the headstone, perched there like a crown, was a daisy chain of flowers woven together to form a circle. Black-eyed Susans.

At the center of her head, it felt like a series of rubber bands, which had been slowly stretched to their breaking point, began to snap one by one. Five or six headstones away, the squirrel stood on its hind legs and stared at her, as if in anticipation of something momentous.

When she returned home, Ted was napping on the sofa. Susan was seated at the dining room table drawing pictures in a spiral-bound notebook. Laurie leaned over the girl's shoulder and saw that all the pictures were of circles.

"Why are you drawing those?"

"It's fun." Susan set down a red crayon, picked up a black one, and began tracing the original circle. She was pressing so hard that the paper crinkled. "Abigail showed me how to do it."

"Was Abigail here today?"

"No."

"What's so fun about a circle?"

"It's not a circle," Susan said. She set the black crayon down and picked up a green one.

"It isn't? What is it, then?"

"That thing out front."

"What thing?"

"You know," said Susan. "The wishing well."

Laurie had been stroking her daughter's hair. Now she stopped, her fingers pausing in mid-stroke.

Susan dropped the green crayon, then selected a sparkly gold one from the box. "That's a pretty color," Susan said admiringly. "Don't you think that's a pretty color, Mom?"

"Yes," she said. "Very pretty."

Laurie turned and walked back through the house. She felt like an ambulatory corpse. In the kitchen, she stood staring at the refrigerator, which was burdened with more drawings of circles. After a time, they began to look like eyes staring out at her.

Dusk had cooled the air. Laurie located a flashlight in the basement, threw on a sweatshirt, and went out the front door. She trampled the high grass as she crossed the yard, stopping at the foot of the old well. Ted had placed bricks on each corner of the plywood cover to give it a bit more security. Laurie knocked the bricks off with her foot. She squeezed her fingers between the plywood and the stone rim of the well and gave it a shove. The plywood scraped along the stone, revealing a semicircle of darkness underneath it.

Laurie dropped to her knees, clicked on the flashlight, and shone it down into the hole. Far below, a pinpoint of light winked back at her. The surface of the black water looked like it was maybe fifteen feet below the mouth of the well. How deep the water was, she could only guess.

In bed that night, after a quick session of lovemaking—something they hadn't done in quite some time—Laurie said, "What would it take to drain that well?"

CHAPTER 23

Because she'd been on edge lately, Ted asked very few questions. (There was another reason, too, although he didn't like to think about it; each time the thought surfaced in his head, he found himself batting it down like a fisherman swatting at the hump of an approaching crocodile with the oar from his johnboat.) Humoring her, he found a hardware store in town where he purchased a portable sump pump, an extension cord, and a fifty-foot garden hose. Back at the house, he attached the garden hose to the pump, then trailed the opposite end of the hose down the driveway and out into the street. He tucked the final few feet of hose down an open storm drain. If a cop happened to cruise by he might catch a fine, but he didn't care.

"Please note that I am being a good husband and doing everything you ask without question," he said as he removed the bricks from the plywood board over the opening of the well. "So, with that in mind, will you please tell me what this is all about?"

Laurie and Susan sat on the porch steps watching him work. A red ice pop dribbled down Susan's hand and her mouth looked like a vampire's.

"You mentioned Liz Rosewood's realtor friend," said Laurie. "I think you're right—we should call her out here to look at the house as soon as possible. But first, I'd like to get it in better shape. That well is not only an eyesore, it's a hazard. We're going to have to fill it in."

He shucked the sheet of plywood off the well. A smell like old garbage rose up and tugged at the hairs in his nose. "I can get a bunch of dirt and just fill the sucker in."

"Maybe. Or it might have to be cemented at the bottom. You sometimes have to do that to old wells so they don't collapse and become sinkholes."

"Yeah?" He had no clue. This was the first well he'd ever encountered in his life. However, he wasn't going to balk. He was glad she was in agreement with him that they needed to unload the house, even if it meant taking a hit because of the lousy market. Money from the sale could buy him a few more years working on his writing without having to supplement their income by taking on additional jobs. He even indulged himself in a fantasy where he quit the Fish project by walking up to the overblown beluga and telling him what a rambling piece of self-indulgent garbage his novel was. This notion, however unrealistic, brought a thin smile to his lips.

Susan finished her ice pop and bounced over to him just as he was lowering the sump pump down into the hole. "Can I help?" she asked.

"In a minute."

"What can I do?"

He could see the surface of the water roughly fifteen

feet below. He fed the pump down into it by the cord, hand over hand, until it was submerged beneath the black water. He pointed to the extension cord that was coiled like a snake in the grass. "See the end of that?"

Susan scratched her head and looked blankly at the extension cord.

"The end of the cord, Susan," he said, pointing to the tri-pronged bulb at the end.

"Yes!" She picked it up.

"Go inside and plug it into the wall. Give yourself enough slack."

"What's that mean?"

"Unwind the cord so you have enough of it to take with you."

She bent, let out several feet of slack, then raced up the stairs and into the house.

"She's getting big," Laurie said from the porch steps, watching her go. Ted clearly heard the maudlin tone to his wife's voice.

Down in the hole, the sump pump began humming beneath the water. Ted had one foot on the garden hose; after a few seconds, he felt the hose swell up as the water funneled through it. He gave up a few more feet of cord and let the sump pump sink to the floor of the well. *Just a few feet of water. Not so deep.* He estimated it would take a couple of hours for the entire well to drain.

Laurie drew up beside him and peered down into the hole. "I threw some things down there when I was a kid," she said, a hint of melancholia still in her voice. "I wonder if they'll still be down there."

"I don't see why not. Where else would they go?"

"When I was a kid, I thought they would disappear and turn into wishes."

He liked the idea of that. "Maybe they did."

"Some, maybe." She smiled but did not look at him. "Sadie threw things down there, too."

For a second, he didn't know whom she was talking about. But then he remembered, and he wondered if she had been honest with him in her reason for wanting to drain the well.

"Thank you," she said, and kissed him on the cheek. Then she turned, went up the stairs, and into the house.

I hope there's nothing down there. The thought came at him like a pop fly to left field. *Nothing but stones and mud.* He didn't know why he felt this way, and that troubled him further.

Susan bounded out onto the porch. "Did I do it?" she called to him, leaning over the porch railing. "Did it work?"

"It sure did, sugar pie."

"Yay!" she cheered. "Now what?"

He wiped his hands on his jeans. "Now we wait."

Steve Markham called about an hour later, and there was triumph in his voice.

"Tell me the good news," Ted said, grinning to himself. Having just checked on the progress of the well, he was out in the front yard with the cell phone to his ear.

"Here's the deal," Markham said. "It'll be a lunch meeting in the city, face-to-face, this Friday. It'll be you, me, Fish, of course, and Fish's agent. She's a real ball-buster dyke, but she's also in agreement with us on this, at least to an extent. She knows Fish is a prick and has already convinced him to hear us out."

"So he hasn't necessarily conceded to letting me go ahead with the original outline—"

"No, but he hasn't told us to fuck off, either. And considering that's his typical modus operandi, I'd say we're looking like a couple of sweepstakes winners right about now, my friend."

"Brilliant. I'm sure I can convince him in person."

"Yes, I'm sure you can, if you do it properly. Kid gloves, you know? These overblown artist types, you have to coddle them, fawn over them, tell them their shit smells like strawberries and their piss tastes like champagne."

"Is that what you do to me?"

Steve Markham laughed. "You're still in Maryland?"

"Yes."

"How soon can you get up here?"

"To the city? I can leave Friday morning and be there for lunch."

"The meeting is set for eleven-thirty at Rao's. I suggest you come in the night before. The last thing we need is for you to drive up Friday morning, blow a flat, or if there's fucking construction on 95, and we both know there's *always* fucking construction on 95. . . ."

"I'll have to check with Laurie."

"There's one other thing, too."

"What's that?"

"I took a shot in the dark here, and nothing's set in stone yet . . ."

"Spit it out."

"I had a meeting yesterday with the guys at the production office about this whole mess. Apparently, the producers had no idea John Fish was such an egomaniacal asshole, and they all agreed you were in a tough spot on this. More than that—they agreed that if you pulled this off and got this thing to work, they'd be happy to work with you again."

"That's wonderful."

"No, no—hear me out. I told them about that play you'd been working on before taking the Fish project, the one about the ex-priest and the prostitute."

"You did what?"

"They want to sit down and talk about it. Right after we're done with Fish's bloated ass, we're heading to their office for a meeting about it."

Ted's head felt light and fuzzy. "Are you shitting me?"

"I shit you not, good sir. But let's not start jerking off about this yet, Ted. It's a meeting, that's all. But we've got their ear, so let's make it something more."

"Count on it," Ted said.

At the bottom of the well, the pump began making gurgling, belching sounds. Ted peered down and saw the pump propped up on a mound of tarry black muck. The water had finished draining.

"What in the name of Christ is that *noise?*"

Ted laughed. "It's my career coming back up the toilet. I'll see you Friday, Steve. Thanks."

Laurie and Susan watched as Ted hauled the pump up out of the well. It dripped water and there was black muck stuck to it. Ted set it down in the grass. The black muck smelled incriminatingly like raw sewage. Together, the three of them peered down into the well at the soupy black sludge on the bottom. Laurie handed him a flashlight, which he pointed down into the hole. The shallow beam illuminated the crenellations in the sludge and glistened off clusters of brownish suds.

"Snake!" Susan shrieked. She thrust an arm down into the hole and pointed. "Daddy, snake! Snake!"

Indeed, he caught the smooth black slither wending through the muck. "There's probably more than one down there."

"That old man said so," Susan reminded him. "Remember that day we got here and he said there were snakes in the well? And you said he was lying, that he was pulling on my legs, and that there were *no* snakes in the well, Daddy—"

"Yeah, yeah, I know what I said."

"What's that?" Laurie said.

He saw it, too—a quick twinkle as the flashlight's beam fell upon a particularly nasty-looking mound of sludge. Some plant-life sprouted from the sludge like slick, wet hair, and Ted had to pass the flashlight's beam back and forth over it a few times before he caught the twinkle again. When he did, he held the beam on it. Something sparkled up at them from the darkness.

"I have no idea what that is," he said.

"Wishes," Laurie said.

"Ooh," said Susan. "Go get 'em, Daddy."

He clicked the flashlight off. "Why don't *you* go get 'em, Snoozin?"

"I'm not afraid of snakes," she countered.

"Yeah, well," he began, but said no more. He wasn't all that crazy about snakes himself. Nor was he keen on the idea of somehow climbing down into that stinking pit. It looked like those Vietnamese prisons they showed in the movies. He'd probably break his neck trying.

"It's a diamond," Laurie said.

Ted snorted. "Yeah, right. It's probably a piece of glass or tinfoil or something."

"No," Laurie said. "It's a diamond. One of my mother's diamond earrings."

Ted blinked at her. "You . . . threw your mother's diamond earrings into the well?"

"Not me."

He opened his mouth to ask for clarification, but then remembered everything she had told him about the girl named Sadie from her childhood. She had told him about the time Sadie had wanted her to steal her mother's diamond earrings. She had threatened Laurie with a used tampon the girl kept in a shoe box. The story had been too incredible not to be true and, anyway, what reason would Laurie have for making up such a horrific tale? He realized now that he hadn't heard how that story had ended, though he could piece it together now—she had stolen the earrings, given them to Sadie, and Sadie had chucked them down the old wishing well. *What kind of little girl does something like that?*

"There's a ladder in the basement," Laurie said.

"Hold on." Ted grabbed her wrist as she turned to head back to the house. "What are you saying?"

"I'll go down there if you don't want to. It's okay."

The smile she offered him was so innocent and pretty, it nearly shattered his heart.

"You're out of your mind wanting to go down there. You'll break your neck."

"And *snaaa-aakes*," Susan caroled, wagging an index finger as if to reprimand someone's naughtiness.

"Those earrings are worth a lot of money," Laurie said. She didn't try to pry her wrist free of his grasp. "Not to mention that they belonged to my mother. There's a lot of other stuff down there, too. I'm sure of it. Ted, I just want to *see*."

What is going on with her? This isn't my wife. This isn't the woman I married. I don't understand any of it.

Gradually, his fingers opened up around her wrist. "You've got some air of obsession about you," he told her. "I wish I understood it."

That sweet smile still lit up her face. "It's my healing process," she told him. "Let's call it that, okay?"

Good, he thought. *Because "obsession" makes me too uncomfortable.*

"Stay here," he said. "I'll go get the ladder."

The ladder went down into the hole, the legs sinking a few inches into the fetid sludge at the bottom. Due to the narrowness of the well, the ladder stood almost vertically. Ted jockeyed it into the most secure position he could find, wedging it between two dimpled niches in the stone. He had equipped himself with a flashlight, a plastic garbage bag, a pair of bright yellow rubber dishwashing gloves, a broken broom handle nearly three feet long, and a wire coat hanger stretched into an approximate hoop covered in a pair of Laurie's nylons, which Ted thought looked like a makeshift pool skimmer. He had fashioned a plastic shopping bag around each of his sneakers, and they were held in place just below the knees with several rubber bands.

"Just keep the ladder steady against the stones," he instructed Laurie before descending. "Hold on to it. I don't want the damn thing wobbling all over the place."

Laurie gripped the extended legs of the ladder, one in each hand. "Be careful."

"Be careful, Daddy," Susan repeated, glancing almost forlornly at him and then down into the pitch-black hole in the earth. "Watch out for that snake."

He swung his right leg down into the well and set his foot on the second rung down from the top. He felt the ladder sink lower into the muck another couple of inches. Gripping the sides of the well with both hands—he had tucked the flashlight, rubber gloves, the broom handle, and makeshift skimmer into the rear waistband of his jeans—he slowly lowered himself until his left foot came down on the rung just below his right foot. The ladder sank down another inch or two, and he waited for it to settle before continuing his descent.

It was like sinking into a grave. The smell was no better—a putrid, eye-watering stench that came at him in a nearly solid cloud. Small flies and gnats dive-bombed his head; he swatted the larger ones away while still keeping a strong grip with his other hand on the rung just above his head. He imagined their tiny pinprick corpses stuck in the sweat on his forehead. Halfway down, he glanced up and saw the faces of his wife and daughter gazing down at him. They looked impossibly far away, as did the opening of the well itself, as if it had shrunk to the size of a softball while he wasn't looking.

Two rungs up from the bottom, he stopped. The well was just slightly roomier than a manhole, and it was with some contortion that he was able to reach behind him, select the broom handle, and withdraw it from his waistband. He crouched as best he could, propping one foot flat against the wall of the well while the other balanced on the rung of the ladder, and drove the broom handle down into the peaty black sludge. It sank down several inches before it struck what felt like solid stone underneath. He felt some relief. *That's not as bad as I'd thought.* For all he knew, it could have been a bottomless chasm that dropped straight to hell.

Releasing his grip on the broom handle, it remained standing straight up out of the muck. *I claim this land in the name of Ted.* He reached around his back again and felt for the flashlight, grabbed it, switched it on, and cast its harsh white beam down on the floor. He caught sight of the black snake retreating into a crevice between two stones, where the mortar had worn away. There were other critters down here as well—mostly bugs. Fat black beetles trundled through mossy, dark green strands of what looked like sea grass while spotted slugs appeared to respire—expanding, then deflating— each time the flashlight's beam passed over them. Earthworms as thick as fingers squirmed and sought solace deeper into the mud. Whitish grubs wriggled up from a tarry swath of black slime; he could hear their collective movements, a sound grotesquely similar to squeezing a handful of wet noodles. There were other critters down here aside from the bugs, but these were all dead and in varying stages of decay—several water-bloated mice and a decomposed bird were among the ones he was able to identify.

With the flashlight propped under his left armpit, he grabbed the broom handle again and, like a witch stirring a cauldron, drew tracks through the muck. Before he stepped down into that mess he wanted to make perfectly sure there weren't any other critters hiding beneath the mud. Particularly critters with teeth.

He realized pretty quickly that he would not be able to bend down with the ladder in the well with him. There just wasn't enough room. Plus, it was slowly sinking into the mud, causing him to wonder just how deep into the earth the well went. He stepped down into the sludge and felt his plastic bag–wrapped sneakers sink into it.

"Hey," he called up the channel, his voice reverberating till it made no sense to his own ears. The opening at the surface was no bigger than a dime now. "Pull the ladder up!"

Laurie didn't respond, though her silhouette was still framed in the tiny lighted hole directly above his head. So was Susan's. He was about to repeat the order when the ladder rose up out of the muck with a sucking, squelching sound, and began to ascend back up the throat of the well.

"Shit," he grumbled, quickly swiping at his face and hair as bits of gunk rained down on him. *Didn't think that part through.* Once the ladder was lifted out of his way and the gunk had ceased dripping down on him, he directed his attention to the muddy heap in which he stood. Again, something sparkled as it caught the beam of the flashlight. It was partially covered in mud, so Ted crouched down, tugged on the rubber dishwashing gloves, and picked it up. It was a solid gold wristwatch.

CHAPTER 24

The items Ted found in the well included approximately seventeen dollars in loose change, a man's gold wristwatch with a cracked crystal face, a single diamond earring (he had located only the one), a woman's brooch that sprouted calcified tumors that looked like dried toothpaste, a few similarly calcified keys, what appeared to be the metal clasp from a girl's barrette, a simple platinum band that looked almost identical to Ted's wedding ring—and was in surprisingly good condition—though it was not Laurie's, a tie clip, a money clip, and various bits of cheaper jewelry that had been reduced to reddish bits of rust. Yet the most unsettling thing was a child's plastic baby doll, its pink body reduced to a curdled tallow hue marbled with bluish veins of rot, its features faded into nothingness from its submergence for God knew how long in that swampy, fetid water. Ted had found other things while sifting through the gunk, straining the muddy water through the coat hanger with the pantyhose stretched across it like a miner panning for gold—countless buttons, bottle caps, the rubber sole of a shoe, and other bits of garbage, all of which he left down below.

After Laurie and Susan lowered the ladder back down the hole, Ted climbed up with his plastic garbage bag dripping foul water onto the lawn. The poor guy was perspiring and smelled awful. Laurie took the bag from him while offering him a conciliatory smile. She felt as though she were on the cusp of some grand discovery, some penultimate revelation. The sensation was not dissimilar to dizzying vertigo.

While Ted hosed himself off in the yard, Laurie took the bag around to the side of the house where she entered the kitchen through the side door. Susan followed close at her heels. Laurie placed the plastic bag on the counter, stopped up the sink's drain, then dumped the items out into the basin. Susan dragged over a chair, climbed up, and peered down into the sink and at the items it held.

"Pirate treasure," Susan said, her voice full of awe.

Laurie rinsed off the items beneath a lukewarm spray. The nicer jewelry cleaned up better than the cheap stuff. The gold watch had been her father's; she remembered stealing it from a little hand-carved box he kept in his study and giving it to Sadie at Sadie's behest. She hadn't wanted to do it but Sadie held some power over her. Similarly, she remembered stealing the diamond earrings from her mother's jewelry box. Sadie had worn them a few times to school but never at home and never around Laurie's parents. When Laurie had asked for them back—her mother had become frantic trying to locate them throughout the house—Sadie had refused. She had laughed and warned Laurie that she would get the shoe box again. *It has flies on it now,* Sadie had said of the bloody tampon in the box. *Big black flies. And if you tattle on me, I'll make you put it in your mouth with all those big black flies on it. I'll make you put it* down there, *too*. Then one day Sadie had stopped wearing the earrings. Only now did Laurie realize where at least one of them had ended up.

Laurie blinked. The power of the memory had been strong and sudden. At her elbow, Susan was staring at her with a mix of apprehension and confusion in her dark eyes. Laurie summoned a smile for her daughter. After some hesitation, Susan offered her one back.

"Where did all this stuff come from, Mom?"

"From years and years of people throwing it down in there," she said.

"Why would someone throw jewelry down a well?"

"Sometimes people do silly things, Susan."

"I bet those things have snake poop on them."

"I'll bet some of them do," Laurie said.

The side door banged as Ted came into the kitchen. He had his sneakers in his hands and the cuffs of his jeans rolled up. His hair was wet and slicked back. "That's some booty, huh, ladies?"

"There was only one earring down there?"

"As far as I could tell. There are some cracks in the mortar and a small drain in the wall. The drain had a mesh covering over it but it was all rusted and there were pieces missing from it. I guess the other earring could have gotten washed away. Not to mention I don't know how deep that sludge is on the bottom. There could be a triceratops skeleton down there." He ran a hand through his wet hair, then sniffed the palm and made a face. "You think any of that stuff is worth anything?"

"Some of it, maybe. The diamond. Maybe the gold

watch, though I'm sure the works are ruined. It was my father's."

"How does a man's gold watch wind up at the bottom of a well?" When Laurie didn't respond, he said, "I'm gonna grab a shower."

With her thumbnail, Laurie attempted to scrape some of the calcification off the face of the brooch. This had also been her mother's, passed down to her from Laurie's grandmother. She felt sick to her stomach just holding it.

"I knew it," said Susan. "I knew we'd find real treasure."

"Yes." Laurie set the brooch down on the kitchen counter. "Why don't you go upstairs and clean yourself up, too?"

"Okay." Susan hopped down from the chair and scampered off.

Laurie picked up the doll. Water streamed from the seams where its limbs met its body. Its face looked like that of a burn victim, its features melted and indistinct. She turned it upside down and heard what sounded like a stone tumble through its body.

Something crashed in the parlor. Laurie jumped, knocking the earring into the sink. The diamond stud rolled around the basin, though before it could disappear down the drain, Laurie caught it. She set it back on the countertop and then went out in the parlor.

Her father's urn had been knocked off the fireplace mantel. It lay in pieces at the foot of the hearth, its grayish, powdery contents in a dusty heap in the center of the broken pieces. It looked like a prehistoric egg someone had dropped, its yolk turned to ancient dust.

"Susan?"

But Susan didn't answer. Laurie crept closer and saw the approximation of a partial footprint in the ashes. When a cool breeze struck her back, she turned around and saw one of the parlor windows was open. She expected to find dusty footprints leading to the window, but there were none. Cold, she shut the window, locked it. Then she swept up the broken bits of urn and her father's ashes into a dustpan, and dumped them unceremoniously into the kitchen trash.

When she turned around, she found herself staring at the plastic doll on the kitchen counter. It lay facing her, its blank eyes staring right through her. She had dropped it on the counter when she heard the crash from the parlor, but now it looked as though it had been perfectly positioned to watch her from across the room.

She went to it, brought it over to the sink. She moved the arms up and down, spilling more gray water into the basin. Gripping the head, she gave it a sharp twist and jerked it sideways until it popped off. It could have been an actual corpse for how rancid the smell was coming out of it. She turned the doll upside down, leaking black sludge into the sink. Something else tumbled out as well, the item she had mistaken for a stone when she initially upended the doll. But it wasn't a stone. It was a large brass key with the number 58 engraved on it.

Laurie spent the rest of the evening wondering if she was losing her mind. By dinnertime, she suggested they order pizza, telling them she was too tired to cook. Ted pulled a face, but didn't comment. Susan cheered.

When the pizza arrived, they ate in the parlor. Mourning the loss of the Victrola, Ted selected similar music from his iTunes playlist and cranked up the speakers on his laptop. Susan no longer laughed at the old music; she now listened to it with her eyebrows knitted together and her mouth set in an appearance of concentration that showed some hint of approval.

"Could it be true?" Ted said as they were halfway through a Schubert composition. "Has the obstinate young *ragazzina* actually begun to appreciate the music?"

Susan wrinkled her nose. "It's just okay," she said, snapping from her trancelike stare at the computer screen. There was pizza grease at the corners of her mouth.

"I can't believe they took the phonograph but left the records," he said. "Do you care if I keep them? Or did you not want them to come back to Hartford with us?"

Laurie blinked and looked at him. She had been in a fog and hadn't fully been listening. "The records? No, that's fine. Keep them if you want." She shrugged. The slice of pizza in the plate on her lap had hardly been touched.

"Are you feeling okay, Laurie?"

"I'm still just a little tired."

"You should go to bed early tonight."

"You're probably right."

Ted sipped at a lowball glass of amber liquor—more of what he'd been scavenging from the liquor cabinet since their arrival at the house. When he set the glass down, he said, "In all the commotion today, I forgot to tell you that Steve Markham called. The meeting with

Fish is set up for Friday afternoon in Manhattan. He's also got us a meeting right after with the producers to talk about something else I've been working on. You know that play about the ex-priest and the prostitute?"

"This Friday?" she said. It was already Tuesday.

"I'll leave early in the morning and drive back after the meetings. You won't even have time to miss me."

"You won't be too tired? Maybe you should go up the night before."

He laughed. "Now you sound like Markham."

"I just don't want you to blow your opportunity."

"We'll talk about it later," he said.

After dinner, Susan practiced for forty-five minutes on the piano while Ted sat beside her, instructing. Several times he corrected her finger placement on the keys and showed her how to work her thumb under her hand to "glide" to the next key to create a more fluid scale. Restless, Laurie looked in on them every once in a while, though she found it nearly impossible to sit in one place for any sustainable length of time. Several times she went into the kitchen to look at the items Ted had salvaged from the well. Some were laid out on a square of paper towel—the watch, the ring, the diamond earring, and a few other things. Some of the other items that had been more corroded—the brooch, the keys, most of the coins—were soaking in a pot of mineral acids, which Laurie had located in the basement under the stairs among other sundries. Some of the corrosion had come apart, but she could already tell that the image on the face of the brooch was gone for good.

Here they are, Laurie thought, *all of Sadie's evil se-*

crets. What horrible wish did you make on that brooch to punish me and keep me in your grasp, Sadie? What evil thing did you hope for? That my mother would die? How about the gold watch? Were you trying to orphan me, you little monster? Thinking of this now, it astounded Laurie at how calculating and manipulative Sadie Russ had been. She tried to think of Susan behaving in such a fashion—she was just about the same age as Sadie had been when she died—but she found it impossible. There were uncharted depths within her daughter, just as there were in all little girls, Laurie knew, but she did not believe Susan was capable of anything even remotely as wicked. *And if Sadie Russ has truly come back as Abigail Evans, to what purpose? To exact some kind of revenge on me? Did she break into this house and murder my father just to lure me back here after all these years?* This last thought was outlandish enough to snap her back to reality. Sadie Russ had been dead for almost thirty years. People weren't reincarnated as other people. Or, if they were, they didn't look the same, and they certainly didn't come back seeking revenge. Yet . . . those things Abigail had said to her . . .

For what purpose? To what extent?

When Laurie came back out into the parlor, Ted and Susan were just finishing up a duet of "Camptown Races" on the piano. As the final notes sustained, Ted slung an arm around his daughter and squeezed her. They were both grinning goofily at each other. When they sensed Laurie behind them, they turned around, still grinning.

"Did you hear us, Mom? Pretty good, huh?"

"Very good. But it's time for bed now."

Susan groaned.

Ted rubbed his daughter's head and said, "Tomorrow's another day. Get up early and start fresh."

Susan swung her legs over the piano bench and stood up. "I can't wait to tell Abigail about the pirate treasure we found in the well today."

"I don't want you to play with Abigail anymore," Laurie said.

Both Susan and Ted turned to look at her. The matching expression on their faces would have been comical had they not looked *so much* alike at that moment—so much that they could have been one complete person split suddenly into two.

"How come?" Susan said.

"Because I don't like her. She's a bad influence."

Ted looked like he wanted to smile—like he thought she might be joking with him—but he couldn't quite get there. "Are you serious, Laurie?"

"You should have seen her the other day down at the park," Laurie said. "She was out of control. She threw rocks at some girl and hurt her, made her cry. And then she wouldn't listen when Liz called her over."

"The other girl threw rocks first!" Susan countered.

Laurie glared at her daughter. "No talk backs."

"It's not fair!"

"Hush up for a second, Susan," Ted told her. "Laurie, what exactly happened?"

"Just what I said. She was out of control, and she's certainly not the type of girl our daughter should be playing with."

"There's no one else here," Susan moaned.

"Susan knows better than to do what some other kid does." Ted was trying to be diplomatic, but Laurie thought he just sounded condescending. "She's old enough and smart enough to know right from wrong."

"You didn't see what I saw, Ted. This is not up for discussion. I've been thinking about it for a few days now." She turned back to Susan, whose eyes were red and glassy now. "Do you understand me? I forbid you to play with that girl."

Susan kicked one leg of the piano bench. "That's not fair! I hate it here!"

Laurie laughed. "You're the one who wanted to stay in this house." She looked at Ted. "The both of you."

"I hate it here and I hate *you*!" Susan shouted.

"Susan—"

"You're always so *mean*!" she cried, then took off down the hall.

Laurie shouted her daughter's name once more, demanding that she return to the room until she was excused, but Susan's footfalls were already pounding up the stairs. A moment later, the bedroom door slammed.

"Disrespectful brat," Laurie breathed.

"Hey." Ted stood from the bench and went over to her. When she tried to sidestep him, he gripped her by the wrist and tugged her toward him. "What the hell's the matter with you?"

"*Me?* Oh, that's rich. Our daughter's running wild, with no discipline whatsoever, and *I'm* the problem?" She jerked her wrist free of him.

"Susan is *not* running wild and she has *plenty* of discipline. She's a damn good kid and you need to loosen up a bit. Enough is enough, Laurie. We've both been very patient with you throughout this whole thing, but I can't sit idly by while—"

"*I'm* the mother and *she's* the child! It's not you and her against me, it's supposed to be you and me against *her*."

"No one needs to be against anyone."

"All you *do* is sit idly by. That's all you've ever done, leaving me to be the heavy. You play with her, you teach her piano, you have a great relationship, she hugs and kisses you, and that's wonderful for you, because Mommy's the bad guy. Mommy's the monster."

"That's incredibly unfair."

"And what the hell do you mean you've both been patient with me throughout all of this? My father died. What do you want, a medal?"

"Keep your voice down," he told her.

"If that girl comes by the house asking for Susan, you send her home. I don't want her coming around here."

She fled from the room before he could say another word. In the kitchen, she put the remaining slices of pizza in the fridge, then crushed up the pizza box and stuffed it in the trash. There was cold coffee in the pot on the stove. She poured some in a mug and heated it in the microwave. Her hands shook as she brought the mug to her lips.

Ted came in, a grim expression on his face. What bothered Laurie most was that he didn't look angry. It was how he had regarded her in the days after the highway incident—a combination of concern and pity. He folded his arms and wandered toward the kitchen table, looking like he contemplated pulling out one of the chairs, but remained standing in the end.

"Can I ask you something?" he said. The timbre of his voice matched the quality of his expression.

"What?" It came out in a bark.

"Are you planning to leave me?"

She set the mug of coffee on the counter but didn't answer. What surprised her was that Ted's question *didn't* surprise her. She couldn't quite say why that was . . . but she had sensed the tension between them for some time now, even before coming to this house.

"Don't take it out on Susan if this is really about us," he said.

"Ted—"

"And don't think I haven't noticed," he said, gesturing toward her. "You haven't been wearing your wedding ring. You haven't bothered to contact a realtor about selling the house. . . ."

"We just got the name and number from Liz the other night."

"Come on, Laurie. You didn't need to wait for Liz's friend's business card. You could have called someone on your own, someone else. And when I brought up selling the house, you brushed me off, but you wouldn't tell me why."

"You think I'm planning to leave you and move in here?" she said. The idea wasn't just absurd—it was frightening. The thought of staying here permanently, living in this house again. . . . It would be like being sucked into a vacuum and suffocating.

Ted dragged a chair away from the table but still

didn't sit in it. "I'm at a crossroads here, Laurie. I can't figure you out. It's like you're . . . punishing me. . . ."

She said nothing.

"I don't know if you want me to say it and put it out on the table, or if you rather I say nothing and you go on quietly torturing me."

And then suddenly she knew. "Don't say it," she told him. Her voice trembled.

"I had an affair, Laurie."

The *No!* she wanted to shout at him got caught halfway up her throat. She stood there with her mouth hanging open, no sound coming out.

"It was a stupid, selfish, careless thing. It's been over for a long time now and I haven't seen her since."

It was as though she were listening to him from the other side of a padded sanitarium wall. His voice was distant and her ears were plugged with balls of cotton.

"You've always been closed off to me, Laurie. You've kept your secrets and I've kept mine. But those secrets are breaking us apart. I'm telling you about what I've done because I want the admission to save us."

"I don't want to hear this."

"That's the problem! A year and a half ago, you and I were living two separate lives. That's no way to sustain a marriage and it's certainly no way to raise a little girl."

She couldn't look at him. Her face burning, her eyes leaking, she looked at the floor.

"I can only do my half, Laurie. We're a team. We're partners."

"Some team."

"We *both* need to come clean, Laurie. Not just me."

"I don't know what you're talking about."

"I'm talking about secrets. I've told you mine. Now you need to tell me yours. If we're going to survive it, we've got to be straight with each other. No more secrets, no more separate lives. We're one, Laurie. We've got to come clean."

"I've got no secrets. I've never had an affair. I've never cheated on you."

"Then what is it? It's something else."

"It's *nothing*!"

"Is it about your father? Or that girl? That . . . Sadie?"

"There's *nothing*!"

He released a shaky exhalation. The chair legs scraped across the floor as he slid it back toward the table. "Then we're both doomed," he said. His footsteps were nearly silent as he left the room.

You fucking creep, you fucking coward, she thought . . . yet she was unsure whether she meant Ted or herself. . . .

At the counter beside the sink, she looked down on the corroded items that still soaked in the acid bath. In the pot, the water had turned a milky greenish-yellow. She strained the water into the sink, then placed the cleaned items on the paper towel beside the others. The decapitated doll head glared blindly at her from the countertop. Laurie's hands shook. The metal backing of the brooch looked newer from the bath, but the cameo picture was gone forever; the blank white bulb on which it had been etched looked like a single eye, blind with cataract. The keys had come clean as well, though there were still remnants of calcification along the teeth and stuck in the grooves. Yet of all the items, it was the key with the number 58 engraved on it that held her attention.

When she returned to the parlor fifteen minutes later, the lights were off and the room was empty. She went down the hall and looked up the stairwell to the second-floor landing. The door to the master bedroom was shut, which meant Ted had gone to bed. *Bully for him.* She returned to the parlor to sleep on the sofa, but first she made sure all the doors were locked and all the windows were secure. She went upstairs and made sure the padlock was still on the belvedere door. If Abigail was getting in through the busted window, she at least wanted to make sure she couldn't get into the rest of the house. She checked the lock on the side door, too. Teresa Larosche's words ghosted up through the fog of her brain—*something about locking up the passageways, that passageways let it in and out like a turnstile. He actually said that—like a turnstile.*

Passageways. In her mind's eye, she saw Sadie scaling the tree and crawling out on the limb to peer down into her father's greenhouse. She saw her lose her balance and swing down off the limb, falling, falling. . . . The sound she made crashing through the glass roof of the greenhouse was like two automobiles colliding.

My secret is that I was happy you died, Sadie. You Hateful Beast, what do you want from me now? Have you come back to torture me some more? She peered out the window in the door, expecting Abigail to emerge from the darkness, her hair done up the same as Sadie's, wearing the same oversized and outmoded clothes, and pointing a damning finger at her.

* * *

The dreams that plagued her that night as she slept on the sofa were unforgiving in their brutality. Sadie made a guest appearance in a few of them, the flesh flayed from her face in gray and red ribbons. Her eyes were gelatinous white orbs that wept snotlike yellow fluid that congealed in her lashes. She wore one of her outdated checkerboard dresses, just as she had in real life. As Laurie gaped at her, the girl hiked the hem of the dress up to her chest. Her belly was a flat white canvas lacerated with startling crimson hash marks. Like Christ on the cross, a rib-exposing wound gaped along her left side. It suppurated a fluid as dark and fibrous as menstrual blood, the nearly black streaks ribboning down her hip, thigh, calf. A blackish discharge dribbled down her inner thighs.

I want to touch you and I want you to touch me, the Sadie-thing said, *and if you don't, I will wish horrible things to happen to your parents. I will wish them to die and you'll have no one left. You'll go to an orphanage, Laurie, and you'll be all alone for the rest of your life.*

And then Ted was there with Sadie, the two of them copulating like beasts, Ted's dark skin in perfect juxtaposition against the slick colorless white of Sadie's flesh. Ted humped and his back arched, each notch in his spine cut in sharp relief beneath his sweat-slickened flesh. As Laurie looked on, horrified, Sadie turned her head and grinned at her. Her teeth had been replaced with sparkling diamonds. Her eyes were black onyx stones.

I feel it in me, Sadie said just as a swarm of white moths burst from her diamond-encrusted mouth. *I feel it in me and it hurts, Laurie. It hurts.* The laughter that followed was not of this world.

Laurie made the grand discovery the following afternoon, just as Mr. McCall's movers were upstairs in the master bedroom disassembling the bedframe and a gnomish woman carried out the Wedgwood china, each piece individually wrapped in brown paper, from the curio in the dining room. The house was slowly being liberated of its last remaining clutter, leaving behind woundlike spaces where furniture had previously been. Laurie chose to think of it as a holy cleansing, a rebirth, a baptism.

Susan was out playing in the backyard. Alone. Abigail Evans hadn't come by and Laurie was silently grateful. Ted had left early that morning, while Laurie pretended to be asleep on the sofa, dressed in his running gear. He had been gone for hours now. He went running more frequently when he was having a difficult time with his writing, but also when there was trouble between them. That was preferable to his excessive drinking, which was his other crutch. She found she didn't care, and was thankful that the son of a bitch had taken to the streets while she'd slept instead of trying to confront her again. With them both gone—and with the exception of McCall's movers shuffling about upstairs while the gnomish woman (whose name Laurie had forgotten) scuttled back and forth from the dining room to the front door—the house was mostly silent.

The business card for Harmony Simmons, Liz's realtor friend, was still on the refrigerator. Laurie considered calling the number, if only to prove Ted wrong, and even went as far as picking the phone up off the wall, but then decided against it.

To hell with Ted. To hell with him.

One of McCall's men poked his head in through the kitchen door. He was a sturdy-looking dark-skinned fellow with the muddy black eyes of a hound. "We got the bedframe loaded in the truck, Mrs. Genarro. We're just gonna take the cabinet and then we'll be out of your hair."

McCall had decided to purchase the liquor cabinet as well, so Laurie had spent some time removing the liquor bottles—most of which were now empty—and placing them in a rough metropolis on the top of the piano. Laurie came out into the parlor and watched McCall's men work. One man—this one blond guy with hypnotizing blue eyes—tipped the cabinet into the waiting arms of the other man. Together, they maneuvered the item around the sofa, the loveseat, the piano, and out into the hall. Something clattered on the floor in their wake but the men didn't seem to notice. Laurie peered over the couch and saw it was the shattered picture frame and the folded photo of her father and his two business companions, which Ted had found in the sleeve of one of the record albums.

"Ma'am," one of the men called to her from the foyer.

Laurie hustled down the hall in time to open the front door for the two men. They grunted as they negotiated the cabinet out the door and down the porch steps. She followed them out—the day was overcast and the trees seemed to reach up and claw at the sky, desperate for rain—and tipped them four dollars each. When the truck pulled away, Laurie saw the Wedgwood woman standing behind it, peering down the open throat of the well. Ted hadn't closed it back up after his spelunking expedition. Laurie approached the woman—Martha? Marsha?—and saw the almost hypnotic appearance of her face.

She reached out and gently touched the woman's arm. "Are you okay?"

"This," said the woman as she jabbed a finger at the open well, "is very dangerous."

"Is it?"

The woman's pinched face turned toward her. Their noses were less than five inches apart and Laurie jerked her head back.

"You have a young daughter, don't you?"

"Yes. Susan."

"Very dangerous to keep this open like that," said the woman. "You should shut it up."

"We had a lid on it until yesterday. . . ." Laurie waved a hand over the plank of wood and clumps of bricks that lay strewn about in the grass beside the well.

The woman winced and turned her head away from the well's opening. "Smells like death down there, dear. It would be a smart idea to put the lid back on."

"Yes. Okay."

A smile suddenly creased the old woman's face. Her teeth looked like coffee beans. "I'll let you know how the china sells," said the woman. She was taking it on consignment and hadn't paid anything for it upfront.

"Thank you," said Laurie. She realized the woman

only had her father's phone number and address, but she didn't give the woman her cell number or contact info for the house in Hartford. *I don't care if that china sells for a billion dollars,* she thought. *Once I leave here, I want to cut all ties and not look back. Leave no tethers behind.*

"Good day," said the woman. She waddled to her car—a Ford Escort whose backseat was crammed with boxes—and drove away.

Laurie looked back down into the well. It had begun to fill back up with water, a cruddy brown soup ringed with frothy white bubbles. And it *did* smell like death— a rancid, raw sewage odor that stung her nose. Feeling cold, Laurie bent and replaced the cover on the well, setting the bricks down around the perimeter to secure it. When she was done, she went around the side of the house to check on Susan. The girl was playing by herself with some Barbie dolls, kneeling in the tall grass. Daisies bloomed all around her and Laurie suddenly wished she had brought her painting supplies. It would take her mind off things.

Back in the house, Laurie gathered up the broken picture frame and the folded photograph and set them both down on the piano top beside Ted's beloved liquor bottles. She contemplated dumping the remaining liquor out in the sink, the ancient bottles in the trash, then decided against it. There was a brownish watermark on the back of the old photo—a perfect stamped circle. She fingered it, then unfolded the photo. Her eyes were drawn to the same things as before—the three men standing before a row of garages while, in the background, the smokestacks of the mill rose up into a monochromatic sky. But then she noticed something she hadn't before . . . or, rather, she attributed more meaning to what she had previously seen. Maybe it was coincidental. Maybe it meant nothing at all. She couldn't tell for sure . . . yet her eyes were drawn to it nonetheless. . . .

The garage doors were all numbered—big numbers stenciled on the corrugated metal doors in white paint. There were seven garage doors depicted here, the numbers on the bay doors ascending until they disappeared off the edge of the photograph. The door on the far right was cut in half by the frayed edge of the photo, but she could still make out the number painted on it, just as clearly as she could make out the chunky padlock on the door's handle. The number on the door matched the number engraved on the key she had found in the body of the baby doll. Fifty-eight.

She waited until after dinner to leave. There were a few reasons for this. To begin with, she didn't want to get caught in rush hour traffic along the Key Bridge, and although Derrick Rosewood had mentioned that much of Sparrows Point was an empty wasteland, she didn't want to run into anyone working out there who might question her trespass. Also, she feared she might look like a lunatic sprinting out of the house the second Ted came home from his run. More than that, she didn't want to make it look like she was fleeing from him; she didn't want him to think she was being a coward. So she went about the rest of the day like someone who had been granted a peek into the future on the pretense that she couldn't share what she had seen with anyone else. Susan was back to her old self—children have short memories—but Ted had been cold to her since their argument last night. She found herself wanting to hate him, but she was only capable of hating herself.

After dinner, Ted and Susan settled together on the sofa to watch a DVD. Laurie pinched the car keys from the kitchen counter and told them she was going out for a while. On his third drink of the evening, Ted had given up trying to rationalize with her. His response was merely an acknowledging nod of his head to show that he had heard her.

CHAPTER 25

Laurie took 695 East and found herself encroaching on the tail end of rush hour. At one point, she pulled onto the shoulder of the road and cried into a wad of tissues. The spell lasted just a few minutes, but when she finished she was completely exhausted. All her strength had been siphoned from her.

It was already a quarter to eight when she got off at the Sparrows Point exit. Beyond the raised concrete ramps of the beltway, sunlight speared through the trees and between the row homes as the sun sank slowly on the far side of the Chesapeake. The commercial shopping centers, restaurants, and housing developments that had flanked various portions of the beltway had vanished; she was now surrounded by sloping gravel pits, cyclone fences, and the occasional bulldozer tucked beneath an exit ramp like a slumbering dragon.

The road narrowed to a single lane. To her right, behind a chain-link fence capped in concertina wire, stood a single-story concrete building with unmarked white trucks in the parking lot. The only sign was a blinking red neon notice behind a panel of smoked glass that read DEPOT CLOSED.

The air smelled fishy. She rolled up the windows and turned on the A/C. Up ahead, orange road cones rose up on the shoulder of the single-lane road. As she approached a slight incline, she could see construction signs dotting the horizon. Yet as she crossed up and over the crest of the road, there were no road crews at work. The construction equipment that stood in the grassy median looked like it had been expediently evacuated in the moments before a nuclear holocaust.

Directly ahead was the wasteland industrial park of Sparrows Point. Along the shore were cargo ports crowded with dark ships that belched smoke into the air and, at the horizon, Laurie could make out the schizophrenic jumble of ductwork and pipes. On the other side of the road stood a complex of redbrick apartments with bars on the windows and a fire escape zigzagging from window to window all the way to the ground. Blinking red lights told Laurie which side roads were off limits. She continued driving until the factories rose up to greet her. They stood like medieval fortresses along the ramparts of the bay, their smokestacks like prison towers, their massive parking lots the color of moat water in the fading daylight. Beacons winked intermittently from the tops of the smokestacks, a warning to careless low-flying aircraft.

Laurie pulled along the shoulder and put the car in park. Her purse was beside her on the passenger seat. She opened it, took out the old photograph, and unfolded it. She wasn't sure exactly where this particular lot was located, and she had no addresses to go by. Instead, she held the photo up and peered past it through the windshield at the crenellated silhouettes of factories along the cusp of the water. She wasn't sure if the water itself was the Chesapeake Bay or one of its tributaries, though with dusk creeping up over the east, it looked expansive enough to be the goddamned Atlantic Ocean. Cargo ships were black specks dotted with Christmas-colored lights far off in the distance.

She thought she recognized the same arrangement of smokestacks in the photo down one of the closed-off access roads. There was an arm-bar blocking the gravel road and a construction barrel equipped with a blinking orange hazard light on the shoulder, but she thought she could hop the grassy hillock beyond the barrel and make her way around it. She switched the Volvo back into drive, spun the wheel, and eased the vehicle up the slight grassy incline of the shoulder. It was a tight squeeze maneuvering the boxy Volvo between the construction barrel and a chain-link fence woven with leafy veins of ivy, but she managed. When she cleared the barrel and the arm-bar, she negotiated back onto the roadway to find the surface bumpy and irregular. The Volvo's steering wheel vibrated in her hands. She tightened her grip on it.

To her right, the factories' smokestacks seemed to have repositioned themselves. She continued along the roadway, slowing down each time a dirt road branched off from it, cutting through the shallow scrim of trees toward the factories and ports. Any one of those dirt service roads could lead her to where she wanted to go. For all she knew, the road she was currently on might dead-end at the cusp of the bay.

She cranked the wheel to the right and took the service road. It proved even bumpier than the previous

road. Tree limbs reached down and scraped the Volvo's
hood. Through the tangle of branches she could see a
thumbnail moon surrounded by many stars.

Just when she thought she had made the wrong
choice—that the service road was actually a conveyor
belt in the middle of the cosmos on which she could
drive and drive and never reach a destination—the trees
parted and the Volvo's headlights fell upon a NO TRES-
PASSING sign the size of an interstate billboard. Beyond
the sign stood a high fence dressed in more concertina wire. Beyond the fence, and at the end of a paved
parking lot that looked like the reflection of the night
sky, were the rambling concrete structures of the factories themselves. The ones in the distance still trailed
white gossamer from their smokestacks, but the ones
here along the point—with the exception of the red and
green blinking lights at the top of the stacks—looked
desolate. They could have been factories on the moon,
for all Laurie could tell.

Again, Laurie compared the photograph to the factories on the other side of the fence. A series of smokestacks midway through the rank of stacks matched up
to the ones in the photo.

Bingo.

The fence was locked, the gates wrapped up in a tight
ball of industrial chain and several padlocks. But age or
vandals—or a combination of the two—had seen fit to
smash a ragged hole in the meshwork a few yards from
the entry point. The opening didn't look large enough
to accommodate the Volvo—not without submitting the
vehicle to potential damage, anyway—but she could
certainly pass through it on foot. Yet the thought of

doing so frightened her. The parking lot itself looked at least a quarter of a mile long, and while there were industrial-sized vapor lamps at intervals throughout the parking lot, none of the lamps were working. It was as dark as infinite space. And once she reached the factories themselves . . . what hideousness might be lying in wait for her there? After all, it had been Sadie— Abigail—who had led her out here. Was she willing to trust the child?

The Vengeance, she thought. *The Hateful Beast.*

Still, she believed she had found that key at the bottom of the well for a reason. The fact that the number carved onto it matched the garage number in her father's photograph—a photograph her father had deliberately hidden in the sleeve of a record album—couldn't just be coincidence.

Laurie got out of the car. The air was acrid with pollutants from the steamships and the factories. Beneath her feet the ground seemed to rumble with the pulse of invisible machinery. Her ears picked up a motorized whine emanating from someplace nearby; her mind flashed images of great earth-moving cogs and wheels, of a system of pulleys and ropes just below the surface of the earth, keeping nature in harmony with itself. One careless move on her part could upset the whole balance of the universe. As it was, she felt as though she had inadvertently stepped through a tear in the fabric of space and time—that she was both simultaneously in the past and the future, watching herself from various different angles all at once.

It was silly, of course. She was standing in the woods at the cusp of a rundown industrial park with a key

in the hip pocket of her jeans and an old photograph
in her hand. The only thing momentous about all of
this was the fact that she would have to explain her
whereabouts to Ted when she eventually came home.
She folded the photo and stuffed it in her back pocket.
Crouching down, she crept beneath low branches while
snagging her feet on brambles. Things very close to her
that had been hiding in the woods took to their feet—or
hooves—and trampled through the underbrush. One of
them sounded disconcertingly large.

The opening in the fence was indeed large enough
for her to pass through, though she did so heedful of
the broken, rusty corkscrews of metal that practically
hummed with tetanus. She didn't see the small ravine
on the other side of the fence until she planted one foot
down into it. She managed to grab a handful of the fence
before she fell. Cold water instantly soaked through her
sneaker, her sock, and the cuff of her pant leg.

By the time she climbed up out of the ravine, grasping at tangles of weeds for handholds, and onto the solid
ground of the parking lot, she already felt bested. Invisible flies droned around her head and she was sweating
profusely. Although she was thin for her size, she rarely
did any cardio and was already wheezing for breath.
Yet here she was: She had been allowed admittance.

The walk across the parking lot felt like it took forever. Her footfalls were hollow thuds that seemed to
echo out over the bay while her labored respiration
found a rhythm similar to the underground droning of
machinery. *I'm being assimilated.* Once, she thought
someone was following her. When she stopped and
looked around, she could see no one—she was the soli-

tary island in the sea of black asphalt—but she was still not one hundred percent convinced. If Sadie Russ could come back as Abigail Evans and murder her father, was anything truly off limits?

The factories loomed over her as she approached. They were tremendous beasts, spewing fetid breath from smokestacks into the black night while glaring at her from blinking red and green eyes. At the end of the parking lot, a second fence circumnavigated the factory grounds. This fence was lower and she could have climbed over it easily enough if she had to, but she decided to walk its length and see if there was an easier way in.

There was—an open gate through which passed a stamped concrete walkway. She went through the gate and followed the walkway between two skyscraper-tall buildings. The buildings may have looked abandoned and out of use, but she thought she could hear electrical currents pulsing behind their steel and brick walls. *Old buildings have ghosts, too. Machines are living things with souls. They're in there right now, crying out to me. They're no different than people.* For whatever reason, this made her think of Sadie Russ's headstone in the cemetery behind the park.

The walkway emptied into another parking area. There were storage sheds along the far side of the lot, and beyond the sheds she could see the silhouette of the Key Bridge backlit by a lavender sunset. She took the photo from her pocket and examined it again. Frowning, she realized the walkway had led her around to the wrong side of the building. Well, she was here now, so she continued in the direction she had been headed.

She passed large sunken bays at the bottom of a concrete slope. There were old tractor trailers here, tagged with graffiti and leprous with rust. The windows along this side of the building were pebbled and situated behind wire meshwork. Over one iron door, a faded sign read LOADING. Over a similar door . . . well, the sign was missing, but she assumed it wasn't out of the realm of possibility that it had at one time read UNLOADING.

Out of nowhere, she felt giddy. Christ, she almost felt *good*.

The row of garage doors began halfway down this side of the building. There were sodium lights above some of them, casting sickly yellow puddles onto the ground. The first garage had a 12 on the door—faded but still legible. It was followed sequentially by 13, 14, 15, and the like. She had no idea what had happened to 1 through 11, but didn't waste time worrying about it. Some had padlocks on the handles and some didn't. Seeing the garage doors in real life, something occurred to her that she hadn't realized when she'd first seen them in the photograph. The doors were about the same size as a standard garage door on a house, but these sons of bitches looked like they were made of corrugated steel. They looked *heavy*. Even if the key in her pocket fit the padlock on door 58, she doubted her ability to open it on her own.

At door 22, the walkway gave way to a swampy pool of dark, stagnant mud. She climbed overtop a series of propane tanks and dropped down onto gritty cement on the other side. Along the coastline, great steel crates were stacked like monstrous Legos. Directly above her, long metal chutes that reminded her of log flumes deviated from a single iron turret. There was writing on the side of the turret but she couldn't make it out in the dark. The chutes crossed the gap from this building to the surrounding ones, to include a structure that looked like a water tower emblazoned with graffiti.

A shadow retreated from the walkway and disappeared into the darkness. Laurie caught it in her peripheral vision and whipped her head around to follow its retreat. But the darkness was too great to see beyond the pooling sodium lights.

"Abigail?" she said, her voice shaking. She would have thought speaking the child's name aloud in this place would have made her feel foolish, but it didn't. She was frightened. "Is it . . . Sadie?"

No figure emerged. No sounds came through the dark.

It's my overworked imagination. That's all.

She hoped.

On the far side of the building, the numbers on the doors jumped from 32 to 45. This was just fine with Laurie, since the muscles in her legs were beginning to ache. Overhead, the looming smokestacks had once again assembled themselves into position so that they looked just like their counterparts in the old photograph. Laurie felt something flutter at the back of her throat. She walked across metal steam grates—she could hear industrial pumps working far down below, reminding her of the Morlocks in H. G. Wells's novel *The Time Machine*—and passed through an assemblage of concrete bollards before she found the door she had been searching for.

Garage 58 was no different than all the others, with

one exception—the padlock looked newer. The other padlocks she had seen had been great hulking blocks of rust that probably wouldn't open to any key in the known universe. While the padlock on 58 had suffered from some exposure to the elements, there was still some shine to it. Laurie felt a sinking feeling in the pit of her stomach. At that instant, she knew with certainty that the key in her pocket was not the key meant to fit this lock.

Regardless, she took the key from her pocket, slipped it into the padlock . . . and turned it.

The lock popped open.

It was the kind of door that slid open from left to right on a track. The track was corroded and uncooperative. And Laurie had been right—the door *was* heavy, but she was able to pry it partway open by administering incremental jerks on the handle. She stopped when the muscles in her arms felt like rubber. The door had opened only about a foot and a half. It was enough for her to squeeze through, even though the thought of doing so made her heart beat faster. Lightheadedness overtook her. When a cargo ship unleashed a bleat on an air horn far out on the bay, she nearly leapt out of her skin.

Once she had sufficiently calmed down, she turned back to the foot-and-a-half opening. The darkness inside was nearly a solid thing. Silently, she cursed herself for forgetting to bring a flashlight. What had she suspected, anyway? But then she remembered the fob on her keychain, the one she had gotten a few years ago from First National Bank of Hartford. It was a whistle—Ted called it a rape whistle—equipped with a tiny LED lightbulb. She fished the keys from her pocket and pressed the button that activated the light. She couldn't remember the last time she had used the light and she had never changed the battery, so she was fairly surprised when the light blinked on and carved a pencil-thin path through the opening in the garage door.

She squeezed through the opening and moved the miniscule beam of light around. The room itself was not much wider than the door. It was maybe twenty feet deep, though she couldn't tell for sure due to the amount of clutter in the place. Boxes and wooden crates were stacked nearly to the ceiling. Amputated machine parts lay strewn about like the bones of dinosaurs. Musty sheets made shapes in the gloom, causing her to guess at the items beneath. The whole garage stank of grease; she could actually taste it at the back of her throat.

I have no idea what I'm looking for. . . .

Had the key not worked—had it not fit the lock—she could have turned around and gone home, satisfied that this had all been one big conspiracy in her head, and that she was imagining everything. There would have been comfort in such a notion, even though it simultaneously put her sanity on the firing line.

She ran a hand along the wall, found the light switch, toggled it. Nothing happened.

Of course.

Her sneakers scuffed along the cement floor as she approached the nearest stack of boxes. The cardboard was brittle and shimmered behind a gauzy veil of cobwebs. When she opened the flaps of the top box, a spi-

der the size of a silver dollar scuttled out and dropped
to the floor. Laurie shrieked, her keychain jangling. The
spider darted between the slats in a crate and Laurie
toed the crate off to one side, grimacing.

The box was filled with tools. The boxes on either
side of it were filled with stacks of papers so old that
the pages were as brittle as autumn leaves and the
print had all but vanished. She spent the next twenty
minutes peering inside containers, lifting the lids off
wooden crates, and getting on her hands and knees to
gaze beneath sheet-covered antiquities. Nothing she
found struck her as out of place. After a bit, she went by
the opening in the door where the night air cooled her.
She coughed into one cupped hand and it felt like she'd
purged her lungs of a clot of sawdust.

There was a dusty leather album wedged between
several rusty aluminum paint cans. The album itself
wouldn't have garnered her attention had she not made
out the clear but faded name running down the spine—
LAURIE. She felt something flutter in her chest. As
she approached it, the light shook. She remembered the
album from her youth. The pages were construction paper on which she had drawn her earliest pictures. It had
been her first art book, and when she and her mother
had moved out of the house on Annapolis Road, Laurie
had thought it was lost forever.

Why is it here and not in the house? And then on the
heels of that, she thought, *Is this what I was meant to
find out here?*

She pried it off the shelf amidst a plume of dust.
There were orange rust stains on both the front and

back covers. Propping the album on one of the sheeted monstrosities, she opened the cover. The drawing on the first page was of a family—a father, a mother, a little girl. Big ear-to-ear smiles spread across all their faces. In the background was a house with a belvedere on the roof. The next few pages showed similar drawings. Then there came a parade of animals—sheep, cows, dogs, pigs, mice, horses. *Ponies,* she corrected her adult self. *Those aren't horses, they're ponies*. The clumsy print at the bottom of the page said LAURIE, AGE: 7. *It's true—I've stepped through a time warp. Hello, Alice, welcome to the rabbit hole*.

She turned the next page and found a drawing of two little girls. The drawing was crude—just a few levels above stick figures—but she knew the girls in the drawing as sure as she'd recognize her own reflection. One of the girls was her, the sandy hair made with jagged scribbles, the eyes too far apart on the circular head, the clothes sensible and drab. The other girl was Sadie. Sadie's hair had been done with both a brown and red crayon, blended to create a luxurious russet color. Sadie's dress was a blue-and-white checkerboard pattern. It was the same dress Abigail Evans had been wearing when Laurie first saw the girl running across the backyard.

Laurie turned the page, but there were no more drawings. If this was what she had been meant to find, its significance was lost on her. Just as she was about to close the scrapbook and slide it back onto the shelf, she realized that there was a manila envelope clipped to the inside back cover. She unfastened the clip, her fumbling fingers carving streaks through the layer of dust that coated the envelope. It was sealed, so she tore it open. A plume of dust wafted out.

She shook the items out onto the cover of the album—a series of photographs of various sizes, some taken with a Polaroid camera, others developed into eight-by-ten glossies, though these had dulled considerably with age. The photo that landed on top appeared to be a candid shot of a young girl, perhaps five or six years old, perched on a bench in a park or playground. The girl wasn't looking at the camera—her head was turned away so that her face was in profile—and something about the composition of the shot made Laurie uncomfortable. She did not recognize the girl in the photo . . . yet the cheap plastic doll the girl held in her lap was readily identifiable, even if all its features were now melted away, its nude plastic body veined with mold.

Laurie sifted through the other photos and found a similar theme in each of them—candid shots of little girls. They played in sandboxes, they climbed trees, they bounced up and down on seesaws. There were close to fifty photographs in all, many of the girls appearing in several photos. What was even more disturbing was that in these reappearances the girls were wearing different clothes, had their hair done up in a different fashion than the picture before. They weren't taken on the same day.

She began to feel ill. Hastily, she swiped the photos back into the envelope and was about to stick the envelop back inside the scrapbook, when her elbow struck one of the tin cans on the shelf. It fell over and rolled to the floor. The sound it made as it struck the cement was like a gunshot. She peered over the sheeted machine parts and saw the can roll in a half circle along the floor before it came to rest beside a faded tarp bound with rope. Laurie squeezed between the sheet-covered machine parts and kicked the can out of the way. The light from the key fob caught a constellation of mouse turds arcing across the concrete floor. Laurie bent down and pressed on the tarp. It crinkled but gave little resistance. Whatever was beneath it was soft.

The ropes were thick, but mice had been to work on them for some time, and they were held together by mere strands in places. Laurie used the Volvo's ignition key to saw through the remaining fibers. She tossed the ropes away, lifted one corner of the tarp, and directed the small beam of light beneath it.

More mouse droppings, dead crickets—the big striped ones with the arched backs that Ted called super crickets, or "sprickets" for short—and dried patches of what looked like motor oil littered the floor. When something shifted beneath the tarp, Laurie froze. *It's just a mouse, it's just a mouse, it's just a—*

A fat brown mouse scurried out from under the tarp, darted toward the tin can, then continued on toward the dark web of shadows behind the shelving unit. Watching it scurry away, Laurie felt herself breathe again. She turned back to the tarp and found a layer of quilts underneath. They were black with mold and stank like death.

She stood and took a step back. One of the ropes had gotten tangled around her right ankle, and when she took another step, she pulled the rope and another section of tarp with her. At first, the thing that was revealed looked like the twisted root of a tree jutting out between the bundles of quilts. When Laurie realized it was the skeletonized hand of a human being, she cried out.

PART III
IN THE HOUSE
OF MANY WINDOWS:
Sadie

CHAPTER 26

The girl's name was Tanya Albrecht, and she was eleven years old when she disappeared in 1989. School photographs showed a pretty but shy child, her plain brown hair done up in pigtails while owlish glasses exaggerated the largeness of her gray eyes. She wore braces. In two separate school photos taken a year apart, Tanya Albrecht wore the same floral-print dress with the rumpled lace collar. Her family did not have much money.

She was the third child in a family of five. Her father, Hal Albrecht, worked at one of the mills in Sparrows Point, and her mother, Hillary, had her hands full with the children. They lived in a row home in Dundalk, where the playgrounds were nothing but asphalt prison yards and the nearest elementary school had been repeatedly defaced by vandals. Their tiny row house had bars on the windows and Hal Albrecht had put up a BEWARE OF DOG sign on both the front and back doors, even though the Albrechts did not have a dog.

When she was nine, Tanya Albrecht had fallen out of a tree while trying to retrieve a Frisbee that had gotten snared in the branches. She broke her arm in two places. Had she been older, doctors would have mended the injury with metal plates and screws, but since Tanya was just nine years old and still growing, they hadn't wanted to impede the bones' growth. Tanya's arm was set in a cast that went from the base of her fingers all the way up to her shoulder, and she stayed in that cast for nearly four months. After it healed, she often complained to her father that the arm was sore, particularly on cold and rainy days, but she never seemed depressed about it. Aside from her inherent shyness, Tanya was no different than any other girl her age. She joined a Brownie troop with her sister June and they sold cookies door-to-door throughout the rundown Dundalk neighborhood to earn badges for her brown sash. Her grades were average and she had a few friends who would sometimes ride the school bus home with her so they could play in the Albrechts' postage-stamp backyard, or across the street in the salvage yards. The salvage yards were off limits to kids, secured behind twenty-foot chain-link fences adorned with signs warning that ALL TESPASSERS WILL BE PROSECUTED! These signs, which were riddled with bullet holes, didn't keep out the neighborhood kids—and a few of the neighborhood drunks, too—and there were plenty of interesting things to find while hunting around the salvage yards. When Tanya disappeared in the spring of 1989, the salvage yards were the first place local cops went to search for her body.

In 1988, Hal Albrecht was laid off from his job at the steel mill. He put on a good face and even fantasized about picking his family up and moving them out of Dundalk and away from Sparrows Point for good. He

said he'd like to go to Florida, which is where some
older friends of his had relocated after retirement. But
Hal hadn't retired—he'd been laid off in the wake of
big changes in the industry. He needed to find another
job, just as most of his coworkers needed to find other
jobs after facing similar layoffs. Hal did not have a
college education—he'd just barely made it through
high school—and the job search in 1989, despite eco-
nomic prosperity for much of the country at that time,
was demoralizing. Hillary Albrecht began taking in
"homework"—mending dresses, suits, slacks for local
neighbors who felt sorry for them—as did their eldest
daughter, Caroline. Hal got a job working nights at a
7-Eleven while going on job interviews during the day.
On weekends, and because he knew some of the dock-
hands from his days at the mill, he picked up some
hours at the shipyards. It was untaxed pay, under the table as they say, and although it helped put food on their
table and while Hal was genuinely grateful, he didn't
know how long he could keep up such a sleep-deprived
schedule. As it turned out, he maintained that impossible schedule up until the day his daughter disappeared.

On April 28, 1989, around eleven-thirty in the morning, Hillary Albrecht handed a brown paper bag to her
daughter Tanya. It was Hal's lunch, which he had forgotten to take with him to the shipyard that morning—
a corned beef sandwich, a plastic cup of apple sauce,
a wedge of apple streusel wrapped in cellophane that
Hillary had baked the night before, and a can of Diet
Coke. It was not the first time Tanya—or one of the
other girls—had to run lunch to their father. The man
had become a roving zombie and he had begun to for-

get a good many things, Hillary knew, and the thought was not without compassion.

"You know the way to go," Hillary said to Tanya as the girl pulled on her sneakers at the kitchen table, her father's brown bag lunch balanced in the crook of her lap.

"Yes," Tanya said, exasperated. They had gone through this a hundred times before. "Be like Dorothy. I remember."

To "be like Dorothy" meant that once she crossed Kingland Terrace and stepped foot into the industrial park, she was to locate the cement path that had been spray-painted bright yellow—the "yellow brick road"—until she reached the bank of terminals down at the port. To veer off the yellow brick road could be dangerous—there were too many things out there that eagerly awaited the nimble fingers and tasty toes of a curious young girl.

Hillary watched her daughter lace her sneakers while she cleaned the countertop. Later, when describing to police what her daughter had been wearing, she told them of the sneakers. They were fake Chuck Taylor's— the Albrechts could not afford real ones—which the kids endearingly referred to behind their parents' backs as "Fucks." Before leaving, Tanya offered her mother a sweet smile. Hillary knew her daughter might never be what society considered a "real beauty"—June was the prettiest of the three girls, at least in the traditional sense—but Tanya had a brilliance inside of her that sometimes managed to shine out, usually when you least expected it. Her smile held that brilliance, radiating it across the tiny kitchenette in the Dundalk row house. And although she had no idea why, Hillary forced herself to take a mental snapshot of that smile, impressing it upon her brain the way prehistoric bugs impressed themselves into sediment which, over millennia, fossilized to permanence. It was the last time Hillary Albrecht would see that smile.

The last person on record to see Tanya Albrecht alive was a man named Chester Karski. Karski lived by himself in a one-bedroom flat on the corner of Kingland Terrace and Highpoint Boulevard. His front windows faced Highpoint, which was a crumbling tributary of a roadway through which patches of blond grass sprouted in the summer. His single bedroom window looked out upon the more nicely paved blacktop of Kingland Terrace and the plateau of parking lots of Sparrows Point beyond. This section of Kingland ran beneath an overpass—one of the extensions off the Key Bridge—and even in broad daylight, Karski could see people moving around beneath the shade of the overpass, no doubt up to no good. On this particular afternoon, Karski had been sweeping grit off his front porch when little Tanya Albrecht came walking up the street. She was carrying a brown paper satchel and wore a pleasing little smile on her face. From where he stood on his porch, Karski could hear the girl humming happily to herself while she kicked the occasional pebble out of the road.

"Hi there, Dorothy!" he called to her. "On your way to see the great and powerful Oz?" Chester Karski was in on the yellow brick road game; he had walked it a few times in his life, too, back before he retired from the shipyards.

"Yes, Mr. Karski!" Tanya called back. "My dad forgot his lunch again!"

"You tell him I said hello."

"I will."

"And you be careful, darling, crossing that road."

"I will!" She raised a hand high and waved it back and forth over her head.

Karski returned the gesture. When the girl reached the intersection of Highpoint and Kingland, Karski paused in his sweeping to make sure the girl made it across safely. He did not realize he'd been holding his breath until she reached the opposite side of Kingland. Yet it wasn't the road Karski worried about. As Tanya crossed beneath the shade of the overpass, Karski went back inside his house, down the hall, and into the bedroom. He peeled the plastic shade away from the window and peered out. Tanya was a speck on the roadway, her shadow stretched out of shape and trailing behind her on the pavement. Karski averted his eyes, peering now into the dark depths beneath the overpass. It was just about noon, still a bit early for the hoodlums to take up residence beneath the overpass, but that didn't mean some strung-out crackhead hadn't spent the night down there. *She shouldn't walk through there on her own. Not at her age. She's a little bit of a thing.* On this morning, however, Chester Karski could see no one. By all appearances, it seemed the Albrecht girl was alone. It gave Karski much relief.

Tanya never made it to the bank of terminals down by the port. In fact, there was no evidence Tanya ever crossed onto the factory grounds. Had the overpass not been there, and had Chester Karski kept watching out his bedroom window, he might have seen what had happened to the girl. But the overpass *was* there, and by the time Tanya Albrecht had encountered her abductor, Charles Karski was making himself a peanut butter and jelly sandwich for lunch.

After an hour had passed without Tanya's return, Hillary went out onto the porch and peered down Kingland Terrace toward the intersection of Kingland and Highpoint. She saw no sign of her daughter, although this did not worry her. It wasn't unusual for one of the girls to spend the lunch hour with their father before heading home. But when another hour ticked by, Hillary began to worry. Again, she went out onto the porch and looked toward the intersection. Again, there was no sign of Tanya. This was when panic set in. Even if the girl had decided to share her father's lunch, she should have been back by now.

Hillary called Merle Daniels, who rode dispatch in the shipyard's front office. Yeah, Hal was still on the docks. No, he hadn't seen Tanya come through. Sure, he supposed Tanya could have gotten through without him noticing—"It ain't like I'm Saint Peter keeping guard over the Pearly Gates, Mrs. A," he said—and promised he'd check with Hal and call her right back.

When the phone rang five minutes later, it wasn't Merle Daniels, but Hal himself. "No, I worked through lunch and never saw her," he said. "What time did she leave the house?"

Hillary told him.

"Maybe she cut a detour over to the Barrows' place,"

Hal suggested, though his own voice did not sound very hopeful. Tanya was friends with Jennifer and Anne Barrow.

"Maybe," Hillary said, twisting the phone cord around her index finger. The silence that followed this comment hung between both of them like the aftermath of some tremendous explosion. "I think—"

"Call the Barrows," Hal said. "If she ain't there, let me know, and I'll come home."

Tanya wasn't at the Barrows' house. Gloria Barrow answered the phone and advised that she hadn't seen Tanya all morning, and that her own two girls were up in their bedroom playing Chutes and Ladders. Hillary thanked Gloria, hung up the phone, and once again found herself talking to Merle Daniels in the dispatch office. This time, even Merle sounded unnerved. "I'm sure she's fine, Mrs. A," he promised her, though Hillary thought she sensed a different truth in his voice.

Hal arrived home ten minutes later. By this time, the two other Albrecht daughters were standing with their mother on the porch while, in the kitchen, the two Albrecht boys ate late lunches of tuna fish sandwiches and chocolate milk. Hal drove around the neighborhood in his Ford pickup, cruising down every dead-end street and alleyway. He must have crossed over Kingland Terrace five or six times. Once he reached the old railroad tracks, it felt like his stomach was full of live snakes. He didn't want to head home; he thought heading home would be akin to accepting this horrible reality, and he didn't want to accept it. Yet he knew the police would have to be called. Had it been one of his older daughters, he might have neglected to call the cops, choosing to wait for his daughter's return in a folding chair on the front porch, a Camel smoldering between his lips, a switch from the birch tree out back in his hands. Hell, June and Caroline missed their curfew three nights out of the week on average, and couldn't be counted on to show up for dinner without rolling through some tall tale about why they were late. Tanya, on the other hand, was never late. She respected her curfews—she respected her *parents*—and she was not apt to get caught up along the way like her sisters. Which was why Hal Albrecht had a very bad feeling when he ultimately turned the pickup truck around and headed back toward Highpoint Boulevard.

His bad feeling only increased when, halfway down Montclair Street, he saw a crumpled brown paper bag on the side of the road. Hal pulled over, got out of the truck, and picked up the bag. He opened it. Had it not been for the block of apple streusel wrapped in cellophane that Hillary had baked the night before, he might not have broken into a full-fledged panic.

The cops arrived at the Albrecht house at approximately 3:45 P.M. Hillary gave the officers a description of the clothes Tanya had been wearing while Caroline hunted for some recent photos of the girl. The officers took a lot of notes then radioed in for assistance. Caroline turned over a few school photos of Tanya to the officers. Since this was a time before AMBER Alerts, the best the officers could do was issue a BOLO through dispatch with the girl's descriptors. When a second patrol car showed up, rack lights flashing, the officers took to the streets. Hal got back into his pickup truck, along with Tom Murray and Will Williams, and resumed his own search. A few of the other neighbors began walking through the neighborhood, which was not a particularly good neighborhood to walk through after the sun went down. Two more officers went door-to-door, asking residents if they had seen Tanya Albrecht that afternoon. The officers only got one confirmed sighting, from Chester Karski. In the days that followed, Karski would be the closest thing the county police had to a suspect in the disappearance. Karski knew they were suspicious of him, but he also knew that he had done nothing wrong. If it took subjecting himself to the cops' redundant questioning in order to put them back on the right track and find Tanya Albrecht, so be it. He was interrogated—*interviewed,* the police detectives called it, always a friendly smile on their face—three times. The third time, Karski brought his rabbi with him, a wizened relic in a black tunic who spoke with a heavy Polish accent. Throughout the *interview,* the rabbi said nothing. Karski was amiable enough, answering all of their questions . . . or at least the ones he was able to answer. Yes, he had seen the Albrecht girl earlier that day. Yes, he had spoken to her. Yes, she had spoken back. No, the Albrecht girl had never been in his home. Yes, the police were more than welcome to search his one-bedroom flat. No, they wouldn't even need a warrant—he would give them permission. When the interview was over, Karski left without a word, feeling the worse for wear. His rabbi followed him out, saying, "Shalom" to the detectives as he went.

Karski's house was searched, but no evidence was uncovered. He was officially dropped as a suspect . . . which meant the police no longer *had* a suspect. At one point, the FBI was notified, but details of what they accomplished—if anything—were vague at best. The only other piece of evidence ever uncovered in the case was one of Tanya Albrecht's imitation Chuck Taylor's, lying in a muddy ditch on the side of Kingland Terrace, only a few yards from the overpass. There were no tire tracks in the dirt, no burnt rubber on the pavement, and no additional signs of a struggle. Briefly, the neighborhood hummed with speculation that the Albrecht girl had possibly known her abductor. More locals were questioned by police, but these were all longshots that proved fruitless. In 1993, the Albrecht family relocated to Baltimore after Hal got a job with Domino Sugar. The new tenants that moved into their Highpoint Boulevard row home agreed to keep a laminated sign on their front door. It read:

Tanya baby we moved to a new house in baltmore.
We didnt never give up lookin for you. We always love you.
You come find your way home you come to the new house
We got your old bed and all your toys here waiting for you Tanya baby.
We love you!

The Albrechts' new address was printed below this note.

By all accounts, the new tenants left the little laminated sign on the front door until they were evicted in 1998.

CHAPTER 27

It was Detective Freeling who told Laurie Genarro this information. Of course, he hadn't been one of the detectives to work the case—in 1989, Freeling hadn't even been on the force yet—but he was familiar with it, and brought with him the original case file. Inside the file were several witness reports, along with the school photos of Tanya Albrecht that had been provided to the officers that night by her older sister Caroline. Laurie asked to see the photos, which Detective Freeling handed over with hesitation. The girl looked fragile, hopeless. For some reason, Laurie thought she also looked familiar. She thought of the skeletonized hand poking out from the tarp back in the godless, industrial mausoleum of garage 58, and shivered.

It was closing in on midnight. Laurie, Ted, and Detective Freeling sat around the kitchen table while three cups of coffee sat untouched and cooling in front of them. Susan had already gone to bed by the time Laurie had come back home, and the girl had slept through the detective's assertive pounding on the front door. Laurie had waited to call the police until she arrived back home, her mind incapable of putting all the pieces together due to the strength of her disbelief until she was back in the house. Now, the house seemed preternaturally quiet. Laurie wished someone would speak again, but at the same time, she did not want to hear anything else Detective Freeling might have to tell her.

"Of course," the detective said after a while, "we won't be one hundred percent sure until her dental records are examined. But the arm—the one she had broken in two places when she fell out of the tree at age nine—still shows signs of the fractures. The body is badly decomposed, but the size of the remains looks to be about the right age. And, of course, there was the other sneaker."

The other imitation Converse sneaker had been uncovered about an hour ago, as a search team went through the rest of the garage. It left little doubt.

"Will the family be notified?" Laurie asked.

"We're tracking them down at the moment. It looks like Hal, the father, died a couple of years ago. Mesothelioma or something, I think. Last known address was some place out in Woodlawn. The kids would all be grown and moved on by now."

"So who actually owns that garage unit?" Ted asked.

"Well," Detective Freeling said, "that's where it gets mucky. Company called Bartwell owns the land, including the shipyards, but leases the buildings—including those garages—to some Russian corporation, who has been working out of there since 2008 or so."

"Russian?" Ted said.

Detective Freeling shrugged. "It's not unusual. Hell, back in oh-six, George W wanted to sell off the whole goddamn Port of Baltimore to Dubai, for Christ's sake. It was big news around here." He sipped some of the lukewarm coffee.

"Aren't there any records to show who owned it back then?" Laurie asked. "Back in 1989 when Tanya Albrecht disappeared?"

Detective Freeling's lips narrowed and his eyebrows arched. He looked passively over the paperwork from the Albrecht girl's case file that was spread out across the table. "I wouldn't get your hopes up about that."

"It was his," she said flatly. "My father's."

She remembered the photo in her back pocket and handed it over to Detective Freeling now. The detective looked at it closely, flipped it around to glance at the back, then set the photograph on the table.

"That was with my father's stuff," she said. She pointed to the door with the 58 painted on it. "That's it right there."

"It could have gone through a dozen different hands since then," Ted offered, but even he didn't sound convinced.

We all know the score, she thought. *Are we trying to kid each other?*

"You said yourself there had been speculation that Tanya Albrecht might have known her abductor," she said to Detective Freeling. "My father sold his share of the mill and retired sometime in the early eighties, but he would still have known some of the folks working there in 1989. He knew the layout of the property, knew the workers . . . but he lived out here, removed enough from their society to be forgotten."

"But what reason would he have to abduct the girl?"

Ted said. He was trying damn hard to not only convince her but to convince himself, Laurie could tell.

"What reason does *anyone* have for abducting and murdering *anyone?*" she retorted. "It would have been so easy. He lived here alone, no one ever came to visit him, and he had access to that whole facility even after he'd left. Maybe her death was an accident—I don't think it was, but I guess it's possible—and he just stowed her away in that garage. Maybe he meant to go back for her once things settled down. And maybe enough time finally passes and he figures, what the hell, and leaves her in there to rot." A final thought struck her like a mallet to a gong. "Maybe he even *forgot* about her. After all that time, I mean. The dementia . . ." She looked intently at Ted. "Maybe that's why he had been tearing this house apart. Maybe he was looking for the key, but in his dementia, he had forgotten what he'd done with it."

It felt like bolts tumbling into place inside her head.

"Laurie . . ." Ted stood up.

"Wait." She lashed out and gripped him just above the wrist. "The last phone call I had with him back in Hartford. He began talking nonsensically, or so I thought at the time—"

"Laurie, he was *sick*."

"He called me Tanya," she said. "Twice. On the phone. I didn't think anything of it then—who would?—but now . . ."

Ted went silent. Slowly, he lowered himself back in his chair. Across the table, Detective Freeling's eyes volleyed between the two of them. After a moment, he said, "Mrs. Genarro, are you sure about that?"

"As sure as I am sitting here. As sure as there's the body of a dead girl in that garage in Sparrows Point." But then she paused. She glanced down at the open case file and at one of the old school photos of Tanya Albrecht. "I've seen this girl before," Laurie said.

One of Freeling's eyebrows arched. "Yeah?"

"Hold on." She stood up and left the room. When she returned less than two minutes later, she carried with her Myles Brashear's photo album. She set the album on the table, opened it, and flipped to the appropriate page. "Here," she said, pointing to the photograph of a young girl peeking out from beneath the shade of a highway overpass. "That's her. That's Tanya Albrecht."

Freeling spun the album around so that he could get a better view of the photo. He said nothing as he looked at it, although the exhalations from his flared nostrils were quite loud.

"Holy Christ," Ted muttered. He looked ill.

"Yeah," Detective Freeling said eventually. He nodded, though he seemed saddened to do it. "Yeah, that's her, all right."

"I think there's more, too," Laurie said. She went to her purse on the counter and dug out the manila envelope she had found clipped to the back of her childhood scrapbook back in that horrible place. She opened it and upended it, scattering the photographs about the table. "Tanya wasn't the only girl I found back at that storage facility."

Both Ted and Detective Freeling picked up a photograph each. A deafening silence fell down upon them. It lasted for several heartbeats.

"Who are all these girls?" Ted said eventually, setting the photo down on the table.

Detective Freeling looked up at her. "These were with your father's stuff?"

"Yes."

"What does this mean?" Ted said.

"I know," Laurie said. "I know what it means."

When she didn't continue, Detective Freeling rubbed his forehead and, peering down at the display of photographs once more, said, "There were a rash of disappearances back in the eighties throughout the Delmarva area. All of them young girls. Nine, I believe, in all. Including Albrecht. None of them were ever found."

"He was stalking them," Laurie said. "Taking pictures."

"Jesus," Ted said. The word juddered out of him. "These can't be the same girls."

"There's eight different girls in all those photos," Laurie said. Then she pointed to the photo of Tanya in her father's album. "Tanya Albrecht makes nine."

Ted just shook his head. His eyes looked distant, unfocused.

"I'll need to take these as evidence," Detective Freeling said. "We can ID them at the station."

Laurie handed him the envelope.

With a sigh, Detective Freeling filed the papers into the case file and then closed it. Along with the photos of the girls, he had included the photograph of Laurie's father and the two other men, but she didn't protest. When he requested the photo of Tanya from the album, Laurie took it out from its plastic sleeve and handed it to him. He stared at it in unabashed amazement, then slid it, too, into the case file.

"I'd like to have you come down to the station tomorrow and give a formal statement," Detective Freeling said. "Whenever is most convenient for you."

She nodded. "Of course."

"I can't promise you what will come out in the newspapers in the next few days, though I presume you'll be heading back to Hartford sooner than later?"

"As soon as we have a realtor look at the house," Laurie said.

"These things can be . . . tough . . . on families." There was more than just a hint of compassion in Detective Freeling's voice. "I'm sure you understand."

Both Laurie and Ted nodded.

Detective Freeling stood. "I'll see myself out. And of course I'll keep you both apprised of anything else we uncover."

"Will you let me know if you're able to contact any of Tanya's relatives?"

"Sure."

"Thank you, detective."

Smiling wearily, the slender blue case file tucked beneath one arm, Detective Freeling wished them a good night.

"I don't know what to say," Ted said. When she didn't answer, he said, "I don't know what to do."

"Whatever you want," she said. She emptied the coffee cups in the sink, then wiped down the counter. Exhaustion pulled on her shoulders like a backpack full of sand. After leaving Sparrows Point in a fit of panic, she was halfway along the beltway toward home before she was able to regain some composure. When she had glanced up at her reflection in the rearview mirror, she wasn't at all surprised to find that she had been crying. Now, just a few hours later, that trip out to the desolate factories of Sparrows Point seemed like it had happened in another lifetime.

Ted stood up from the table. "Your mind must be reeling. I can't imagine what this is like for you."

"I don't need your compassion or your sympathy," she advised him. "This changes nothing between you and me."

"I'd like to talk about that, if you'll let me."

"I don't think so, Ted. It's very late and I've been through enough bullshit this evening."

"Maybe you should rethink coming with me on Friday. You and Susan."

"There's nothing to rethink. Susan and I will be fine here on our own. And I think you should leave tomorrow instead of waiting till Friday." She looked at the clock on the microwave. It was after midnight. "Today, I mean."

"I don't like the idea of leaving you two alone in this house."

"It isn't the house. There's no menacing spirit here. I'm a grown woman and I can take care of myself."

She threw the crusty dishrag in the sink. On the counter, the remaining items that had been recovered from the well still sat on the paper towel. There were half a dozen more keys among the swag. How many other doors were there? How many other locks waited to be opened? The possibilities were horrifying.

"At least let me come to the police station with you tomorrow," he said.

"I can handle that on my own."

"Laurie, you're being pigheaded."

"Am I?"

"Stop it. Please. Let's talk."

"I've got nothing to say to you."

Her back was toward him but she could hear him sigh loud enough. She knew the look that would be on his face—that hurt, pouty, boyish look of indignation. She had seen it plenty of times in the past.

"It's like you don't even care," he said. "Any other wife would have . . . would have asked questions about . . ."

She turned and smiled coolly at him. It took all her strength. "You want me to ask who she was? When it happened? How did it start?"

"At least we'd be talking."

"I don't want to know those things, Ted. I'm tired and I'm sad and I'm lonely. Thing is, I've been lonely for a while now. Why is it you care all of a sudden?"

"I've always cared."

"Have you?"

"Stop answering me with rhetoric."

She rinsed her hands beneath the faucet, then dried them off on a fresh dishtowel. The decapitated head of the plastic baby doll watched her from the counter with blank eye sockets. "You should get some rest if you're going to drive back tomorrow."

"I can leave Friday morning instead, just like we planned."

"We planned nothing."

"You know what I mean. Come on. Cut it out."

Folding her arms across her chest, she turned around to face him as she leaned back against the edge of the counter. "Here's the deal. You leave tomorrow for your big meeting. You stay there when it's done. Once I'm able to get a realtor out here to look at this place, Susan and I will take a train back. I'll use the money we've made already from the sale of the furniture, so you won't feel it in your bank account."

"This isn't about *money,* Laurie."

"No. It's about fidelity. Or your lack thereof. Either way, once Susan and I get back to Hartford, you and I can talk. I think that's reasonable. We've got a daughter to think about in all this, and it would do her no good for me to scream and shout and throw your shit out into the street. Which, truth be told, is what I'd really like to do."

There was nothing for him to say to this. He simply stared at her, a dumbstruck look on his face. For the first time since she had known him, he actually looked his age. There were dark patches beneath his eyes with spidery crow's feet at the corners. His skin looked sallow and nearly transparent. Blood vessels as thin as hairs networked across his cheeks. His appearance gave her some dark satisfaction.

"Okay," he said at last, and left the kitchen.

Though exhausted, she needed a shower. While under the tepid spray, she wept quietly for a full ten minutes, her sadness confused by the fusillade of betrayal she'd felt in the past forty-eight hours. A husband whose infidelity forced her to reexamine herself. A father whose black, unfathomable secrets had just floated to the surface. The only solace she found, which beckoned to her like the pinprick radiance of a distant star, was in the probability that she had been wrong about Abigail Evans after all. Sadie Russ had come back all right, but it hadn't been to continue tormenting and torturing her. She had come back to reveal a truth that had long been hidden—that her father had done unspeakable things to little girls. Perhaps it was Sadie's way of atoning for the evil she had brought unto Laurie when they had both been little girls. Perhaps this was Sadie Russ's salvation from beyond the grave. With some despondency, Laurie wondered what would happen to Abigail Evans now that Sadie's work was done. Would the girl return to her normal self, no longer the vessel needed for Sadie's handiwork? Or would the girl simply blink out of existence altogether, as if she had never truly existed in the first place?

CHAPTER 28

Ted left before noon. Laurie was asleep upstairs, on the mattress that had been left on the floor after McCall's haulers had taken the bedframe. Ted had spent the evening on the sofa downstairs, and he had already relocated his luggage to the foyer so that he wouldn't disturb Laurie when he left. As it was, she had already been awake for about an hour, hearing him fumble around downstairs, until she finally heard the front door open and close. A moment later, she heard the Volvo's engine start up. The urge to go to the window and watch his retreat was strong, but she resisted. Once the sound of the engine dissipated, she lay on the mattress staring at the shapes that seemed to coalesce then disengage in the stucco ceiling.

At two-thirty, an unmarked police car pulled up the driveway. A fresh-faced cop in a frumpy brown suit knocked on the front door. Laurie had just finished showering and her hair was still wet. She pulled her hair back into a short ponytail as she hurried to the front door.

"Hi, Mrs. Genarro. Detective Freeling said to pick you up and bring you to the station for your statement."

"I'm just a few minutes behind," she said, propping open the door and waving him inside. "Would you like something to drink?"

"No, ma'am." He spoke with a heavy Baltimore accent that stretched out his words and made them sound lazy. "I'm just fine, thank you."

Upstairs, she poked her head into Susan's bedroom. Susan sat on the edge of her bed lacing up her Keds. The girl looked despondent. Laurie wondered how much of the discussion her daughter had overheard last night.

"You okay, kiddo?"

"Tummy feels yucky."

"What's wrong with it?"

"It just feels yucky."

Laurie pressed her lips to the girl's forehead to gauge her temperature. "You don't feel hot."

Frowning, Susan shrugged.

"There's a cop downstairs waiting to take us to the police station. You ready to go?"

"Will he turn on the lights and sirens?"

"Probably not, but it wouldn't hurt to ask."

The cop, whose name was Freddy Shannon, did not turn on the lights and siren, though he did seem amused by the request. Instead, he let Susan sit up front and listen to the squawking radio while Laurie sat in the back.

"Have you ever been in a car chase?" Susan asked.

"Nope," Shannon said.

"Have you ever shot somebody?"

"Nope."

"Have you ever done that thing where you give somebody electric shocks?"

"You mean a Taser?"

"Yeah, that's it!"

"Nope."

"Oh. Well, have you ever seen a dead body?"

"Sure have," said Shannon brightly.

"Really? Oh, wow, was it all nasty like in the movies?"

Laurie cleared her throat and said, "Susan."

"No, ma'am," Shannon said to Susan, though his smiling eyes glanced up at Laurie in the rearview mirror. "Wasn't nasty at all."

"No?"

"Nope. Was quite peaceful and nice. The fella was done up in his favorite suit and tie and there were all these beautiful flowers all around him."

Susan made a face that suggested she smelled something awful. "Who was he?"

"Uncle Hubert," said Freddy Shannon. "Was a real nice funeral."

The police station was a squat redbrick building with flagpoles out front. Freddy Shannon led them inside, through a vestibule where women sat behind bulletproof glass, down a hallway carpeted in garish fire-retardant berber, and into a small office. The office was empty of personnel, but there were two desks piled high with clutter. A dry erase board hung from one wall, the ghosts of ancient cases still faintly visible despite having been erased. The only photo on the wall was of the governor.

"Can I get you guys a soda or something?" Shannon said.

"No, thanks," Laurie said before Susan could interject. "We're good."

"Detective Freeling got caught up with some other business, but he should be here in a couple of minutes."

"Thank you."

When Shannon left, Laurie sat down in one of the two empty chairs that faced the nearest desk. Susan went over to the dry erase board and picked up one of the markers. She popped the cap off, then looked at her mother. "Will they care if I draw?"

"They might arrest you for vandalism."

Susan snapped the cap back on the marker, then claimed the empty seat beside Laurie.

When Detective Freeling arrived a few minutes later, he had his shirtsleeves cuffed to the elbows and a hasty air about him. A gun and gold shield hung on his hip. He apologized for keeping them waiting. "Things popped up this morning, which I'll tell you about momentarily," he said.

"More information about the girls?"

"Not exactly," Detective Freeling said as he dropped down behind the desk.

"Mommy, what girls?"

"Detective, is there a place where my daughter can wait while we do this?"

"Of course." He jumped up and went to the door, opened it, and shouted someone's name down the hallway. When he turned back around, his face was red. "I wasn't thinking. I'm sorry."

"Not a problem."

"Will Mr. Genarro be joining us?"

"My daddy left," Susan said before Laurie could respond. "He went back to Hartford without us."

One of Detective Freeling's eyebrows went up. He looked at Laurie.

"He had a business meeting in Manhattan," Laurie explained.

"Oh," said the detective.

An attractive young woman with a boyish bob of hair appeared in the doorway. She wore sensible rimless glasses, a tweed pantsuit, and a lanyard around her neck. She smiled brightly at both Laurie and Susan.

"Susan," Detective Freeling said, "this is Miss Debbie. She just intercepted a whole shipment of illegal unicorns, princess gowns, pixie dust, and mermaids. Would you like to go with her and take a look?"

Susan's jaw unhinged. Laurie laughed.

"You're terrible," Miss Debbie said to Detective Freeling. "Susan, hon, I'm Debbie. We don't have any unicorns or mermaids or whatever, but we do have a litter of puppies in the sally port, if you'd like to come see them."

Susan sprung up out of her chair. "Yes, please! Can I, Mom?"

Laurie nodded. "Go on."

"Neat." She bounded over to Miss Debbie, then followed the woman out into the hallway.

Detective Freeling shut the door and returned to his desk. "Don't worry, she'll be fine with Debs. Cute kid."

"Thank you. Detective, I've never done this before. I wasn't sure what to expect."

"Oh, don't worry, it's no big deal." He was rifling

around the desk drawers in search of something. "I'll just turn on a recorder and have you tell me everything you told me last night. Couldn't be simpler." He frowned, then rubbed his forehead. He had big hands. "If I can *find* the recorder."

She pointed to the breast pocket of his shirt, where something small and mechanical-looking stuck out. "Is that it?"

He glanced down, then smiled at her embarrassedly. "Yeah, that's it." He pulled the recorder out and fiddled with it. "This ain't even my office. Normally, we'd do this at my desk, but it's a cube, and there are about twenty other bucket heads moping around back there right now. Here." He swiped some papers off to the side to clear some room on the desk. "I'll turn it on, do a little preamble, and then you just tell your story. Don't get nervous, it's not a big deal. If you flub it up real bad, we can kill it and start again. Sound good?"

"Let's do it."

Detective Freeling hit the record button and then set the recorder down on the desk. He glanced at his wristwatch—a digital Casio that looked like he'd probably had it since high school—and said in a strangely official voice, "This is Detective Brian Freeling, Anne Arundel County Police, Eastern District." He recited the time and the date, then nodded for Laurie to go ahead.

When she had finished, Detective Freeling switched off the tape recorder and dropped it back in the breast pocket of his dress shirt.

"Don't forget it's there," she joked.

"Oh. Ha ha, yeah, no sweat. It'll probably wind up going through the wash tonight." He got up and dragged his chair around to her side of the desk, then sat down. "Hey, listen, I said I had some more news for you. It's about your dad."

"Oh. I thought you said it had nothing to do with Tanya Albrecht."

"It doesn't. It has to do with your dad's death."

She realized she was fumbling with the clasp on her purse. She stopped.

"He didn't fall out that window," Detective Freeling said. "He was pushed."

"Someone—" she began, then cut herself off. Suddenly, her face felt very hot.

"We got a confession and made the arrest this morning."

"Who?" The word squeaked out of her. She thought for sure he was going to say, *Some little girl named Abigail Evans. Ever heard of her?*

"Teresa Larosche," said Freeling. "She was your dad's nighttime caretaker."

Laurie shook her head. "No. That can't be."

"Her fingerprints were in the third-floor room— on the inside of the doorknob, around the windowsill where your father went out. I went back to her apartment for a second interview, just to sew up the loose ends, and she must have figured that I knew something that I didn't. When I started asking about the fingerprints, she broke down and confessed."

"When did this happen?" Shock had dried out her mouth, making it difficult to speak properly.

"Early this morning. She's in lockup now. Been co-operative all morning."

"I don't . . . I don't understand. What . . . what exactly happened?"

"She's a very disturbed young lady, Mrs. Genarro. You've met her once, correct?"

"Yes. She's the one who gave me the key to the room on the roof. She seemed worried about something—scared, even—but she didn't strike me as someone who would . . ."

He showed her his palms, as if to say, *Well, folks, there you have it.*

"Why did she do it?"

"Because he frightened the hell out of her," said Freeling. "When she first started talking, I thought she was setting herself up for a self-defense argument, but she didn't go there. My guess now is that a good lawyer might try to get her to plead to temporary insanity."

"Because he *frightened* her?"

"I know, it sounds ridiculous."

No, she thought. *It doesn't.* Even now, she could hear Teresa Larosche's words thundering through her head, clear as a bell: *And do you want to hear something ridiculous? After a while, he started to convince* me *of it. And I started to think, shit, what if he's right? He seems so certain,* what if he's right? *Soon, I started waking* myself *up just to go around the house and make sure the doors were all locked. And, see, that freaked me out even more because, you know, just like I said—what if his dementia was contagious? What if it had somehow seeped into me?*

"It doesn't sound ridiculous at all," she said. "Not after last night."

"She asked to speak with you."

"Teresa?"

"Normally, we wouldn't bother, but in this case . . . well, it would be strictly for your benefit, not hers. Unless you don't want to, of course."

She didn't know how to feel about this.

"I just thought you might have some questions," Detective Freeling said. "This whole thing came out of nowhere. I just thought it might do you some good. Like I said, she's been cooperative. She hasn't even requested an attorney, despite her boyfriend's protestations."

"Toby," she said.

"Ah, you've met the inimitable Toby."

"No. Teresa mentioned him the day we met."

"He's a piece of work." He stood up. "Like I said, Mrs. Genarro, it's up to you. If you just want to get home, I'll have Freddy take you back right now."

"No," she said. "I'd like to speak with her."

CHAPTER 29

Teresa Larosche sat in a cell by herself at the end of a cellblock that was rank with the stink of perspiration. Detective Freeling led Laurie down the cellblock past other jailed offenders, each one looking like a caged animal awaiting euthanasia. There was a folding chair set up in the hall facing Teresa's cell. It reminded her of when Jodie Foster went to talk with Anthony Hopkins's character in *The Silence of the Lambs*.

Teresa Larosche was seated on a bench, her head down, her bleached hair hanging over her eyes. She wasn't wearing the Hannibal Lecter–style jumpsuit that would have completed the visual, but a plain black T-shirt and jeans. The laces had been removed from her sneakers and she wore none of the jewelry she had worn on the day Laurie had met her for coffee. When the young woman looked up at her, she could see that there was no makeup on her face, either. Her eyes looked haunted.

Detective Freeling placed a hand on Laurie's shoulder. "When you're finished, just come back down the hall and push the intercom button by the door." He smelled like aftershave lotion.

"Okay. Thanks."

Once Detective Freeling was halfway down the hall, Laurie sat in the folding chair. In the cell, Teresa's eyes were red, bleary orbs that leaked wet tracks down her cheeks. She looked much older than the woman whom Laurie had met at the Brickfront coffee shop, though only slightly more frightened.

"I'm sorry for lying to you," Teresa said.

"But not for killing my father," Laurie said. "Why did you do it?"

"Because he was poisoning me. Because he was getting into my head and I had to stop him from doing that."

"Why didn't you just quit?"

"It wouldn't have done any good. Even when I wasn't there—you know, during the day—it was like he was still inside my head. Remember that movie I told you about? The crazy guy and the psychiatrist or whatever?"

"I remember."

"You know what I'm talking about, don't you? You feel it, too."

"In the next few days, there will be a story in the news about my father. I can't tell you about it now, but you'll know what it is when it happens. So while I don't know exactly what you're talking about, it isn't hard for me to comprehend just how horrible he might have been toward you. Believe me on that."

Teresa hung her head again. The part in her scalp looked very pink.

"How did you do it?"

"I told you the door was unlocked, but I didn't know

how it had gotten that way. Well, that's not true. I unlocked it. He swore someone was up there, trying to get
in. At first he wanted the door locked to keep them out,
but then he wanted to go up there and confront who-
ever it was. That's when I really started to get scared.
I thought I heard someone up there, too. So I left the
door unlocked. In the night, he got out of bed and went
up there. He began screaming. Then crying. I went up
and he was there, naked, shouting at the walls. Tears
were coming down his face. He had . . . there was . . .
my God, this huge fucking erection. And he had taken
a . . . um, he'd defecated on the floor, too. And then I
couldn't be sure if he was crying or laughing.

"When he saw me, he called me someone else's
name. I could feel his sickness crawling around in my
brain. He had a sickness in him, just like my old man
had his *own* sickness. Those things poison a person.
Well, I was done being poisoned."

Teresa looked up at her. The young woman's face
had gone slack.

"He pointed to the broken window, said that's how
they'd been getting in the house. He had cut himself on
the glass, too, and was bleeding all over the rug."

"So, wait," Laurie said. "The window was already
broken?"

Teresa nodded. "He was so *big*. I kept shoving him
backward, I guess to keep him away from me, but also
to shut him up, shut him up, shut him up. I thought the
only way to stop the poison from going through my
veins was to *shut him up*."

She spoke those final three words through clenched
teeth.

"So you pushed him out the window."

"To shut him up," Teresa said, her voice now a whisper.

"What name did he call you?" Laurie asked, wondering if she would actually say *Sadie* or *Abigail,* but knowing that it would be the same name her father had mistakenly called her during their last phone call—*Tanya*. But it wasn't Tanya's name, either.

"It was *your* name, Mrs. Genarro," Teresa said. "It was *Laurie*."

Susan complained about stomach pains the whole ride back to the house. This time, they were chauffeured by a uniformed officer in a squad car. Laurie and Susan both sat in the back behind a mesh cage like animals. The officer said nothing until he got lost and had to ask for directions to Annapolis Road. When they arrived home, Laurie located some Tums with her toiletries and gave two to Susan.

"Blech," Susan bemoaned. "Tastes like chalk."

"Why don't you go lie down and I'll call you when dinner's ready?"

"What's for dinner?"

"How about spaghetti?"

"Okay."

Once Susan had gone upstairs, Laurie poured herself a stiff drink from the remaining bottles on the piano. It tasted like turpentine and she nearly gagged. She thought about the events of the past couple of weeks . . . and found she was wrapped in a blanket of unease concerning the status of her own sanity. This hadn't

been some ghost story. There was no menacing presence haunting her and pointing out clues. There was
no Hateful Beast, no Vengeance. Her father had been
murdered by Teresa Larosche. Perhaps the only ghosts
in this tale were the ones that plagued her father's dete-
riorating and guilt-ridden mind as well as the ones that
no doubt populated Teresa Larosche's nightmares. She
had believed in the return of a vengeful spirit the way
small children believe in Santa Claus. What did that say
about her sanity?

Ted is right. I need to get out of this house.

In the kitchen, Laurie dialed Harmony Simmons's
number. She got the realtor's voice mail, left a message,
and hung up.

She was halfway through cooking dinner when Susan appeared in the kitchen doorway, sobbing. Laurie
hurried over to the girl.

"Honey, what's wrong?"

"Blood," Susan whimpered. "It's really true!"

At first, Laurie didn't understand. But then she did,
and she smiled warmly and hugged the girl. Susan's
arms hung limply at her sides while she moaned into
her mother's hair.

"It's not so bad," Laurie said. "Come on. Let's get
you upstairs and cleaned up."

While Susan soaked in the bathtub, Laurie found
some Tampax pads in her purse. She explained to Susan
how to use them.

"I don't like it," Susan grumbled. She had filled the

tub with bubbles and there were some in her hair. "I don't want it."

"It happens to every little girl when they become a woman." For whatever reason, this made her think of Teresa Larosche, and how she had looked sitting in that jail cell, no jewelry on her fingers, no makeup on her face, no laces in her sneakers. *She was once a little girl, too. What horrors did she face at the hand of her own father?* The world, she knew suddenly, was full of innocent little girls turned mad.

"Are you angry about it?" Susan asked.

"Are you kidding? No, hon. What's to be angry about?"

"I don't know."

"I guess I'm just a little surprised. It's happened so early."

"What does that mean?"

"You're still pretty young."

"I'm going to be eleven next month."

"That's still pretty young."

Susan said, "I want Daddy to come back."

CHAPTER 30

It was still dark when Ted awoke Friday morning. Moments ticked by before he realized he was back in his own bed in his own house in Hartford. He lay there for a while, smelling the familiar smells, while the room slowly brightened with the dawn. He was grounded enough to recognize that this might not be his bedroom for very long. This might not be his house.

He had spent the drive yesterday replaying not only the argument with Laurie, but the events in his life that had led to that argument. Not just the affair with Marney—how careless he had been in hindsight—but his overall approach to his relationship with Laurie. How many hours had be spent moody and despondent because of his floundering writing career? How many conversations had he dominated with his bellyaching? In hindsight, it was a wonder that she hadn't left him sooner, and taken Susan with her.

Thinking of Susan made his face burn. Would Laurie really leave him? Would she take Susan and disappear?

That's impossible. Where would they go?

What if she stayed in that house in Maryland? What if Laurie and Susan *never* came back?

He got up, pulled on his running gear, and was outside jogging along Tamarack Street just as the early morning sun threw reddish spears through the trees to the east. The street climbed toward a grade in the hillside. The houses there were grandiose—all brick fronts, marble porches, balconies atop the porticos—and it was still early enough in the morning to see people climbing into SUVs, BMWs, and Mercedes for their morning commutes. By the time he reached the park at the end of Tamarack, he was firmly back in the working middle-class neck of the neighborhood. The park itself was nothing but a weedy basketball court. On the next street over, a row of Ryder trucks stood in the parking lot of a rental facility. Beyond the facility, the spire of St. Mark's rose up against a still-dark sky.

Back at the house, he showered for a good forty-five minutes. He made himself breakfast with whatever was still edible in the refrigerator—eggs, toast, grapefruit juice, a few grapes that had already started to wither and looked unappetizingly like some small mammal's testicles. He was calm while he cooked and while coffee brewed in the gurgling stainless-steel machine. But when he sat down to eat, he found his calmness—along with his appetite—had deserted him. In his chest, his heart thudded furiously against his sternum. His pulse hadn't slowed down since he'd come back from his run. *Heart attack?* That would be poetic—his first morning alone and he drops dead with no one around to call the paramedics. Brilliant.

He dumped the food down the garbage disposal,

forced down the grapefruit juice, grimaced. On the refrigerator, Susan's artwork made his heart hurt. At some point, he found himself holding the portable phone. He dialed Laurie's cell number, placed the phone to his ear, listened to it ring. When it went to voice mail, he hung up.

Something didn't feel right.

He arrived at Rao's a half hour early for the meeting. There were tables outside and it was already promising to be a nice day, but he didn't feel like waiting around to be seated. He went directly inside to the bar. There was an attractive girl in a man's white shirt trolling back and forth behind the bar. A male bar-back with a bald pate and severe black eyes stacked soapy glasses on a spongy green mat beside a stainless-steel sink.

He ordered a Laphroaig from the bartender, then drummed his fingers restlessly on the bar top. The drink arrived and it smelled like a fire pit. He tossed it down, felt his intestines backfire like an old Plymouth, then ordered another. He had his cell phone out and was staring at it as if confused by its existence when the second drink arrived. Ultimately, he dialed Laurie's cell phone number again. He had no speech prepared, didn't know what to say. He simply felt awful about how he had left things with her. She had been hit with too much over the past forty-eight hours and she had been hanging on by a thread even before that. He shouldn't have left them home alone.

The phone rang a few times and then went to voice

mail. He disconnected, then hit redial. This time, it went straight to voice mail without ringing.

"Goddamn it."

Steve Markham arrived a few minutes later and sat on the stool next to him. "Christ, you look nervous," Markham said.

"Hey, Steve. Good to see you." Ted checked his wristwatch.

"Relax, will you?" Markham said, clapping Ted on the back. He ordered a vodka and cranberry from the bartender. "The meeting will go fine. In fact, we've got some time to relax. Fish's agent called. He's running about an hour late."

"Christ," Ted said. "An hour?"

"What's wrong? You've got someplace else to be? You look too thin, by the way. How's things going in Virginia?"

"Maryland."

"Wherever. Laurie doing okay?"

Ted emptied his second drink and set the glass down hard on the bar. His hand was shaking. "You know, Steve, she's not. Not really." He sat up straight, looking around the restaurant. "This was a mistake," he said.

Markham frowned. "The hell are you talking about? You've been begging for a sit-down with Fish ever since you started on the project."

"I don't mean the meeting. I just . . . I shouldn't be here." He checked his watch again. His cell phone. Was Laurie so angry at him that she wasn't answering his calls? Or was something else going on back at that house?

*Why would I think that? I've got no reason to think
something bad has happened.*

Yet he couldn't shake that feeling that Laurie was in
trouble. And not just Laurie—Susan, too.

"Are you on something?" Markham said.

Ted dropped cash on the bar and got off the stool.
"Look, Steve, I can't stay. Tell Fish I'm sorry, but something came up and I need to get home."

"*What?*"

"I'm sorry," he said. "But it's an emergency."

"Are you fucking with me? You busted my balls
about setting this up and now you're just going to bail?
Is this some kind of joke?"

"I wish it was."

"What about the meeting with the producers? We're
supposed to head to their office when we leave here.
This is a big goddamn deal, Ted. Please tell me you're
pulling my leg."

Ted squeezed Markham's shoulder. Then he turned
and hustled through the lunch crowd toward the doors.

"This is your career!" Markham shouted after him.
But by that time, Ted was already out on the street and
running to his car.

CHAPTER 31

Laurie awoke to the vibration of her cell phone. Sprawled out on the mattress in the master bedroom, she pawed around the floor for her purse. Beside her, Susan moaned and muttered something unintelligible, though Laurie could tell she was clearly agitated about being disturbed. Her purse was on the floor beside the mattress, beneath a clutter of yesterday's clothes. She dragged the purse closer and dug out the phone. Ted's name and cell number blinked on the digital display. Laurie felt a knot tighten up in her stomach. She hit the IGNORE button and the call was silenced. The clock on the phone's display showed it was 12:41 P.M. There were missed call icons on the screen, and when she clicked on these, she saw they were from Ted, too. Why had she and Susan slept so late? She powered down the phone and tossed it back in her bag.

Rolling over, Laurie rocked the girl gently. "Hey. It's late. We slept till lunchtime."

Susan groaned and pulled the sheet up over her head. "Don't feel good."

Don't feel well, Laurie internally corrected her

grammar—an unpleasant habit she had adopted from Ted.

Laurie climbed up off the mattress. Her back ached. In just her panties and a T-shirt, she went to the bathroom, brushed her teeth, washed the sleep from her eyes. Susan had been up much of the night with cramps. Laurie had tried to talk to the girl about all the changes going on in her body, and how it was actually a wonderful thing despite how awful Susan felt. Susan had not been interested in hearing how wonderful it was. On her way out the bedroom, she shut the door so the kid could sleep.

Downstairs, the house was gray. The sky beyond the windows was overcast. Clouds the color of ash congregated over the trees in the backyard. An unseasonably cool wind funneled into the kitchen when Laurie opened one of the bay windows. At the stove, she put on a pot of coffee and silently wished for a newspaper. She wasn't terribly hungry but found herself peering into the refrigerator at one point, looking at everything but not seeing a thing. In the end, she decided to take a long, hot shower. The need to get clean was very strong.

Outside, the roll of thunder was long and sonorous, like a passing locomotive.

It was nearly one-thirty when Ted finally broke free from a snarl of traffic and the highway opened up. He sped along I-95, dodging slower vehicles while honking at the ones that simply refused to get out of his way. He had already called Laurie's cell phone three times, leaving enough time between each call in hopes that she would cool off. Each time his call went to voice mail.

This had been a bad idea. He knew he shouldn't have left them behind in that house.

Calm down. You're going to kill yourself driving ninety-five miles an hour and what good will that do anyone, Teddy-biscuit?

He wondered now just how long this sense of dread had been bobbing around in his stomach. It had been roiling inside his guts since leaving Maryland. Yesterday, when he had pulled the Volvo up the driveway of their house in Hartford, he had felt an unsettling black shadow fall against his back—an unseen presence breathing down his neck. For the second time in just over a week, he thought about his old childhood nightmare—of waking up in an empty house, his parents gone, his dog gone. Only now it wasn't a dream. Laurie was gone. Susan was gone. Ted Genarro was finally and permanently ostracized from the people he loved the most.

You're thinking crazy. She told you to stay away and now you're just going to go running back to her? Do you really want to do more damage? Maybe she's right—maybe she just needs some space for a while.

Up ahead, traffic was already beginning to slow. It was just over a four-hour drive to Annapolis.

I should have written down the house's phone number and called her on the landline. Damn it, I wasn't thinking!

He could have called information, but he didn't know the address off the top of his—

But he did. It was programmed in his GPS. He

turned the GPS on and waited until it booted up. He scrolled through the RECENTLY FOUND locations. Myles Brashear's address was at the top. On his cell phone, he dialed 411, then gave the operator the address of the house on Annapolis Road. A few seconds later, an automated female voice recited the number to him. The automated voice advised him that if he pressed 1, he would be connected at no additional cost. He pressed 1.

She was in the middle of toasting some bread when the phone rang.

"Hello?"

"Mrs. Genarro, this is Detective Freeling. Is this a good time?"

"Sure, detective. Is everything all right?"

"I wanted to keep my promise," he said. "A positive ID has been made on the body this morning. It *is* Tanya Albrecht. We've managed to locate Tanya's sister June living out in White Marsh. She's been notified of the discovery, although she wasn't told about your involvement. She's in the process of contacting the rest of her family."

"Oh. Well . . . I guess that's . . ."

"Yeah, I know. You were gonna say you guess that's good, but it seems like a strange thing to say, given the circumstances."

"I feel like I want to do something for those poor people."

"That's kind of you, but I'd lay low for the time being, if I were you, Mrs. Genarro. You can never tell how family members may react to this sort of thing. Yeah, it's been about twenty-five years, but maybe you never get over something like that, you know?"

"I don't think you do," she admitted. "What about the other girls? The ones in the photos?"

"I've contacted the various police departments who worked those missing persons cases back then. As of now, I've only heard back from three of them. They sent over photos of the missing girls." There was a pause before he added, "They're a match to three of the girls found in your father's photos."

Laurie closed her eyes. "What about Teresa Larosche?"

"She's still in custody, charged with second-degree murder. She hasn't made bail. Still hasn't asked for an attorney, either."

"I still can't believe it. . . ."

"Have you seen the news?"

"It's on the news already?" she said, though she was hardly surprised.

"Don't worry, your name wasn't mentioned. We're calling you 'an anonymous source.'"

"But it's only a matter of time, isn't it?"

"I really don't know how it'll play out."

"I see."

"Anyway," he said, sighing heavily, "I just wanted to hold up my end of the bargain. You hanging in there?"

Hadn't Ted said something similar to her recently? She remembered thinking of those inspirational posters where the kitten dangles from the tree limb.

"Just like the cat," she said.

Detective Freeling made a sound that approximated, "Huh?"

"I'm doing just fine, detective. Thanks for all your help."

"Yeah. Likewise."

She had just hung up the phone when it surprised her by ringing again.

"Detective Freeling?" she said into the receiver.

There was static over the line. It wasn't Freeling's telephone, but a less reliable connection. A cellular phone. Someone said something but the voice was muffled, the words incoherent.

"Hello?" she said.

The line went dead.

When she turned around, Susan was standing in the doorway. She had on baggy sweatpants and a T-shirt with a soccer ball on it. Her hair was matted and her eyes looked half-lidded.

"I was just making some toast," Laurie offered. "Would you like some?"

"Not really hungry. My head hurts."

"There's ibuprofen in my purse upstairs."

"Yeah, I found it. I already took some."

"You know I don't like you taking aspirin without my supervision."

"I just took one. I'm not a dummy." She set something down on the counter on her way to the refrigerator. "Found that in your purse, too."

It was her wedding band.

The urge to laugh accosted her. She didn't give into it, for fear it would begin as laughter but slowly migrate toward hysteria. She slid the ring onto her finger.

Susan opened the refrigerator and stared at the contents with disinterest. "It smells funny in here," she said.

"Maybe some of the food has started to rot."

"Not just in the fridge," she said, closing the door. "The whole house."

Laurie smelled it, too. It was like there was something behind the walls, rotting. It reminded her of the well in the front yard, and that awful smell that had risen out of it. Shaking her head, she took the toast from the toaster oven and set the slices onto a plate. "Could you get me the butter from—"

At the opposite end of the house, someone knocked three times on the front door. Had someone begun playing the trumpet in the next room, the sound wouldn't have been less startling. Laurie slipped out of the kitchen, through the parlor, and down the hall. She glanced out one of the front windows on her way to the door and could see no car in the driveway. She opened the door to find Dora Lorton standing there. Dressed in a black square-shouldered coat and clunky black shoes, the woman looked like a widowed Italian grandmother.

"Ms. Lorton. I didn't see your car. . . ."

"I parked it in the street. I can't manage it up the driveway without bumping a few trees. Felix gets furious. May I come in?"

"Please. I was just making some toast. Can I get you something?"

"Some coffee would be nice."

"Have a seat and I'll put some on."

"Nonsense. You finish your business and *I'll* put some on. I still know my way around the place, assuming you haven't moved anything."

"It's all where you left it."

They passed through the parlor and Dora paused to survey the missing liquor cabinet.

"We've had some interest in my father's stuff," Laurie said, and immediately winced inwardly at the apologetic tone she heard in her voice.

In the kitchen, Laurie sat at the table and ate her toast while Dora—still in her square-shouldered coat—put on a pot of coffee. Susan had retreated to her bedroom to read, perhaps unnerved by the older woman's presence. Gemlike specks of rain appeared on the bay windows.

"I saw the news this morning," Dora said. "There was no mention of your name, but I recognized the Sparrows Point facility from that old picture he used to have hanging on the wall. Before he smashed the glass and tore it out of the frame, that is. I'd spoken to Teresa Larosche, too, and she told me what you told her—about keeping an eye on the news. I was able to make the connection."

"I found her," Laurie said. "The little girl. Tanya Albrecht." She explained about the keys in the well and how one of them matched the lock on garage 58. "I went there Wednesday night and found her body."

Since the newspapers and TV news had left out her name, she assumed this was new information to Dora. Yet the old woman's expression didn't change.

"There's more," she went on, almost breathlessly now. It was as if she needed to get it off her chest. "I'm not supposed to talk about it yet, but you're going to hear about other girls. My father . . ." Her voice trailed off.

"I feel I owe you an apology," Dora said. She retrieved two mugs from the cupboard and set them down on the counter. "More than one, perhaps."

"Don't be silly."

"Please, Mrs. Genarro." Her thick-soled shoes made hard, flat sounds on the tile as she tottered over to the refrigerator for the milk. "It took some courage for me to even come here today, so let me go on with it."

Laurie nodded. Finished eating, she now broke apart the remaining bits of crust in her plate.

"I was hard on you when you came here. My reproachful behavior toward you when we first met was misdirected. It was not my place to judge the relationship you had with your father. I am sorry."

"Thank you."

"My sister lives in Boca Raton." She dropped her voice to a conspiratorial murmur and added, "That's in Florida. She's got four children, all grown now, of course. I was never able to have children. It was the reason I never married. That's difficult enough, but I carry Felix's weight in that regard, too."

"I don't understand. Your brother Felix?"

"He's never said as much, but I know him well enough to know that because *I* never married, *he* never married. We grew up in a different time, Mrs. Genarro, and ours was a close family. Our parents were very poor and our father died of emphysema when I was still very young. A girl needs a father, Mrs. Genarro. Little girls are like clay waiting to be molded. The father reserves the right to mold it—reserves it *solely*, Mrs. Genarro—and she is happy to let him. But if he is not around, strange hands are eager to come into the mix and lay their own impressions in the clay."

The coffee began to percolate on the stove. Brown water spit up into the glass bulb in the lid of the coffeepot.

"I speak metaphorically because we both understand what I mean, correct?"

"Yes."

"After our father died, Felix became very protective of me. He has always been a good brother, and I am very grateful for that, but I am also sad for him, too. Perhaps had I married, he would have let go and lived his own life. But I never married, Mrs. Genarro, and Felix never did, either. It was as though we'd become husband and wife by proxy."

"He must care for you very much."

"And I for him," Dora said. "See, in a way, my brother became my father, and our fathers are the ones who hold the lamplight so we can find our way in the dark. Teresa Larosche is a perfect example."

"How do you mean?"

Dora poured two cups of coffee, which she carried over to the table. She expelled a great huff of air as she settled herself in the chair opposite Laurie.

"That girl had problems her whole life. Her father was abusive. Not just to her, either, but to her mother as well. She told me that right here in this house, on nights when she'd arrive early for her shift just to talk. It was toward the end, when she began to grow scared about being in this house alone at night with your father. It wasn't some confession or some great revelation, like Saint Paul seeing Jesus on Damascus Road. It was just talk and, some nights, we found ourselves going down that old road. She never seemed bitter about it, or even bothered by it at all."

"She told you she was afraid to be in the house?"

Dora got up, brought the milk and a tea spoon over to the table, and sat back down. She poured a healthy stream into her coffee, then stirred it.

"She asked if I heard noises during the day, noises like she heard at night."

"What noises?"

"Sounds like someone other than your father in the house."

"Did you?"

"No."

"I saw her in jail," Laurie said. "She asked for me and I spoke with her. She apologized for what she'd done. She tried to explain it, though I'll admit I didn't understand much of it."

"She is a troubled young girl," Dora said, her eyes downcast. It was easy to see she felt protective of Teresa Larosche. Perhaps childless Dora Lorton felt some stewardship over the young woman who was so desperately in need of guidance. *My brother became my father, and our fathers are the ones who hold the lamplight so we can find our way in the dark.*

"She said my father was afraid someone was trying to get into the house. She said that after a while, she began to believe him. She started to hear someone else in the house, too. She knew there was no one there but became paranoid that my father's . . . dementia"—she had almost said *insanity*—"was finding its way into her brain, too. That's why she felt she had to kill him."

There had been no one holding the lamplight for Teresa Larosche. This notion caused a pang of sadness to resonate at the center of Laurie's chest. *There had been no one.*

"My father called the intruder the Hateful Beast. The Vengeance. I can see how that could frighten someone as fragile as Teresa Larosche. Heck, it frightened me when she told me. Until I realized what he was really talking about."

Dora Lorton pursed her lips. "Oh? And what was he really talking about?"

"Tanya Albrecht, the girl whose body I found in that factory garage. Other little girls, too. Maybe it was the guilt that had finally caught up with him, but I don't think that's true. I think his brain—in the throes of dementia—turned on him, attacked him. Made him believe they were coming back to get him."

"Yes!" Dora said this with surprising energy. "Yes, he sometimes mentioned a young girl, though he never spoke her name. I assumed it was you, dear. His mind had become very . . . muddy . . . and he would often slip in and out of the past."

"At first I thought it was a reference to a girl named Sadie Russ. She lived next door when I was a kid and she died when she fell through the roof of my father's greenhouse. I assumed he carried guilt over that, though my mother and I didn't stick around long enough to know for sure. But it hadn't been Sadie at all—it had been Tanya Albrecht and the other little girls."

Which means I have been losing my mind the past few weeks, accusing an innocent girl, poor Abigail, of being a monster, she thought.

Both women jumped when the telephone rang. Laurie got up, turned off the ringer, then sat back down.

"What will happen to Teresa Larosche?" Laurie asked, gripping the handle of her coffee cup.

"I don't know, dear."

"Once I sell the house, I'd like to help her out in some way. I think she needs to be admitted to a hospital, not sit in some jail cell."

Dora said nothing to this, but Laurie could tell by the look on the older woman's face that the sentiment pleased her. After she finished her coffee, her big-shouldered coat rose up from the chair.

"It's time I leave."

"Thank you for coming by. It means a lot."

"You take care of yourself," Dora said. "And that little girl of yours, too."

Little girls are like clay, Laurie thought, walking Dora to the front door. *Little girls, little girls . . .*

When she returned to the kitchen, Susan was there rummaging through a box of cereal.

"Let me make you a proper lunch," she told the girl.

"I'm just in a snacky mood."

Laurie dumped Dora Lorton's coffee into the sink, then replenished her own.

"Are we gonna still live with Dad when we go home?" Susan asked suddenly.

"Honey, why would you ask that?"

"I don't know. Because I heard you guys fighting."

"Could you sit down for a minute? I want to talk to you."

Susan dragged one of the kitchen chairs out, then sank down onto it.

Laurie returned to the table with her fresh coffee, and sat opposite her daughter. Dora's words still echoed in her head. "Your father and I are dealing with some issues right now, but you don't have to worry about it. I don't want you worrying about any of it. Your father and I love you very much and we wouldn't do anything to hurt you. Do you understand?"

Susan nodded, but there was a vacant look in her eyes, like she was unwilling to affix herself to any of Laurie's words.

"Honey," said Laurie. "I know you sometimes think I'm too strict with you. I see how you are with your dad, and I think that's wonderful, and I know you and I have . . . well . . . a different relationship. I'm strict because I worry about you. I feel the need to protect you. This world is full of awful things, Susan, and I want to make sure nothing ever happens to you."

"What would happen to me?"

"Nothing will happen," said Laurie. "I won't let it. I love you very much. Do you know that?"

Susan nodded her head. "I love you, too, Mom."

"Good," Laurie said, smiling softly.

To her surprise, Susan stood and came to her, wrapped her thin brown arms around Laurie's neck. Laurie hugged her daughter back, feeling the thinness and fragility of her frame within her embrace. When she finally let go, it seemed too soon.

"Hey," Susan said. She went over to the bay windows and peered out at the gray, overcast backyard. "There's Abigail."

Laurie stood and came up behind Susan. Abigail was out in the yard on her hands and knees, digging a hole in the ground with a stick. Auburn hair hung in tangles in front of her face. Her feet appeared to be bare.

Laurie set the coffee cup down on the table, then went to the side door where she kicked on her shoes. "Stay here," she told Susan. "I'll be right back."

Outside, the wind was cold and misty with rain. The sun was barricaded behind angry black clouds. Laurie cast no shadow as she crossed the lawn and stopped in front of the hole Abigail was digging.

The girl looked up at her. Her eyes were large and curious, set in the smooth, pale oval of her face, but she did not seem surprised to find she had a visitor.

"There have been a lot of apologies going around today," Laurie said. She crouched down and met the girl's eyes head-on. "I guess it's my turn. I've been rude to you, Abigail. I'm sorry. I apologize."

Abigail's lower lip twitched. For a moment, it seemed like her eyes unfocused before that quiet curiosity filled them back up again.

"Stop," Abigail said. "Stop it."

"Stop what?"

"Calling me that."

"Stop calling you Abigail?"

One of Abigail's grubby little hands reached into the hole. She dug around in the loose dirt. She wasn't just being playful—she was looking for something.

On shaky knees, Laurie stood up.

"Eeny, meeny, miney, moe." Abigail's voice was grating—the sound of carving knives being scraped together. "Can Susan come out and play?"

Not saying a word, Laurie took a step backwards.

"We'll make wishes together," Abigail said. "Good

wishes." Beneath the dirt, she found what she was looking for. She gathered it between her thumb and index finger and brought it up so that even in the sunless afternoon it sparkled. It was the missing diamond earring.

"Sadie," Laurie managed. She could feel her windpipe constricting.

"Can *Susan* come out and *play*?"

"No. You should go home."

"This isn't my home."

"You know what I mean."

"But it *was*," Abigail said. "It *was* mine."

Laurie felt like she was struggling to breathe underwater. Briefly, she closed her eyes and took a deep breath. When she opened them, Abigail was still kneeling there, holding the diamond earring. She hadn't moved.

"Stupid," Abigail said. But no—she didn't just *say* it. The word *snarled* out of her. "Stupid. Stupid *bitch*."

Laurie took another step back. She wanted to run but couldn't convince her legs to cooperate. Her entire body felt numb.

Abigail laughed. It sounded like two people laughing at once, one laugh overlaid atop the other.

"I came back for you, Laurie. I waited and waited and now we're together again."

Laurie wheezed out, "What do you want?"

Abigail's dark eyes narrowed. That stunning auburn hair framed her face. "Eeny, meeny, miney, moe. You. To come. With me." A hint of a smile swam briefly across her face. "Or the other one."

"What other one?"

Abigail pointed toward the house, where Susan watched from the kitchen window.

"No," Laurie said.

"Eeny, meeny—"

"Go *away!*"

Abigail brushed a strand of that wavy auburn hair behind her right ear. At first, it looked like there was grease or perhaps ink running down the right side of Abigail's face; it started at her ear, coursed down the curve of her jaw, down her neck, and soaked the collar of her checkerboard dress. It was blood. Abigail brought the diamond earring to her mangled ear, pressed it to the flesh. A muddy squelching sound broke the silence. When Abigail brought her hand down, the diamond remained seated in the bulb of bloody tissue.

And that was when it all rushed back to her—*the morning commute to the university on I-84, the radio turned to an easy listening station, the weather pleasant. Traffic slows as she approaches the interchange. She eases down on the brake and happens to glance out the window at the car sliding into place beside her. There is a middle-aged couple in the front, the man behind the wheel wearing a baseball cap, the woman with her hair pulled back in a blondish ponytail. The car rolls up a few more inches, and Laurie sees a little girl in the backseat—a girl who turns to her, her eyes hollow black pits, her auburn hair matted with blood and spangled with dead leaves. Bits of broken glass shimmer like confetti in her hair, her eyebrows, her eyelashes. Great slashes have been cut like gills along her cheeks and the sides of her neck. One pink ear dribbles blood so thick it is almost black while a diamond stud winks out from all that madness—*

This broke her paralysis. She turned and ran back

into the house, slamming the side door shut behind her. Susan watched her in a state of utter perplexity, one hand filled with Cheerios frozen midway to her mouth.

"Mom . . . ?"

"Get away from the window," Laurie said.

"Huh?"

She reached out and grabbed Susan by one shoulder. Susan shoved her hand away, spilling cereal on the floor in the process. For a moment, they stared at each other, a corresponding look of terror on both their faces.

Outside, Abigail swished past the bay windows and disappeared around the side of the house.

Suddenly unsure if she had locked the side door or just slammed it shut, Laurie dove for it, toppling a kitchen chair in the process—*clack!*—and reached for the dead bolt. But the lock had been changed by Dora Lorton and now required a *key*—

The spare sat on the kitchen counter. Laurie snatched it up, hurried back to the door, jammed the key in the lock. It turned audibly. A heartbeat later, Abigail's plain white face appeared in the rectangle of glass in the upper portion of the door. Laurie stared. Their mutual respiration fogged up the glass. When Abigail placed one grubby palm against the glass, Laurie made a small hiccupping sound and jerked backwards. One finger began tapping against the window. The nail was black, the knuckles smudgy with dirt.

"Go away!" Laurie shouted at the monster.

Abigail's finger screeched across the glass. It moved past Laurie and stopped on Susan.

"No!"

"Mom . . ."

"Get in the other room, Susan!"

"What are you *doing*?"

"Susan!"

Crying, Susan ran into the parlor.

On the other side of the window, Abigail opened her mouth and rolled back her thin lips, exposing all her teeth. Her tongue squirmed.

Laurie hurried over to the bay windows. She closed and latched the open window, her breath coming in quick little gasps now, strands of hair swinging down across her face. She could no longer see Abigail—the rectangle of glass in the door was starkly, incriminatingly vacant—but the black-eyed Susans were swaying at the base of the patio as if recently disturbed.

What about the front door? Had she locked it after Dora Lorton left? *What about the other windows? Maybe all the locks have been turned. , , ,*

She was so terrified of the idea that she was momentarily incapable of movement. Some strange buoyancy made it feel as if her stomach was gradually elevating up through her esophagus. When she broke her trance, she turned and ran into the parlor. Susan was not there. The windows in the parlor were closed, but she couldn't tell if they were latched. Ted had pried the nails from the frames so they could open the windows when they wanted, circulating some fresh air through the house, yet now she wished he hadn't. She ran to them, checked them one by one. They were all locked.

Glass can be broken. She thought about the busted window in the belvedere.

In the foyer, she found the front door unlocked. Fear clenched her in its fist. She screamed Susan's name but

Susan didn't respond. She turned the bolt and heard the lock slide sturdily into place. *She could already be in the house*. Then she thought of Susan. *Susan could have gone out!*

"Susan! Susan!"

Susan was weeping from somewhere in the house. She couldn't pinpoint the exact location. *Sound travels funny here.* Lowering her voice to a more reasonable tone, though unable to keep out the tremolo, she said, "Susan? Honey? Where'd you go?"

Susan's sobs grew louder but she still did not answer.

Laurie took three silent steps toward the stairs. Susan was perched halfway up the staircase, her hands pressed into her lap and her face a slick red map of tears. When she saw her mother, the tears came harder. Her lower lip shook and her chin wrinkled. *Walnut chin,* Ted would have said.

"Hey," Laurie said, placing a foot on the first step and a hand on the banister. "What's the matter with you?"

"What's the matter with *you?*" the girl sobbed. "You're *scaring* me!"

"I'm only trying to protect you." She ascended another step.

"I want Daddy to come home! I want Daddy!"

"I'm going to fix it, okay? I'm going to make it all better." Two more steps. "I just want to make sure you're safe first, Susan. I love you, honey. You know that I do. I'm not going to let anything happen to you."

Susan lowered her face and cried into her lap.

"Come with me," Laurie said, stopping two steps below Susan. She reached out and rubbed the girl's head.

She could feel the smoothness of her skull beneath her thin hair. "We'll get you safe. Safe as milk."

Susan struck out and swatted Laurie's hand off her head. "No!" she shouted at her mother, simultaneously gripping the banister and pulling herself to her feet.

Laurie snatched the girl's forearm with both hands and dragged her the rest of the way up the stairs.

Ted was less than an hour from the house when the storm hit. It didn't begin slowly and graduate to a full-on thunderstorm; instead, it dumped out of the sky all at once, bringing traffic along the interstate to a screeching halt. Cursing audibly, he rolled up his window and tried Laurie's cell phone again. Like the previous times, it went straight to voice mail. Similarly, the house phone kept ringing and ringing until an operator disconnected the line.

When he began to see signs for the Harbor Tunnel, he leapt up onto the shoulder and rode the rumble-strip to the exit. Two police cars sat on the other side of the median, but the rain must have made a traffic stop seem about as appealing as a tooth extraction to the officers, and neither vehicle pursued him.

There was an eight-inch butcher's knife in one of the kitchen drawers. Laurie gripped its handle, then retrieved the flashlight from the counter, where Ted had left it after his expedition down into the wishing well. Susan's cries were muffled now, but she could still hear them rattling around in her head. Outside, rain pattered against the bay windows. At the edge of the patio, the black-eyed Susans bobbed and whipped about, as if puppeted by strings.

Laurie undid the bolt on the side door. She turned the knob, opened the door, and was instantly accosted by a cold, rain-speckled wind more befitting of late winter than early summer. The storm had arrived. Before stepping out, she scanned the area. Trashcans stood against the siding to her left. To her right, wildflowers had been reduced to spongy green mats by the storm. The fence that ran between the two properties was overgrown with vegetation. The trees beyond resembled dancing, shambling black smears.

"Abigail." Her voice was flat, toneless.

She stepped outside, shut the door, then quickly locked it with the key. She followed the walkway around to the back of the house. Directly above, large mottled storm clouds pulsed with an unearthly light. When the next whip crack of thunder resounded from across the river, Laurie felt its reverberation in her back teeth.

Intermingled with the sounds of the storm was a steady banging noise.

Where are you, Abigail? Or was Sadie fully in control now?

She approached the fence and peered down beneath the whipping branches of the willow tree. The banging noise was the door in the fence; not properly latched, it slammed repeatedly against the fence post in the wind. *The passageway,* Laurie thought. She grabbed the door and shoved it all the way open. Rain splattered her face and soaked her shirt. On the ground, small footprints were quickly filling with brown water.

Over the storm, she thought she could hear Susan screaming for her. It took all her will to block out the sound.

A checkerboard dress passed through the trees up ahead.

I'm going to kill you.

She pursued, the knife leading the way.

The idea to call 911 didn't come to him until he saw the massive swarm of taillights blocking all lanes of I-97 South. Even if he was overreacting—

Of course you are, Teddy-biscuit. Didn't I tell you that a hundred times?

—he would still feel better having the police check things out.

And what will they find when they get there? A pissed-off wife who doesn't want to talk to her cheating husband right now? I'm sure the local boys in blue will be plenty pleased about that.

"Fuck it," he said and dialed 911.

"Nine-one-one, what's your emergency?"

"I've been trying to reach my wife at home but she's not answering the phone."

"How long have you been trying to reach her?"

"A few hours. I'm worried something's happened."

"Is your wife sick, sir?"

"No. She's . . . I don't know. . . ."

"Is she expecting a call from you?"

"No, no." His mouth was dry. "She's angry with me."

"What's your name, sir?"

"Her name is Laurie."

"No, sir—*your* name," said the woman. "What's *your* name?"

"Ted Genarro. I've got the address, if you could send a car by—"

"Do you have any reason to believe your wife is in any type of danger, sir?"

Go on. Tell her you got a vibe, tapped into some bad juju. I'm sure cops hear that sort of thing all the time.

"Fuck," he blurted, then killed the call.

She was freezing, her teeth knocking together in her skull by the time she reached the greenhouse. Great swirling puddles expanded along the dirt path. At one point, lightning struck a nearby tree and sent a branch roughly the width of a telephone pole plummeting to the earth. Glimpsed through the treetops, the sky itself had deepened to the color of blackboard slate.

The knife quivered in her hand as she approached the greenhouse. The canvas rippled in the strong wind while rivulets of rainwater cascaded down the creases. There was no sign of Abigail, and the canvas covering the greenhouse didn't look as if it had been disturbed, but there were also plenty of places to hide. The tree with FUCK carved onto its trunk clawed at the gunmetal sky with barren, skeletal limbs. The branch Sadie had toppled from all those years ago still extended out over the roof of the greenhouse, its bark the color of marrow.

She approached the front side of the greenhouse. Wind whipped at the canvas covering, making it bulge and ripple in places. She peeled back one of the canvas flaps to expose the blackened glass door beneath.

The rope that had held the door shut—the rope she had untied on her previous jaunt out here—was still gone, though it was no longer on the ground where she had left it. She managed to work some fingers between the door and the frame, and pulled. The door squalled open about five or six inches. Blackness seasoned with the heady aroma of rotting vegetation stood just beyond the doorway. She switched the knife to her weak hand, flicked on the flashlight, and stepped inside.

It was moist and humid, like a rainforest. Had the sheet of canvas not covered the structure, she still did not believe much light would have been able to penetrate the blackened, moss-caked windows. Jumbled shapes resolved themselves out of the gloom, vaguely plantlike. The air wasn't fetid as much as it was merely *earthy*—an orchestra of organic perfumes.

As the flashlight played across the remains of her father's greenhouse, Laurie realized that she was looking at a man-made structure that had wholly and unwaveringly been usurped by Mother Nature. After Sadie's death, her father had shut down the greenhouse and, to the best of her knowledge, had never returned to it. What plants he'd kept inside hadn't died; on the contrary, their roots had burst through their terracotta pots and the corrugated tin flooring in search of soil and water . . . *and had found it.* The interior of the greenhouse had become a swampy black jungle, the air so fragrant with pheromones that it was difficult to breathe. Water dripped from perhaps a hundred places, tapping against leaves and draining into puddles on the floor. Large flies curtained the air. She took a step forward and her foot sank down into an inch or so of putrid black bile.

A shape stood partially hidden behind a curtain of dense foliage. Laurie flicked the flashlight over it. The checkerboard dress looked incongruous, even with its mud-colored blood soaking through the fabric. The girl wearing it was no longer Abigail Evans. It was Sadie Russ. Lacerations streamed red across her otherwise cadaver-white face. The darkened knots of Sadie's nipples were visible beneath the sodden fabric of the dress. Her hair was a wet, twisted tangle that framed her face. Only her eyes looked alive—piercing, lucid, lighter in color than Laurie had remembered.

She found she was no longer afraid.

"Why did you come back?"

Sadie's lips peeled back into a hideous clownlike smile. "To take you back with me," she said. It was Sadie's voice, but it was still somehow Abigail's voice, too—two little girls speaking simultaneously from the same mouth.

"Why?"

That grotesque smile did not falter. "Find the circle."

In response, Laurie tightened her grip on the knife.

Sadie laughed. It was an adult man's laugh now. "You can't kill me. I'm already dead," she said.

"I won't go with you."

"Then I'll take the other one," Sadie said. "I'll take Susan. If I can't have you, I'll have her. *Let me have her.* I'll break her neck and make a wish out of her. I'll throw her down there in that dark hole with all your father's girls. It'll be the best wish I've ever made. Eeny, meeny, miney—"

"Why are you *doing* this?" she sobbed. The knife trembled in her hand.

"Because I'm the Vengeance. I'm the Hateful Beast." Sadie extended a pale white arm ribboned with deep cuts and pointed to a spot on the floor, perhaps a foot or two in front of Laurie.

Laurie redirected the flashlight to the spot Sadie had pointed out. The floor was a squishy cushion of mud networked with plant roots. With her sneaker, she cleared an arc through the mud to reveal the corrugated tin floor beneath.

"The circle," Sadie hissed.

Indeed, there was a small circular grate covering a drain, perhaps just slightly bigger in diameter than a softball, set into the floor. It reminded her of the drains in the locker-room shower stalls where Coach Linda had made all the girls take showers after gym class back in high school. Two flathead screws were bolted into the grate. Trembling, Laurie sank to her knees. With her thumbnail, she dug crud out of the groove in the head of each screw. Using the blade of the knife, the flatheads unscrewed willingly enough. The grate itself gave more of a protest. She wedged the blade of the knife around the edge of the grate until she was finally able to pop it off.

She looked down the drain but saw nothing but darkness. She thought of those pictures Susan had drawn and stuck to the refrigerator: They hadn't been pictures of the well after all, but of this drainpipe. She could hear water running below and, even as she stared at it, rainwater spilled down into its mouth. Then she remembered the flashlight. She directed the beam down into the hole . . . and saw the box.

It was a rusted tin piece of garbage that, at one time,

402   *Ronald Malfi*

might have been a cigarette case. Someone—her father, most likely—had wedged it halfway down the throat of the drain, to the part where the pipe narrowed and prevented it from falling all the way down. Laurie retrieved it, the casing scabrous with rust. There was a small release button on one side of the metal box. To cut her flesh on it would be to welcome a whole host of infections into her bloodstream, so she was cautious when she pushed it. The box sprung open.

There was a grimy plastic bag inside. It looked like a Ziploc bag. There was something inside, though the bag was too grimy and foggy with age for her to clearly make out what it was. She opened the bag and shook the item out into her hand. It turned out to be several items, although they were apparently part of a set. Old Polaroid photographs.

It took her several seconds to realize what she was looking at. But by the time she turned to the fourth photo in the stack, *she knew.* The variations of the flesh tones . . . the crease that could be the bend of an elbow or a knee or something else . . . the places exposed that should have never, ever been exposed, not on a child, a little girl. She didn't know who the girl—the *victim*— was until she saw the fearful, blank-eyed face appear in one of the photos. Then, in another, she could clearly make out Sadie's profile. Potting soil beneath the fingernails, Myles Brashear's big hand covered Sadie's mouth in yet another photograph. Touched her buttocks in another photo. Touched her in worse places in yet another. . . .

Unable to look at the rest, she dropped the stack of

photos to the floor. She tried to stand, but found that she couldn't. Her face burned and it was becoming difficult to breathe. She realized she had been crying.

When she turned to Sadie, she expected to find that the girl had vanished. But she was still there, having in fact taken a step closer to Laurie while she had been going through the photographs. The girl's bare feet were black with mud. There was an absence of expression on her face.

"I had no idea he did those horrible things to you. You weren't evil. An evil man did evil things to you, but *you* weren't evil. You just needed someone to help you."

"He did it right in here, in this place." Sadie's voice was flat, unemotional.

"Sadie, had I known, I would have helped you. I would have."

"You knew."

"Honey, no—how could I know such a thing?"

"Because I told you."

"I just thought you were a bully. I just thought you . . . for some reason, that you'd *changed*. . . ."

"I told you what he was doing to me. You called me a liar. We climbed up the tree so I could show you where he did it to me. Right in here. Right in here."

"No, no—*you* climbed the tree. I watched you."

"You didn't want me to tell on him," Sadie said. "You thought the police would take you away from your family so you didn't want me to tell on him. He kept doing it and you didn't want me to tell."

Laurie tried to speak but couldn't. Suddenly, a part of her had returned to that afternoon, watching Sadie climb the tree, her cheap black shoes scrabbling for purchase on the low-hanging branches. *Had* she gone up, too?

"You didn't want me to tell," Sadie droned on, "and you got mad at me. You said I was making it up. You got very mad, Laurie."

Had she gone up? Had they *both* been on the branch that day? Insanely, she thought of that inspirational poster again, the one with the kitten dangling from the branch with the caption that read HANG IN THERE!

"You got mad," Sadie said. "You—"

"No!" Laurie shouted. She dropped the flashlight and clamped her hands to her ears. "No! Stop it!"

Had she gone up there and gotten mad?

"—pushed me," finished Sadie.

Laurie screamed until her throat ruptured. In her mind's eye, she could see Sadie losing her balance, swinging down one side of the limb, her hands laced together around the limb . . . then snapping apart as she dropped through the roof of the greenhouse. She could *see* it, just as she had seen it a hundred times before in her nightmares . . . only this time, her perspective had changed. The angle was different. This time, she watched Sadie Russ fall to her death while she sat up in the tree. She watched Sadie from above.

Weeping, Laurie collapsed to the floor. Only vaguely was she aware of Sadie's dirty bare feet shuffling toward her.

"So now I've come back for you."

"I won't go," Laurie sobbed into the dirt. "I'm sorry, I'm sorry, I'm sorry—"

"Then I will throw Susan down the well and wish you dead."

"*Please—*"

"Eeny, meeny, miney, moe. Who's it going to be?"

Laurie propped herself up. Her whole body hitched with sobs. As she stared at Sadie, the little girl's wounds began suppurating. Blood spilled from the gashes in her throat while great red magnolias bloomed beneath her filthy checkerboard dress. For the first time, she could see the jagged geometry of broken glass jutting from the girl's ghost-white flesh.

"I've been following you forever," Sadie said. "I'm always just off to the side, watching you. You saw me that day in the car." Sadie's lips stretched into a grimace. "You couldn't handle it so your mind shut down. It was fun for a while—I like games—but now I'm tired of it. So if you won't do what I say, I will play with Susan. We'll play *hard,* Laurie. I'll haunt her and drive her mad. I'll do *things* to her. Don't you remember the terrible things I can do?"

Laurie sobbed.

"I can get at her any time I want. You know that's true. There's only one way to protect her. Kill yourself."

"Please . . ."

"It's you or your daughter," Sadie said.

"Okay," she moaned. "Okay—*me*. I'll pay for it. Please—leave my daughter alone."

"Kill yourself and I will," said Sadie.

Her vision bleary, she felt around for the knife.

"No," Sadie barked. She extracted a triangular wedge of broken glass from one of her wounds, and extended it toward Laurie. "Use this. The same glass that cut me."

The glass was weightless in her hand. She managed to come to a kneeling position once again. When she looked at the glass, a part of her recoiled at how dirty it was . . . and then she laughed at the absurdity of such a thought.

"Cut," said Sadie Russ.

Laurie cut.

Ted had to smash a window to get in the house. No one had answered when he knocked on the door. He went around to the side of the house, but the door there was locked, too. He picked up a large stone from the garden and was about to send it hurling through the bay windows when he thought he heard Susan's voice screaming for him. He looked around and couldn't see her. The storm was playing tricks with his head. Then he sent the stone sailing.

"Laurie? Susan?" His voice echoed through the kitchen and out into the parlor. The house was dark and silent.

He raced out into the front hall and paused again, this time *certain* he had heard Susan screaming for him.

Upstairs, he realized.

He took the stairs two at a time, then froze at the top of them. The bedroom doors all stood open . . . yet Susan, whose screams he could still hear, sounded impossibly far away. Then his eyes fell on the door to the belvedere. It was closed and locked with the padlock.

"I'm here, Susan! I'm here!"

He rammed his shoulder against the door four times before the frame split. He kicked it the rest of the way off its hinges just as Susan came streaming down a set of narrow stairs. She dove into his arms, sobbing hysterically.

"Okay, okay," he said, smoothing her hair and kissing her hot cheeks. "Calm down. It's okay."

She shrieked, "Mommy!"

"Where is she? Where's Mommy?"

"She went into the woods! I saw her! She went into—" She buried her face against him.

Ted scooped her up and carried her downstairs. He set her down in the kitchen.

"Daddy, no—"

"Call nine-one-one, pumpkin. Can you do that?" He touched the side of her face.

"Where—"

"I'm going to get your mom."

Susan's chest hitched. Before he could leave, she threw her arms around his neck and hugged him tight. He kissed the side of her face, then reluctantly broke the embrace.

"Do it now," he told her. "Do it now, Susan."

He didn't have the key to unlock the side door, so he climbed back out the window. He hadn't realized he'd cut himself until he was jogging down the wooded path and saw that the front of his shirt was soaked in blood. A sharp pain radiated from his left side.

When he reached the clearing, he saw the door of the greenhouse standing open. He rushed inside and was quickly attracted to a dull cone of light issuing from the floor. It was a flashlight. A second later, he saw Laurie. She was sprawled out seemingly dead on the floor surrounded by a black jungle of dripping, stinking plants. Both her wrists had been cut open and she lay there with the bloodied, jagged piece of glass pressed to her throat.

Ted rushed to her side, shoving the broken shard of glass away. He listened to her chest and felt for a pulse. Counted. For a minute, he couldn't differentiate his heartbeat from hers. But then he could. She was still alive.

He gathered her up in his arms and ran back to the house.

CHAPTER 32

When Ted came back from the bathroom, Detective Freeling was seated in one of the molded plastic chairs in the waiting room of the hospital. Ted didn't recognize him at first. Freeling spotted him and rose quickly. They were in the middle of shaking hands before Ted recognized him.

"I'm sorry to hear about this," Detective Freeling said. He looked haggard and deflated, though Ted was fairly certain he looked even worse. "Will she be all right?"

"She's stable. The doctors said she passed out after doing her wrists, but that she didn't lose too much blood."

"Thankfully."

"Had she not passed out and got to her throat . . ." He didn't complete the thought.

"How about you? You holding up okay?"

"Sure."

"And . . . Susan, was it?"

"She's fine. She's with the neighbors. I didn't want her to see her mother like this."

All pertinent questions dispatched, Detective Freeling

looked suddenly at a loss for words. He sawed an index finger back and forth beneath his lower lip while his eyes darted fervently around the hospital waiting room.

"They've been keeping her pretty sedated," Ted said, offering the man a lifeline. "I haven't actually spoken to her yet."

"I see."

"I can't imagine what . . . what state she'll be in when she comes around. I'm almost afraid for her to wake up."

Detective Freeling put a hand on his shoulder. It was a firm grip and a genuine gesture, but there was little comfort in it.

"I'll leave you to it, then," said the detective. "Was there anything you needed? Anything I can do?"

"No. I've got it all taken care of."

Detective Freeling nodded. His hand slipped off Ted's shoulder and sought solace in the pocket of his trousers. The detective looked like he wanted to say something more, but in the end, he settled for a meager little smile that made him look no older than a frat boy. When he left, he did so silently.

The man who woke him up had stale breath and large gray eyes behind thick lenses. He wore a white lab coat.

"She's awake, Mr. Genarro."

They had her hooked up to machines through a series of tubes and brightly colored wires. Electronics beeped and pulsed on the rack beside her bed. She was propped up on several pillows, her body shrunken beneath the white cloth gown she wore. Her complexion was ashen and her eyes looked too big for her face. She stared despondently at him as he came into the room. Both her wrists were heavily bandaged.

"How are you feeling?"

"How did you find me?" Her voice was hardly a wheeze. "How did I get here? I don't remember."

"I came home. Susan saw you go off into the woods. I found you in that greenhouse. You'd cut . . . you'd hurt yourself pretty badly. You were unconscious when I got there."

"Susan?"

"She's fine."

"Where is she?"

"She's fine. She's safe. Babe, relax. Your heart monitor's racing." He took one of her hands in his. Hers was cold. "Laurie, what happened? Why'd you do this to yourself?"

"It was Sadie."

"Who?"

"The little girl who lived next door to me when I was a kid," she rasped. "The one who fell through the greenhouse—"

"And died," he finished. "Yes."

"She came back. She was going to hurt Susan if I didn't . . ." Her eyes went distant. She tried to struggle up off the bed but it took little effort for Ted to keep her down.

"You need to relax, Laurie. You need to lie here and get better. Do you understand?"

"You and Susan have to get out of that house."

"We will. As soon as they let you out of this place, we'll all leave together."

"No," she croaked at him. "You have to do it *now*."

He squeezed her hand gently. "Okay, okay. We will."

"Promise me."

"I promise. Scout's honor."

"Ted, that girl was in the house. My father wasn't just hearing noises—*she was really there*."

"That's not true, Laurie. Sadie is dead."

"No. Sadie is Abigail. She's been in our house while we were there, too."

"No, she hasn't."

"You don't *know*, Ted. Remember the cuff links? My father's cuff links? Susan *hadn't* been lying—it was Abigail who'd come into the house and taken them. She had my mother's diamond earring and she was digging it out of the same hole where she and Susan had been burying—"

"Susan took the cuff links."

Laurie's lower lip quivered. "What?"

"I didn't tell you. I spoke with her like I said I would and she admitted that she had taken the cuff links from your father's study. She was too ashamed to tell you so she told me. So, you see, no one was in the house. No one but Susan took those cuff links. You see?"

Even as her facial muscles relaxed, the terror in Laurie's eyes did not abate.

"What?" he said. "What is it?"

"That's true? What you just told me?"

"Yes."

"Then . . ."

"Then what?"

"Then I'm crazy. I'm crazy, Ted. If none of it is real, that means I imagined it all. It means I'm out of my—"

"It means you're stressed. Your father just passed away and you've had unresolved issues with that. Then you made that discovery—you remember it, right? The girls—"

She closed her eyes. "Yes."

"Laurie, your father was a very bad man. You were lucky to have been taken from him when you were a kid."

She opened her eyes and just stared at him.

He leaned in and kissed the side of her face. It was like kissing a wax sculpture. "Then there's you and me. Mostly me. I'm no good. We can talk about that once you're better. I just want to tell you that I'm sorry. Incredibly sorry."

"I know you are. It's okay. We can work through it, can't we?"

He felt something lurch forward in his chest. "God, yes. Yes, we really can, Laurie. I'm sorry. I'm so sorry."

"I want to work it out. I want us all to be happy—you, me, and Susan."

"That's all I want," he said.

She smiled thinly at him, then turned away. He could see her eyes welling up with tears, and once again she looked very fearful.

"You're not crazy," he told her. "You're going to be okay."

She whispered, "Okay." Then she smiled at him, which caused her cheeks to come to points. "Okay. Thank you."

"Can I get you anything before I leave?"

"No, I'm fine."

"Good. I love you."

"I love you, too."

He turned and went to the door but she called him back.

"When I get out of here," she said, "I've got something to tell you. It's something that happened a long time ago—something I did—but I feel the need to tell you. And maybe this way you won't ever let me forget it. Maybe this way it'll set things right."

He nodded.

"It was a terrible thing," she said. "I'm my father's daughter, after all."

He was surprised to find himself close to tears.

It was almost midnight by the time he arrived back at the house on Annapolis Road. The storm still raged and there were downed trees blocking the driveway. He parked as close to the house as he could, then raced across the yard with the collar of his sport coat tugged over his head.

The house was dark. The Rosewoods had been kind enough to take Susan off his hands and let her sleep over. She had been so rattled by what Laurie had done that she hardly seemed like herself. She was eager to spend the night with Abigail, and Ted considered that a small victory.

He fixed himself a drink, then languished on the sofa in the parlor, the lights off. The sound of the rain kept lulling him in and out of sleep.

They would all require some recovery. Not just physically, but emotionally. Laurie would need to speak with a therapist—he had insisted on it after her inexplicable blackout on the highway last year—and this time he wouldn't take no for an answer. He was willing to seek counseling to salvage their marriage, too. It was important to him, though perhaps he hadn't realized just how important until he arrived back in Hartford without them. They would have to be open and honest with each other from here on out—no more secrets, no more lies. No more living separate lives under the same roof.

In that case, you're off to a good start, Teddy-biscuit, he thought now, his mind already retiring to some shadowed corner of half-sleep. *The woman was not even conscious a full five minutes and you were already lying to her face.*

She'd said, *That's true? What you just told me?*

He'd said, *Yes.*

Maybe some lies are good lies, if they help a person, he convinced himself. *Does it really matter that I lied to her about the cuff links if it makes her feel better?* He had never asked Susan about it. In fact, he had forgotten about it until Laurie brought it up again tonight.

Soon, his thoughts collided with other thoughts. He dreamt he was a grown man sleeping in a child's bed—his own childhood bed—only to be awakened in the middle of the night by the terrible clash of thunder. When he went to look for his parents, he found their dusty corpses spun in spiderwebs propped up in their bed. Downstairs, in the dog crate, Stooge had been turned inside-out, his entrails gleaming like wet, purple

snakes in the moonlight. Then, at another point in the
dream, he thought he heard the distant wails of a little
girl—Susan?—calling out to him in the night. Shriek-
ing. After a while, the cries went silent.

When he awoke in real life, it was because the
telephone in the kitchen was ringing. In the midst of
Laurie's madness, she had also shut the ringer off on
the phone—he had realized this yesterday, while waiting for Laurie's doctor to call. Outside, the storm had
stopped. Daylight crept up over the trees. Birds sang
brightly.

"Hello?"

"Hi, Ted, it's Liz Rosewood from next door. I'm
sorry to wake you so early, but I just got up and Abigail told me about Susan getting upset in the middle
of the night. Ted, I had no idea she went back over to
your place, and I'm completely embarrassed. I've already scolded Abigail—she should have told me and
I would have come over and sat with Susan until you
came home."

Ted scratched his forehead and stared at the glisten-
ing raindrops on the bay windows.

"Anyway, I just wanted to apologize. Is Susan all
right?"

"To be honest, she isn't up yet. I haven't seen her. I
didn't even realize she was here last night."

"I hope you're not upset."

"Not at all."

"How's Laurie?"

"She was awake. We spoke for a little bit."

"Will she be okay?"

"I think so." What he almost said was, *I hope so*. It was what he meant, anyway.

"Well, I'm glad to hear it," Liz said. "I'll bring some lunch by for you and Susan later today."

"Please don't trouble yourself."

"I insist."

"All right. Thank you."

He hung up the phone, filled up the coffeepot, then wandered out into the front hall. Peering through the windows, he could see the damage left behind in the wake of the storm—the felled trees, the trash strewn about the yard, some of the fence pickets broken. Apparently, the wind had been strong enough to tear the plywood cover off the well, bricks and all.

He climbed up the stairs and went down the hall to Susan's bedroom door. The door was closed. He knocked on it.

When she didn't answer, he knocked again.

When she still didn't answer, he opened the door, poked his head in, and called out, "Susan?"

The room was empty. He stood there for a few seconds, puzzling over this. Then he went back downstairs and searched the rest of the house, but she wasn't there. By this time, he was replaying the phone call with Liz in his head and wondered if he'd misunderstood her. He considered calling her back up for clarification, but in the end, decided he would just walk next door.

It was cold outside. He went down the porch steps and cut across the yard, pausing to survey the bricks that had been tossed about, the sheet of plywood that lay discarded on the lawn. *Must have been some wind last night.*

He kept walking across the lawn, then paused. Some nonspecific disquiet had settled all around him. It was as if he'd inadvertently walked through a spider's web. Something didn't sit right.

He turned around and cut back toward the house, stepping over the discarded bricks and maneuvering around the sheet of plywood. Crickets sang in the overgrown grass. A cool breeze rustled the leaves in the trees.

He peered over the side of the well and looked into the darkness.

Don't miss Ronald Malfi's next chilling novel of
supernatural suspense

BONE WHITE

Coming soon from Kensington Publishing Corp.

Keep reading to enjoy a sample excerpt . . .

I

The man who walked into Tabby White's luncheonette around seven in the morning on that overcast
Tuesday was recognized only by a scant few customers, despite the fact that he had been a resident of that
town for the better part of thirty years. He came in on a
gust of cold wind, a withered husk of a man in a heavy
chamois coat with wool lining. There were bits of leaves
and grit in his salt-and-pepper beard, and the tip of his
nose and the fleshy pockets beneath his eyes looked red
and swollen with chilblains. The thermal undershirt he
wore beneath the coat looked stiff with dried blood.

Bill Hopewell, whose family had lived in the town
for three generations, was the first to recognize the
man, and even that took the accumulation of several
minutes' scrutiny. By the time he realized the fellow
was old Joe Mallory from up Durham Road, Mallory
was seated at the breakfast counter warming his hands
around a steaming mug of Tabby's hot cocoa.

"Is that you, Joe?" Bill Hopewell said. Tabby's was
a small place, and despite it being breakfast time, there
were only about half a dozen customers. A few of them
looked up from their meals and over at Bill Hopewell,

who was seated by himself at one of the rickety tables before a bowl of oatmeal and a cup of strong coffee. Those same few then glanced over at the scarecrow-thin man in the chamois coat hunched over Tabby's breakfast counter.

The man—Joe Mallory, if it was him—did not turn around. Far as Bill Hopewell could tell, he hadn't even heard him.

It was the look on Tabby White's face that ultimately prompted Bill to climb out of his chair and mosey over to the breakfast counter. Tabby White was about as friendly as they came, and it was rare to catch a glimpse of her when she wasn't smiling. But she wasn't smiling now: She had served the man his requested cup of hot cocoa with dutiful subservience, and was now watching him from the far end of the breakfast counter, backed into the corner as far as she could go, beneath a wall clock in the shape of a cat whose eyes ticked back and forth like the wand of a metronome. There was a look of apprehension on Tabby's face.

"Hey, Joe," Bill Hopewell said as he came up beside the man and leaned one elbow down on the breakfast counter. When the man turned to look at him, Bill momentarily questioned his assumption that this was, in fact, Joseph Mallory from up Durham Road. Mallory was in his fifties, and this guy looked maybe ten years older than that—maybe more. And while Joe Mallory had never been overly concerned with personal hygiene, this guy smelled like he hadn't bathed in the better part of a month.

The man turned and grinned at Bill Hopewell. Through the wiry bristles of his beard, the man's lips were scabbed and wind-chapped. There was a patch of black frostbite, abrasive as tree bark, at one corner of his mouth. The few teeth remaining in Mallory's mouth looked like small wooden pegs.

"Where you been, Joe?" Bill asked. "Ain't nobody seen you in a long time."

"Been years," said Galen Provost, who was watching the exchange from a table near the windows. "Ain't that right, Joe?"

Joseph Mallory turned back around on his stool. With both hands, he brought the mug of hot cocoa to his lips and slurped. A runnel of cocoa spilled down his beard and spattered in splotches on the Formica countertop.

Bill Hopewell and Galen Provost exchanged a disconcerted look. Then Bill turned his gaze toward Tabby, who was still backed into her corner beneath the cat clock with the ticking eyes, gnawing on a thumbnail.

"This is fine cocoa, Tabs," Mallory said, the words coming out in a sandpapery drawl. "Mighty fine."

At the mention of her name, Tabby bumped into a shelf and sent a bottle of ketchup to the floor.

"What you got all over them clothes?" Galen Provost said from across the room. Everyone was watching now.

"Is that blood on your clothes, Joe?" Bill Hopewell asked, his tone less accusatory than Galen's, despite the directness of his query. Perhaps, Bill thought, Galen wouldn't have been so boisterous if he'd been standing right next to Mallory, where he could see the dirt collected in the creases of Mallory's face, the white nits in his hair and beard, and what looked like old blood beneath the man's fingernails. If he could see how *off* Mallory looked. Bill cleared his throat and said, "You been up in them woods, Joe?"

It was at that point that Joseph Mallory started to laugh. Or perhaps he started to cry: Bill Hopewell wasn't sure at that moment which one it was, and he would still be undecided about it much later, once Mallory's face was on the TV news. All he knew was that the noise that juddered from old Joe Mallory's throat sounded much like a stubborn carburetor, and that tears were welling in the man's eyes.

Bill Hopewell pushed himself off the counter and took two steps back.

The laughter—or whatever it was—lasted for just a couple of seconds. When he was done, Mallory swiped the tears from his eyes with a large, callused hand. Then he dug a few damp bills from the inside pocket of his coat and laid them out flat on the countertop. He nodded in Tabby White's direction.

Tabby White just stared at him.

Mallory's stool squealed as he rotated around toward Bill Hopewell. With some difficulty, he climbed down off the stool. His movements were labored and stiff, as if his muscles were wound too tight, his bones like brittle twigs. Those dark streaks across the front of Mallory's shirt were also on his coat and his pants, too, Bill realized.

"Well, they're up there, the whole lot of them," Mallory said. His voice was barely a rasp. Later, Bill would have to relay what he'd heard to Galen Provost and the rest of the patrons of Tabby's luncheonette, who were just out of earshot. "They're all dead, and I killed 'em. But I'm done now, so that's that." He turned away from Bill Hopewell and looked at Tabby. "Val Drammell still the safety officer 'round here?"

Tabby didn't answer. She didn't look capable.

"He is," Bill Hopewell answered for her.

"All right," said Mallory, turning back to Bill. He nodded once, as if satisfied. "One of you folks be kind enough to give him a call? Tell him I'll be sitting out by the church waiting for the staties to come collect me."

"Yeah, okay," Bill said, too stunned to do anything else but agree with the man's request.

"Much obliged," said Mallory, and then he turned and ambled out into the cold, gray morning.

"Tabby," Bill said, not looking at her—in fact, he was staring out the window, watching the gaunt form of Joe Mallory shamble up the road in the direction of the old church. "Best give Val Drammell a call, like he says."

It took Tabby White a few seconds before she understood that she had been spoken to. She moved across the floor toward the portable phone next to the coffee station—one of her white sneakers smeared a streak of ketchup along the linoleum, but she didn't notice—and fumbled with the receiver before bringing it to her ear.

"Val," she said into the phone, her voice reed-thin and bordering on a whine. "It's Tabby down at the luncheonette." There was a pause, then she said, "I think I'll turn you over to Bill Hopewell."

She handed Bill the receiver, and Bill set it against his ear. He was still watching Joe Mallory as he ambled up the road toward the church. At the horizon, the sky looked bleached and colorless. It promised to be a cold winter. "We got something here I think you should come take a look at," he said, then explained the situation.

2

It was a quarter after eight in the morning when Jill Ryerson's desk phone rang.

"Major Crimes," she said. "This is Ryerson."

"Ms. Ryerson, this is Valerie Drammell, I'm the safety officer up the Hand. I had your card here and figured I'd give you a call on this situation we got out here." It was a man's voice with a woman's name, she realized. He spoke in a rushed, breathless patter that was difficult to understand.

"Where'd you say you're calling from, Mr. Drammell?"

"Up the Hand, ma'am." Then the man cleared his throat and said, "That's Dread's Hand, ma'am."

The name was familiar—it was too unique to forget—but in that moment she couldn't remember how or why she knew it. But something had happened there, maybe within the past year, and she had somehow been involved.

"What's the situation out there, Drammell?"

"Listen, I got a guy here, a local fella, named Joe Mallory," Drammell explained. "Says he killed a bunch of people and buried their bodies in the woods here.

He's got . . . well, what looks like blood on his clothes, dried blood. It don't look fresh. He looks . . . he don't look right, Ms. Ryerson—er, Detective. I'm calling the right number, ain't I? This is the right number?"

She assured Drammell that it was, and said she'd be there as soon as possible. After she hung up, she stepped out of her office and peered into the squad room. Mike McHale sat behind the nearest desk.

"Dread's Hand," she said. "Where's that?"

McHale just shrugged his shoulders. There was a road atlas on the credenza behind McHale's desk, and he leaned over and grabbed it, eliciting a grunt as he did so. He opened the atlas on his desk and scrutinized one of the area maps.

"VPSO out there just called. Said he's with some local guy who claims he's killed some people."

McHale looked up from the map, frowning. "Yeah?" he said.

Ryerson shrugged.

"Here it is," McHale said, tapping a finger against an enlarged map of Alaska's interior. "Way out there in the hills. Should take us about an hour and a half, I'd guess," McHale said.

Ryerson curled up one side of her mouth in a partial grin. "Us?"

"What kind of guy would I be, letting you run off chasing murder suspects on your own?"

"Then you're driving," she said.

They found Drammell seated on a bench outside the village church beside a wasted scarecrow of a man with a frizzy beard that came down past his collarbone. Ryerson and McHale got out of the cruiser and approached the men. Ryerson spotted the coppery-brown streaks of dried blood along the front of Mallory's long johns and around the cuffs of his pants. Not that she put much stock in it right off the bat—this guy could have been butchering critters in the woods for the past couple of days, for all she knew—although there was something in Mallory's gray eyes that chilled her when he first looked up at her.

"I'm here to make my peace with it," Mallory said as they approached.

"What's 'it'?" Ryerson asked.

"C'mon and I'll show y'all," Mallory said. He used Val Drammell's shoulder for support as he hoisted himself off the church bench. Drammell made a face that suggested he was disgusted by the man's touch, although he didn't make a move to shove the man off him. When his eyes shifted toward Ryerson, he looked relieved that they were here and he could transfer this problem to them.

"Just hold on a minute," Ryerson said. "This fella Drammell here called and told us you killed a few people out this way. Is that right?"

"Yes, ma'am," said Mallory.

"Is this something you done recently?"

"Oh no, ma'am. It's been quite some time for me."

"Where are they?"

"That's what I was goin' t' show you, ma'am," Mallory said. He pointed toward the cusp of trees that wreathed the foothills of the White Mountains.

"That's where they are? Up there?"

"The lot of 'em," Mallory said.

"People," Val Drammell interjected. "Says he's buried some *people* up there. Just so we're clear here."

"I understand," she said to Drammell. Looking back at Mallory, she said, "That's what you're telling us, right? That you killed some folks and buried them up there. Is that right?"

"As rain," Mallory said.

She glanced at the tree line before turning her gaze back to Mallory. Those woods were expansive and the foothills could be treacherous. Not to mention that Mallory looked malnourished and about as sturdy as a day-old colt. "How far?" she asked.

"We can walk it, for sure," Mallory responded, although judging by his appearance and by the way he'd utilized Drammell's shoulder as a crutch to lift himself off the bench just a moment ago, Jill Ryerson had serious doubts about that.

"I think maybe you need to see a doctor first," she said to him.

"Time enough for that later," said Mallory. "I ain't gonna expire out here, ma'am. First I'll show you where they are. It's important I show you where they are. This is all very important."

She glanced at McHale, who looked cold and uncertain. He shrugged.

"All right," Ryerson said. For some reason, she believed him—that it was important he show them where they were, right then and there. As if there wouldn't be a chance to do it later. She got an extra coat from the cruiser's trunk, and helped Mallory into it. Mallory peered down at the embroidered badge over the breast, a bemused expression on his wind-burned face.

"Well, lookit that," he muttered, fingering the badge.

Mallory took them up into the woods, a walk that took nearly an hour and covered a distance that Ryerson, in her head, calculated to be just over a mile. Had she gone back for the car, it would have been possible to drive less than halfway up the old mining road: After about fifteen minutes of walking, the road narrowed to maybe three feet in width, and there were times when they had to climb over deadfalls and step around massive boulders in order to keep going. And then the road vanished altogether, surrendering to sparse stands of pines and Sitka spruce and large boulders furred with spongy green moss.

"If this is someone's idea of a practical joke," McHale said to no one in particular midway through the hike, "they're getting brained with my Maglite."

Ryerson let Mallory lead the way. She hadn't cuffed him—it would have been too difficult for the man to climb through the woods with his hands cuffed behind his back—but she had surreptitiously frisked him when she'd helped him into the parka, and she had felt no weapons on him. Besides, she still wasn't convinced this guy wasn't just some crackpot. Lord knew there were enough of them out here. Nonetheless, she kept her eyes on him as they walked.

"How'd you get my name and number?" Ryerson asked Drammell as they climbed toward the cups of the wooded foothills. "The name of this town sounds familiar, but I've never been out here before."

"Two troopers came out here about a year ago looking for a fella," Drammell said. "Far as I know, they never found the guy. When they left, they gave me your business card. Said I should call you if the fella ever turned up." Drammell frowned and added, "He never did."

Yes, she remembered now. She'd gotten a call about a year ago from the brother of a man who'd gone missing out this way. The man had traced his brother back to Dread's Hand as the last known place he'd been. Ryerson had taken the call and filed the paperwork, but she hadn't come out here herself. Instead, she had dispatched two troopers to Dread's Hand to check things out. She couldn't be positive at the moment, but she believed they managed to recover the man's rental car.

"You guys ever find the fella?" Drammell asked.

"No," said Ryerson.

Despite his weakened physical condition, Mallory appeared to have no difficulties on the walk. McHale and Drammell, on the other hand, were both wheezing by the time they reached a vast clearing. It was right here, Joseph Mallory explained, that he had buried the bodies of eight victims whom he'd murdered over a five-year period. He seemed certain about the number of victims, less certain about how long he'd spent killing. "Time," he suggested, "acts funny out here."

Ryerson and McHale exchanged a glance.

"You understand what you're telling us, don't you?" said McHale.

"Of course." Mallory glared at McHale, indignant. "I ain't stupid, son."

"No, sir," McHale said, and Ryerson detected more than just a hint of sarcasm in his voice.

"This is a big area," Ryerson said. "Is it possible to narrow down a location?"

"There are many locations," Mallory informed her. "Come on, then."

He pointed out the general vicinity of each unmarked grave, which covered an area of just about ten acres of woodland, in Ryerson's estimation. And although Ryerson had been right there standing beside him, inspecting the somber look on Joseph Mallory's wind-chapped face as he murmured, "One soul here, 'nother far yonder," she continued to believe that there were no bodies buried here at all, and that Joseph Mallory was just another backwoods crackpot with dried elk blood on his clothes who wanted his fifteen minutes of fame with the state police out of Fairbanks. After all, it was evident that the old man was one cherry short of an ice cream sundae, as Jill Ryerson's father had been fond of saying.

"That does her," Mallory said once he'd finished walking Ryerson, McHale, and Drammell all over God's green earth (although there was nothing green about this Alaska forest in the middle of September— the ground was as cold and gray as the trunks of the Sitka spruce). The whole thing had taken over two hours—a few times Mallory got confused as to a specific location while other times he just needed to rest— and they still needed to walk back down out of the woods, but despite the cold, Ryerson had overexerted herself and was sweating beneath her uniform and parka. She instructed Mike McHale to mark each spot as Mallory pointed them out, and McHale had jammed sticks into the earth and tied a Kleenex to each one for quick reference.

"You don't really think there's people *buried* here, do you?" McHale asked her at one point, his voice low, his hot, coffee-scented breath against the side of her neck.

"No, I don't," she said. "He just seems confused. But let's do this thing by the book, in case we're wrong, okay?"

"Roger that," said McHale.

"I'm going to cuff you and take you back to Fairbanks for now," Ryerson told Mallory once he finished pointing out all eight unmarked graves. "Would make me feel better if I got a doctor's eyes on you, too."

"I feel fine now," Mallory said, standing there in that clearing. He closed his eyes and tilted his reddened, wind-chapped face to the sky. Sores ran along his cheekbones and suppurated at his lips. It looked like he might have some frostbite in places, too. "But we've been spending too much time out here. I've already scrubbed it off once. Let's get back to town before it gets grabby again."

Jill Ryerson might have asked him to elaborate on what he meant by that statement had Valerie Drammell not spoken up then: "Yeah, let's get back to town. Like, right now." He was looking around, as if expecting someone to walk out of the trees and join them. A ghost, maybe.

"You both should cordon off the area and take some pictures," Ryerson suggested, looking from Drammell to McHale. "Let's treat this as a crime scene. I'll radio for assistance when I get back to the car. I'll contact the ME's office in Anchorage, too, just to put them on notice, in the event that, well . . . our friend here knows what he's talking about."

"Of course I do," grumbled Mallory, scowling.

"Me?" Val Drammell said. "Me stay here, too?"

Ryerson thought he sounded like Tarzan at the moment. "You're not obligated, but we could use the help, Mr. Drammell," she told him.

Drammell nodded, though it was clear he didn't want to be here. The ground speared by McHale's sticks with their Kleenex flags was an unsettling visual, and no doubt the past hour and a half sitting with Mallory on that church bench had creeped the poor guy out. He put a cigarette in his mouth.

"No smoking, please," Ryerson said. "Crime scene."

Drammell stared at her for the length of two heartbeats—long enough for Jill Ryerson to think, *Okay, here we go, let's flex those man muscles now*—but then he took the smoke out of his mouth and propped it up behind his left ear.

"You don't want help taking him back to the car?" McHale asked as Ryerson placed Mallory's hands behind his back and snapped the cuffs on him.

"I can manage," she said. "Let's just secure this place. And let's keep any locals from coming out here, too."

"No locals would come out here," Drammell said, but he did not elaborate.

*   *   *

Once they got into the police car back in town, Ryerson recited Mallory's Miranda rights.

"Don't have no need for them rights," Mallory said from behind the wire cage in the backseat of the cruiser. "Don't have no need for no lawyers, neither. I confessed all my sins. That's about it, ain't it?"

"I'm just telling you the law, Mr. Mallory," she said, firing up the engine and cranking the heater to full force. A small group of onlookers stood across the road, watching the situation, clouds of vapor spiraling from their open mouths. To Ryerson, they all looked like refugees deposited on the shores of some foreign country.

She drove slowly down the main street, which alternated between rutted dirt and white gravel, while the onlookers all turned their heads in unison to watch their departure.

"You feel like giving me your motive for killing those folks?" she said.

"No," Mallory said.

"No motive?"

"Don't feel like giving it," he clarified.

"How come?"

This time, Mallory didn't answer.

"How 'bout their names?" Ryerson said. "Care to tell me who they are? Were they locals?"

"Don't feel like speakin' their names aloud, ma'am, though I don't expect you to understand," Mallory said. "Don't rightly recall any of their names at the moment, to be honest. That part was never important."

"Is that right," she said.

"I suspect you'll find out in time, though. And that's fine."

"If this is some game you're playing with us, Mr. Mallory, you should just tell me now so we can avoid a lot of unnecessary work."

"Game?" he said.

"If you're trying to fool with us, in other words," she said. "If there are no bodies up there, I mean."

"Oh," he said, "they're up there, all right, ma'am. God help us, they're up there."

Jill Ryerson had her doubts.

Ninety minutes later, Ryerson deposited Mallory at Fairbanks Memorial and into the care of two fresh-faced troopers while McHale and Drammell secured the wooded clearing and awaited the arrival of backup, which included sniffer dogs and a technician schooled in using ground penetrating radar. Ryerson did not think too much of it until she got a phone call sometime later from McHale, who was still on the scene.

"You better get out here, Jill," McHale said, and she could detect a note of brash excitement in his voice even though he was trying his best to keep himself under control. "We've got a body."

Connect with

Us

Visit us online at
KensingtonBooks.com
to read more from your favorite authors, see books
by series, view reading group guides, and more.

Join us on social media

for sneak peeks, chances to win books and prize packs,
and to share your thoughts with other readers.

facebook.com/kensingtonpublishing
twitter.com/kensingtonbooks

Tell us what you think!

To share your thoughts, submit a review,
or sign up for our eNewsletters, please visit:
KensingtonBooks.com/TellUs.